Chris Bonnello is an autistic author, speaker and special education teacher based in Nottingham, United Kingdom. Since 2015 he has been an autism advocate through his website, Autistic Not Weird (https://autisticnotweird.com), winning multiple awards for his work and delivering speeches as far away as India and the Sydney Opera House. In his spare time, he is a Rubik's cube geek and a chess nerd. The Underdogs series, which began in 2019, is his first published venture as a novelist.

... Underdogs series

'This action-packed dystopian drama following a group of neurodivergent teens is hugely popular ... An admirably unusual book, and one that serves real purpose ... Bonnello is writing the books that ...

leisure & culture DUNDEE

'A

an

bo

Michael Grant, author of the Gone series

'This filmic, page-turning, edge-of-the-seat dystopian master-piece does exactly what its title suggests: propel the reader straight into the action. If you thought *Tooth and Nail* was hardcore, *Acceleration* surpasses it: the plot twists to a whole new level, the lens is wider, the characters deeper. It has all the thrills of an action adventure with the added bonus that you can zoom into the characters' innermost thoughts. Bonnello's insights into his neurodivergent cast are especially acute. Ambitious, brutal and brilliant: Bonnello's best book yet'
Patience Agbabi, author of the Leap Cycle series

'Chris Bonnello's *Underdogs* is a singular achievement – a taut, thrilling, fully rendered vision of dystopia that teaches valuable lessons about the contributions that people with atypical minds can make when given the chance'
Steve Silberman, author of *NeuroTribes*

'*Underdogs* introduces us to a band of neurodiverse young people, and the story explores the way their self-esteem has been ground down in the past, and how the support, acceptance and love shown to them by each other, and by their wise and kindly leader, restores their sense of worth. This is a great read, and it comes with the added message of the value of diversity and difference'

Carol Povey,
former Director of the National Autistic Society

'The Underdogs series sits proudly on the bookshelf in our Haven classroom, which is an inclusive space in a mainstream secondary school. Our young people highly value the representation of neurodivergent characters'

Sam, 46, student support mentor

'Underdogs is a fantastic series! I love that I can relate to some of the characters, especially when they express the struggles they had at school. The storyline is exciting with a lot of added logic and strategy which most novels don't include. Chris's wit and humour shine through, even though it's a serious plotline about war. I would highly recommend it!'

Nye, 12, autistic reader

'Underdogs introduces something vital to the neurodivergence advocacy movement: quality, diverse representation in fiction. As a person with diagnoses of autism, ADHD and mild dyslexia, it means so much to me to see that, and I know I won't be alone. These are more than fab books: they are also important ones'

Jenny, 28, autistic reader

'Finding a book with characters my sons could identify with? Priceless. Not only are they encouraged but I continue my learning journey alongside them'

Susanna, 42, mother to autistic sons

UNDER DOGS: ACCELERATION

CHRIS BONNELLO

unbound

First published in 2022

Unbound
Level 1, Devonshire House, One Mayfair Place, London W1J 8AJ
www.unbound.com

© Chris Bonnello, 2022

Text design by Ellipsis, Glasgow

A CIP record for this book is available from the British Library

ISBN 978-1-80018-088-8 (paperback)
ISBN 978-1-80018-089-5 (ebook)

Printed and bound in Great Britain by Clays Ltd, Elcograf S.p.A.

1 3 5 7 9 8 6 4 2

To my cousin Corwin. We've come a long, long way
since Sonic the Hedgehog fan fiction.

And to all my students, who I know will grow up to become
awesome autistic adults. Even the ones who keep telling me
that nobody is buying my books.

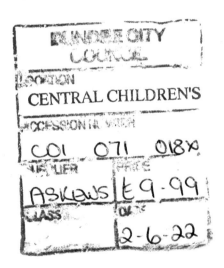

The Underdogs of Spitfire's Rise
as of June 20th, Year One

First name	Last name	Age	Notes
Kate	Arrowsmith	16	Secondary student, Oakenfold Special School, Harpenden. Diagnoses: Autism, Severe Anxiety.
~~Charlie~~	~~Coleman~~	~~16~~	~~Secondary student, Oakenfold Special School, Harpenden. Diagnosis: ADHD.~~
Gracie	Freeman	15	Secondary student, Oakenfold Special School, Harpenden. Diagnosis: Global Development Delay.
Alex	Ginelli	22	Deputy store manager, Fixit hardware store, Bancroft Road, Brighton.
Mark	Gunnarsson	18	Post-16 student, Oakenfold Special School, Harpenden. Diagnosis: unclear.
Jack	Hopper	17	Post-16 student, Oakenfold Special School, Harpenden. Diagnosis: Asperger Syndrome.
~~Joseph~~	~~McCormick~~	~~64~~	~~Lecturer in Mathematical Sciences, Greenwich University.~~

Thomas	Foster	9	Year 4 pupil, St David's Primary School, St Albans.
Lorraine	Shepherd	52	Nurse, Queen's Hospital stroke unit, Luton.
~~Raj~~	~~Singh~~	~~15~~	~~Secondary student, Oakenfold Special School, Harpenden. Diagnosis: Dyslexia.~~
Ewan	West	16	Secondary student, Oakenfold Special School, Harpenden. Diagnosis: Autism (PDA profile).
Simon	Young	14	Secondary student, Oakenfold Special School, Harpenden. Diagnosis: Down's Syndrome.
Shannon	Grant	17	Daughter of Great Britain's autocratic dictator, Nicholas Grant.

And the highest-ranking staff of New London Citadel:

First name	Last name	Age	Notes
Nicholas	Grant	55	Undisputed ruler of Great Britain.
~~Iain~~	~~Marshall~~	~~43~~	~~Head of Military Division.~~
Nathaniel	Pearce	42	Chief of Scientific Research.
Oliver	Roth	14	Primary assassin.

Prologue

War was hell, except when it was boring.

Alex Ginelli took a sip of coffee, and checked his watch. Comms duty in the attic of the Boys' Brigade hall was perfect for those who wanted to fight against Nicholas Grant without sticking their necks out. And Alex had done enough of that during the course of the war – fighting alongside the thinning army of Underdogs in the hope that they'd one day defeat an innumerable army of cloned soldiers, and free the British population from Grant's gargantuan walled Citadels.

That morning, Alex was grateful for the rare opportunity to take a back seat. As one of the few surviving Underdogs without special needs (as capable as the Oakenfold crew had proven themselves to be), he had lost count of the number of times he had been called to the front line. Comms duty was a rare relaxation opportunity for him.

The strike team in New London – the first team to go in since the one-year anniversary of Takeover Day – were almost on their way back out again. As far as Alex was aware, nobody had died this time.

He looked to his left at Gracie Freeman: the fairly useless fifteen-year-old dipstick, and his comms partner for the morning. Alex believed she was fifteen anyway. She looked it, but acted twelve if not younger. Gracie was spending her free time the same way as she spent the rare minutes when the strike team called: twirling her hair between fingers that had been starved of varnish for thirteen months.

Alex still felt offended that she had asked to sit on his left, so that she wouldn't have to look at the three-inch scar on his right cheek. Her choice would have been understandable, if the scar were still healing and not perfectly settled in his face. However long the war (or Alex) would last, the scar in his dark skin would be a permanent reminder of his experience of being captured and cloned... and the day Ewan came up with an idea to distinguish the real Alex from his clone soldier counterparts.

Alex tried giving some thought as to how his clones came into being – how his capture had resulted in his cloning, what the production process had actually been, and so on – but his brain brushed it all away. He laid a finger on the puckered flesh of his cheek, and wondered whether most deep scars looked like that after a month.

That long? Yeah, I guess it's been a month since McCormick.

When his mother had passed away, Alex's overbearing father had given the least helpful advice imaginable: that 'no matter who dies on you, it doesn't take forever to get over them and start living again'. As the years had passed, Alex had started living again and living well, but 'getting over' the loss of his mum had been impossible. Now it was the same at Spitfire's Rise.

A month on from the explosion that had killed Dr Joseph McCormick (and Grant's Head of Military too, although nobody seemed to care about his death by comparison), life had started to sprout among the Underdogs again. Jokes were being made in the living room. People were talking about the old man and smiling. But nobody was getting over McCormick. The man had led the charge against Grant for almost precisely a year, and had been a father figure to everyone he had left behind. Even Alex, although he had concealed those feelings well.

There were ten Underdogs left now. Less than a third of the number they had started with after Takeover Day, when Grant's clone armies had launched their attack across Britain and imprisoned its population in the Citadels. But even after thirteen months of warfare, and losing two thirds of their guerrilla army, McCormick's loss was by far the hardest to adapt to. He had been the group's centre of gravity. There had been a sense of civility and community with him at the helm: a house filled with order and love at the same time.

The phone on the desk buzzed. Alex reached out and grabbed it. To Gracie's credit, she at least looked vaguely interested. Alex noted that it was a voice call rather than a video call. The team must have been too busy for a face-to-face conversation.

'Yep.'

'Alex, it's Ewan.'

'What's the latest?'

'You were right,' Ewan's voice boomed down the phone. 'It's New Oxford. We don't know when.'

'Have you thought about finding out?'

'Yes, actually. Stand by.'

It was interesting, hearing the recent change in Ewan's tone. McCormick had named the sixteen-year-old as his successor, although Alex believed it was a responsibility the lad was neither mentally nor emotionally ready for. Ewan was doing his best to fill the mould, bless him, but the strongest jelly poured and refined through the toughest crucible would still come out as jelly.

Alex couldn't blame the lad for trying. But Ewan would have to work hard to develop a *real* leadership voice: one that was firm and controlled yet effortless (like the voice Alex's father used during his taekwondo lessons), rather than the forced, high-volume-low-pitch bellow that made him sound like he was *trying* to be a leader.

'So where are you now?' asked Gracie. Alex raised his eyebrows. The phone was against his ear, but Ewan's attempt at a leadership voice must have been audible even where Gracie sat.

'Floor T. Research room. We won't get all the details here, but it's not like we can breach an officers' sector again. We've only just got enough time for—'

'What about the others?' asked Alex, just to see how Ewan would react to the interruption.

'Alex, let me bloody talk. Mark and Simon are right here, no injuries. Mark's at the computer right now, but it's logged out.'

There was a muttering in the background, clearly Mark. Alex could make out his voice saying something about a password.

'No, Mark,' whispered Ewan. 'No idea.'

'If you're looking for a password,' said Alex, 'leave the room, find a place where some poor clone's already logged on, and hijack his workstation.'

'No time, Alex,' called Mark. 'They know we're in the Citadel. It's now or never. What would you guess?'

'Probably a set of random letters and numbers.'

'These are clones,' said Ewan. 'It won't be anything complicated.'

'What about "password"?' said Gracie.

Alex rolled his eyes. There was no way they would guard sensitive information behind something so obvious.

'I mean, think about it,' said Gracie. 'The screen says, "enter password", so you can literally do what it says, and enter the word "password"! It's clever when you think about it.'

'Gracie, every idiot on Earth—'

'Typing it now,' said Mark. Alex sighed. Over the phone, Ewan did too.

Alex understood how time pressures affected people's judgment. He had been on both of the recent big New London missions: the one when they had destroyed the clone factory (although he had spent most of it being held prisoner in a bungalow), and the one when they had taken down the AME shield. On the last mission in particular, time limits had almost forced him and Ewan into making fatal mistakes.

Alex heard the press of the enter key through the phone. Mark must have hit it hard.

'Nope, it wasn't—'

Music started to play from the computer, very loudly.

It was 'Seven Nation Army', by the White Stripes. A song older than Alex, but one he knew well. The thumping bass drum and foreboding guitar riff got into his mind...

A little *too far* into his mind...

'Why the hell are they playing this?' Ewan asked, the volume of his voice fading in Alex's mind.

'That's a weird alarm,' Gracie laughed, her voice fading too.

At that moment, everything solidified in Alex's subconscious. His brain took its commands from the music, and accepted what had to be done.

He felt his hand reaching for his gun, then stopping as his brain realised it would be too loud. Instead, his hand reached for the knife in his belt.

There was no independent thought in his mind, no respect for consequence. Just the smack of the bass drum, and Jack White's slow guitar.

When Alex stood up and threw his chair out from under his legs, Gracie didn't know how to react. Her face remained blank even when the hunting knife emerged in his hands, and she had no time to move before Alex plunged it into her stomach.

Alex's brain would not give his true personality a moment of influence, merely passing the music's instructions to his body. He pulled the knife out of Gracie and drove it deep into her side. She yelped and fell to the attic floor, the knife sliding out of her body as it stayed gripped in Alex's hands.

Alex's other hand remained clenched around the phone, which emitted only one sound audible to Alex's ears. Through the music he couldn't even hear his snarling breaths rasping through his throat, his furious low-pitched yells, or Gracie shrieking on the floor.

He knelt down and stabbed her again. Her fingers, too weak to make a difference, grasped for his face. They didn't take much effort to avoid.

The fourth stab landed between Gracie's neck and collar bone. It caught an artery.

Alex pulled the knife out and started to raise—

The music stopped.

'Right, unplugged,' said Ewan's voice. 'Let's not get a password wrong again. Couldn't hear myself think.'

The world was clear once more. Alex – the *real* Alex – caught his breath, and glanced around.

Beneath him, Gracie was dying.

Why the hell did I just do that?!

Was it me? Really, I mean?

The dying teenager certainly believed so. In the dimmed glow of half a dozen camping lights, Gracie Freeman's blood was dark as crude oil. Her face – wide eyes, open mouth, quivering jaw, head twitching with each heartbeat but beginning to slow – displayed a level of panic he had never seen before, or ever imagined he could cause with his own hands.

What was I thinking?

Was I even thinking?

What did that music do to me?

'Alex, we're out of time,' finished Ewan. 'I'll call you when we're out.'

Ewan did not wait for an answer. The phone cut out, leaving Alex and his victim alone in the attic of the Boys' Brigade hall. Tears fell from Alex's eyes.

Gracie was using the last of her energy to mouth a word.

'Why?'

'I... don't know,' said Alex, as she died.

Chapter 1

Oliver Roth felt uneasy when Grant called him to Floor B. It was an unusual feeling. The great Nicholas Grant had never made him uneasy before.

He used his keycard against the door to the stairwell between Floors C and B, and took a deep breath after the door had closed behind him. The rebels had escaped New London's Outer City walls before he could even make it downstairs to confront them, and Grant wouldn't be happy. Still, calling a whole meeting about it was a surprising response.

His missed opportunity to confront the Underdogs was extra annoying since they still believed him to be dead. Following that duel in the burning Experiment Chamber last month, when Ewan had shot him four times in his concealed Kevlar and left him to fry, Roth's enemies had every reason to believe that he was gone. Especially since the only Underdog to have seen him alive afterwards had been blown up before he could contact his allies. Today, Roth had missed the perfect chance to see the oh–it's-not-fair look of shock on Ewan West's face by appearing on the battlefield out of nowhere alive and well.

Roth scanned his keycard again at the entrance to Floor B

and was met on the other side by Nathaniel Pearce, who had clearly been waiting.

What the hell is Grant's smarmy smart-arse Chief Scientist doing here?

Stood barely taller than fourteen-year-old Roth, Pearce positioned himself head-on with his trademark grin plastered across his face, perhaps trying to look authoritative. He couldn't look intimidating in the traditional sense, with his weedy frame and unmanaged hair, but he made Roth uncomfortable with his far too relaxed manner and general sliminess.

Slimy. That was the right word, and it described him to perfection. Nathaniel Pearce was the type of creature that Roth couldn't imagine having had acne as a teenager, as the spots would have just slid off his face.

'Ah, Oliver,' Pearce said. 'We're going to Iain's office. Nick's already there.'

'Iain's office?' Roth laughed. 'Seriously?'

'He has his reasons. And he doesn't want me to spoil them. Come along.'

Roth followed, noticing the disdain in Pearce's voice, despite the man's grin. That lifted Roth's spirits a little. If something annoyed Nathaniel Pearce, it was likely to be good – or at least entertaining.

Oliver Roth hadn't seen the office since the night Iain Marshall had died in it; when the prisoner in the room had exploded with such force that the whole AME computer had been annihilated, along with everything else in the room, including Marshall. Even after a month, Roth was surprised they'd finished scraping Joseph McCormick off the walls.

A couple of Floor B workers shot a glance at Roth as he passed. Perhaps he looked out of place with his combat boots marching across the carpeted corridor, with sweat dripping from his forehead and a loaded assault rifle instead of a suit and tie. Or maybe the stares were because of his reputation. They were in the presence of Nicholas Grant's fourteen-year-old master assassin, slaughterer of countryside rebels – and occasional punisher of staff members when required. Their facial reactions were predictable, and Roth didn't mind them.

Marshall's office was up ahead. The floor in front of the entrance had been recarpeted, with an ever so slightly different colour that made it stand out awkwardly from the rest of the corridor. Roth noticed himself slowing down, enough for Pearce to glance backwards and check on him.

This room was where my life began, he thought. *The good life, anyway.*

His mind, very briefly, went back to the early meetings he used to have in that office, alone with a man he admired; when Iain Marshall, war veteran of twelve years (who had not yet told him about his eight as an arms dealer), had been a rare person Roth had looked up to. At twelve years old, in a Britain that existed before the clones took over, not many people had held that status in Roth's life. Their meetings had largely been theoretical training sessions, with Marshall teaching him about military strategy, weapons, and the dirtier tactics that Marshall-Pearce's youth training programme had not dared to touch.

Marshall had never talked about Oliver Roth's *real* reason for being there, of course. He had been too smart to discuss it in a place which had compulsory CCTV and potential lip-readers on the other side. The subject only came up during their field trips and training sessions in the forest. Once upon a time, young Oliver was going to prevent Takeover Day from ever happening by assassinating Nicholas Grant himself. Clearly though, Marshall had lost his nerve and never given the signal.

Roth felt no guilt about the little fact that he could have

stopped Takeover Day before it began. It had been Marshall's decision rather than his own. It had also been perfect blackmail material – the ability to walk up to Grant and spill the beans any time he liked – but Roth had never needed to actually make any threats. Marshall had been careful enough to give him everything he ever wanted in order to buy his silence.

Roth sighed as he realised the true reason why he felt so uneasy, and why he missed Iain Marshall. His leverage was gone; all of his unspoken power vanished in that explosion. He no longer had the unquestioning support of Grant's Head of Military.

He walked into the office, and found himself in unfamiliar territory. All trace of the explosion was gone, not a charred stain in sight. It looked like the room had been rebuilt altogether rather than just redecorated.

At the new desk, placed on the opposite side of the room to where the old one had been, Nicholas Grant sat in a large leather chair.

'Oliver,' he said, in a voice that could perhaps have been called friendly, 'take a seat.'

Another leather chair had been placed on the other side of the desk. Grant stretched out a welcoming hand. Roth knew right away that this wasn't about his failure to contain the rebels that morning.

'Do you actually need me here?' asked Pearce.

'Yes,' said Grant. 'This is a formal ceremony that should be witnessed by the most valuable people in the Citadel. Unless you don't consider yourself that valuable?'

Pearce said nothing, and stood with his back against the door. Roth sat down in the chair, and browsed the paper placed on the desk for him to read. It was a contract of some sort, as far as he understood.

Provisional terms of role reassignment – Oliver Gabriel Roth, the title said.

'Formal ceremony?' he asked. 'You should have let me get changed.'

'I thought you'd feel more comfortable in your current outfit.'

He's not wrong, thought Roth.

'So what's this about?' he asked.

'You're getting promoted,' answered Grant with an enthusiastic grin. 'You're one signature away from becoming my provisional Head of Military Division.'

Oliver Roth had a lifelong habit of not letting his emotions show on his face, but it was difficult when surprises were landed on him. His eyebrows rose to the top of his head, his mouth opened, and his eyes stared into Grant's like a man who had won the lottery and been caught in a car's headlights at the same time. His concerns about the three escaping rebels left his mind altogether.

'I'm Iain's replacement,' he gasped.

'The youngest field marshal in history.'

'Why me?'

'There aren't many other candidates, in all fairness,' Grant replied as he leaned back in his leather chair. 'I have a few other ex-military personnel on my payroll, but none of them have modern, post-Takeover experience like you. Keith Tylor would have been perfect back in the day, before he came down with that bad case of multiple stab wounds. So that leaves either you or some colonel downstairs, and you're the one I believe in most. Besides, I'm sure Iain would have wanted it.'

You'd be surprised what Iain Marshall would have wanted.

'Do I still get to serve in the field?' Roth asked.

'Yes, you'll still get to run through the corridors killing

rebels. Except now you'll do it with *real* authority. And this office will be yours once it's finished. It may be a couple more weeks, but I'm sure you understand.'

Roth flipped through the contract, pretending to understand all the legal words.

'Wait,' he asked, 'so how come we *still* haven't rebuilt the clone factory two months on, but this office can be completely fixed in a matter of weeks?'

Pearce guffawed from the entrance.

'And that sentence right there,' he said, 'is why you're provisional Head of Military and not Chief Scientist. You clearly have no appreciation for the complexities involved with building a factory that produces armies of imitation humans.'

'I don't care about the "complexities" either,' Roth said. 'If my maths is right, we've got another two months before the last New London clones reach their four-month lifespan and collapse into dust. Now as Head of Military—'

'*Provisional* Head of Military,' said Pearce, grinning.

'Whatever. As the number-one military guy in Great Britain, I'm concerned about my New London army being a few months from extinction, and me having to rely on imported clones to keep us going. Why do your creatures live for such a short time anyway?'

'Because biological replication is complicated,' said Pearce. 'That's the child-friendly explanation. You should see how fast they heal though – it's a nice side effect of their bodies developing at a faster speed. Can *you* heal a broken arm in a day and a half?'

'I wouldn't know, Nat, it's usually me doing the breaking. Put your arm across my desk and I'll give you a child-friendly demonstration.'

'Oliver,' Grant said with a discreet laugh, 'don't threaten your closest colleague.'

'Why not? Iain and Nat fought all the time. I'll take Iain's job, but I'm not becoming Nat's new best friend.'

'I'm guessing you won't be taking Iain's wife and daughters, either,' Grant scoffed, perhaps in an attempt to quell the rising mood with offbeat humour.

'Good guess,' Roth replied. 'How's poor Mrs Marshall doing, by the way? Is she OK after losing the husband she loved *so* dearly?'

'Hannah's doing fine,' Pearce said behind him with subtle laughter: a low-level chuckle with an air of superiority, as if he knew something about the Marshalls that Roth did not. Roth wondered what it meant, before realising he didn't care. He grabbed a fountain pen that Grant had left next to his papers, and found the dotted line.

Then something strange happened. Roth had not heard McCormick's voice for a month, and had only ever met him once, but he recognised the man's soothing tone the moment it entered his head.

The world is full of young people who think their futures are already decided, just because they've been instructed to believe it.

Roth had tried to argue against McCormick at the time. Even now, he did his best to ignore the words in his mind.

Even though we don't get to decide what happens to us, we do get to choose how we respond. And even if people tell you your future is predestined...

Roth shook his head, and hoped that Grant wouldn't notice.

He remembered his miniature breakdown on the night McCormick died: when he came to realise that he had already made every meaningful decision that would decide the course of his life. When he had realised that, in all likelihood, it really was too late for him.

Helplessly obedient to his boss, despite being the only

person in the room with an assault rifle, Oliver Roth signed the dotted line. And just like that, he became the second most powerful person in the whole of Great Britain. Only provisionally though, according to the exact wording.

Provisionally, Roth thought. *I wonder what the catch is here...*

'OK, job done,' Pearce said, stretching his arms. 'Can I go now?'

'Has Gwen arrived?'

'Not as yet.'

'Then no, you can't.'

Roth smiled. He didn't know much about Gwen Crossland, except for her now-famous work on the Ginelli Project, but he knew to keep his distance from her. After Marshall's death, someone in Grant's health department had recommended her to Roth as a psychotherapist who could help him. Roth had obviously declined: the less influence that tiny, well-spoken hag held over his brain, the better off he would be.

Suddenly, she was there. Stood in the entrance, next to Nathaniel Pearce.

Holy crap, she even moves like a bloody poltergeist.

'Nicholas,' she said, although her lips barely moved.

'Nick, if that's OK,' Grant corrected her. 'Are you ready?'

'My bags are packed, and my equipment is in safe hands. But my work on Floor G is not yet complete.'

'How long, may I ask?'

Roth noticed how polite Grant was being to Gwen Crossland. He could not tell whether it was genuine politeness to a lady from his own generation, or politeness inspired by fear.

'I should be done by the end of the morning,' she answered. 'I'm just waiting for Nathaniel's company. He should join me to observe the Acceleration experiment.'

'I'll tell the vehicle port operatives you'll be joining them at lunchtime then,' said Grant. 'You should make it to the transport mid-afternoon, preparation should be ready by the evening, and you'll be there before midnight. Enjoy New Oxford, both of you. It's strikingly similar to New London, except the staff are less interesting.'

'In my experience,' finished Crossland, 'it's the "interesting" staff who are the most problematic. Nathaniel?'

She walked away with Nathaniel Pearce in tow, leaving Roth on his own with Nicholas Grant.

'Why are they going to New Oxford?' asked Roth.

'They're going to engineer the greatest one-day bloodbath in human history,' answered Grant. 'I'll fill you in later. In the meantime, you've got a bloodbath of your own to organise. Did you notice how your promotion is—'

'Provisional, yeah. So… how do I make it permanent?'

'By successfully completing your next mission. One which will prove beyond doubt that you're worthy of the new title.'

Grant leaned forward, placing his elbows on his desk and interlocking his fingers. The expression on his face turned bitter.

'It's not often I admit to making mistakes, Oliver. But the biggest mistake I ever made was underestimating Joseph McCormick. He and his band of countryside wildlife were able to reach our upper floors and stop us from becoming invincible, all because I didn't think they were worth paying attention to.'

Stop making excuses, you old fart. You've been paying attention to them ever since your daughter jumped ship, and you've made it personal. I mean bloody hell, you even made their old school the main AME test centre.

'So it's time to deal with them once and for all,' Grant continued. 'And I know you've focused a lot of effort on them since the Takeover. You've dispatched six of them personally, haven't you?'

'Eight.'

'Good lad. Now last time I checked the list, only nine names on it belonged to people who are still alive. Ten, if you include my backstabbing daughter. I need you to make it *zero*. And from now on, we're not waiting for them to come to us.'

Oliver Roth went over Grant's sentences word by word in his mind, just to double- and triple-check he had interpreted them right. But whichever way he looked at it, the message was the same: Grant no longer wanted Shannon alive. After everything she had done to them – running away from New London, stabbing Keith Tylor to death when he had come to recapture her, then providing the intelligence and tools for the Underdogs to destroy the clone factory (even the loss of their AME research had been partly her doing, since she must have shared the login details of the scientist she and Lambourne had hacked) – evidently enough was enough. The death of Grant's daughter was now a vital part of his vision for success.

'They fear you, Oliver,' Grant continued. 'And with their leader gone, they'll fear you more than ever. And I'm assuming you want the honour of finishing them off?'

Roth nodded. He would still have the element of surprise over the Underdogs, since they believed he was gone from this Earth. But he tried to ignore the memory of why his advantage existed.

Roth wanted to feel proud, as if his feigned death had been deliberate trickery on his part. But more than anything he felt the shame of failure, and leftover pain from the burn scars across his torso. He hadn't revealed to anyone how much of a wreck his bare chest looked.

Even Grant seemed to have forgotten about Roth's supposed death. He had just mentioned the Underdogs' fearing him in the *present* tense. Evidently, the event had fallen out of

Grant's mind in the maelstrom of bigger carnage that had happened that night.

And that was OK. Reminding Grant of the truth would involve revealing the failure that led to it.

'What do you want me to do?' Roth asked.

'That countryside hideout they have… Spitfire's Rise, I think they call it.'

Surely he's not asking…

'Sir, there must be a million square miles of—'

'I'm going to give you until the end of the day,' Grant interrupted, 'and then you're leaving New London. Take as many soldiers as you see fit, and whatever resources you feel you need. And do not return to this Citadel until you have found Spitfire's Rise and destroyed it.'

Chapter 2

Ewan took a last cautious glance around the countryside as Mark opened the trapdoor. It was just a formality of course, with clones so rarely seen outside of the Citadels these days, but he felt the need to check anyway.

'Well done, guys,' he said. 'You did well today.'

Mark ignored him, although Simon gave some kind of vague smile.

Huh, even the tiny parts of leadership aren't easy.

Ewan was the last one through the trapdoor, and the last to reach the end of the thin and dusty tunnel that brought them to the cellar's entrance. Ahead of him, Simon found the handle among the mud wall that concealed the doorway. Kate had occupied many hours hiding the door behind a fascia of clayed mud, so that any invaders would only see a dead end rather than a door – it was more a disguise than a practical defence, but it had occupied her and kept her comfortably isolated during her frequent anxious moments.

Simon turned the handle and opened the door outwards, walking into the cellar with Mark close behind him. Ewan passed the Memorial Wall on the way to joining them as they packed their weapons away, and took great care to ignore

McCormick's name chiselled at the bottom of the list. It was difficult to lead with him watching.

It hadn't been half as difficult when the man was alive. The uncompromising reassurance of Joseph McCormick – the unrelenting belief and faith he had displayed so genuinely – had found its way past Ewan's PDA-ridden instincts and allowed him to become his own lead soldier, without the deathly fear of other people's expectations and unspoken demands. Well, without *some* of the fear anyway.

With the old man dead, it hadn't taken long for Ewan's anxieties to return. He could already feel the creeping little demands setting him on edge like they did in the pre-McCormick days, and the temptation to disobey all of them regardless of whether they were right. He could fight off such feelings well enough, but the fighting drained his energy. He was so *tired* with McCormick gone, and anxious to the point of being frightened by the sight of a chiselled name in a bloody rock.

Mark and Simon finished their work and headed upstairs in silence, leaving Ewan to call comms on his own.

The phone rang at his ear three times without answer, which was odd. Maybe Alex had popped to the loo, and Gracie was being her usual lazy self.

Or maybe it's not laziness, Ewan thought. *Maybe her hesitation to take responsibility is because of fear. Perhaps it always has been.*

Ewan would never have expected it, but his empathy for Gracie was growing by the day. In recent weeks he had begun to remember the insidious fear of other people's judgement, which Gracie must have grown up fearing too. It had never truly vanished from his head, even after society vanished on Takeover Day, but in his new leadership role he felt the overbearing pressure of other people's disapproval stronger than ever.

He was surprised when Alex finally answered on the sixth ring.

'Hello?'

'Did I catch you sleeping, Alex?'

'No... what's up?'

It wasn't Alex's usual confident voice, but Ewan was too worn out to investigate.

'We're home. Your duty's over. See you in a bit.'

'Yeah, sure. Bye.'

The phone went dead before Ewan could react. But he wasn't complaining. The farm was waiting for him, and the sooner he reached it the better.

Ewan wondered whether it would have been cosier and more intimate to meet Shannon in the small room through the other tunnel, which they affectionately called the engine room, but he knew it would have been too noisy. The thermal blocker that kept their heat signatures safe from scanning equipment was completely silent, but the adjacent petrol generator wasn't. He made his way along the tunnel under the neighbouring house, and climbed up the stepladder into the makeshift farm. There, as agreed the previous night, Shannon Grant was waiting for him.

Growing up, Ewan had never believed himself to be the type of person to have a serious romantic relationship. Not through any fault of his own, despite other people's assumptions about him, but because he couldn't imagine making himself that vulnerable. But when he entered the farm he found the one person on Earth who had fought her way past his spiky defences, and into the warmer parts of his mind which he almost feared to use. And she happened to be the daughter of the world's most nefarious dictator.

Shannon reached for him and brought him into a hug. They had even moved on to kissing on most days, but Ewan didn't have the energy for it after his long trip back from New London. And kisses had to be genuine, otherwise there was no point.

Tell him his daughter's a great kisser, came his own voice in his head.

The memory of those words made him flinch. Just to score a point against the late Iain Marshall, Ewan had boasted about his relationship with Shannon during a phone call on the AME mission. The information had probably been passed on to Nicholas Grant, which meant the dictator would know something that made Ewan vulnerable. (And on top of that, Ewan didn't like talking about women that way. They were worth more than that.)

He told the voice in his head to shut up. It was only trying to make him feel guilty, and using his inbuilt hatred of himself to look for things to—

'What's wrong?' Shannon asked as the hug came to an end. 'You're struggling.'

Ewan shuddered. Shannon's ability to read him like a book of ABCs was both a comfort and a concern: a comfort because there was less for him to put into words, and a concern because – even in a house of unperceptive special-ed teenagers – his feelings were no longer secret.

'Ewan?' she asked. 'Is everyone safe?'

The worry in her voice forced him to give a reassuring answer.

'Yeah. Yeah, we're all fine. Just feeling the pressure today, that's all.'

'It's your first proper mission as leader. Everyone understands.'

Ewan kicked some soil around with the tip of his boot, hands in his pockets. He focused his mind on his physical surroundings – a trick that sometimes helped with his anxieties

– and heard the irritating electric buzz of the lights above the vegetables, felt the creak of the thin floorboards around the soil, and noticed the pattern of the peeled wallpaper that had once belonged to McCormick and Polly's neighbours.

This time, however, the distractions didn't help and he remained anxious.

'I don't *want* people to understand,' he said. 'I want them to be clueless about how stressed I am. Visible strength is everything.'

'You don't have to be invincible, Ewan. McCormick wasn't invincible.'

Ewan shot her a dirty look, which he regretted.

'Sorry,' she said, 'I didn't mean it like that. *Emotionally*, he wasn't invincible. And he wasn't ashamed of it either.'

For a while, Ewan didn't respond. When he did, he spoke with a meek gasp, his eyes pointed far away from her face.

'I'm afraid, Shannon.'

'You're at war, Ewan. How else are you supposed to feel?'

It's not just that. I've been at war for a year. But people are looking at me now, far more closely than before.

I'm afraid of the Underdogs depending on me for motivation and guidance, the same way we depended on McCormick.

And worst of all, I'm afraid of depending on you.

Shannon, without exaggeration, was his closest friend in the world. Not just because she was an understanding and accommodating girlfriend, but also because most of her competitors were dead. Ewan had loved his family, especially his dad, during the years when he had hated the rest of the world. He had loved Charlie, although not admitted it until after Oliver Roth had got to him. He had loved McCormick, and was grateful that the man was observant enough to have noticed.

It was a terrifying pattern. The love of Ewan West seemed to be a death sentence.

'Do you want a few minutes alone?' Shannon asked. Ewan nodded. After one more quick, non-intrusive hug, she climbed down the stepladder and left him by himself.

Ewan took as little time to steady himself as he could get away with. The group would need him to lead a meeting as quickly as possible, and the sooner it was over the better. Two minutes of long breaths later, with nothing but soil, hot lights and moist air for company, Ewan made his way back to the cellar and up the stairs to the ground floor.

When he walked into the living room, most of the remaining Underdogs were already waiting. Mark must have spread the word. He and Simon were already there, on the same sofa as Shannon. As Ewan looked around at the rest of his team, he was struck by how important they secretly were to him when he wasn't intimidated by them. Thomas Foster, who hadn't yet reached his tenth birthday but was capable of raising the spirits of an entire house. Jack Hopper, the trustworthy friend with whom he had survived New London's Inner City, stimming his fingers already in anticipation of Ewan's words. Kate Arrowsmith, who had survived the Inner City with him too, as well as the strike on Oakenfold *and* the AME mission.

Kate's last month had been even worse than Ewan's, and he was willing to admit it. She had watched her boyfriend Raj die in front of her, blown apart by the shield that had surrounded Oakenfold. She had kept her strength up in the days that followed, only to lose McCormick at the end of it all. Since then, her whole personality had vanished. A month on, her body hung around Spitfire's Rise, but the real Kate Arrowsmith had not yet returned.

Ewan bit his lip, and performed a quick head count. Everyone was in attendance except for the comms team and Lorraine, but Ewan knew better than to try summoning their reclusive nurse from the clinic. She hadn't been the same since

McCormick's death either… most likely due to her own compliance with the plan that had killed him.

He decided to start. The comms team weren't back, but their absence would mean two fewer judging faces in the crowd. He felt safer starting without them.

'Right,' he began to his audience, most of whom fell silent for him. 'Better make this a quick one, because we don't have much time to muck around.'

And the less time I spend talking, the less time I'll spend feeling judged.

'What about Alex and Gracie?' asked Mark.

'If they're late they're late. They know everything already and I'm not delaying this just because they're slow. Anyway, we didn't get as much as we wanted from the computers, but we got enough. Grant has been making plans to transport a ton of stuff from New Oxford to New London. The data suggested—'

'Only a ton?' asked Jack. 'That's barely anything in industrial terms.'

'Not a literal ton, you numpty.'

Name-calling people for interrupting you. Wow, McCormick must be looking down at you with bloody admiration.

'But yeah,' Ewan continued, 'a load of equipment or something. The data didn't say exactly what, but it's pretty obvious. Long story short… they're planning to shut down New Oxford.'

A confused silence fell among the room.

'Why on Earth would they do that?' asked Thomas.

'They wouldn't, unless they didn't need it anymore. Why have two Citadels when one will do the job?'

'You don't mean…' gasped Shannon.

'Yeah. In thirteen months, so many people have died in New London *and* New Oxford that the survivors can fit into one prison together.'

It wasn't until he saw Thomas' reaction that Ewan realised how casually he had spoken the sentence. His year as a soldier had desensitised him to the horrors of war, to such an extent that even the most horrific facts had become no more than facts. Meanwhile, the nine-year-old boy on the carpet in front of him still took the news as if those countless people had died in front of his eyes.

Ewan reached for the most obvious coping strategy. He disregarded his feelings before they could take root in his mind, and moved on.

'They're reducing the number of Citadels, then,' said Shannon, 'from an unknown number to another unknown number.'

'Yeah,' Ewan answered, irritated that such a vital piece of information had been kept from Shannon during her year on Floor A, and irritated at himself and his friends for not having memorised how many Marshall-Pearce complexes existed before Takeover Day – back when they were known only as 'research centres'. Their pre-Takeover selves could never have known how important that number would one day be. 'So my guess is, they'll keep the essentials going in New Oxford – their Cerberus defence missiles, their clone factory and so on – and they'll leave enough human staff to operate it all, but their prisoners and anything being used to keep them alive will get transported over here. We can expect a ton of convoys – not actually a ton, Jack – and once we know which routes they're taking, there'll be loads of chances to strike.'

'Question,' declared Mark. 'If they're transporting equipment that'll keep prisoners alive, why the hell would we get in their way?'

'Because the longer we stop the equipment from arriving, the longer it'll take to transport the prisoners. And looking at the bigger picture, any disruption will slow Grant's progress towards whatever his ultimate grand master plan is.'

'I don't want to put my life on the line to slow him down,' Mark grunted. 'I'd rather *stop* him.'

Next to him, Kate was nodding. Contributing as much to the discussion as she felt able to.

'It's this or hanging back,' said Ewan. 'Besides, we don't know what we'll find when we raid those convoys. Could be useful stuff.'

'Could be stuff with a tracker planted,' said Mark. 'Something they're just dying for us to bring back here.'

'Useful for information, even if we don't bring it home. Either way, we're not lying here and waiting for the whole thing to be over.'

'That's your executive decision as our grand leader, is it?'

'Actually, yes. It is. Meeting dismissed.'

Ewan turned his head away from his audience, hoping it was enough to claim victory. An argument against Mark would never have gone his way. And even if it had, the argument's existence alone would be considered a win for Mark. It was better to not engage with him.

At some point I'd better tell them what the attack plans are. Or how we'll even work out which routes they'll take. But I've got to know for myself first.

The groan of faux leather seats sounded around him as the Underdogs rose from the sofas. Nobody spoke.

When Ewan wandered out of the living room, he caught sight of Alex opening the door from the cellar. His face froze and his chin dropped, like a child being caught stealing cookies from a cupboard. Clearly, he was guilty about getting back so late.

'You took your sweet time,' said Ewan.

'Yeah, sorry.'

Some time later, Ewan would realise how weird it was that Alex had apologised for something.

'Where's Gracie?'

Chapter 3

Alex had expected his hand to freeze as it landed on the clinic door handle, almost in fear of the woman inside and the conversation that lay in wait. Instead, his fear of the rest of the house forced him to hurry.

It had surprised him how easily Ewan had been fobbed off by his answer. Perhaps he had stuff occupying his own mind. The sentence 'she'll be a few minutes' had resulted in the predictable answer of 'why the hell weren't you with her the whole way back', but his dismissive 'I can't force her to stay with me, mate' had stopped the conversation dead. Alex had not shed his opening tear until he was halfway up the stairs.

There were not many tears, yet. He was too nervous to cry, for now.

Lorraine shot him a hostile glare as he approached. Alex closed the door behind him, and stood as far away from her as he could manage.

'I... need to talk,' he said.

Lorraine huffed, and turned her head away.

She hasn't been the same since we blew up McCormick. I guess it takes a while to get over causing something like that.

OK, that's not quite fair. McCormick died because of Grant and

Marshall and all those twats. All Lorraine did was give him an easy way out if his situation became hopeless.

But still, she carved him open and planted a fistful of NPN8 inside his abdomen. Not something she'll forget any time soon. And she knows we won't forget either.

'It's about the night McCormick died,' Alex said. It was the most reliable way of grabbing her attention.

As predicted, her head drifted back in his direction, and her eyes started to pierce his own.

'I talked to you on the phone that night,' he said, 'but I don't remember it. There's just a blank space where...'

Lorraine closed her eyes, just for a moment, in what seemed like either pity or irritation. Alex couldn't tell which.

'All I know,' Alex continued, 'is that I was captured, cloned, then held in a bungalow for a few days, and they tried forcing me to give away where we live. I lied and said it was Lemsford, then got out when the others escaped... and my memories of it were taken away. But I know there's more to it than that.'

'Really?' asked Lorraine.

Alex hadn't expected to actually hear her voice. Its grumpiness took him aback.

'I only know because Shannon let it slip a week later,' he said. 'We talked about the mission, and she mentioned the phone call and then fell deathly silent, like she was trying to conceal something from me. I badgered her about it until she talked, and she told me that I'd forced *myself* to forget about it... and "trust me, Alex, there's a good reason you did". So I trusted her and took it no further. But now I *need* to know.'

'Why?' asked Lorraine. 'What changed?'

Alex had no idea how to answer. So he didn't.

'Shannon was right,' Lorraine continued. 'You said you wanted to wipe all memory of it from your head, and we all agreed it would be the best thing for you.'

So it's true... I really did wipe the memories myself?

'Normally,' finished Lorraine, 'the worst part of any type of anxiety is not knowing. But not in this case. We told the others what they needed to know – about your capture, how you lied to misdirect our enemies, and how you can't remember the events anymore. But the other contents of that phone call really are best left forgotten.'

'I don't need to know what we talked about,' Alex said, unsure if he was telling the truth. 'I just need to know... was music involved?'

The expression on Lorraine's face changed from one that Alex couldn't decipher to another he couldn't decipher. Was it sympathy? Remorse? Fear? Either way, Lorraine took a long time before responding. Maybe it was her nursing instincts from a whole world ago, instructing her on what she could and couldn't tell her patients.

'If you have to ask, you must have worked it out,' she said.

'So that's a yes?'

'Tell me what you're thinking, Alex.'

Alex took the longest, most relaxed breath he knew how to take, as if preparing for a taekwondo grading performance. Once he said the words, they could never be unsaid.

Then again, bodies that had been stabbed to death could never be *un*stabbed to death, so his situation was already irredeemable.

'I think there are pieces of music that... force me to think or do things,' he whispered. 'I think there was something that happened on the clone factory mission... it's the first blank space in my memory I can think of... and Grant or someone planted something in my mind to be triggered by certain songs...'

The thump-thump-thump began in his brain.

No, he yelled at himself, *whatever it takes, I can't have it in my head. Keep it out. Keep it out at all costs...*

'And?' asked Lorraine.

Alex hadn't realised he had stopped talking.

'And I need you to tell me, *right now*, if I'm a danger to anyone in this house.'

Well that's a bloody stupid thing to say.

Then again, she doesn't know Gracie's dead yet.

'Alex, I'm a nurse. The hospitals may be gone, but I'm still under my oath of protection. If I truly believed you posed a risk to the other Underdogs, I'd have told Ewan myself.'

It was strange how comforted Alex felt by that.

But even so, Gracie was still dead. And he wouldn't have many minutes before people asked the kind of questions he couldn't dismiss.

'What else did I tell you over the phone that night?' he asked.

'Nothing that would help you if you found out.'

'You'd be surprised.'

'Well this is my judgement,' she snapped, 'not just as a nurse, but as the matriarch of this house and as the only *real* adult left in Spitfire's Rise. It was Shannon's judgement too, despite her moment of unhelpful blabbering later on. Given the information I have, you are better off never finding out. And unless you present me with information that would change my mind, that will *remain* my judgement.'

Clever cow, thought Alex. Leaving aside the 'only real adult' comment – a clear swipe at him, aged twenty-two and the second-oldest Underdog left alive – she was forcing his hand. Giving him a firm answer, unchangeable unless he dropped his act and just told the truth.

He put on a brave face, and pretended to believe his plan would go well.

'*I* believe I might be a danger to other people,' he began. 'And before you ask why, I don't have to tell you how. I don't *need* to give you any details. They don't matter. Because you've now had a person coming up to you and *telling* you they're a danger to others. According to that oath you think still matters, you have to change your approach now. So get yourself out of your own backside and just tell me what I said over the phone, because you're endangering the others if you don't.'

He knew he would be met with either a loud, semi-abusive response, or with complete silence. Thankfully, it was the latter.

A whole minute later, as if she were trying to make the experience as awkward as possible, she spoke.

'You won't like what you're about to hear.'

'I don't have to like it. I just have to know it.'

Alex suspected that before the death of McCormick, the argument would have been harder to win. But after a month of self-destructive seclusion, perhaps Lorraine cared a little less about whether her judgements remained as professional as before.

'After you were captured in the clone factory control room,' she said, baldly, 'you were subjected to experimental treatment by a psychotherapist called Gwen Crossland. She used the influence of songs to switch your memories on and off, and used them to hold you inside that bungalow to keep an eye on you. Obviously she planned for you to give away the name of our village, but thankfully you never knew it to begin with. She'd tried the same thing with Daniel Amopoulos some months ago, but he hadn't known either.'

Lorraine spoke slowly, but the information was still too much for Alex to take in. The other Underdogs had all known about his capture (and had been kind enough to not keep reminding him about it), but the news of Gwen Crossland's 'treatment' was a total shock.

'What were the two songs?' he asked.

'You never told us,' Lorraine huffed. 'You were quite adamant that we would never find out, and we decided to respect your wishes. You were just that desperate to never remember the details.'

'OK, you've made your point, but still...'

'You want the details anyway. OK. Do you want to talk about how the Alex Ginelli clones were created?'

Alex nodded. He had never seen them for himself, but there was no question that they existed. Jack and Gracie had killed *three* of them in Lemsford.

Her experience of fighting me didn't help her in the end...

'Did you ever wonder *how* Grant cloned you?' Lorraine asked.

Alex opened his mouth, but no words came. For the month that had passed since the AME strike, he had never even questioned it. His brain had felt unsettled yet satisfied, somehow content with the answer being absent from his mind.

'How?' he asked.

'How are clones normally made?'

'Well...' said Alex, 'there are these cloning pods in the factories. A volunteer walks into them, they get scanned, and...'

Alex paused, and his jaw dropped.

'You've known that for a month,' Lorraine replied. 'You taught the rest of us after you found out. And you *never* applied this knowledge to your own situation? You never thought it might have been exactly the same process with you?'

It never occurred to me, Alex thought. *Every time I wondered where my clones came from, my brain just went blank, like it was trying to avoid the answer. I knew I had clones and I knew how clones were made... but until this moment, my brain never allowed me to connect the two thoughts.*

What else is my brain telling me to avoid thinking about?

'You were the volunteer, Alex,' Lorraine continued. 'Turns out you walked into a cloning pod and you *allowed* yourself to be cloned.'

Alex slapped both hands over his forehead. He wouldn't have done that, surely?

'You made a deal with Grant and Crossland,' Lorraine spat. 'Let yourself get cloned and give away Spitfire's Rise, in exchange for your life. Thankfully you escaped before they could find out you'd lied – if you'd been caught, they'd have removed your brain, extracted its memory signature and added it to your clone models, in the hope that your clones would remember the way home.'

'Wait... can they really give clones memories of their previous lives?'

'*Can* they? It was literally what they had planned for you! You may not like the thought of making a deal with Grant, but you assured us that's what you did. It was necessary to keep yourself alive, and you felt like it was a small price to pay.'

'Could you say it a little more judgementally, please?' he asked sarcastically.

'You've already put us in danger once, Alex. And we forgave you. Now whatever it is that's making you think you're a danger to us *again*, my honest guidance is to spill the beans to more than just the cranky old recluse in the clinic. If you keep it to yourself, the others might not be so forgiving this time.'

It wasn't the answer Alex had wanted. He still clung on to the hope that Gracie would just be remembered for dying of her own stupidity, getting lost on the way home or something like that. It wasn't like they'd ever find her body, which had been thin enough to drop through the manhole in the street outside the comms unit.

He could preserve himself for a little longer, couldn't he?

But what if I say nothing, and one day it happens again?

A few minutes ago the song nearly got back inside my head. Could I have killed Lorraine if I'd not fought it off?

Alex remembered his many years of watching gory zombie movies, and how in every single bloody one of them, there'd always been one crap character who got bitten and infected but decided not to tell the others. He had despised those one-dimensional characters, and despised movie tropes in general (not least because 'the token black guy usually dies', or 'any black man and black woman will automatically fall in love'), but he recognised that he was a living equivalent of the same dilemma. If he were bitten by a zombie, he wouldn't be the type of person to hide it, would he?

Except – at that moment at least – he was. And he would remain so, unless he grew some extra bravery.

'Is there anything else?' asked Lorraine.

Alex shrugged.

'If you have more to talk about, then talk to me. If I've satisfied your curiosity, leave me alone. But don't hang around in the clinic to avoid facing the others.'

'What, like *you've* done for the past month?'

'*Get out*, Alex.'

Alex did as he was told, careful to not push his luck any further. He turned to the door, his thoughts already turning to the enormity of what he had just learned.

He hadn't just been captured. He had *let* himself be cloned. His loyalty in staying at the bungalow had been brought upon him by this Crossland person, rather than his own free decision. And now he had killed a fifteen-year-old. Under influences beyond his control, but had killed her nonetheless.

They must have set every computer alarm in New London to that song. Hoping I'd be there to hear it, and stood right next to my allies... Well, their plan went mostly right.

37

Wow, Dad would be so proud of me.

Two steps into the hallway, Kate burst out of the women's bedroom in combat gear.

'Alex, get ready,' she said. Perhaps she had meant to sound commanding, but all he heard in her voice was weakness.

'Ready for what?'

'Finding Gracie. Ewan's getting all of us to go out looking. He's afraid something bad's happened to her.'

She ran down the stairs without another word. Alex followed, in silence too.

Chapter 4

Ewan was angry at Gracie. So angry, he was already preparing the speech he was going to dump on her once she showed up. It was becoming a staple habit of Ewan's leadership: preparing his sentences well in advance so he wouldn't stumble over his words during important moments. He had done it for most of his life whilst coping with general conversation, but his new role made it essential for him to not humiliate himself with verbal incompetence.

The armoury was filling with soldiers. Shannon and Mark had been as fast as expected, and Jack had not been much later. Simon was there too, leaving just Kate, who had gone looking for Alex.

Meanwhile, Lorraine and Thomas were set to have Spitfire's Rise to themselves. If seven Underdogs weren't enough to find Gracie, a nine-year-old boy and a reclusive ageing nurse would be unlikely to make a difference.

'So, is there a plan?' asked Mark.

Damn it, Gracie... you made me lead twice in the same morning.

Ewan turned away from the Memorial Wall to answer.

'We stay together as much as possible,' he began, 'and only branch out in pairs when necessary. And we *don't* call out for her, no matter what happens. We don't know who else is out there. If we haven't found her by the time we reach comms, we spread out and cover every reasonable route back home. Radios on and active at all times, in case she ran into something dangerous.'

Mark nodded, and turned his attention back to the shotguns. Ewan raised his eyebrows, surprised that his orders had been obeyed without question.

Even when there's nothing to complain about, I'm still seeing phantom threats to my leadership.

Kate entered the cellar, followed closely by Alex. Ewan immediately noticed the expression on his face.

Alex was terrified. Not nervous in the general sense, or even Kate-style anxious. He looked like a man whose world had just ended.

One of his shaking hands rose, and beckoned Ewan over to the stairs. Normally Ewan's first instinct would have been to refuse any command, physical or verbal, in a defiant statement of 'screw you'. But this time, he could tell something was wrong. He walked over to Alex and positioned his ear to receive a whisper.

'We need to talk,' Alex said. 'Privately.'

'Right now?'

'*Right* now. Before everyone leaves.'

Ewan drew his head away from Alex's mouth, so he could stare at him with interrogating eyes.

'You know something,' he said. It was not a question.

'In the farm,' Alex replied. 'Don't tell the others.'

'Well they're right behind us, and ready to start chanting at the Memorial Wall.'

'Just tell them to wait. They'll obey you. Bring Shannon. And a gun.'

Without another word, Alex slipped through the cellar like

a ghost, and entered the tunnel to the neighbouring house without anybody noticing. Ewan considered his options, but knew there was no other choice to make. He walked over to the shelves and grabbed a handgun for himself, then approached Shannon and tapped her on the shoulder.

'Shannon,' he whispered, 'I need to borrow you. Alex wants to talk in the farm.'

'What?'

'I don't know either. Just come with me. Please.'

Shannon headed for the tunnel, and was halfway through the door when Ewan addressed the remains of the crowd.

'You're going to have to wait a minute, guys,' he said, to a chorus of confused faces. 'I need to ask Alex about something before we go.'

'Along with Shannon?' asked Mark. 'And a gun?'

Ewan didn't answer. He vanished through the door to leave Mark, Kate, Jack and Simon to mumble amongst themselves. At the other end of the tunnel, Shannon was halfway up the stepladder that led into the farm. He followed her up, to the sight of Alex holding out a long coil of rope.

'I brought this with me,' Alex said, still whispering for some reason. 'Ewan... remember what you did after my clones were discovered?'

'What, tied you to a chair, ran a blood test and gave you that scar across your cheek?'

'The chair bit, yeah. Assuming I was the enemy until proven otherwise. I need you to do it again now.'

It was such a bizarre request that Ewan could have laughed, were it not for the dead seriousness in Alex's face. That, and the simple fact that he would never suggest something so ridiculous if there weren't a real sense of danger.

'You're unarmed, right?' asked Shannon.

'Yeah,' said Alex, tossing the rope over to her and sitting

himself down in the chair at the side of the soil. 'Ewan, guard me until she's finished. I don't know whether the song will creep into my head again.'

His last sentence had been said slowly and deliberately, with his eyes pointed right towards Shannon. In response, she froze in place.

Ewan had never been good at interpreting subtle, between-the-lines communication, but that had been an obvious signal. It was a reference to some kind of information that Alex and Shannon would understand, but Ewan would not.

'Oh…' she breathed, before leaping behind the back of the chair and getting to work. Ewan asked her for details, but got no immediate answer. Not before Alex's hands and feet were securely bound.

Ewan took long breaths. He was the only person in the room who didn't know what was going on, and the apparent urgency of it made him all the more agitated.

'Before we begin,' said Alex, his eyes to the floor and his voice subdued, 'I could have chosen to keep this a secret. I *could* have kept this to myself, and nobody would ever have known. Remember that. Remember that I chose to tell the truth anyway.'

Ewan had no idea how to react.

'We'll remember,' said Shannon, reassuringly. 'Tell us everything.'

She had always been better at knowing what people needed to hear. Alex lifted his head, his face wet with tears, and spoke.

'I know what happened to Gracie.'

Ewan's heart accelerated.

He needed – *needed* to know the truth, but Alex's face revealed that nothing happy would come from the discussion. Ewan had already worked out that the news would change the war, and he instantly wanted to avoid learning about it. But he knew the longer he went without knowing, the worse off he would be. It was time to get it over with.

'Alex?'

'She's... and I'm so sorry... she's...'

Injured or dead, Alex – which is it? Just say one of the words and get it over with!

'Dead...' he mouthed, but no voice came out.

Ewan and Shannon stared at each other, unable to process the information. There was abject disbelief at first: how the hell could Gracie die on a trip to comms? What could the danger possibly have been? Was it an accident, or had she been deliberately killed?

Was someone coming for them too?

Ewan turned back to the man who had pleaded to be tied to a chair, and asked him how Gracie Freeman had died.

'Shannon,' Alex replied, 'I just talked with Lorraine. She told me everything about the memory blanks. Everything I told you both on... on AME night. Well, she told me enough anyway.'

Lorraine knows what the gaps in Alex's memory are?

Shannon does too?!

Why did they keep it from me?

'I know music was involved,' Alex continued, 'and I know this woman called Gwen Crossland did it. And—'

Ewan marched up to the chair and pointed his handgun at Alex's forehead.

'*What the hell happened to Gracie?!*'

Alex gulped and gasped, but no words came out. At his side, Ewan could see Shannon shaking her head.

Screw it, he knows I'm not going to shoot him either way.

Ewan lowered the handgun, and Alex strung a sentence together.

'Ewan... Gracie died when the alarm went off in New London. The one that played... "S–Seven Nation Army".'

Alex rocked his head back and forth, as if trying to get something out of his mind. Most likely, trying to prevent the song from taking root in his head.

Ewan's brain tried and failed to make sense of the situation. He remembered the loud blasts of music from that computer next to Mark and Simon, but to him the situation had ended when Mark pulled the plug out of the wall. How could Gracie have died miles away while it was going on?

'And... how did the music kill her, exactly?' he asked.

'*You* killed her, didn't you?' asked Shannon, somehow not unkindly.

Ewan shot an astonished glance at her, but found sorrow in her face rather than anger.

'The song got stuck in your head,' she continued, 'just like the two that switch your memories on and off. Only this one took control of your mind and... made you kill her.'

The tears were in full flow from Alex. He nodded, wordless.

'And you asked to be tied to that chair in case the song gets into your head again.'

Another nod.

Ewan's outrage was addressed by Shannon before it even had time to build up.

'Don't judge him too harshly, Ewan,' she said. 'You've never known my dad. You don't know what he can do to people.'

I know what he did to my family and Charlie and McCormick and everyone else...

Ewan felt so hurt: just for once, and in this particularly vulnerable moment, Shannon's fiery, driven nature wasn't pointed in the same direction as his own. He and Shannon were so rarely misaligned.

'Don't judge him harshly?!' he shouted, perhaps too loudly. 'Gracie is *dead*! And *he* bloody did it!'

'Not the real me,' Alex gasped.

'He's right, Ewan,' said Shannon, her voice rough but kind. 'The *real* Alex chose to be honest with us, stopped you from sending out a pointless search party, and chose to face the consequences of his actions.'

Ewan clawed at the sides of his head. There was no arguing with Shannon, which made the situation so much harder to process.

'Make me understand, Alex,' he snarled. 'Because seriously, I don't have a clue whether I should keep you alive.'

Alex didn't react to the threat. Perhaps he didn't even disagree.

'Lorraine said...' he began, 'she said that I told her and Shannon about two songs that switched my memories on and off. I read about them in a report, but I didn't read anything about a third song. Maybe it was in a different report, or somewhere I didn't have time to read. I don't know... but it makes me violent. An irrepressible, horrifying kind of violent. Gracie never stood a chance. I think Grant wanted me to be part of the team that heard it in New London, so I'd have... I'd have killed you all there. I don't think he was aiming to kill anyone at comms.'

Despite all of Ewan's strategic prowess, no useful thoughts entered his mind. The only things that made sense in his world were the gun in his hand and the killer before him. An involuntary killer perhaps, but a killer nonetheless. Ewan had never been Gracie's biggest fan, and his rage was exacerbated by the knowledge that he had undervalued her so much while she was alive. There was guilt in Ewan's mind as well as anger: Gracie Freeman had deserved better in life, she had deserved better in death, and now she deserved revenge.

Something stopped him from taking the thoughts further. And even though Ewan's mind was a foggy place at that moment, he recognised that there were both strategic and moral reasons for compassion towards Alex.

The problems are not the person. The Oakenfold Code, that mantra that all of us agreed on back at school. It applies to Alex too. Shannon's right – the real Alex Ginelli chose to talk to us about this.

Ewan thought further, and came to realise something new about Alex: that if it weren't for his age and his lack of neuro-divergence, Alex would have fitted right in at Oakenfold. From his masking – pretending to be stronger and less vulnerable than he was – to his lifelong sense of isolation, and now some of his actions being beyond his conscious control, perhaps the cocky neurotypical guy had more in common with his Oakenfold friends than they had given him credit for.

'Ewan,' Shannon whispered to him, bringing him back to reality. 'There's a clever move we could play here.'

Ewan said nothing, but looked at her with a doubtful expression.

'I was in comms during his phone call that night. I heard what he said. And there's no way he could have told us everything in the three minutes he had.'

She turned to Alex, and offered an idea that gave Ewan an objective to focus on.

'We need to find out what those other two songs were. Let's switch his memories back on, and find out what else he knows.'

Chapter 5

Oliver Roth was conflicted. He wanted to hate Grant for expelling him from New London for the foreseeable future, and making him prepare to live in the wild countryside like some kind of rodent (or even worse, one of the rebels). But at the same time, he also wanted to thank Grant for the opportunity to annihilate Spitfire's Rise personally.

It'll be worth it once it's done, he thought to himself. *Once the word 'provisional' is dropped from my promotion, and I become Head of Military for real. I just need to endure the crappy stuff first.*

The lift arrived at Floor G and Roth stomped out along the corridor as loudly as he could. Despite being grateful for the opportunity, he *wanted* to feel annoyed at that moment. And there was a second reason for his annoyance too; he was walking in its direction at that moment, with neither Grant's knowledge nor consent.

It was a long way to Gwen Crossland's lair. He had enough time to swing his rucksack in front of him and dig through it to double-check his supplies. The food, drink, sleeping bags and ammunition would be carried by his private army of 500 clone soldiers, but some things he only entrusted to himself.

Electronic map, check. Super-strength torch, check. Night-vision binoculars, check.

Thermal tracker, check.

Roth smiled. When he truly thought about it, the hunt for Spitfire's Rise would probably be a challenge worthy of him. Perhaps some kind of masterpiece if he did everything right. And perhaps it was only the lack of a comfy bed and thrash metal on demand that put him off.

Roth slung the rucksack over his shoulder again, and checked the signs along the rooms at his side. He wasn't far away now.

Grant had called Pearce and Crossland's project 'the greatest bloodbath ever seen' or something like that. And Roth would move Hell and Earth to at least know what it was about. Hopefully they hadn't already left for the transport that would take them to New Oxford.

He turned around the last corner, and found a bulky man in combat uniform awaiting him outside Gwen Crossland's door.

Ah, crap. I forgot I'd told him to meet me here.

Grant had known Roth well enough to know that days or weeks without a human to talk to would drive him mad. And besides, a second-in-command was always useful on ambitious missions. Having been offered the pick of the bunch, Roth had chosen the perfect partner for the hunt for Spitfire's Rise: an older man with significant military experience, but a level of intelligence just low enough to make Roth feel superior.

The man lunged forward with an outstretched arm, towering over Roth but with an unthreatening, semi-foolish smile.

'Oliver Roth?' he asked, as if the ginger teenager could be anyone else.

'Yep,' Roth grunted, accepting the handshake.

'Good to meet you. Congratulations on your promotion.'

Evidently the word had got around quickly.

Provisional promotion, Roth was tempted to correct him, but decided to hold his tongue. Already, the word 'provisional' was becoming his least favourite in the dictionary: an irritating thorn in his side, piercing his entire sense of worth. A thorn that needed to be extracted as soon as possible.

Perhaps it was how Grant had planned for him to feel.

'Thanks,' he replied to the soldier. 'Just remind me what your name is?'

'João. Colonel João Pereira.'

Colonel. This guy outranked the great Ewan West's dad. By two levels, if I remember right.

Pereira didn't look much like a colonel. The bulk of his body looked like it could have been pure muscle in the past, but thirteen months of inactivity and good food had turned it into useless flab. Perhaps even more than thirteen months. Even in the old days, colonels hadn't served in the field.

'Joe-ow Pereira?' Roth mimicked. 'What kind of name's that?'

'Brazilian. Two generations back.'

'Yeah, but... *Joe-ow?*'

'Yes, João.'

'Did you bite your mother when she was naming you?'

Pereira's expression changed, as if his expectations of Oliver Roth weren't being met. Roth was OK with that. It was good to spring surprises on people. It kept them from settling into their comfort zones around him.

'What's the plan, Oliver?'

'Well, Colonel,' Roth began, with a hint of mockery directed at Pereira's expired rank, 'I don't know how much Grant has told you, but we're heading for Spitfire's Rise.'

'Where?'

'Ewan West's hidden headquarters.'

'Who?'

'Terrorist Faction 001, for bloody hell's sake. The guys that blew up the clone factory and made us rely on imported soldiers from New Reading. The ones who took out the AME shield and stopped us from becoming invincible, remember?'

'Ah. Didn't realise they were important enough for a name.'

Roth rolled his eyes, but Pereira had some kind of point. Ewan and his remaining friends probably felt they'd survived the war so long because of their deviousness or ingenuity or whatever. In truth, Grant could have marched clone armies up through the whole of Hertfordshire and razed every village to the ground, and he could have done it a year earlier. The biggest reason for the rebels' survival was simply that Grant hadn't considered them a valid threat.

Evidently, the loss of the clone factory and the AME shield had changed his mind. The Underdogs' admirable successes were about to be their undoing.

The Underdogs, thought Roth. *When I talk about them aloud I call them Terrorist Faction 001, like every other staff member in New London. But in my head I call them the Underdogs without a second thought.*

Am I getting overly attached to them?

'So what's the plan?' asked Pereira, interrupting Roth's thoughts.

'We're taking five hundred clones,' Roth continued, reaching into his rucksack to fetch out his electronic map, 'three hundred normal, one hundred biorifle. The other hundred are the new scout model Nat's been playing around with, the ones with night-vision eyes and enhanced optical detail and so on. We're heading north. Look here,' he said, pointing to the screen. 'The enemies' break-in points have all been through the northern wall. And their retard school was up in Harpenden, which is also north. Wherever they were by the end of Takeover Day, it wouldn't have been too far from where they started.'

Roth switched on the map, solar powered to last for weeks in open fields, and zoomed in on his first ports of call.

'We'll head towards Lemsford first,' he said. 'I don't know what you know about the Ginelli Project, but a guy called Alex lied to us and said that's where their base was…'

He took a moment to remember whether he'd asked for zero Ginelli clones to be attached to his team. When he remembered the aggressive wording of his email to the deployment manager, he nodded to himself, satisfied. It would avoid confusion once they reached Spitfire's Rise and hunted the real Alex.

'…so the rebels must be familiar with the place,' he finished. 'We'll look for clues there, and head further north if we don't find anything.'

Roth heard laughter from the other side of the door. It sounded like the wry chuckling of Nathaniel Pearce pretending to find something funny. The sooner João Pereira was gone, the better.

'And have you got any ideas on how to speed up the process?' Pereira asked. 'There are quite a few doors to knock on in Hertfordshire.'

'Well this might save some time,' said Roth, bringing out the thermal tracker. 'Anything bigger than a badger will get picked up by this. If we go far enough north, they'll appear on it. Then we send in the troops.'

Pereira nodded, but seemed unsatisfied.

'What?' asked Roth.

'Why didn't we use thermal tracking technology before now?'

'We did. Two months ago.'

When Shannon and Lieutenant Lambourne escaped. We found nothing more than a bunch of non-combatants hiding at a health centre, but Keith being Keith, he slaughtered them all anyway. Should have 'accidentally' killed Shannon while he was at it, no matter how much Nick wanted her alive at the time.

Roth thought back to Grant's face – blank but somehow still bitter – as he had said that *all* the Underdogs needed to die, including his daughter. He wondered what the inside of Shannon Grant's head looked like, having been parented by a mother who died before she'd finished infant school and a father who literally wanted her dead. Her mind was probably messed up enough for her to be a perfect fit for the Underdogs.

'So,' Pereira continued, 'if we didn't find Terrorist Faction 001 with thermal tracking back then, why would we find them with it now?'

Roth knew the answer, but it wouldn't satisfy Pereira. Keith Tylor was entirely to blame, having scanned far enough north to reach Hertford but stopping once he found human activity in the health centre. It was only by happy coincidence that he had found Shannon in the first place he looked; if the man had been blessed with even the slightest common sense, he would have searched further north for other potential hide-outs too.

That's a clue already, Roth thought to himself. *Wherever Spitfire's Rise is, it must be further north than Hertford. If it isn't, Keith would have found it first time round.*

'Don't worry, I've got a plan,' he said dismissively. 'Anyway, could you wait here for a moment? I've got a quick meeting with Nat.'

Without waiting for an answer, Roth slapped his keycard against the pad, and the door slid open for him. Colonel Pereira took the hint and shut up.

On the other side of the door, Nathaniel Pearce looked surprised to see him. Gwen Crossland did not. She didn't really look like anything.

'Hmm, I thought you might be interested,' she muttered.

'I might not be back here for a while,' said Roth, scanning his eyes around the room in search of clues. 'It was either now or never. So, what are you up to?'

He had half-expected Pearce to insist he turn around and leave, but instead he got the man's trademark grin. It was probably harder to justify ejecting Grant's new Head of Military.

'Why not take a look?' he asked. 'Assuming that's OK, Gwen?'

He felt the need to ask her permission. Knowing Pearce, that's more likely fear than respect.

Just like Grant. Is there a man anywhere in New London who doesn't fear her?

Crossland gave a subtle nod, almost without even moving her head, and Pearce led the way towards the door at the back of the office. Along the other side was a long corridor, bordered on the left side by one-way glass.

Before he even looked through it, Roth could guess what kind of sight awaited him. Pearce was grinning like a eugenicist making a new discovery, and Crossland wore a silent, unassuming expression. It was something they both took quite seriously, in their own ways.

Roth looked through the window and saw twelve terrified people. None of them matched any clone model Roth was familiar with. They were clearly humans.

There were six on the left, dressed in yellow jumpsuits. A couple of the faces looked familiar, from the staff parties Roth used to turn up to before he stopped being arsed. The other six people on the right wore green jumpsuits, and looked noticeably dirtier, thinner, and with more worn faces. Roth did not recognise a single one of them.

'So, who are you betting on?' asked Pearce. 'The staff team or the prisoner team?'

'Huh?'

'Gwen asked for twelve subjects – real, human subjects – to test whether this will work the way we predict. It was my idea to pick six failing staff members rather than just twelve prisoners.'

'Yes,' said Gwen, 'and unsurprisingly, the suggestion of teams was yours as well.'

'Might as well have a side to cheer for. I think our guys can do it. Oliver, what do you think?'

Roth wasn't sure whether he said it to defy Pearce, or whether Ewan's team had taught him to respect untrained common people, but he bet on the prisoners. Whatever the bet was for.

'Gwen?'

'I know better than to make offhand predictions, thank you very much.'

'Suit yourself. Ready when you are.'

Gwen walked to the other end of the room, although her body seemed perfectly still above her waist. It was almost as if she were hovering to the control panel.

At that moment, Roth recognised one of the women.

Sandra Zeigler... replacement Chief Architect for the northern wall...

She stood, motionless, on the wrong side of the two-way mirror, dread in her widened blue-green-grey eyes. Roth knew that Sandra had never liked him, especially after what he had done to her predecessor, but he found no pleasure seeing her in a yellow jumpsuit.

Two months ago, after Roth had blown a hole into the

Inner City with a laser cannon (aiming for a group of Underdogs, of course), Pearce had ordered him to torture an architect named Adnan Shah – to punish the man for not fixing the hole fast enough. Marshall's intervention had stopped Roth's torture and saved the man's life... only for him to have died from heart failure a week later. There were lasting consequences to an encounter with Oliver Roth.

Sandra Zeigler worked in the fabric trade back in the old world. She had nothing more than a foundation degree in architecture... I remember being in the room when she tried to refuse the promotion. Iain made me watch the ceremony, to try and make me feel guilty for Shah's death.

No wonder she's failing at being Chief Architect. And whatever's happening in here, she won't deserve it.

'Oh,' said Pearce, 'and you know what's funny? I found an Oakenfold staff member for this.'

Roth gave Pearce a mocking glance.

'Really?'

'Yep. Skinny young guy, red hair, third from the right. Daniel Berry, I think his name is. Taught computing as a student teacher. According to the records, it was his final placement before Takeover Day stopped his teaching course dead. Poor lad.'

'And you think him being here is going to affect his former students in any way?'

'It was more of a challenge,' said Pearce, 'to see if I could find someone connected to them. I was actually after someone completely different, but Mr Berry was rather helpful in finding that person too. Anyway, now his usefulness has expired and he can't help us in the wider battle. So he's here.'

Daniel Berry didn't look like the kind of man who had worked in a school. But trapped inside a clinical room in a coloured jumpsuit behind a two-way mirror, most humans wouldn't look like their real, pre-Takeover selves.

'Heads or tails?' asked Pearce.

'Tails.'

Pearce tossed the coin, which landed on heads.

'Bad luck. My side goes first. Gwen, could you please play song number one?'

'Yes,' replied Crossland as she did something with her laptop, 'and as requested, I'll set them to alternate every thirty seconds.'

'Excellent. In your own time, please.'

Crossland leaned towards a nearby microphone, pushed a button, and started to whisper.

'Fourteen minutes past eleven,' she began, 'June twentieth, Year One. Final phase of practical experimentation underway. Acceleration, research trial four. Commencing.'

Music started to emanate from inside the chamber. It was a song that Roth didn't recognise, but clearly the yellow-suited people inside the chamber did. And they were *angry* at hearing it.

The prisoners in green froze in horror as the six yellow-suited staff members charged towards them, fury etched into every muscle of their faces. There were no weapons in the chamber, so they just used their fists. Sandra Zeigler thrust her whole arm into the face of the prisoner in front of her, who dropped the hands he had held up in submission. The force of the punch sent his head into the wall behind him, and suddenly his body lost all responsiveness and collapsed to the floor.

The other five staff members acted the same ferocious way. The man closest to the mirror had a prisoner by the throat and was sending punch after punch into his cheek. The aggressors were barely recognisable as humans.

After thirty seconds, the music stopped. Further screams became audible through the glass: some from the surviving three or four prisoners, others from the six staff members who came to their senses and realised what they had done.

The music's controlling them...

If it wasn't so frightening, Roth would have admired it. But before he could get his own feelings straightened out in his mind, a second song began.

The surviving green-suited prisoners, scared and victimised mere seconds earlier, leapt to their feet with the exact same anger in their eyes. The yellow-suited staff members, still reeling from the horror of what they had done, were hopelessly unprepared for the response.

Roth turned away from the bloodbath, but tried not to look too horrified in case Pearce checked his reaction. A younger Oliver Roth might have enjoyed it. Perhaps a pre-McCormick version of him, although he tried not to give the man too much thought.

Roth looked back once the music stopped, and counted the living bodies. Sandra Zeigler had survived, sheltered at the far end of the room. Evidently she had lived because the other staff members had distracted the enraged prisoners in green. Daniel from Oakenfold had half his attention on the dead staff member who lay before him, and the other half on his wrist, visibly broken from the strength of his own punches. In total, Roth judged the score to be three staff members against three prisoners, although their fitness varied.

The first song played again, and the following thirty seconds left only Daniel Berry standing out of the prisoners. In the precious seconds of silence between songs, Daniel and the three staff members wasted time pleading with each other – half of them through fewer teeth than usual – but Roth couldn't hear their words. Whatever they said made no difference, and the frenzied computing teacher killed two of the staff members before the second song ended: even with all three of them working together, it had been easy enough for him to smash two of their heads together until they fell lifeless to the floor. Sandra Zeigler was left as the only staff survivor.

'One of yours and one of mine,' said Pearce with childlike curious joy. Gwen Crossland had her arms folded, not looking especially interested in the sporting side to her experiment.

As the first song played one final time, Sandra had the obvious upper hand. Roth watched, eyebrows raised, as she pulled her opponent's head to her armpit height and secured an arm around it. One enthusiastic jerk later, Daniel Berry from Oakenfold suffered a broken neck at the hands of the northern wall's Chief Architect.

The experiment ended. Crossland stopped the music and Sandra regained her senses. The last prisoner fell to her knees in wide-eyed shock, and the chamber fell into a haunted silence.

'So… what was all that about?' asked Roth, trying not to sound too disapproving.

'Population control,' answered Crossland. 'We made early steps into it during the Ginelli Project, but time constraints didn't allow us to investigate its full potential.'

A door opened at the far end of the chamber and a platoon of armed clones entered. The shaking Sandra Zeigler appeared too preoccupied to notice their presence, her gaze resting lifelessly at Daniel Berry's corpse. Nor did she give much of a reaction when they filled her with bullets, as if she still posed any sort of threat. In turn, the clones checked the other eleven human bodies and seemed satisfied.

'You realise, of course,' chuckled Pearce, 'it would be dangerous to release one of these subjects back into society. It's not like we can deprogram them or anything. Trust me, it's the best thing for the rest of us.'

Roth nodded, although the expression on his face probably didn't match his agreement.

'And this is something to do with New Oxford?'

'Replicating it on a larger scale, yes. Gwen, are you happy?'

'I feel satisfied that our hypotheses still stand, and that this experiment can have wider applications.'

'Splendid. Looks like I can give Richard Unsworth a call and tell him to babysit for me.'

Pearce brought his mobile phone out of his pocket, pushed his screen a few times, then raised the phone to his ear.

Richard Unsworth... Wasn't that the admin guy from the AME project? He's filling in as Chief Scientist while Nat's away?

As Pearce started talking, Roth's vague memories of the man's name started to reawaken. If it hadn't been for Unsworth's account being hacked by Ewan (as well as Shannon and Anthony Lambourne before him), all their research would never have been deleted that night. The man had narrowly avoided being cast into the Inner City as punishment for the breach – and Roth hadn't been called on for disciplinary measures either. Truthfully, Roth would have expected to see the man occupying one of the now-bloodstained yellow jump-suits, rather than taking charge in Pearce's absence. Perhaps, following recent crises, lucky Richard Unsworth had been considered too important to lose.

Pearce hung up his phone and looked directly into Roth's eyes.

'I suppose we'd better go then,' he said. 'Oliver, best wishes with your own little mission.'

It was a not-so-subtle way of telling Roth to leave. He took the hint and left without a word.

The plan was to spend the next ten minutes in the corridors of Floor G, gently recovering from what he had just witnessed.

Sadly, that idiot Colonel João Pereira awaited him outside Crossland's office.

'Right,' he began, 'are we ready to leave?'

Oliver Roth wore his best leadership expression, and wiped the image of the twelve dead bodies from his mind.

'Yeah,' he replied. 'Very ready.'

Chapter 6

Kate could follow orders as well as she always had, but it was no longer with enthusiasm for winning the war. Performing her duty as an Underdog soldier just meant doing as she was told for the approval of other people. It was like the masking she had always done in mainstream education, but with even more depressing undertones.

Losing Raj had been a large part of her collapse into anxious apathy. Blowing up McCormick had been another. Sure, Ewan and Alex had pushed the button too, but that little fact was firmly at the back of her mind. She had still leapt at the chance of taking care of the detonator, clueless about what it would truly mean. Since then, responsibility had stopped being a heartfelt interest of hers.

Nonetheless, she had joined Ewan in the farm as commanded. For some reason, he still saw her as fit to include.

Alex, tied to his chair in front of the crowd, was sweating. To be fair, everyone else was too. The first rule of Spitfire's Rise had always been 'don't take loaded weapons beyond the cellar', and today they were breaking it. And all because Gracie was dead, killed by one of their own.

'If you've got anything to say,' said Alex with his eyes to the floor, 'say it now and get it over with.'

'You're a murdering twat,' said Mark.

'Not helping,' said Ewan.

'I'm not saying it to help. I'm saying it because it feels good. Gracie was a tapeworm but she was one of us. And now we've got two less hands to carry guns with, so yeah, I feel pretty—'

'*Mark*,' Shannon snapped, marching across the room and staring up to his face, 'this isn't *your* discussion, and this isn't about *you* or *your* feelings. This is the part where you shut up and listen to more important people.'

Kate had no idea how Shannon had managed it, but Mark didn't say another word. She looked around at the others, and found similar reactions of surprise. Simon looked openly stunned, his eyes so wide they barely stayed in their sockets, and even Alex managed a weak, inaudible laugh. Ewan, of course, was staring at her with that face he always had for her. It wasn't quite a smile or anything *traditionally* romantic, but it was full of respect and admiration.

They were all who had turned up for the questioning. Kate and four others. Thomas was too young, and there was no dragging Lorraine out of the clinic. Jack, for unclear reasons, had refused to enter the room.

He cared about Gracie.

Not that he ever did anything about it… he avoids romance like the plague. But he cared about her, in his own way.

'Let's get this started,' said Ewan. 'We all know why we're here, so I won't waste time explaining. Alex—'

'I don't remember the song. And my memory stops when Kate ran off and left me in the Alpha Control Room.'

Kate gasped, and felt the staring faces without seeing them.

But Simon stepped forward, pointed at Alex and Kate in turn, sticking out his bottom lip in protest.

'OK, fine,' said Alex, 'I told her to run. But that *is* where my memory ends.'

Kate felt herself able to relax. It was good to have friends looking out for her, even if they didn't use words.

'Well, let's see what we can do about that,' said Ewan, bringing a small black smartphone out of his pocket. Kate had never seen it before.

'Hey, that's my phone!' said Alex. '*Literally* my phone, from the old days!'

'Yep,' said Ewan.

'Where did you find that? I haven't seen it since the beginning!'

'Should have looked after it better,' said Ewan. 'Mark, you might as well explain.'

'I nicked it,' the giant grunted.

Kate watched the disbelief on Alex's face, the discreet laughter of Mark, and wondered how McCormick would have reacted to the way his youngsters were handling the situation.

'Well why not?' Mark continued. 'None of us knew what the future was going to hold. For all we knew, we were only going to be staying here a few days. I took what I could from whoever I could, just in case.'

'Don't take it personally, Alex,' said Ewan with a huff. 'He stole Charlie's too. And Ben Christie's. Hell, he'd have stolen half the house if he'd been able to hide it.'

'Yep, all true,' said Mark, pressing buttons until the screen of Alex's phone lit up. 'And I've been charging this ever since Ewan gave us the news about you. Remember the passcode?'

'Why the hell should I give it to you?' asked Alex.

Kate sunk her head. They had an enormous opportunity

here to unlock valuable lost information – some of which could change the course of the whole war – but the hostile atmosphere was doing them no good. Not that she was helping with her ineffective silence.

'We're going through your music library until something interesting happens,' said Mark. 'Don't worry, we'll miss out "Seven Nation Army". Code, please.'

Kate watched Alex as his face morphed from offence to acceptance. Perhaps he had reached the same conclusion as her: that the only hope for progress involved pushing his pride away and doing what needed to be done.

'One three nine seven,' Alex gasped.

'A square on the keypad,' muttered Mark. 'How imaginative.'

As Mark entered the code, Kate had to remind herself that using the phone was safe. If comms was far enough out of detection range, Spitfire's Rise would be out of range too.

'Are you sure this is a good idea?' Alex asked. 'What if they infected me with a hundred trigger songs? What if one of them forces me to burn this place down? What if another makes me destroy the thermal blocker so we're all traceable?'

'You're tied to a chair,' Mark replied, bringing up the playlist of songs on Alex's phone. 'I think we're safe.'

Kate glanced across at Shannon, who had an all-too-familiar look of guilt on her face. Perhaps she was feeling dreadful about how she and Lorraine had never suspected a *third* trigger song, let alone a hundred. Objectively, there was nothing for them to feel guilty for: all their intelligence had pointed at exactly two trigger songs. But guilt, like anxiety, didn't need an objective reason to exist.

The first two minutes of song-searching passed, comprising of multiple ten-second openings in alphabetical order by artist. The boys soon started to bicker about how long the process would take: Ewan insisting that the whole day was expendable, Mark insisting it would be tiresome but offering no suggestions, and Simon making sign language symbols few people understood. Meanwhile, Kate noticed Shannon heading towards her.

'Between you and me,' Shannon whispered, 'Alex's taste in music is actually pretty good.'

Kate smiled, but only out of politeness. Masking her feelings in order to give the correct response, again. Even with someone as genuine as Shannon.

Mark had reached Danzig, a group Kate had never heard of, before the next dispute began among the boys.

'For what it's worth,' Shannon whispered again, 'my dad's people were never as civil as this.'

Kate gave her a confused expression in response.

'Seriously,' she continued. 'Iain Marshall and Nathaniel Pearce hated each other. Used to be best friends, and then my father came along. Iain Marshall used to love Hannah and their children too, before Takeover Day turned them against each other. Even Oliver Roth and Keith Tylor were mortal enemies. My dad spreads hate wherever he goes.'

Kate still remembered Keith Tylor with genuine fear, nearly two months after Shannon had killed him with his own knife. Her memories of Oliver Roth were hardly pleasant either; in fact, having not seen his dead body for herself, she was almost reluctant to believe he had even died in that Experiment Chamber. After a year of fighting him it felt like the boy was immortal, even death itself bowing to his will.

'So whenever you see your guys arguing,' Shannon finished, 'remember they're still the friendly side. The New London staff could never have had the bond you have.'

'Did they put aside their differences for Takeover Day at least?' Kate asked. 'The day they all finally got what they wanted?'

Shannon shuddered.

'I… I didn't s—'

Alex's phone switched away from David Guetta and started playing Deep Purple. The opening guitar riff sounded for 'Smoke on the Water', and Alex froze.

'Keep playing it,' were the only words he could gasp before his eyes squeezed themselves shut and he started to shake in his chair.

He shook with such force that the soil under the floorboards trembled beneath them. Kate watched the others bend their knees, perhaps preparing to run. Ewan raised his rifle, just in case.

Alex bent forward as far as his restrained body would let him, and then threw himself backwards. Halfway between one of her brother James' meltdowns and an exorcism gone wrong, it looked as if he were trying to throw his brain out of his head.

All this happened because I turned and ran from the clone factory control room two months ago, Kate thought to herself, her mind following its natural habit of looking for things to blame itself for. *I had no ammo, but still… surely I could have done something to stop Alex going through his capture and his suffering, and to stop Gracie dying the way she did…*

She regained her concentration, and found Alex crying. Properly crying, and with voice too.

Kate didn't know how to react any more than the others in the room. Alex had never cried in front of them before, even when Ewan had given him that scar, and he had always gone to a visible effort to maintain his carefree, invulnerable manner. She looked across at the other Underdogs, and found them staring at each other too.

Alex lifted his head and opened his mouth, most likely trying to talk. His erratic breaths stopped him each time, and half a minute passed before he choked out an opening sentence.

'My father's dead...'

A sudden hush fell upon the farm. Kate was no expert at discerning different types of silence, but imagined it to be a blend of sympathy and confusion. It certainly was in her own mind.

Dean Ginelli. His taekwondo coach first, his father second.

Wait, how would he—

'Gwen Crossland had him murdered,' Alex gasped in realisation, 'because they asked me where Spitfire's Rise was and I lied to them... I told her we lived in Lemsford, and that's where the clones later found Jack and Gracie... so they knew I was lying and killed Dad...'

Kate could barely piece together what Alex was talking about, and had never heard of Gwen Crossley or whatever her name was. Shannon, however, took a calm step forward and knelt down.

'I'm so sorry,' she said with a cautious hand on his shoulder. 'I had no idea about that part. I can understand why you didn't tell me.'

All eyes fell on Shannon.

'I couldn't...' were the words Alex's lips imitated.

'You knew?!' Mark bellowed towards Shannon. Kate almost leapt out of her skin. Mark, for all his ferocity, almost never bellowed.

'I knew enough,' said Shannon, not bothering to turn around, 'and so did Lorraine. We told you guys everything you needed to know, and nothing more. Alex's clones had no memories, so Spitfire's Rise was still hidden. Everything else was personal to Alex, and we respected that.'

'What happened to the Shannon Grant who held a knife to Thomas' throat?' asked Mark. 'You need to learn how to disrespect people again. Right now, you tell us *everything*. For starters, who the hell is Gwen Crossland?'

'An experimental hyp—'

'A hideous bloody Womble,' Alex interrupted, 'with special bloody mind powers.'

'Womble?' Kate asked, having never heard the word before.

'You know, those rat-like puppet characters from that old children's show. Long snouts, far too hairy, uncomfortable to look at.'

'I know them,' said Ewan. 'I'll remember the description for when we go after her.'

'Whatever,' said Mark. 'Keep going, Shannon. Tell us everything Alex told you over the phone, 'cos I've not got time to listen through his tears.'

Shannon stood up, turned around, and explained every detail.

That Alex, while trapped inside the Alpha Control Room, had been the victim of an experimental hypnotherapist called Gwen Crossland.

That he had agreed, under the threat of severe pain, to be cloned and betray the location of Spitfire's Rise in exchange for his own life.

That he had spent the next three days conditioned into staying at a nearby bungalow, believing he was waiting for his four teenage friends to escape from the Inner City prison… when in reality Crossland was keeping him there to interrogate him.

However, the fact that he had sacrificed his father for the safety of the Underdogs was just as new to Shannon as it was to Kate.

She was close to tears of her own. It was only at that moment that she understood the person Alex was, underneath the exterior he had been taught to maintain by the father he had lost. She realised that he had spent a good portion of his life masking his difficulties in a similar way to herself, and the mask had slipped the very moment he remembered the death of his father.

'I'm sorry,' Kate said, trying to rid her brain of her own guilt at leaving him that fateful morning.

'Don't be,' Alex answered. 'He disowned me with his last words. I don't have to feel too bad about it.'

And there it was. Alex Ginelli's mask had been reattached.

'I think,' said Ewan, as kindly as he could manage, 'it's time to tell us what else you remember. The stuff you *didn't* tell Shannon and Lorraine over the phone.'

'In my defence,' Alex said, 'I was running around New London trying to take down the AME shield so we wouldn't lose the war. I didn't have *time* to remember everything.'

'So you forgot the bit about killing people at random?' asked Mark.

'I remembered the parts mentioned in the report I was reading. And the questions that were already in my mind. Like, for example, *are my friends safe in Spitfire's Rise?* Once I knew I hadn't betrayed you... there wasn't time to go swimming in other lost memories. You were safe, my dad was dead, and that was enough to deal with.'

'Alex,' said Ewan, 'we're here and listening now. Tell us the rest, before the memories fade.'

'They won't fade. As long as I don't hear the other song, they'll stay with me forever. And before you ask—'

'Did your new memories bring back what the forgetting song is?' Mark interrupted.

'Yeah. It's "Barbie Girl". Don't laugh.'

Nobody even smiled, which Kate saw as a kindness. Alex closed his eyes and tilted his head back. Whether he was truly trying to remember or just escaping the conversation, Kate couldn't tell.

After a full minute in silent reminiscence, he began.

'"Seven Nation Army" was the *third* song,' he started, 'but it was separate from the Ginelli Project. Gwen said it was a separate area of Pearce's research, called... wait, that can't make sense...'

Simon shrugged, and stared hard.

'Give me a moment, OK? I think it was called the Acceleration project. I'm not sure how that makes sense though...'

Kate couldn't work it out for herself either. Acceleration of what?

'What do you know about it?' asked Ewan. 'What's it about?'

'Conditioning people to violence. They didn't tell me much while they were working on me in the bungalow. But you know its effects.'

Kate looked over her shoulder, and pictured the Memorial Wall in the cellar next door. The name of Gracie Freeman was just waiting to be added.

The more of us die, the more my dead boyfriend and my dead mentor will be pushed up the list and forgotten... before I've even learned how to handle the loss of them.

'Is there anything else you haven't mentioned?' asked Shannon. 'Anything you know about the inside of—'

Kate could sense the interruption before it came. Alex's deepening eyes went straight to Shannon's, and he breathed heavily enough for his chest to double in size.

'Me?' he asked. 'What about *you*, Shannon? You've been here nearly two months, and you *never* thought to tell us your father's master plan? *Why* he's doing everything he's doing? You just figured you'd keep it to yourself?'

Kate expected Shannon to flinch or cower. She did neither, and just shrugged.

'He never told me,' she answered. 'His plan was to surprise me with Takeover Day, and then...'

There was a shudder in Shannon's voice that Kate recognised far too well: the shudder of regretting a sentence halfway through.

'And then?' Alex asked.

'And then explain his plan to me once the prisoners were contained. But he never did.'

'Just couldn't be arsed, could he?' asked Mark sarcastically. Shannon didn't answer.

There was something in Shannon's communication that had seemed odd to Kate. After many years of hiding her own feelings – usually not very well – it was obvious to her when other vulnerable girls did the same. There were clearly some details missing about how Takeover Day had gone for her.

Then again... maybe there's a reason we've never asked her about it. With us losing our families, and her in luxury on Floor A, maybe we never wanted to know.

'Crossland had no issues sharing it with me,' Alex snarled, 'even with the one-in-a-million chance of me escaping alive and remembering it later—'

'Alex,' Shannon interrupted, 'you need to tell us. This is completely new, even to me.'

'OK. He's culling the human population.'

Silence.

The farm fell so quiet that Kate could hear her own breathing. The buzz of the lights emerged again, along with the gentle squeak of the floorboards beneath her trembling feet.

'Seriously, that's the grand plan,' Alex continued. 'Just kill as many humans as possible until the planet is saved from us. Your father's an eco-nut, Shannon. And not one of those "let's use renewable energy" eco-nuts – he's one of those "Earth would be better off if we kill all the humans" eco-nuts. He's planning to take over the rest of the world just like he took over Britain, and then wait long enough for the population to decrease to a "safe" level. Then he'll age the clones to death, release the last humans, and restart civilisation.'

Kate's best chance at avoiding her own anxiety was looking at everyone else's reactions. They didn't help. Shannon looked more devastated – and more betrayed – than everyone else combined.

Nicholas Grant raised her. Bought her birthday presents. Took her to school. And that same man is planning to bring the whole of humanity within an inch of extinction. Worst of all, he's capable of actually doing it.

'There are nine of us left,' Alex continued. 'But the numbers don't matter. We *have* to win this war, whatever the odds, whatever the cost. Because it's not just about freeing the British people anymore. It never has been.'

Alex straightened his back as much as he could, and wore an expression of forced steadiness that Kate recognised all too well. He was trying to be brave.

'If we lose this war, most of the world's population is going to die. McCormick gave his life believing our fight was *less* important than it really is. That's why the cost doesn't matter. It's why I'm not going to make the same mistake twice – I'm *never* getting rid of my memories again. Forget the pain of remembering – the facts are too important. And it's why you can never, ever release me from this chair until the war ends, with one result or the other. In case I kill another one of you. My freedom's not worth it.'

Despite everything Alex had done, Kate couldn't help but admire his courage. It was still there within him, a stronger part of him than she had previously realised.

'Alex,' said Ewan, 'do you think there are *other* memories

hidden inside you? Any inside info about Grant that might help us?'

'Well if there are, it's all unlocked now,' Alex muttered. 'I just need to think about them consciously... bring them to the front of my mind.'

'What do you mean?'

'Can *you* remember every single thing that's ever happened to you, without putting any thought into it?' Alex asked. 'Or instantly recall every fact you ever learned? Can *you* remember all your times tables without having to think... You know what – never mind, Ewan. What I mean is, even with a flawless memory you still need to *think* about stuff to make it appear in your head and remember it properly.'

'So how about you sit here thinking about what you did with Crossland, and see what you can uncover?'

Alex's face dropped even further.

'I'm scared to look, but... I mean, I'm afraid of what I might remember myself hearing or doing. Fear of the unknown becoming known, I guess. But I'll do it. You go off on your mission, and I'll remember whatever I can.'

When Kate looked up, she found Ewan nodding. But before anyone could move, Mark gave a strong huff like he sometimes did before talking.

'Well,' Mark said, 'looks like I'm the first person here to work out something important.'

'And what's that?' asked Alex.

'What Nicholas Grant plans to accelerate.'

Chapter 7

Ewan had the road atlas right in front of his eyes, but he couldn't focus on it. He hadn't had enough time to process the day he had endured. In one day, he had woken up in the countryside, broken into New London, stolen some research, headed home, learned about the death of Gracie, tied Alex to a chair and interrogated him. It was early evening now, and he was about to leave Spitfire's Rise again to lead another team on a completely new mission.

And that didn't even include the worst part: the truth behind Nicholas Grant's long-term goals for the planet.

Ewan looked at the wavy blue line that represented the M40. Perhaps Grant's vehicles would take that route, but the country roads were likely to be clearer. Ewan's plans would be educated guesswork, nothing more. And perhaps not even that educated, given the weight on his brain.

Acceleration, he thought, rubbing his fingers against the corner of the atlas until the paper came apart. *That's a word I'll grow to hate very quickly.*

Throughout his short, intense life, Ewan had tried a number of coping strategies for stress and anxiety. Only a few of them had worked for more than a week. But one of the better strategies had been to picture the worst way something could possibly go wrong, and make a plan for how to deal with it. After that, all the less-bad options became bearable in his mind too.

Even in the old days it had been tricky. With a logical imagination like Ewan's, the worst-case scenario in every situation would be death. A bad day at school could theoretically end with coming home to find his dad had had a heart attack. But once he restricted his imagination to *reasonable* outcomes, his anxiety levels improved.

Then came the day his parents actually died. After that, the worst-case scenario – even the *reasonable* worst-case scenario – had been the death of Great Britain and the permanent imprisonment of its people. It had taken him half a year to learn how to deal with that possibility, by remembering that if worst came to worst, the rest of the world's population would still live on peacefully.

That dream was over. Now, the worst-case scenario was extinction in all but name. It would take far longer than half a year for Ewan to learn how to deal with that.

There was a knock on the door, and Ewan remembered that he was in his bedroom looking at a map. He slapped the atlas closed and threw it into the gap between the bed and the far wall, and tried his best to look natural. Nobody in Spitfire's Rise had ever been allowed to know about the atlas's existence, except for Ewan and McCormick. Anyone with the slightest sense of direction could have used it to work out the name of their village.

'Who is it?' he asked.

Jack walked into the room, looking forlorn. It was his bedroom too, so he didn't have to knock, but Ewan was grateful to him for being considerate.

'You alright, Jack?'

'Never mind that,' Jack said hurriedly. 'What's the plan?'

Ewan looked at his friend with a sceptical face.

'Jack, you're the most transparent person I've ever known. If you're not alright just save us some time and tell me.'

'*Me* transparent?' Jack asked, sitting down on his sleeping bag and covering his face with one hand. 'I could tell the moment I walked in you were doing something you didn't want me to see. Don't worry, I won't ask. Just tell me what the plan is.'

'You didn't come in here to ask about the plan,' Ewan replied, taking the opportunity to change the subject back to Jack. 'You know I'm telling the team in a few minutes anyway. So, what's on your mind?'

'Who do you think?'

Makes sense, I guess. He hasn't mentioned her since it happened, so he must have bottled it up.

Ewan bit his lip. The relationship between Jack and Gracie, or lack thereof, had always been an inside joke among the Underdogs. Today, it had become less funny.

'Do you think she knew I cared about her?' asked Jack.

'Yes,' answered Ewan. Straight answers worked best for both of them.

'But I never really... *said...*'

'Did you need to say it?'

'She deserved better than what I gave.'

Jack's hand hadn't moved from his face. Ewan decided he wasn't going to get through to him by standing over a bed on the other side of the room, so he walked over and sat down on the floor next to Jack – deliberately by his side so there'd be no pressure to look at each other. But it was more for Ewan's comfort than Jack's. For an emotional teenager with natural manipulation skills, Ewan wasn't good at manipulating his own emotions.

'I hate to say it, Jack,' he began, 'but Gracie didn't have many friends here. Don't get me wrong – she was one of us. She was valued. But... she didn't have many *friends*. E—'

'Is that supposed to make me feel better?'

'I was about to say "except you". Let me finish the bloody sentence, mate.'

'Huh, OK.'

'You meant something to her. When a lot of others didn't.'

Although Ewan couldn't see his face, there was a tremble through Jack's body. Trembling was usually a sign of fear, cold or guilt. Ewan suspected it was the latter.

'I... never gave her what she wanted,' Jack gasped.

'What was that?'

'A flock of burning cats. Use your bloody imagination.'

Ewan rolled his eyes.

'So... sex?'

'I don't know whether she wanted *that*. But... she wanted my... companionship.'

'You couldn't even give her that?'

Ewan held his breath. As usual, he hadn't noticed the hurt-fulness in what he was saying until the words had left his mouth. Jack gave his answer regardless.

'Remember when you sent me to find that new house, on the night of the AME mission? When we thought Spitfire's Rise had been found? Not one moment after we settled in, she tried to get with me. And I had to tell her... I'm not attracted to girls in the way she wanted.'

'You're gay, then?'

Jack shrugged.

'Not really. Or maybe that's... I don't know. I'm just not attracted to anyone. I'm nothing, really.'

'You're not nothing, Jack.'

'Might as well have been. To her.'

'You may be many things, but you're not nothing. *Nothing* could make you nothing, mate.'

Huh, maybe if I put that advice in a blender it would come out making sense.

Ewan couldn't get his head around Jack not being attracted to anyone, but decided not to ask questions since he wouldn't be good with the answers. He adjusted himself on the carpet beneath him and used the sleeping bag to warm his hands.

'For what it's worth,' he began, 'I've kind of been in a similar position before.'

'Really now?' asked Jack.

'Inside the Inner City. Don't tell the others, but… I tried to kiss Kate. And she couldn't give me what I wanted either.'

'She was going out with Raj back then.'

'Yeah, that's right,' Ewan answered.

A little voice reminded him that Kate and Raj's relationship hadn't been public knowledge until after they'd arrived home from the Inner City. He knew that Jack was clever enough to calculate the timeline himself, but he still wondered whether Kate and Raj had trusted Jack with the information long before they'd trusted *him* with it.

'What's your point?' asked Jack.

'Gracie probably didn't feel that bad. When I was in her kind of position, I ended up being happy with the friendship I had.'

'You ended up with Shannon. That probably played a small part in you being fine with it.'

Ewan's hands clenched themselves together, and the blood heated in his veins.

Shannon had nothing to do with it, he thought but didn't want to say. *Once Kate turned me down, I made myself accept it. For her sake. Kate deserved a friend who respected her enough not to chase her.*

He pictured his parents back in the old days, sitting him down and explaining the importance of respecting women. Perhaps Dad had been annoyed with his lack of respect for Mum. Or maybe they were afraid of what kind of trouble his PDA would get him into if he disrespected half the world's population. Or maybe they were just trying to turn him into a decent human being. Ewan didn't know whether he passed the 'decent human being' bit, but he had at least picked up their lessons.

'Let me ask you something,' Jack said. 'When Kate didn't go out with you, do you think she felt guilty about it? If you died today, would she spend the rest of her life wishing she had been able to *change herself* to accommodate you?'

Ewan decided to be honest.

'No.'

'Well then,' said Jack, rising from his sleeping bag and marching for the door, 'that's the difference between Kate and me. I know you tried, Ewan, but our situations don't compare.'

Jack was out of the door and on the landing before Ewan could think of a response.

Ewan hit the floor with a clenched fist and swore to himself. There probably hadn't been a way of helping Jack anyway, but he had hoped for better than his friend storming out.

Try not to feel too bad, he thought to himself. *McCormick wouldn't have solved it in one conversation either.*

His mind wandered, trying to uncover what McCormick might have said in a similar situation. But Ewan's brain and the old man's brain were just too different. For all of the strengths that existed in Ewan's complex mind, his strengths were his own and McCormick's had been McCormick's.

However, the thought process did give him an idea. Ewan reached behind the bed for the hidden atlas, walked out of the bedroom and looked into the rooms around him to check that everyone else was downstairs. Without any witnesses, he opened the hatch to the attic, fetched out the stepladder from the airing cupboard, and climbed up.

The inside of the attic was dark and smelled like cold wood, and it was dusty enough to force a run of coughs from Ewan's throat. It felt as aged as he had always imagined it to be: by McCormick's request he had never been up there before, until needing to fetch the atlas for himself that morning. But as he laid it back in its place, he had a general idea of what other treasures would be around.

The first thing he found, just to check it was still there, was an envelope of confidential material they had gathered from New London. Inside, right at the top of its contents, he saw the folded sheet of paper Shannon had brought with her the first time she entered Spitfire's Rise. He opened it out, and glared at it in disgust.

First name	Last name	Age	Notes
Kate	Arrowsmith	16	Secondary student, Oakenfold Special School, Harpenden. Diagnoses: Autism, Severe Anxiety.
~~Charlie~~	~~Coleman~~	~~15~~	~~Secondary student, Oakenfold Special School, Harpenden. Diagnosis: ADHD.~~
Gracie	Freeman	15	Secondary student, Oakenfold Special School, Harpenden. Diagnosis: Global Development Delay.

And so on.

Well bloody hell… When I get a moment, there's yet another name I'll have to cross out.

Ewan folded the paper and placed it back in the envelope, then kept searching.

It didn't take him long to find McCormick's memory box. When he opened it, the first object his fingers touched was a photo frame, which he took out to reveal a picture of a surprisingly young Joseph McCormick on a dull-looking beach. His happy expression perfectly matched the young woman's next to him, a lady who must have been Barbara. Perhaps it had been their honeymoon photo or something.

Ewan expected to feel emotional at the sight of McCormick, but instead he felt confused. It was the first time Ewan had seen his face since they had separated in New London. But the photograph was of a young man in his mid-twenties, decades away from becoming the leader who had brought the Underdogs together under his roof.

How the hell did you ever lead people like us? Ewan asked the photo.

The photo did not reply. Ewan didn't even feel like he had communicated with the version of McCormick etched in his memory. The framed photo may have held a special place in McCormick's heart, but it meant nothing to Ewan. He rested it back in its box, and decided not to waste any more time disturbing the old man's things. It was still his house, after all.

Well, Polly's really.

Polly... I wish I'd had a chance to know you before I did what I did.

Ewan shook his head. He had not known what he had wanted from visiting the attic. Perhaps to feel his mentor's presence, or find inspiration from being around things that the man had valued.

At that moment, Ewan realised the truth. The contents of the house valued most by McCormick were the people downstairs in the cellar, waiting for Ewan to lead them. He edged back towards the open hatch, unfulfilled and unrewarded.

I took everything I could from his guidance while I had the chance. I can't ask any more of him now. The Underdogs are mine to lead, and mine alone.

The task was not an easy one, and Ewan still had doubts about him being the right teenager to lead his people. The point was driven home by the sight he found when he descended the stairs and passed through the living room to get a drink from the kitchen. Jack had found a much more capable friend to talk to about his worries, sat next to Simon and pouring out his worries about letting Gracie down. The selectively mute boy with learning difficulties was his usual caring self: watching, listening, smiling sympathetically, and nodding in understanding. The sight of Simon and Jack's friendship would have been lovely to watch, if it didn't remind Ewan of his own shortcomings.

The Underdogs may be mine to lead, he thought as his shaking hand grabbed a glass, *but I'm only good for shooting clones. When it comes to supporting real people, my skills died with McCormick. Without him showing me how it's done, the others are so much more capable than me.*

When Ewan arrived in the cellar, he found the rest of his team assembled. Shannon, Mark and Simon were in combat uniform as commanded, with the others gathered around next to the armoury – even those uninvolved in the mission. Everyone but Alex was there, including Thomas. With only nine Underdogs left alive, every opportunity to be together was a good one.

'I still don't get it,' said Thomas to whoever would listen. 'If Grant wants to kill everyone, why doesn't he just use nukes?'

'Because he doesn't want to destroy the world,' Shannon

answered, 'he just wants to remove the humans from it. Nukes would destroy the world he thinks he's saving.'

Ewan scowled, and wondered which of his soldiers had disclosed Nicholas Grant's plans to Thomas. Unless the child had overheard someone explaining them to Lorraine, since she had also been absent from the farm.

He glanced at Lorraine as she stood next to the exit, with a cold stare directed at nowhere in particular. Even if nothing else could drag the group nurse out of her solace in the clinic, duty and responsibility could. Placing her on comms with Kate might have been one of Ewan's brighter ideas.

'My friends,' he said, flattening out a crumpled piece of paper in front of him, 'a moment of your time, please.'

Ewan noticed, and presumably everyone else did too, that he was talking to the group like McCormick had.

He opened up the paper to reveal a pencil-drawn road map: one which the Underdogs had used for several months, with Ewan pretending he had drawn it from memory (even inventing a childhood special interest in maps that he'd never had). The bigger roads had been scribbled in thicker and pressed harder into the paper, labelled with road names in Ewan's shoddy handwriting. A big rectangle with a question mark inside denoted everything within the Luton-Stevenage-St Albans triangle, where Spitfire's Rise lay.

'I'm going to be honest with you,' he began. 'I don't think we can *guess* which route they'll use to transport stuff from New Oxford to New London. But with four of us going out tonight, we can split up and guard two roads. I'm picking the M40 and the A481.'

He checked that his paper was being held the right way up, and pointed a finger at each route in turn. He noticed that the second road was actually the A418, but hoped to continue without anyone correcting him. He was pointing to the right line at least, even if his reading and number skills remained crap.

'If they can plough a clear path through the motorways,' he continued, 'they'll use the M40 down to the M25 and follow it round. If they think the quieter roads are better, maybe they'll head for Aylesbury and then use the A41. They *could* take winding countryside roads but they'll be difficult for large transport vehicles, and a single blockage could pretty much end their journey.'

'So who goes where?' asked Mark.

'You and Shannon can take the A418,' he answered. 'Simon and I—'

'You're letting your girlfriend go off with me?'

Thomas laughed, not understanding that it may have been inappropriate. Thankfully, his laughter was met with silence from the crowd.

'She's not my property, Mark,' Ewan answered. 'Besides, you need her to look after you.'

Ewan looked at Shannon, who appeared halfway between surprised and offended. She had clearly assumed herself to be with Ewan by default. Ewan flashed his eyes towards Simon, then back. Shannon nodded, having clearly understood.

Simon's one of the most trustworthy people I know. But everyone knows he needs assistance. He's better off with me alongside him.

'So yeah, us four will head out now. Kate and Lorraine, you know what to do on comms. Jack, Thomas... enjoy the quiet, I guess. Let's go.'

The team started to move, and while they were busying themselves around the Memorial Wall, Ewan jogged across the room and tapped Jack on the shoulder.

'I need to know I can leave you here with Alex,' he whispered. 'Safely, I mean.'

Jack stared back at him, noticeably hurt.

'Alex is a victim too,' Jack snarled, or making a noise as close as he ever got to snarling. 'I don't like him, but I don't exactly blame him either. And no, I won't shoot him or anything. His memories are too valuable to us.'

Ewan nodded, and decided not to press the issue.

In truth, he didn't want to blame Alex either. He had far too much experience of committing horrible acts when his anxiety meltdowns struck and his rational mind was absent. (On the outside, of course, they had looked like horrific bouts of anger, and the other primary school children must have *believed* it to be anger when he had used their chairs to smash windows.) After a lifetime of being blamed for actions taken during his most vulnerable and uncontrollable moments, he didn't want to be a hypocrite by doing the same to Alex.

But all the same... Gracie was still dead.

He's not the first Underdog to literally kill an innocent person in a meltdown, his brain said to him. *The only reason you got away with Polly was because nobody saw it except you and McCormick, and the old man had the grace to keep it a secret.*

How do you know McCormick wasn't in love with Polly when you shot her dead on Takeover Day? He wouldn't have told you if he was. He wouldn't have wanted to hurt you with the truth. Maybe you'll never know the full extent of the damage you did.

Ewan gritted his teeth and tried to force his thoughts away from Polly. But as nasty as his brain was being to him, it was right: he couldn't claim innocence in the unintentional death of McCormick's housemate while blaming Alex for his own involuntary actions.

'Ewan?' said Shannon.

Brought back to his senses, and putting on his best faked expression of confidence, Ewan joined the rest of the Underdogs at the Memorial Wall and they all linked hands.

Two missions in one day. Except now we're one fewer, and the stakes are so much higher. I know I've thought this before, but there's no way we can win this war, surely.

Ewan shook his head.

Stuff it. That's a long-term problem. Let's just succeed today and go from there.

'To honour those who gave everything they had,' Ewan said to the Memorial Wall, 'we will give everything *we* have. To honour the dead we will free the living... united by our differences.'

'United,' was the response from far too few surviving Underdogs.

Chapter 8

Despite her long-standing negative self-perception, Shannon knew she had plenty to be proud of in her short life. Not least abandoning her father, playing a role in the destruction of the clone factory, and joining the Underdogs.

That evening, she had given herself another achievement to be proud of. She was heading through the countryside in the dark again, and doing so in total fearlessness. Keith Tylor's voice popped up in her head whenever she felt unsure of herself, but it no longer controlled her fear levels like it once had.

This was not her first mission as an Underdog. She had gone to Luton Retail Centre with Ewan that one time, but that had been in broad daylight with someone she had been growing to care about. This was in the dead of night, with only Mark Gunnarsson for company.

But at least the bicycles helped to speed things up.

The night breeze cooled Shannon's face as she glided down the A418. She had no idea how her friends had gone for thirteen months just *walking* everywhere, when there was a bicycle shop in Harpenden with no shortage of spare merchandise. When she had asked, Ewan had said something about not being able to hide bikes safely around New London without them being discovered. But perhaps he was making excuses for not coming up with the idea himself. He and Simon were pedalling down the M40 at that moment, set to reach their vantage point in three hours instead of twelve.

The ride was enjoyable. Danger or not, Shannon felt free. There was something beautiful and liberating about the wind against her face, a sensation nobody could experience in New London's Outer City, or even in Spitfire's Rise.

Mark was five seconds behind her. But he hardly would have talked to her anyway, even if they had been walking side by side.

'*Stop*,' he yelled, in a voice loud enough to make Shannon brake without realising.

She turned around and saw him at a standstill, his face dipped and focusing on the road. She turned her bike around and headed back, hoping it was important enough to interrupt her freedom for.

Of course it's important. If it were tiredness, he wouldn't let me know.

'Did you feel that?' he asked, with an unusually quiet voice.

'Feel what?'

'The bump in the road. Come here, slowly.'

Shannon swung herself off her bike and wheeled it back towards Mark. Other than the general rumbling beneath her wheels, she had not felt anything worthy of her attention. But something had concerned Mark.

When she arrived, there was a thin rope-shaped line pulled tight across the road, flat on the tarmac and only visible when viewed up close. Shannon didn't know what it was, nor did she want to touch it.

Mark rested his bike on the ground and followed the mystery line to the bushes at the side of the road.

When he pulled the branches to one side, he found a small pile of plastic explosives.

'Holy crap,' he whispered, taking several steps back.

The branches fell back in place as he let go. Shannon looked back at the discreet line across the road which connected to the explosives.

'Touch-sensitive material,' she said. 'Why didn't we set it off when we rode over it?'

'Maybe we were too light,' Mark said, running to the other side of the road and uncovering a second batch of explosives behind the opposite bushes. 'These were designed for proper vehicles, not bikes.'

Shannon's first instincts told her to cycle as far from the explosives as possible. But her battle instincts – the side of her that had been tired of running from her father and wanted to take every fighting opportunity that came her way – told her to look around. Nobody would leave such valuable resources along the roadside without keeping an eye on them.

It didn't take her long to see the farmhouse a hundred metres from the roadside.

'Mark,' she whispered, 'I'm willing to bet my life savings that there's a bunch of clones inside that place.'

Mark looked where her finger pointed, and huffed. 'Well the British pound is useless these days, but I'm pretty sure you're right. Let's check it out.'

Shannon hid her bicycle in the densest bush available, and gazed at the distant farmhouse. There were two storeys, which made her bite her lip in concern. If a platoon of clones lay within, they would get to attack from an elevated position.

Mark had already raised his shotgun and started his march across the field. Shannon followed, her rifle pointed towards one of the windows. She wondered whether the theoretical enemies in the farmhouse would be prepared for attackers approaching on foot, or whether they were just there to clear up the mess once a big enough vehicle came along to set off the explosives.

With that in mind, a thought struck her.

'Mark, I just realised something...'

'Say it.'

'I don't think there are clones in that building.'

'Changed your mind already? A few seconds ago you bet your life savings on the complete opposite.'

'Yeah, but I just realised... whoever set up that trap was expecting their enemies to have heavy vehicles.'

'So?'

Shannon looked across the field that surrounded them. There were no ditches. No fences. No hay bales. Nothing to shelter her. She hoped she was right, otherwise she and Mark would be dead the moment someone looked out of a window. There was a bright enough moon for them to be visible without night-vision goggles.

'Think about it, Mark. How many of my dad's *enemies* have heavy vehicles?'

'What, so he won't set any traps? Come on, this is the same guy who commissioned the Cerberus system to guard every single coordinate in the sky. He covers all his bases. There are enemies in there until proven otherwise.'

Shannon didn't want to agree with Mark, but she knew that caution was the best approach. Besides, if the trap *was* her father's, it meant he definitely wouldn't be using that road for transport. It was worth checking just to find out—

There was a flash at the window.

A tiny one, like glass reflected in moonlight. As if from the front of a telescope changing position. Or a rifle scope.

The blood fled from Shannon's face, and she gasped. Next to her, Mark started to run.

'Someone's there,' he said as he sped off. 'You head for the window and distract them, I'll sneak to that side door!'

Sure, let me get shot first, she thought, picking up the pace herself.

It was little comfort that the rifle scope had moved away from the window. For all Shannon knew, there were other enemies in the house ready to open fire.

Nor was it a comfort that she hadn't yet been attacked. Whoever owned the rifle, it would be easier for them to get a kill shot once she and Mark were up close.

She thought of Ewan. Not just in the loving sense, but in a strategic sense too. If the enemies saw her reaching for her radio, it would force them to open fire before she was close enough for a guaranteed kill...

She reached for her belt. Nobody fired.

She removed her radio. Nobody fired.

She brought it to her mouth.

'Ewa—'

Bang, came a sharp noise from the house, and a patch of mud splattered up from her feet.

Shannon froze. Every instinct told her to raise her own weapon and return fire, but the bullet had missed so *neatly*. And in either case, it hadn't been followed by a second bullet. It wasn't an attack: it was a warning shot.

The breath held itself in Shannon's throat, and she looked towards the ground-floor window where the muzzle flash had come from. She did her best not to look over at Mark and give away his position, as he jumped to the mud not many metres from the side door.

It's not one of Dad's regular soldiers. They would never, ever give warning shots.

Shannon took a step towards the farmhouse, nervous about

a second gunshot but moving forward regardless. If the shooter didn't want her dead, they could be negotiated with.

Step by step, each completed footstep a surprise, Shannon approached the window. She must have been thirty metres away when she saw a visible figure on the other side. From twenty metres away, she saw a pair of eyes and a black balaclava. Fifteen metres away, she saw eyelashes and olive-coloured skin.

The woman had her weapon held up and pointed in Shannon's direction. Shannon was cautious, but unafraid. If the shooter had wanted to kill her, she could have done so half a field ago.

'You're a human,' Shannon said quietly. The shooter did not react. She didn't even blink.

In the background, the shadowed image of Mark crept into Shannon's line of sight. He had found the entrance, and made it inside in total silence. He crept up on the shooter from behind, surprisingly quiet by his standards. Shannon maintained eye contact with the shooter, to avoid giving away Mark's position with her face.

Mark had no interest in shooting her dead. He must have had thoughts of interrogation. When he was two metres behind her, he leapt.

The shooter spun round and dashed to the side, leaving Mark to stumble into the spot where she had stood. She bent her knees, spun her assault rifle around like a short staff, then leapt upwards at Mark, driving the butt of her rifle up through his chin.

Just like that, he was unconscious. Eighty kilograms of Mark Gunnarsson fell to the floor like meaty timber, thumping against the living-room carpet with a loud echo.

Before Shannon could react, the shooter's weapon was pointed back at her. No further reaction: just the same eyes, cold but controlled, and the same eyelashes and olive skin poking through her balaclava.

'You don't have to fear me because of him,' Shannon said. 'He's always been a bit of a numpty. And he was probably afraid. You know, with you shooting at me and everything.'

Numpty... It didn't take me long to start talking like the other Underdogs.

At least ten seconds passed before the woman responded. She stepped back, lowered her rifle, and pointed it downwards at Mark's unconscious body.

'If you want him to live,' she barked, 'you drop your weapon right where you stand, and you enter this room through the door at the side of the building.'

She had a heavy London accent, but it wasn't worth trying to analyse her beyond that. Shannon obeyed without question, sparing Mark's life by dropping her rifle and jogging around the side of the house to find the entrance he had left open.

By the time she made it indoors, the woman had removed her balaclava. The rest of her face looked as serious as her eyes, and a long plait of black hair hung from the back of her head. Mark's shotgun was in her other hand, pointed towards Shannon. She held it so steadily that it might as well have been made from cardboard, despite it being held by a single hand at arm's length.

Shannon took gentle steps towards this complete stranger – an enemy who didn't seem like an enemy, despite pointing a shotgun at her and an automatic weapon at her unconscious ally.

'You could have blown us up back there,' Shannon breathed. 'Why didn't you?'

'Two kids on bikes?' the woman answered. 'You're not exactly a fleet of New Oxford tanks.'

Shannon couldn't stop herself from smiling.

'So you're not one of Grant's people,' she said, relaxing her shoulders and dropping her hands. 'Thought you weren't.'

'Yeah, and what are you?'

'Huh… How long have you got?'

'All bloody night. Start talking.'

Well, it's not like I've got much choice. She's pointing the guns, I'm not.

'We're the Underdogs,' Shannon said. 'A bunch of guerrilla fighters who spend our lives trying to sabotage Grant and his people.'

She opted not to mention their achievements: the destruction of the clone factory, the death of the AME shield, and so on. The less this stranger knew, the better.

'Your turn,' Shannon said. 'Why should we trust you?'

'I didn't say you should,' said the stranger.

'Whatever. Who are you?'

No response.

'You can be honest,' said Shannon. 'If you don't like how I react, shoot me afterwards.'

Silence again. The woman withdrew her weapon from Mark's direction, and stepped far enough away from his body that he couldn't leap at her unexpectedly. At the far side of the living room, she laid Mark's shotgun on the carpet, and nudged it to the back wall with her feet before pointing her assault rifle at Shannon instead.

'Captain Emilia Rubinstein,' she said. 'Special Forces.'

Shannon grinned.

'*Special Forces?*' she asked. 'Some of you guys made it here? I thought the British coastline was wrapped up tighter than a grandma's Christmas present.'

'I didn't "make it here",' said Rubinstein. 'I never left this sodding island. Been here since the beginning.'

'How did you—'

'Your turn. Give me your name.'

Rubinstein's rifle was pointed straight at Shannon's face. Her finger was on the trigger. But even then, Shannon decided the most risk-free option was to tell the truth.

'Shannon,' she said.

'Good. So you're not a liar.'

Shannon froze.

How does she know...

'I've spent more than a year with intel making its way to my phone. I never forgot your face.'

There was a twinge in Emilia Rubinstein's eyes. It looked sad rather than angry. But it terrified Shannon deep to the core of her being. Because if Rubinstein knew...

'If we're having this conversation,' Shannon said, 'let's get it over with before Mark wakes up.'

She had hoped dropping Mark's name would result in a change of topic, and that Rubinstein would want to know about him too. She was wrong: Shannon remained the most interesting person in the room.

'Your full name,' said Rubinstein. 'Now.'

'Shannon Rose Grant. My father and I disowned each other a long time ago, and now I'm fighting against him.'

Rubinstein paused. Her body's position didn't change, but there was something resembling compassion in her determined eyes.

'I believe you, Shannon. I really do.'

'But you're not putting your rifle away.'

'No. And I think you know why.'

'I'm harmless.'

'It's not about that. On Takeover Day, a thousand different alerts appeared on my phone. Not that I had time to look, of course. But I read through them over the following weeks and saw your face, and… what you did that day was chilling.'

Shannon dropped her gaze to the floor. She had not realised that complete strangers knew about it.

It had been such a well-guarded secret that not even the Underdogs knew.

'Is it true?' asked Rubinstein. 'Did you really do what the reports say you did?'

'Yes.'

'Then that can only mean one thing. That you—'

'*Yes.* If you're going to say it, say it. While he's still unconscious.'

Rubinstein blinked a number of times. Each time she did, her eyes looked a little sadder.

'In that case,' she said, 'I'm so sorry, Shannon.'

Shannon had not expected that kind of response. Sympathy was usually reserved for the daughters of *good* guys.

'The report told me everything you did,' Rubinstein continued, 'but it didn't say what they did after…'

'It's ancient history now.'

'But you remember it?'

'It'll always be a part of me.'

The muzzle of the rifle began to sink. Shannon had no idea how, but Captain Emilia Rubinstein had seen the face of Nicholas Grant's daughter, and her reaction had been sympathy rather than judgement.

At their side, Mark began to stir.

'Do *they* know what you did?' asked Rubinstein.

'No. None of them.'

'You don't think—'

'*No.*'

Mark's hand made its way to his head. He was conscious, but not yet awake. Not truly.

'Before he wakes up,' asked Rubinstein, 'how many are you on now?'

What business is that of yours? You have no idea how painful this subject is to me!

Mark made an effort to lift his head.

'Five,' said Shannon. 'Now shut up about it, OK?'

'Five what?' Mark moaned.

Shannon flashed a fearful pair of eyes at Rubinstein, who kept her lips sealed.

'Nothing,' answered Shannon. 'Mark, this woman's on our side.'

'Yeah, bloody feels like it.'

Shannon wasn't expecting to smile, but she did. When she looked up, Rubinstein was smiling too.

'Mark,' said Shannon, 'her name's Captain Emilia Rubinstein. Special Forces, apparently. Emilia, this is Mark. Mark Gunnarsson.'

'I won't shake your bloody hand if that's alright,' said Mark, fumbling an arm to the mantelpiece to pull himself up to his feet.

Interestingly, Rubinstein didn't lift her rifle. Clearly Shannon had been seen as the only respectable threat, and even that had only been because of—

'So those explosives out there,' Mark mumbled. 'What's all that about?'

'Classified.'

'Yeah, right. You don't look like you've got many allies here. Are you waiting for some big transport to head from New Oxford to New London? For the Acceleration project, by any chance?'

Shannon's jaw dropped open at Mark's willingness to divulge secrets. But it made sense. Rubinstein wouldn't be the first to open up, so someone had to make the first move. If she were truly an ally she'd be worth sharing intelligence with.

'Your bikes didn't set off the explosives because I keep them unarmed.'

'And because we were too light.'

'Don't flatter yourself. A wandering fox could set them off. I'm saving them for something that really matters. Their main transport probably has room for everything, but just in case—'

'Their main transport?' asked Shannon. 'What *else* could they be using?'

'You haven't worked it out? Didn't your dad ever tell you about it?'

Stop talking about my crap father!

'Huh,' she answered, 'as if he trusted me. Everything I knew, I found out for myself.'

Rubinstein nodded. It seemed that whatever she had previously thought of Shannon, it was now being replaced by genuine respect.

'I'd say you've got about three minutes until you find out. You might want to head outside for this.'

'Why?' asked Mark.

'Trust me.'

'You knocked me out.'

'Then stay in here and miss it, you overconfident, under-qualified thug.'

Mark picked his rifle from the floor, grumbled something inaudible, and staggered towards the farmhouse's exit.

Once he was gone, Shannon looked back at Rubinstein. She didn't know whether she wanted their previous conversation to restart, but the anxiety that sprung from it was unresolved.

'I've got contacts across the world,' Rubinstein said. 'So I know exactly what's about to happen. What I *don't* have is the resources to deal with it myself. You say your people are guerrillas, right?'

'Better than that. Underdogs.'

'So you know how to fight?'

Shannon grinned. 'Yeah. We know a thing or two.'

'Right. Because you blew up the clone factory. You and Anthony Lambourne wrote the software, then your new friends did the job.'

Shannon froze. Again.

'I can't tell you my sources,' said Rubinstein. 'But we know a lot about Terrorist Faction 001. You've done the kind of stuff the rest of us haven't been able to dream of. You've got our respect for that.'

She called us Terrorist Faction 001. That was Dad's name for the Underdogs.

She gets her information from inside the Citadels.

'Did you know Joseph McCormick?' asked Rubinstein.

'Yeah. He was wonderful.'

'Were you close?'

Shannon couldn't stop the memories from flooding back. Her first night in Spitfire's Rise. The slow journey to becoming an Underdog, and all the warmth and acceptance she had been offered along the way.

'He basically saved me.'

'I'm sorry you lost him,' said Rubinstein. 'My contacts saw him as a hero. Even after his suicide bombing.'

'It was *not* a suicide bombing,' Shannon snapped, perhaps too loud. 'He had every intention of getting out alive.'

'Either way, he killed Iain Marshall and wiped out the AME shield. The world owes him a great deal, whether he died deliberately or not.'

A hum started to sound outside the farmhouse. Like the

planes Shannon had vague memories of flying over British airspace, except so much louder.

'Shannon,' said Rubinstein, 'a minute from now we'll be running outside. Before we do, answer me this.'

Shannon felt vulnerable. The kind of vulnerable she hadn't felt since the hours before she met McCormick. She even felt her hands tempted to search around for the nearest bladed object. For the first time since she had fled New London, she had come across a person who understood her for who she truly was. And it terrified her.

'Shannon... how close are you to the others in your team?'

'They mean everything to me.'

'Everything?' Rubinstein asked, her eyes widening with interest. 'So it wouldn't surprise me if you're romantically involved with one of them?'

Shannon didn't know how to react at first, and said the first sentence that came to mind.

'None of your bloody business, you nosy arse.'

'You could have just said "yes". No need to be aggressive about it.'

Shannon rolled her eyes. This woman from Special Forces had dropped into her life from absolutely nowhere, and acted like she had the right to poke around every fibre of her being, because of some intelligence reports she had read.

Where did that question even come from, anyway? she asked herself. *People don't normally ask about your love life when you've just met them, do they?*

Did she already know about me and Ewan? If she's getting her intelligence from someone in New London...

'I've got a wife and two adopted kids,' said Rubinstein, her gaze dropping to the carpet. 'They're in South Carolina right now. Or they were, last I heard. When Special Forces started to get suspicious of Marshall-Pearce Solutions, I couldn't tell my family anything. So I can sympathise with your situation.'

'Don't pretend you can even—'

'But what I *could* do,' Rubinstein interrupted, 'was encourage them to get out of Britain. Take a nice long holiday in the United States. They've been there without me for more than a year, while I've sheltered here spending most of my days like a survivor on a desert island. Once every few weeks I get contacted by someone who outranks me, who's tucked away in a nice posh house in Monaco. There used to be others like me dotted around Britain, but I don't think many of us are left. But you know what occupies my mind most hours of the day, whenever I have nothing else to focus on?'

'Your family.'

'Damned right. My wife and daughters are somewhere across an ocean, and they probably think I'm dead. I wouldn't blame them either.'

The hum outside got louder.

'They deserved to know more than I could give them. I couldn't tell them the truth – not without breaking every kind of regulation we have – I couldn't even tell them how much I loved them when they left for the airport, in case it made them suspicious. And if I had to go back in time, I *still* wouldn't tell them. But there's nothing stopping you, Shannon. Nothing but your own emotions, and fear of how others may react. Who's the lucky lover?'

Rubinstein spoke in such an overfamiliar tone that it was as if she'd known Shannon for years. Almost as if they were actual friends. Shannon huffed. From Rubinstein's perspective, having observed New London life for so long through the many reports sent to her phone – and likely with zero face-to-face human contact since Takeover Day – she probably felt like she and Shannon weren't strangers at all.

Shannon decided to answer the question. Ewan had told her apologetically about the 'great kisser' comment he had made to Iain Marshall, and that would have caused huge waves in New London's high society. Rumours spread fast around the upper floors – even rumours that were true. So perhaps Emilia Rubinstein already knew the answer.

'Ewan.'

'Ewan West?' Rubinstein asked. 'McCormick's head soldier? The problem child turned war hero?'

'He was only a problem child from other people's perspectives,' Shannon sneered. 'To him, he was a scared child in a world designed for everyone else.'

'You *do* love him then,' said Rubinstein. 'That sentence and your tone of voice is enough.'

Shannon headed for the door. The humming grew, and Mark's voice could be heard swearing outside.

'You should tell him what you did on Takeover Day,' finished Rubinstein, with a hand clutching Shannon's shoulder. 'If he's fallen in love with you, he deserves to know. Sooner rather than later... You know why.'

Yeah, thanks for bloody reminding me.

Shannon turned around and stared as hard as she could into Emilia Rubinstein's eyes.

'If Ewan were ever to find out about Takeover Day,' she snarled, 'he'd find out *my* way. My words, my timing, my terms. Got it?'

Rubinstein nodded, and released her shoulder.

'You should call him once you see what's out there,' she called out, as Shannon ran outside. 'The quicker he gets here, the better.'

Shannon didn't answer. She didn't even reach Mark before she saw it.

'You've got to be kidding...'

A patch of the night sky was starless, blocked out by the jet-black metallic cloud that roared as it made its way across the sky.

It was an airship. Hundreds of metres long at least – it was difficult to tell whether it was a massive aircraft at a low altitude, or an even *more* massive aircraft flying high. It sung a loud hum to the countryside beneath as it hovered towards New Oxford, flanked by at least a dozen helicopter defence units, and out of the range of anything the Underdogs could possibly throw at it.

'I wasn't expecting it to be that big,' muttered Rubinstein, who had appeared at her side. Shannon turned to face her.

'What can we do?'

'Like I said, I've not got much in the way of resources. Other than roadside explosives, the bullets in my rifle and the intel on my phone, all I've got is the clothes I'm wearing. Not even a rocket launcher, as if one of those could take down a thing like that.'

Shannon watched in horror as the biggest mode of transport she had ever laid eyes on soared its way across the night sky. Suddenly it became clear how her father could transport a Citadel's worth of resources without relying on 10,000 lorries.

For all our victories to date, for all our determination and all our strategic prowess… we're powerless against anything in the air.

And my father knows it.

Chapter 9

Kate sat on her plastic chair in the attic of the Boys' Brigade hall, her knees tucked up to her chest. She didn't want her feet to touch the floor.

Gracie died here.

Violently, in this exact spot. Just this morning.

Alex had done a decent enough job of clearing up the blood. But not out of decency or hygiene: at the time, he was planning not to be found out. Nonetheless, the knowledge was haunting enough without the blood to accompany it.

To her left, Lorraine's feet were firmly on the floor. She was no stranger to blood, and hadn't been for a long time before Takeover Day.

'Lorraine... how are you doing that?'

Lorraine glanced towards her, with apathy in her eyes.

'Doing what?' she asked slowly.

'Sitting there, knowing that's where Gracie...'

'I spent twenty years putting new patients into beds that people had died in the day before. Or sometimes the same day.'

'But... you *knew* Gracie...'

'You think I didn't know my patients? That I didn't get to

know their families? That I didn't sometimes pop in on days off to look after relatives soon to be in bereavement?'

Kate had no response at first. But for as long as she had known Lorraine, she had seen her as someone to learn from. And with last month's events still cemented in her mind, a lesson in detachment would perhaps be welcome.

'Is that how you cope with loss?' Kate asked. 'You just think "stuff it, happens all the time"?'

'I never said I cope with loss. But it *does* happen all the time.'

Kate couldn't find a way of manipulating the conversation her way. She had never been good at manipulating anything. She decided to just speak her mind. One way or another, there was a lesson she needed to learn before she could become the fighter she had once been.

'How should I deal with Raj?'

Lorraine let out a long sigh, which Kate couldn't interpret.

'Think of another person you lost,' Lorraine said eventually. 'Someone you deeply cared about. And tell me what you learned from it.'

'McCormick,' said Kate, knowing straight away that it was the least helpful choice. Lorraine's face scrunched up at the sound of the man's name.

'Let's not talk about McCormick,' she said with a bitter voice.

'Why not? What did *you* learn from his death?'

Kate didn't want to push, but it had been the first time in a month that Lorraine sounded like she cared about something.

'I learned not to be controlled by *anyone*. Not even those I'm accountable to. McCormick's operation was the one time I compromised my beliefs, and even my core principles as a nurse, thinking I was doing so for the greater good. And look where it got us.'

'The AME shield was destroyed,' said Kate. 'We still get to fight this war, thanks to what you both did.'

'You think that's enough?'

'Of course not... I'm the one who pressed the button.'

She pushed away the memory of Ewan and Alex pressing the button with her. It didn't match the bias in her brain, which told her that she alone was responsible.

She took a moment to try to understand the workings of Lorraine's traumatised mind, but it was likely to be a particular trauma that Kate had never experienced herself. All she knew was that if Lorraine really had learned to not let other people control her, she was applying it in the worst possible way. Kate would have hoped it would lead to Lorraine feeling more independent or autonomous, rather than just shutting herself in the clinic and ignoring other people's existence.

Just because someone learns a life lesson, it doesn't mean they learn it well.

'I'd like to say you get used to it,' Lorraine said, 'losing so many people. But you don't. Death is fresh and painful every time and there's nothing you can do about it. The trick is not to miss them.'

Kate turned her head, her mouth gaping in surprise at that last sentence.

'How do you lose someone you care about and not miss them?!'

'By knowing it won't help them. You can move on happily with your life or spend the rest of your days in mourning, and the other person will be dead either way. Trust me, when I was a teaching assistant I lost a student just after his twelfth birthday, and no matter how much I...'

Kate kept silent, and hoped the conversation wouldn't go in an even more stressful direction. Shannon had told her in passing that Lorraine had left a career in education after the suicide of a student, but she didn't know the details. She was pretty sure his name had been Joey. Either way, bringing him up in conversation would set Lorraine even more on edge than Kate was comfortable with witnessing.

Thankfully Lorraine shook her head, and finished her point without any further mention of Joey.

'Nursing taught me a brutal enough lesson too. If you're in a place where people die all the time, there's simply not enough room in your brain to miss them all.'

Kate rested her face in her hands.

You'd be surprised how much room there is in my brain for hurt. For bereavement. For guilt.

James…

And just like that, her brother was in her mind again. Her profoundly disabled brother, overloaded with learning difficulties in every conceivable area, and also the best man on Earth. The person she would go into battle against impossible odds for, and bring an army to its knees in exchange for even the slightest chance of one day discovering him alive. The young man she and her Oakenfold friends had abandoned in the field on Takeover Day, along with all the other Block One students, for fear of being captured themselves. James Arrowsmith, Kate's own reason for waging a war against Nicholas Grant and a million clones. A war fought in the hope of rectifying the worst decision she had ever been forced to make.

She missed him. Everything about him. His pensive long gaze. The poetic consistency of his evening routine. His excited yelling in the park, and how it scared the more judgemental members of the public so beautifully. She missed his unique communication methods, which didn't correlate with most other people's but expressed exactly what he was feeling. More than anything else, she missed watching the same episode of

David Tennant-era *Doctor Who* with him over and over again, and the sense of security and consistency it brought to both of them.

Those days were gone – perhaps temporarily or perhaps forever – and it saddened Kate beyond words.

And that was no bad thing. Alive or dead, people as wonderful as her brother were worth being sad for.

The pain of missing someone is always worth it for the joy of having known them, said McCormick's voice in Kate's head. *Always.*

'I can't be like you, Lorraine,' she replied. 'I have to miss Raj. I have to miss all of them.'

'Even if it destroys you?'

'It won't destroy me,' Kate said, picturing James' face. 'Each person I miss is an extra reason to fight back and win this war.'

'Then it sounds like you've found your way of coping with Raj's death. Congratulations.'

Silence followed.

Ten minutes of it.

When the silence was broken by the vibrating phone, Kate's hand seized it first.

It was a voice call, not a video call. And its screen held words Kate had never seen on it before: *Unknown number*.

She showed it to Lorraine and shrugged her shoulders.

'Answer it,' Lorraine said. 'If it's an enemy, hang up straight away.'

'What if—'

'If Grant's found our phone number, he's probably tracked it and we're already buggered. Let's at least find out who it is.'

'Fair enough,' said Kate. 'If they find their way here and kill me, you won't miss me anyway.' She pressed the green button and clapped the phone against her ear before Lorraine could respond.

Kate refused to speak first, not even breathing into the mouthpiece.

'Hello?' came the other voice moments later. Kate smiled, recognising the voice immediately.

'Unknown number, Shannon? What's going on?'

'You'll like this,' said Shannon. 'Scrambled phone, can't be traced. As long as we're using this, we won't need to restrict our calls to three minutes. Not anywhere.'

'Where did you—'

'I'm going to pass you on to this woman we found near New Oxford. She calls herself Captain Emilia Rubinstein. Special Forces, apparently.'

It was already too much information for Kate to process. She put the phone on speaker, hoping that Lorraine's brain would be able to handle it better than hers.

'Did you say "Special Forces"?' Kate asked, watching the surprise emerge on Lorraine's face.

'Yeah.'

'Do you believe her?'

There was a pause from Shannon, its reason unclear. 'Yeah. She knows enough about us.'

'So does your father,' said Lorraine.

'Believe me,' said Shannon's voice, 'given what we're up against, we need all the help we can get. Even if there's a risk, she's a risk worth taking. Let me pass you over.'

There was a moment of rustling over the phone, just long enough for Kate and Lorraine to stare at each other in confusion. Apparently, Lorraine had no idea how to interpret the news either. It was just too outlandish.

Then again, perhaps it wasn't to Shannon. She had found other survivors in the countryside before... not that it had ended well.

'Speaking,' came a firm, strong voice that Kate had never heard before.

'Hi... what's your name again?'

'Rubinstein. Captain Emilia Rubinstein. And I'm not going to bother with the ten minutes of "how do I know I can trust you" and so on. I've met Shannon, I've met Mark, and I've already worked out there's no way you're working with Grant.'

'Alright... but same question in reverse. How do we kn—'

'You don't. But your friends trust me, and the longer we talk the more useful you'll find me. I'll tell you as much as I can about Acceleration, about Pearce and Crossland's next steps, and what you *might* be able to do to stop it. What you do with the info is up to you, but if you have better ideas on how to bring down an airship using more reliable sources than me then be my guest and hang up. But after you do, give Ewan and Simon a ring and pass on the directions I'm about to give you. I'm with your friends at a farmhouse just north of Thame, east of New Oxford.'

Kate and Lorraine paused, long enough to reveal that they had no plans to hang up.

'Did you say "bring down an airship"?' Kate breathed.

Oliver Roth rarely wasted time regretting past decisions, but he wished he had chosen a better starting point than Lemsford.

The village had been levelled flat by airstrikes a month earlier, an overreaction by Grant after learning the Underdogs were familiar with the place. Perhaps it had been Grant being cautious, or maybe it had been frustration. After all, Alex Ginelli had escaped their clutches and they hadn't even extracted a location for Spitfire's Rise, leaving them with nothing to show for his capture except an extra clone model.

Destroying a village in anger was a pretty standard response from the same man who had imprisoned a nation.

Roth was sitting on a rock which might once have been part of somebody's wall. He laid the last of the sticks in place for his makeshift campfire, and looked around. He was on the outskirts of the village, but had an unrestricted view right to the other side of it. Nothing stood between him and the far end of Lemsford except charred wooden beams, broken walls and scattered ash. It meant fewer resources to scavenge for him and his 500-strong clone army.

He took the lighter from his pocket and set fire to the paper underneath the collection of sticks. The wind, gentle as it was, would be a risk: there was literally nothing to shelter the fire from the breeze. Nothing in the whole village stood more than a metre high. Roth glanced over to his soldiers and saw that the construction of their tents was progressing well. The biorifle soldiers couldn't do much with one functioning hand each, but they were more active with their left hands and right forearms than Roth had predicted. The fancypants scouts were guarding the perimeter of the village: almost certain to be idle for the night, but it was a good chance to test their night vision anyway.

Roth's army wouldn't need his leadership for a while, so he had the chance to do something he hadn't done since his childhood days: sit by a fire, look up at the stars and just think to himself. He had already spent most of his waking hours under the watchful eyes of those he commanded, so rare time to himself would be priceless.

'Oliver,' said Colonel João Pereira from behind him.

Oh get the hell out of here, you useless, overweight sack of incompetence and get yourself a better name, you twat.

'Hi, Colonel,' he said. 'Is your tent up yet?'

'Just finished,' answered Pereira. 'You got yours up pretty quickly, I see.'

'Yeah... thought I'd get it out the way so I could spend some quality time out here. Just me and the stars.'

Roth had hoped, wrongly, that the hint was clear enough.

'I don't blame you,' came the colonel's answer, sitting himself down at the opposite side of the campfire. He brought his hands close to the little flames, which must have been too small to offer any real heat. 'Nothing relaxes a person like a sky full of stars. It's always helped me to clear my mind.'

To be fair, your mind's pretty empty to begin with.

Roth gave up on his quest for alone time. He could have commanded Pereira to leave him alone, but there would be no point in souring their relationship openly. Like it or not he probably needed the colonel, and would continue to need him until they had found Spitfire's Rise.

'Has your thermal tracker picked anything up?' asked Pereira.

'Just us. Nothing else within ten kilometres. Except woodland creatures too insignificant to show up.'

'Insignificant woodland creatures? Like the rebels, then?'

Roth smiled, but stopped himself before Pereira noticed. Perhaps the colonel did have a rudimentary sense of humour.

'Other than them *actually* being small woodland creatures,' Pereira continued, after taking a swig of his bottled water, 'which I think is unlikely, I'd like to know how they've avoided our thermal trackers for so long. And, privately, I'd like to know why we only utilised the technology once before now.'

Roth shuffled himself closer to the fire, which had grown to a half-decent size and temperature. He decided not to tell Pereira the truth: that the biggest reason the great Nicholas Grant had never found the Underdogs – via thermal technology or otherwise – was simply because he'd never felt threatened enough to look. For all their little sabotage missions over the first eleven-ish months, they had never been seen as a legitimate threat until Shannon had used them to destroy the clone factory. And their annihilation of the AME project had made them too big to ignore.

But Pereira had a point. There was something odd about the lack of thermal clues. When Shannon and Lieutenant Lambourne had run away to that health centre in Hertford, they'd been found in less than a day. Why wasn't history repeating itself, albeit a little further north?

There's no good reason for it. If Keith bloody Tylor could find Shannon that quickly, nothing would stop me.

Wait a second...

A Keith Tylor-related thought struck Roth's mind, which snowballed into a collection of decent ideas. He brought out his electronic map and loaded it up. After a couple of minutes, he worked out something important.

'Colonel,' he barked.

'Oliver?'

Provisional Head of Military, and I still get called by my first name. Bloody hell, I wish my job came with some kind of title.

He shuddered just slightly, as always, at the word 'provisional'. It made his promotion seem fake. It felt like all the glory of being the most powerful British person below Grant was being dangled in front of his nose, close enough to smell but too far away to touch.

Spitfire's Rise needed destroying. As soon as he could do it.

'We're going the wrong way,' he said. 'Wherever Spitfire's Rise is, it won't be along this route.'

Roth beckoned Pereira closer, and the colonel edged around the fire until he could see the screen.

'We're here,' Roth said, pointing to Lemsford – a village

planted right next to the A1, and far to the northeast of New London. 'But Keith Tylor died here,' he continued, pointing to a village called Sandridge – a village a few miles away at the northern tip of St Albans.

'What are you getting at?' asked Pereira.

'Shannon was in Sandridge when she killed him. At some point that night, she found the rebels. Whatever route they use between Spitfire's Rise and New London, it passes through Sandridge, not Lemsford. In fact, it wouldn't surprise me if they used Lemsford as a way of *avoiding* Sandridge after Keith died.'

'So… we should head for Sandridge in the morning?'

'North of it. *And* north of here. This village maybe… Wheathampstead. Either Shannon headed north after killing Tylor, or they found her and *took* her north.'

Pereira nodded, but added nothing.

'Either way,' Roth finished, 'Wheathampstead will be a step closer to Spitfire's Rise. Maybe where it actually is.'

Pereira smiled. 'Good work, Oliver. Perhaps you could have been a detective in a different life.'

'I'm pretty happy with the way my life has gone, thanks. Do you mind giving me a moment? I need some time to think.'

'Sure. See you in a bit.'

It turned out that getting rid of Pereira without commanding him was easy. Diplomacy had never been in Oliver Roth's skillset, but he knew that listening to a few sentences and smiling was enough to satisfy most people. Pereira rose to his feet and wandered away, his head tilted back to gaze at the stars and empty his mind even further.

Roth had sort of told the truth as well. Except he didn't need time to think. He needed time to dream.

It was likely to happen, when he thought about it: actually

finding Spitfire's Rise and slaughtering its residents. Maybe in a few days, maybe in a week, maybe after a Scott-Amundsen style trek that would last for months, or maybe tomorrow. But eventually, the storming of Spitfire's Rise would have to happen, especially if Grant was serious in commanding him not to return before completion.

Roth began to daydream. He daydreamed about a showdown against the great Ewan West: watching him panic with no idea how to defend himself on home ground – against an enemy he had believed to be dead. He daydreamed about facing off against Mark Gunnarsson, whom he had always seen as an evenly matched opponent. About meeting Alex Ginelli, and thanking him for his assistance before putting a bullet in his head.

About Shannon begging before the end. Perhaps he could present her head at the next staff meeting.

About McCormick…

Wait, no. Not McCormick.

Roth hated it when that old dead man invaded his brain. It reminded him of how conflicted his mind could be in its weaker state.

The Underdogs had compassion for each other. The New London staff put their subordinates in death chambers, smiling and taking notes while a gentle woman like Sandra Zeigler snapped the neck of a harmless man like Daniel Berry.

The Underdogs put their lives on the line for each other. Nobody in New London would do that for him.

And the Underdogs were *brave*. Nobody in New London's Outer City had an ounce of bravery.

Oliver Roth was under no illusions. Finding Spitfire's Rise would mean sending 500 clone soldiers to wipe out everyone Joseph McCormick had loved. A lot of friendship and bravery would have to die in the process. McCormick had introduced

Roth to something wonderful, and here he sat, perhaps days away from removing it all from the world.

Then again, it would mean winning the war. And getting back to his room sooner rather than later.

Would I do it though? If I found Spitfire's Rise tomorrow, how would I really react?

Roth shook his head. That was tomorrow's problem. Tonight, he had a warm fire and a clear sky, and the annihilated village around him would look far uglier in the morning. He had a responsibility to relax tonight, and put McCormick and Grant to the back of his mind.

Chapter 10

Ewan braked when the distant farmhouse came into view. Behind him, Simon did the same. It hardly stood out in the dead of night, but it was in the middle of a field and its shape was distinctive enough. Lorraine and Kate had passed on the directions perfectly.

'Best hide the bikes here,' he said. 'They'll be no use in bumpy fields.'

Simon found the thickest looking hedge and buried his bike behind it. Ewan took a moment to inspect the field before him, then hid his bike next to Simon's.

'So someone from Special Forces is in that farmhouse,' he said.

Simon snorted, apparently unable to believe it either.

'Huh, "Special Forces",' Ewan continued, as he hopped over the ditch at the side of the field and made his way onto the lumpy ground. 'Maybe we shouldn't have called ourselves the Underdogs. We should have called ourselves Special Forces. That'd suit us, right?'

He looked to Simon with a grin, thinking it was a clever comment. Simon just huffed.

Ewan understood. More than a year after society's collapse,

some Underdogs had still not made peace with the word 'special'. Even Ewan only used it for self-deprecating humour.

Either way, a touch of humour was welcome at that moment. The airship had only been visible in the distance from the M40, but it had still been terrifying to see what they were up against.

Simon joined him in the field, and they made their way towards the unlit farmhouse in the distance.

'I need you with me when I talk to her,' Ewan said. 'I'm not giving her my trust until I know she deserves it, and if things go bad then two guns are better than one. You up for it?'

'Yeah…' came a shy grunt from Simon's throat.

Wow, he must be feeling confident tonight.

Halfway across the field, the familiar figure of Shannon appeared before the farmhouse and headed in their direction. They met a hundred metres later, and Shannon's first reaction was to give Ewan a long, tight hug.

It was unusual behaviour by battlefield standards. Something must have bothered her.

'You OK?' Ewan asked.

'Yeah. Nervous.'

'About the airship?'

A pause. 'Yeah.'

It was an unconvincing answer, perhaps even a lie, but Ewan decided not to chase it. He could utilise all of his manipulative powers to get to the bottom of her secrets, but turning on manipulation mode for Shannon just wouldn't feel right.

'She's inside,' Shannon continued. 'Dining room.'

'What do you make of her?'

Shannon took a sharp intake of breath, as if wondering how to answer.

'She's trustworthy. And she'll be helpful to us. Just don't expect her to make you comfortable.'

'I'm pretty experienced in people not making me comfortable. Let's see what she's got.'

They reached the entrance to the farmhouse, and saw Mark on guard duty. He nodded in their direction, but said no more.

When Ewan walked into the house, Rubinstein was sat at the dining room table with a dim camping light flickering in front of her face. She had no weapons with her. No visible weapons, anyway. It should have calmed Ewan down, but he wouldn't let himself relax.

Simon stood in the corner of the room, assault rifle in his hands, and Ewan took his seat at the other side of the table.

Before he could talk, Simon started to sign something towards him. Ewan watched, wondering why his friend hadn't worked out he'd never learned British Sign Language, but also very aware that he was being observed by someone he didn't yet trust. In fear of looking incompetent within five seconds of meeting her, he decided to wave his hands around and pretend he was answering Simon back.

Simon looked predictably confused. Ewan just hoped he hadn't answered with something obscene by accident. He turned to Rubinstein and opened his mouth, but she cut him off.

'Your friend was saying "she looks trustworthy",' Rubinstein said. 'I don't know what you were saying back though. Maybe your BSL's more advanced than mine.'

From the opening sentences of the conversation, Ewan already had a reason to feel uncomfortable. He had been caught out by someone who was clearly smarter than him.

'I'm Ewan,' he said, taking the most obvious opportunity to change the subject. 'Ewan West. This is Simon.'

'Pleasure. I've heard a lot about you. I'm Captain Emilia Rubinstein, Special Forces.'

'If you've heard a lot about me, you'll know my record in competitive shooting. So if you've got any extra people here waiting to jump out, you'd best give up on that—'

'Ewan, you were a student at Oakenfold Special School in Harpenden, while it was under the leadership of headteacher Paul Dale. You were expelled from six mainstream schools before Oakenfold, largely due to their inability to accommodate your needs associated with Pathological Demand Avoidance. You are the son of the late Major George West and his wife Martha, you're presumably the leader of the Underdogs following the passing of Dr Joseph McCormick, and although you never earned a criminal record, there are details of meetings you had with the police to discuss your behaviour as a teenager. Oh, and your middle name's Morgan. Need I continue?'

Ewan heard a snort from his side. Simon seemed to find it funny.

How the hell are you finding this funny when I'm clearly this frightened? It must be all over my face right now…

'There is no record at all of you being involved with competitive shooting, although I've no doubt you're highly skilled anyway. Including the BSL attempt, that's the second time you have tried to mislead me in the twenty seconds we've known each other. So let me be clear on this, and I'm saying this without judgement…'

Yeah, right. You sound like the most judgemental non-judgemental person I've ever met.

'I want to put my trust in you, Ewan Morgan West. I *really* do. By the end of this conversation you'll have an idea of how much you're needed, and how much Special Forces appreciate you, even if we were never permitted to make contact. I'm not a hundred percent sure this conversation's even allowed, but if it helps take down that airship I'll make my own choices and pay for them later. But in order for both of us to get what we want, I need you to act like the hero that gets mentioned in all my reports, rather than a teenager who lies to make himself look good. Can you be the hero for me?'

Ewan found himself wishing he could push the reset button on the conversation, walk into the building a second time and start the discussion the way Rubinstein had recommended. The first impressions he had given her had been based on nervousness. Throughout his whole life, most of his negative behaviours had been rooted in anxiety first and foremost.

Two months ago I met the Rowlands for the first time. Even then, trapped in the Inner City with almost no chance of escape, I did a decent job of making friends with them. Why am I struggling now? Did I suddenly become a bad person?

He realised the truth not many seconds later. Things were different now. His leadership responsibilities were pressing down on his shoulders and manipulating his judgements. Since the morning after McCormick's death, most of Ewan's actions had been taken with the long-term goal of being seen as a good leader. Not necessarily *being* a good leader, but being seen as one.

Ewan breathed 'sod it', stood up and left the table. He walked to the back door, not turning round to see how surprised Simon was, and closed his ears to whatever Rubinstein was saying in the background. He stormed outside into the darkness, walked to Shannon at the back of the house, and tapped her on the shoulder. She turned around, concerned.

'I screwed up,' he whispered.

'Then try again,' she replied, with both sympathy and determination written across her face. 'You'll get it right the second time.'

'And if I don't?' Ewan asked, wary of Mark's listening ears not far away in the field.

'Then try a third time. Trying again's what you're good at. Besides… she needs you and she knows it. She may have the intel, but we have the people. She can't succeed without us, so she'll accommodate you screwing up.'

Ewan took a deep breath.

Worth a try, I guess. It's a high-stakes situation, but my leadership strategy hasn't worked so far. And let's face it, she's already worked out what kind of person I am. I can afford to be my real self – the only person I'm good at being.

'Thanks,' he whispered, looking away from Shannon's face to protect his vulnerability. He jogged back to the front door and strolled towards the dining table again, and found himself interrupting a BSL conversation between Rubinstein and Simon. He could not translate it of course, but they were smiling at each other.

The conversation came to an abrupt halt as they saw Ewan. Their hands fell, and their eyes focused solely on him. Ewan took a moment to wipe the anxious thought from his head: that their conversation *must* have been about him and how inept he was.

'Alright,' he said, approaching to take his seat once more. 'I'm sorry. Let's start again.'

Rubinstein could have given any reaction to Ewan's re-entry. But, as Shannon predicted, she accommodated him.

'Good man. Apologies if I was too direct with you. I'm no expert on PDA, but I probably made you uncomfortable with all that. Let me know if I head in that direction again.'

They were refreshing words, dissimilar to anything Ewan had heard from a human's lips outside of his family, Oakenfold, or Spitfire's Rise.

'Alright, cheers,' he said, trying his best to smile at her as he spoke. 'Just remember... the problems are not the person, OK? I'm normally better than that.'

'Oh I believe you, don't worry.'

Ewan raised his eyebrows. Rubinstein was speaking like someone who meant it – not like someone who was *trying* to mean it. Adults like this were rare.

'So what's your story?' Ewan asked. 'How many of you are out here?'

'Just me outside New Oxford. Others dotted around the country. On average, about two per Citadel.'

Ewan leaned back in his chair, trying to process the information. In just a couple of sentences, Captain Rubinstein had turned his understanding of the abandoned countryside right on its head.

'There's a small resistance inside Grant's own staff,' she continued, gazing at the table as if nervous about uttering her words aloud. Ewan remembered how little his father had been comfortable telling him about his job as a major, so he could imagine how much confidentiality meant in Special Forces. 'Albeit a pretty *useless* resistance. The Network – as we call them – can't really do anything except pass on their info to people like me, then wait for me to pass it to my superiors, and then wait for the United Nations to do nothing about it. That, and many of them have already been found and purged. I won't tell you how many are left in the Network, but it's not as many as we need.'

Ewan laid one hand across his forehead, and drummed the fingers of his other hand across the wood of the table. Was this good news or bad? There were more opportunities for inside help than Ewan could possibly have predicted, but Rubinstein seemed far from positive about them.

'And on top of *that*,' she continued, 'Grant knows that

other traitors still exist in his organisation. Did you see the attempted missile strike on New London?'

Ewan nodded. He hadn't witnessed it for himself, but Kate and Mark had. And Raj.

Just days before AME would have gone up, the outside world had tried a one-in-a-million shot of getting past the Cerberus missile defence system and wiping out Nicholas Grant the old-fashioned way. The Underdogs had never figured out whether the attacker was just one country or some grander alliance, but either way it hadn't worked. It was never going to.

'It was stupid for the UN to even try,' spat Rubinstein. 'It wouldn't have worked anyway and now Grant *knows* he has moles working against him. How else could the United Nations have found out AME was so close to completion?'

She was getting emotional. By her standards, anyway. Ewan had his own surprise to deal with too, learning for the first time that the missile attack had been a decision made by the United Nations itself. Nicholas Grant really did have the whole world against him, although he certainly wasn't losing.

'So who else can we trust in New London?' he asked.

She shook her head. 'Not yet, Ewan. I'm not telling you anything that would put Network members at risk.'

'So you're not planning to tell me about Acceleration—'

'Yes I am. But I won't tell you anything that Grant doesn't already know. I trust you as a soldier, but I don't trust anyone to resist torture and interrogation. I'll let you know only what you need to, and only when you need to know it.'

Ewan nodded. There were no counter-arguments that would work.

'While we're on the subject,' Rubinstein continued, 'how on Earth have you not been found? I know at least one of you has been captured in the past.'

Daniel Amopoulos. Wow, it's been a long two and a half months since we last saw him.

'Daniel didn't know our location. Only three Underdogs have ever even known the name of our village,' he replied, with Raj and McCormick on his mind. 'And two of them are dead now.'

'And how did you avoid all their technology? Given your father's association with the military, I'm guessing you used a thermal blocker?'

Ewan kept silent, even though silence was as good as a 'yes'. Simon's terrified face gave it away regardless.

'Don't worry, me too,' she said, reaching into her pocket and fetching out a metal device the size of a table tennis ball. 'Keeps me invisible over a one-mile radius.'

Ewan smiled.

'Ours is *five* miles.'

Rubinstein smiled back.

Ewan yawned, and looked at his watch. It had been one of the longest days of his life in terms of activity, which after a life like his was really saying something. It was time to get down to business before he fell asleep at the table.

'So anyway,' he said, 'why don't you share what you know about Acceleration, so we know what we'll be up against?'

'How much do you already know?'

Ewan decided that the risk of telling her was worth it. Besides, he had already acted like a brat to her once.

'One of our friends was held prisoner by this... hypnotist. Called Gwen Crossland.'

A look of horror swept across Rubinstein's face, a sign of recognition which surprised Ewan.

'One of you met her?' she asked. 'In person?!'

'Long story, but yeah. And she gave away that Grant plans to cull the human population in the long run. "Acceleration" is his way of making people kill each other, to speed up the process, I guess. In the meantime, he's also closing down New Oxford. Looks like time and disease are doing the job for him, and now two Citadels can fit into one.'

The horror on Rubinstein's face turned into anger.

'I've had people in the Network watching New Oxford for over a year,' she said. 'The population hasn't dropped that much.'

'But they're combining New Oxford and New London… by putting the two populations together…'

'Not because the populations are low *already*…'

Ewan looked at Simon. His friend had already worked it out.

'That enormous airship?' Rubinstein said. 'Grant wouldn't build it just to transport equipment too big for the roads. He built it to transport people too, en masse. Nathaniel Pearce and Gwen Crossland are on that airship right now, heading to New Oxford to pick up the first of the equipment… plus the first four hundred subjects to "treat", transport and release into the New London population. Once they've seen how the first four hundred do, they'll fly the airship back for everyone else. We're talking about a slaughter of unimaginable proportions… thousands attacking thousands, and *killing* thousands. Millions, maybe.'

Ewan broke his gaze away and stared down at the camping light that flickered on the table. He tried to rid his brain of the mental image that was trying to form: of New London's Inner City exactly as he remembered it, except filled with screaming Londoners as they ran from unexplained mass murder, committed by members within their own crowd as they tore through the wastelands of wood and corrugated metal.

Ewan knew the best way of beating his anxieties was to calculate his way through them. He started to focus on real, practical options. If there were any.

'How do we beat them?' he asked.

'If you ask me,' Rubinstein said, 'when planning for something big, it's usually helpful to start at the end. What would success look like to you at the end of all this?'

Ewan stared at her, blank-faced.

'Winning the war.'

Rubinstein smiled, which seemed like an odd reaction to Ewan.

'What about in the shorter term?' she asked. 'At the end of this mission?'

'All of us still being alive.'

'Let's try to be more specific.'

'All of us being alive and in good health, and ready to strike again—'

'Look,' Rubinstein said, with a voice identical to the one Ewan's teachers once used when they were doing their best not to snap, 'I know you take things literally. But use your imagination here. What is your team trying to *achieve* over the next few days?'

Ewan did his best.

'I guess...' he started, 'whatever research they've done, whatever methods they've come up with, Gwen Crossland's the only one who can make it happen. By the end of this mission, she needs to die.'

'Good start. Keep going.'

'You said Nathaniel Pearce is on board. If he dies too, it'll slam the brakes on all of Grant's future plans.'

'Anything else?'

'If we can't get rid of Crossland and Pearce, the only way of stopping the New London bloodbath is by making sure the airship never reaches its destination. And even without the bloodbath, if he's using that airship to transport the New

Oxford equipment to New London, we'll have to bring it down anyway.'

Rubinstein nodded. The total lack of surprise on her face suggested that she'd thought of all this herself.

'And we do that by…?' she asked.

'By sabotaging the airship before it even leaves New Oxford.'

'That won't work,' she answered, shaking her head. 'They'll just *fix* it in New Oxford and be on their way.'

'Which just leaves… doing something to it in the air. You want me to suggest blowing it out of the sky, don't you?'

'You really think we have the resources for that?'

Well, don't forget the 400 innocent people on board. Pretty sure they should enter the equation too.

'Then we commandeer it,' Ewan said.

'Which would involve sneaking on board, killing every last clone soldier without exception, and then… well, and then what? Floating over the countryside until further notice? Heading very slowly towards the English Channel without Grant shooting you down on the way?'

'If he shoots us down, the airship never reaches its destination,' replied Ewan, doing his best to control his impatience. 'Didn't we agree that was the objective?'

'Yes, but you also said staying alive was an objective. And I'd say it's the primary one.'

Ewan looked at Rubinstein, confused. He even looked to Simon to check his reaction too.

'Isn't sacrifice an importa—'

'How many Underdogs are left, Ewan? Nine? Ten? That's the problem with heroic sacrifice. Even if you win the battle, you're gone for the rest of the war. If you want to win both, you need to be alive for it. So how do you bring down this airship without dying, given the possibilities we've crossed off already?'

'Take out its engines,' Ewan answered, having used Rubinstein's talking time to brainstorm his answer – which in turn had been a good distraction from the painful thought of sacrifice and the friends he had lost to it. 'Force an emergency landing. It would trap all their equipment in the middle of nowhere, and we could take out Pearce and Crossland while we're on board, but... it still leaves the problem of the four hundred civilians running around the countryside. Grant's clones will pick them off like upper-class bloody foxhunters.'

There was a look of grave sadness on Rubinstein's face.

'Ewan,' she said, 'I think you'll have to assume those people will die whatever you do.'

It was a thought Ewan was unwilling to accept. At his side, even gentle Simon was showing signs of anger.

'You won't like hearing this,' Rubinstein continued, 'but New Oxford's the only safe place for them. The moment they leave, one way or another they're dead. The objective is to stop them reaching New London, not to save their lives. Would you rather four hundred people die in the countryside, or four hundred thousand die in a horrific slaughter?'

Ewan gave Rubinstein a nasty glare, for all the good it would do.

'So this is the plan as I see it,' Rubinstein said. 'You head back to Spitfire's Rise and make whatever preparations you need to. Tomorrow you come back here with your two most reliable friends, and I'll give you details of my contact in New Oxford who can help you break in. I made contact with him while you were on your way here – he has an idea but there's only room for three of you. Once you're on board, you wait until the airship takes off, then destroy its engines. Force a crash-landing – one that doesn't kill you, of course – and escape with as many innocents into the countryside as you can.'

Rubinstein collapsed back in her chair.

'And after that,' she finished through gritted teeth, 'I suggest you run back home... while Grant's forces are distracted picking off those four hundred people.'

Chapter 11

Alex was running out of uncovered memories. He had spent hours conquering the distraction of the bright lights over the vegetables and their insufferable droning buzz, using strategies from his long-gone taekwondo lessons to focus his brain, slowly but surely relearning the information from his lost days. Despite his fear of the unknown becoming known, despite the possibility that each awakened memory would reveal something terrible he had done, and despite the physical sickness at the end of each reawakening – the heavy head and trembling extremities as if waking up from a conscious nightmare – he had dived into each one without hesitation, in the hope that he could uncover something useful that might help his friends.

He could still be heroic in one way, at least.

Alex gazed at the faded roses on the dull wallpaper, which made him look forward to remembering something that had happened outside. Perhaps recalling it would make him feel warm. He had served a long sentence in that chair, and it had felt so much longer with each new memory's reawakening. But there was just one sequence left.

Alex closed his eyes, and remembered.

*

He was at gunpoint, walking down the main street of some dead village. Half a dozen clones were escorting him – with Gwen Crossland personally at his side, her aged Womble-like face even more prim and ugly in daylight. She held onto his telescopic handgun, leaving Alex unarmed.

Alex found himself wishing he had shot her in the face instead of handing his weapon over at gunpoint. It had been a smart move on Crossland's part, switching his memory back to normal at the water treatment centre so he'd be able to tell the others exactly how he escaped. It wasn't until he was out and 'Smoke on the Water' started playing that he had realised how brilliantly Crossland had tricked him.

'There'll be a nice bungalow for you somewhere in this village,' she said in her usual voice, soft yet terrifying. 'I'll let you choose it yourself.'

Alex didn't respond. He was too busy coming up with plans for how to escape, how to rescue his trapped friends, and how to warn everyone about the new Alex clones due for production. But plans were pointless and he knew it. As soon as 'Barbie Girl' started playing, all memory of his plans would be lost.

Crossland's phone rang, its ringtone dull and characterless.

'Hello, Nathaniel,' said Crossland, holding the phone on speaker a few inches from her face.

Alex started to listen closely. Nathaniel Pearce, as irritating as he was, was worth eavesdropping on.

'Is this a good time?' he asked.

'I'm still escorting Ginelli.'

'You've left the Citadel already? You didn't complete the Acceleration experiment first?'

What the hell's Acceleration supposed to be?

'I cannot complete the experiment inside the Citadel whilst delivering Ginelli to his shelter in time for his allies to not become suspicious,' she said. 'He must reach safety within a short period of his apparent escape, or questions may be asked.'

'OK, fine. Anyway, a bit of news which Grant wants everyone aware of. New Glasgow was attacked yesterday.'

Crossland stopped suddenly, and the clones around them took half a step before following suit. Alex just stared at the phone in her hand, far too confused to feel any optimism about the news. Crossland glanced across at him with suspicious eyes, pausing for a few moments before giving Pearce any response. In the end she must have reached the same conclusion as she had before using her speakerphone at all: that even if Alex heard the conversation, he was doomed to forget all about it.

'Attacked?' she asked, curious rather than afraid. 'By whom?'

'An alliance of Americans and Canadians, given the testimony of those captured. Five thousand soldiers, most of them dead now.'

Crossland looked at Alex, perhaps wondering what he knew. Alex shrugged, and dared to smile at her.

'Disabling Cerberus was their first step,' Pearce began. 'Apparently Colin Oswald wasn't as loyal as we predicted.'

'I don't know who that is.'

'Don't bother memorising his name. He'll be dead as soon as his knowledge has been extracted. He was in charge of New Glasgow's defences, and he disabled them ten minutes before the invasion. Oswald was obviously in contact with one of the UN Special Forces morons.'

'And then?'

'Then they lost. Their first wave of missiles struck the outer walls and caused us enough disruption, but five thousand human soldiers against a hundred thousand Glaswegian clones? It was a massacre.'

Alex turned his head away, not wanting the ageing little witch to see his crestfallen reaction.

'What were they hoping to achieve?' Crossland asked.

'Marshall's probably the better person to ask,' Pearce answered with noticeable disdain towards his colleague, 'but in my opinion, they never planned to *hold* New Glasgow. They wanted to steal as much intelligence as they could while dragging our armies into the mountainous Scottish waste-land, so they could send a bigger army to take the southern Citadels. Anyway, I've ordered a credentials check into the twenty-six security leads nationwide and their deputies. And everyone else with access to the Operations Room – not including Nick, of course. A *biological* credentials check.'

'I'm unclear…'

'Call it a truth serum if you like. They'll all tell the truth regardless.'

Alex was still looking away, but could sense the smile on Crossland's face as Pearce had spoken.

'What would we do without you, Nathaniel?' she asked.

Alex perked an eyebrow. It had not sounded romantic, but would at least have sounded kind and warm if Gwen Cross-land had possessed some kind of soul.

'Without me?' Pearce answered. 'Well, most likely Grant would lose his mind and slaughter most of the world.'

'I'm sure he would.'

'I'm quite serious, you know. Subjugating the world's pop-ulation and gradually reducing it is simply Plan A. Plan B, if he were ever to lose access to new technology, would be to reduce the number of living humans the old-fashioned way. Grow enough clones to invade Europe, and sweep across the rest of the world from there. Execute everyone in France except the Parisians, everyone in Germany except those in Berlin, everyone in Spain except those in Madrid, and so on.

Ugly, but fast. He *wants* this to take generations and give the world enough time to adapt, but if worst comes to—'

'I need to go, Nathaniel,' Crossland said, with a sharp, judgemental eye pointed towards Alex. 'You can tell me the rest when we're alone.'

Alex looked around the village to avoid Crossland's expression, his gaze coming to rest on the wide range of abandoned buildings around him: some of them bungalows that had showed no signs of having been abandoned at all except for overgrown gardens, and some of them two-storey houses with their walls eaten away by untended ivy. Crossland said her goodbyes to Pearce, and tucked her phone back in her pocket. She then checked her watch and stared at Alex.

'I need to release you now,' she finished. 'Choose your shelter, make yourself comfortable, and tell McCormick you're safe. Enjoy your alone time, Alex.'

She nodded, and a clone behind Alex wrapped an arm around his neck, tore off the bandage around his shoulder wound, and drove a small knife into his bullet hole, reopening the wound in full.

Alex didn't hear Crossland's exact words as he yelled in pain and his torso warmed with the sensation of leaking blood, but it was something about removing the evidence of him being treated during his escape. The next thing he knew he was running across the village with his handgun back in its holster, the high-pitched tones of 'Barbie Girl' playing from the loudspeaker in another clone's hands. Gwen Crossland and her entourage left the scene in the opposite direction, and before too long they had turned the corner to the main street and were out of sight altogether.

As the music faded, the world clarified itself in Alex's mind and he forgot what he wasn't allowed to remember. Then, with his hand slapped over his gunshot wound, he ran for the nearest bungalow in search of something – *anything* to stem the bleeding. He needed to call McCormick and Simon at comms to let them know he was still alive – and determined to shelter close to the Citadel until the teenagers found their way out too.

Alex stopped reminiscing, as his new memories of that day bled into the memories he already had.

With the closing of that memory sequence, Alex's usefulness as an Underdog came to an end. The last of his memories had been uncovered, his final secrets unearthed. With his fighting days over and his information mine exhausted, Alex's life was now destined to consist of sitting in his chair – a useless, restrained waste of Underdog resources – until the war ended or until he died.

But at the very least, he no longer had to feel afraid of remembering his lost memories. That alone was something of a comfort.

Something moved in the corner of his vision. The tiniest movement, but by far the most significant event in an otherwise boring farm. Alex turned his head just in time to see a shock of black hair vanishing down the stepladder into the underground tunnel.

'You can come in, Thomas. I'm not going to kill you.'

The child crept back up the stepladder and into the farm, approaching inch by inch as if trying to pet an angry dog.

'I… just wondered if you were OK,' Thomas said.

Well at least I still have one friend here.

'Yeah, I'm alright,' Alex answered.

'Really?' the boy asked, confusion twisting the shape of his face. Alex paused.

'Well OK, I'm not. I guess you could say this is the low point of my whole life. And it's not going to get better either.'

Thomas sat down on the floorboards, half a metre from Alex's feet, and looked up at him. Being looked up at was a rare luxury for a man tied to a chair.

'You've got me,' Thomas said. 'I mean, if you think that's a good thing. If you want some company I can stay here with you. I know you didn't mean to—'

Alex cut him off.

'You're right. And thank you.'

To Alex, the nine-year-old at his side had been an unnecessary extra in the Underdogs for as long as he could remember. Right up until Beth died, he had only regarded Thomas as 'Beth's son' rather than a person in his own right. But as the population of Spitfire's Rise dwindled, the influence of each member increased. Thomas' joyous humour and humanity had become so blatant that even Alex could no longer deny it.

In fact, it was time for the boy to get the praise he deserved. Alex felt himself softening, entirely against his own nature – or perhaps the nature his dad had instructed him to have – and spoke with compassion in his wavering voice.

'Thomas,' he began, 'I just want you to know... this may be a houseful of heroes, but you're by far the best person here.'

Thomas wasn't quite sure how to react at first, but after a moment of confusion he took the compliment with bright eyes. 'Thanks, Alex.'

'No problem. I'd give you a hug if I weren't tied here.'

'Ewan and the others said—'

'I know. And I don't *want* you to untie me. They're right. I'm just saying thank you.'

Thomas smiled. It was a delightful smile, which showed the gaps between his teeth and tiny dimples in his cheeks. Alex had never paid attention to Thomas' smiles before, or even smiles in general, but under the circumstances he was growing to appreciate them.

The smile dropped at the sound of footsteps echoing through the tunnel. They emanated from the cellar next door, along with a voice which sounded like Ewan's.

It wasn't long before the strike team were in the farm too, dragging Jack along with them. Nobody was complaining about Thomas being unattended with an apparent psychopath, which suggested to Alex that Jack had been spying on the conversation all along.

Lorraine and Kate completed the set by following the strike team into the farm.

'From now on, all meetings will take place in the farm,' Ewan began. 'It's easier than moving Alex around, and he should be part of this too.'

'Cheers, mate,' Alex replied. He had said it genuinely, but Ewan stared back at him as if he were mocking his kindness. A year of sarcastic comebacks had taken their toll on people's perception of Alex as a person.

Ewan explained the events of the previous night as succinctly as he could. Alex had not been able to look at his watch, and had no idea the night was over. But the surprise paled in comparison with the news of Captain Emilia Rubinstein, and the details that followed were nothing short of incredible.

Oswald was obviously in contact with one of the UN Special Forces morons, Pearce's voice sounded in Alex's head.

'These Special Forces people may be more common than you think,' he muttered. 'And so are traitors in the Citadels.'

All eyes fell on him.

'Excuse me?' said Ewan.

'I've had a long time in this chair to reawaken old memories. I remember human staff talking about traitors as if they were a real problem, not just a small crew of conscientious objectors or whatever. They're a well-organised group… or as well-organised as you can be with Grant watching your tech all the time.'

Ewan nodded. 'Rubinstein mentioned these people called the Network…'

'That'll be them. And they have outside links too. Did you know New Glasgow was attacked by American and Canadian forces the day before we attacked the clone factory?'

When eight people responded with nothing but silence, Alex told them the whole story, in as much detail as he could remember. Including Colin Oswald's name, and his bravery in disabling the Cerberus missile defence system.

'But I'm guessing Rubinstein didn't mention that,' he finished. 'Maybe it was classified or something.'

'Wait,' said Jack, 'you're saying Cerberus can be disabled by one person acting alone?'

'That's the main learning point of the discussion, yeah. Which is encouraging.'

'Yeah,' grunted Mark, 'one person acting alone, all the way up on Floor A.'

'I've got as high as Floor C before,' Alex answered, opting not to mention he had only stayed there long enough to blow up McCormick from the top of the stairwell. 'If I can get there, one of you should be able to get higher.'

'And then what?' asked Kate. 'Meet the same end as Oswald?'

'Well the war's got to end somehow. But that's your information, anyway. It's up to you how you use it. By the way… you'd need to do it twenty-six times. I heard Pearce say there are twenty-six security leads, which suggests there are twenty-six Citadels. I guess we finally know the number. I don't know where they are though – we know there's a London, a Reading, an Oxford, a Glasgow, a... a Brighton...'

There was a pause in conversation, as the remaining Underdogs processed the news of Nicholas Grant owning *twenty-six* Citadels. They had fought for over a year and two thirds of their army had died without even knowing how many fortresses they were supposed to take down. The last nine soldiers looked unlikely to reduce the number: in fact, Alex realised, the upcoming closure of New Oxford meant that Grant himself was set to destroy more Citadels than the Underdogs ever had.

Ewan spoke, blatantly trying to change the subject.

'We need to talk about tonight's strike,' he began. 'We'll have to leave here mid-afternoon to get back to New Oxford in time, and I suggest the new strike team spends the rest of this morning sleeping. We've earned it.'

Simon circled a finger around the group, and shrugged.

'Me, Kate and Jack. We're the strike team.'

Alex raised his eyes, as did half the room.

'Three?' asked Lorraine. 'Thousands of lives at stake and you're sending three of us to deal with it? You had four just for last night!'

'And Rubinstein said there was only room for three people in her plan. I'm picking Jack because we might need a technical geek on the airship, and Kate because she's probably the best fighter we have. No disrespect, Mark, but Emilia wouldn't have knocked out Kate so easily.'

'Yeah,' Mark grunted, 'but w—'

'Which leaves Lorraine and Shannon on comms,' Ewan interrupted before an argument could start, forcing a tiny smile onto Alex's lips. 'Mark and Simon, you're here looking after Alex and Thomas. And that's all nine of us sorted.'

'Quick question,' said Jack. 'What exactly are we doing while we're on board?'

'Taking out its engines and forcing a crash-landing.'

'Oh...'

There was a short silence from a crowd of people yearning for more hopeful details. Ewan offered none.

'But you said there were people on board this thing,' said Thomas, with a wobbly voice.

'There are. And I'll do my best to save them. I promise.'

Mark gave a snort, alongside something that could perhaps be described as a laugh.

'They'll all be hypnotised, you know,' he said. 'If their trigger song plays while you're on board, you've got four hundred mad Alexes trying to rip you apart. So while we're in a position to do some research... Alex, do you need to *hear* the specific song before you get violent?'

Alex was surprised at Mark's blunt, unapologetic tone, and then realised he shouldn't have been surprised at all.

'I don't know,' he answered.

'So if you get it stuck in your head, what happens?'

'I'd never *let* it happen.'

'Try it now. We'll watch.'

Every pair of eyes went to Mark, each of them disapproving. Alex looked away, and chose not to respond. Mark, of all people, had no right to control what went on inside his head.

'Fine then. What if someone sings it?'

I already know the answer to that. I woke up my memories on the night McCormick died just by singing 'Smoke on the Water' to myself.

He had no time to respond verbally. Mark, to the shock of everyone around him, had already started to sing 'Seven Nation Army'.

'Duuuun, du-dun dun dun duuun, duuun...'

'Mark, stop,' someone said. Alex couldn't tell who. His mind was already flooded.

Alex's body, absent from the influence of its mind, started to wrench against the ropes. His hands and feet were stuck fast, but they wrenched anyway. He would rip the chair to splinters if he needed to.

Mark was still singing, although a flurry of other people's hands appeared around his mouth.

Alex realised, as little as he was able to think in his current form, that the chair was not going to break. Even his anger-driven brute strength wouldn't be enough. He jumped forward and brought the whole chair along with him, reaching his head towards the nearest human in the crowded farm and opening his unrestrained jaws.

Suddenly, Alex was back to normal. Mark had stopped singing, but nobody paid him any attention. They were all preoccupied by the screaming young woman in the middle of them.

She screamed like that the first night I met her… after she killed Keith Tylor.

There was a horrible gash across Shannon's forearm, uneven and dribbling with blood. Alex's mouth felt strangely warm, like a nosebleed that had gone the wrong way.

I bit her?!

Shannon looked petrified. Truly, truly petrified. Alex had not believed that someone as life-worn as Shannon could be the kind of person to freak out over a minor arm wound. But then again, she had probably never felt a man's teeth sink into her flesh.

'I'm s-sorry,' Alex gasped, unable to wipe his own tears as he spat her blood onto the floorboards.

'*You're* sorry?' yelled Ewan, turning and clenching his fists. '*He* bloody did this! Mark, what the *hell* were you thinking?'

He sent one of his clenched fists smashing into the bridge of Mark's nose, with a fury that Alex rarely saw in him outside of combat: the unforgiving aggression Ewan could launch when a person he valued got hurt. Mark shuffled back a couple of feet – a surprising distance – before several other Underdogs placed their bodies between him and Ewan. Their angered leader looked an inch away from battling through them in furious desperation to get back to Mark, until Shannon rested a trembling hand against his shoulder. Suddenly, his focus was entirely on her and her bleeding forearm. The anger remained, but his aggression was dying.

'Well now we know what Gracie saw,' Mark answered, not even rubbing his nose in response to Ewan's punch. 'Don't make friends with the prisoners on that airship, mate. They only need to hear a bad impression of their trigger song and you're dead.'

'Whatever,' Ewan snarled as he signalled a hand towards the exit, an aggressive command for everyone to get out. 'Meeting over. Lorraine, look after Shannon. Kate and Jack, get some sleep while you still can. Mark, stay the hell away from Alex. And Shannon. *And* me. Or I swear you'll regret it.'

Caught up in his own searing guilt, Alex would have loved for someone to offer words of sympathy. Hell, to even acknowledge him. But in the shock of the moment, they couldn't possibly have been in the frame of mind to recognise how crushed Alex felt at his manipulation. The farm emptied before he had even caught his breath.

The silence didn't last long. The shock of black hair returned, just as soon as everyone had found something more urgent to focus on.

'You don't have to spend time with me, Thomas,' said Alex. 'Especially not after what just happened.'

'But I want to,' the boy replied, climbing back up the step-ladder and sitting himself down on the floorboards. 'You're still a person, even if people don't treat you like one.'

Alex gave a troubled smile. After thirteen months of regarding this child as more of an annoyance than an ally, he was glad to have the opportunity to see Thomas for the wonderful young man he truly was.

Chapter 12

Roth knew he was heading in the right direction. And not just because his equipment said he was heading northwest. He had never been a real believer in the power of feelings, but he could sense – somehow – that he and his 500 troops were getting closer.

It was like Frodo in *The Lord of the Rings*. Sure, the movies may have been long and filled with sappy do-gooders (maybe the books had been different, but he'd never been arsed to read them), but it had been interesting to watch Frodo's personality collapse the closer he got to Mount Doom. He had been infected by something contrary to his whole being, which only grew stronger the closer he got to his goal.

Except, the reverse was true for Oliver Roth. The closer he got to Spitfire's Rise, the stronger the voice in his head told him *not* to destroy it.

He had spent the last few hours switching his glance between the sunny morning countryside with its wavy-leaved trees and dew-glittering grass, and the thermal tracker in his grip. He was using the tracker in place of his GPS device, since the GPS provided a map and nothing else, whereas the thermal tracker was useful for keeping an eye on his troops' locations too. Their heat signatures revealed a twenty-strong batch of his scout clones half a mile ahead of them, taking the route he had commanded.

With the route predictable for several miles to come, Roth could afford to relax his brain for a while. He brought his eyes back to the abandoned countryside, and tried to remember whether he used to appreciate blue sky back in the old days. He couldn't remember missing it much after his whole life was replaced by Floor A luxuries and shotguns.

'What's the latest?' came Colonel Pereira's voice from behind him.

Somehow, Roth wasn't quite as annoyed by Pereira's existence as before. He wasn't that bad a guy, even if his judgement was inept from a year of inactivity. Besides, having another human to talk to was good. They had even shared breakfast together, despite the irritation Roth had felt but hid.

'Nothing new really,' Roth answered. 'Just following the road for a few miles. Once we reach Wheathampstead we'll take the road north. The leading scout team are looking for evidence of human activity. Nothing so far though... so feel free to spend some hours looking into the empty sky again.'

'It is excellent weather, isn't it?'

'Mid June, I guess.'

'I've always loved the summer. Everyone else bangs on about how beautiful the autumn months are, but I've never understood why. Summer's been my favourite season ever since childhood.'

'Not mine,' Roth answered, wondering why he was expending effort on such a pointless conversation. 'I'll take autumn any day. Redheads like me don't do well in the sun.'

Or at least, that's the stereotype. Gave the other kids another excuse to poke fun at my hair... back when we were young enough for them not to fear me.

'What's wrong with a little sunburn?' asked Pereira. 'Autumn may have pretty colours, but it's only pretty because everything starts dying.'

'Maybe that's why I prefer it.'

Pereira laughed, and Roth pretended that was the reaction he was after. The death and decay of autumn did have some kind of appeal to it, but Roth had never given it much conscious thought.

Thinking back, he wondered whether the appeal of autumn's decay had started with the squirrel.

He had just turned ten, that dull but pleasant age when he would spend most of his days wandering through the countryside outside his house. Not because he appreciated the great outdoors, but just to go somewhere and do something. Mum and Dad had only really spoken to him when asking him to do things, and had never provided much in the way of entertainment or activities to occupy him. So Oliver Roth had grown up finding his own.

His friend – or one of his allies in school, since 'friend' was probably too strong a word – had been given an air rifle as a birthday present for some reason. It had been perfectly legal: air rifles were considered so harmless when used responsibly that they weren't restricted by regular gun laws. Clearly his friend's parents had believed their son to be responsible enough to handle baby firearms at the age of ten.

Except, his friend hadn't been responsible with who *else* got to touch his weapon. It had been quickly passed around the group like an already-opened pass-the-parcel toy. Oliver had already borrowed it twice within three weeks of the kid's birthday.

On one particular day, he was taking it back to his house for some target practice in his back garden. Mum and Dad would notice but not care enough to ask questions. They would step in if they believed he was in danger, but otherwise his ways of occupying himself didn't concern them. There had been very little for Oliver to do as a child: no clubs or sports or even real hobbies – and his parents had banned him from playing videogames in case they made him violent.

Oliver had walked through the forest towards his house with a sense of reluctance; he already knew he was talented at shooting inanimate objects with an air rifle, and the challenge was subsiding already.

That was when a squirrel crossed his path, and changed his life.

No, it wasn't the squirrel that changed my life. It was my own choices. I could have ignored it if I wanted.

It was autumn, and the forest was full of the fancy-tailed rats scurrying around for last-minute nuts before hibernation. They were fast little creatures. Great acrobats. Young Oliver had admired them.

But admiring something and valuing it were different things. Oliver had raised the air rifle, following the squirrel with the rifle's muzzle as it scrambled up and down the nearby tree trunk.

Some elderly adult had once told him that 'the devil makes work for idle hands'. He figured it was a warning against getting bored, or an excuse to get away with bad things when people didn't entertain him enough. Looking back now, at the age of fourteen, Oliver Roth wondered whether his actions would have been the same if he had been walking home with some kind of youth group awaiting him in the evening. Or if his parents had introduced him to board games. Or if he had collected comics. *Something.*

Oliver had fired an air rifle pellet straight into the squirrel's back. It flopped off the tree trunk like a furry sponge and slapped onto the leaf-ridden ground, rolling onto its side and revealing the exit wound on its tiny belly.

Several years on, Roth could no longer remember which sensation he had felt first: the elation of 'wow, that was a good shot' or the daredevil thrill of 'what the hell did I just do?!'

Oliver's first bodily action had been to look around for witnesses, for adults he may have been accountable to.

Accountability changes people's actions more than morals. People are far more concerned about whether they'll get away with something than whether it's the right thing to do.

For a moment, the present-day Roth found himself wondering if he'd just explained the person he had become. He had spent thirteen months being accountable to nobody but Nicholas Grant and Iain Marshall, and his personality had taken the consequences. He shook his head, and thought about the squirrel again.

The squirrel had still been alive. Maybe, if it had found a safe hole to hide in with a decent food supply, it would have ended up surviving. Unless infection was a thing for squirrels too.

But that was a maybe. And besides, no bullet could pass through a body that small without rupturing a few organs. To Oliver's relief and disappointment, none of those little organs were visible outside the exit wound.

There was a second pellet available to him. What he would do with it was simply a matter of his own free will. In his class there'd been some violent kid with blatant special needs (perhaps a younger version of Ewan West), who the teachers had wasted hours talking to about the importance of making choices, and doing so in front of the other children. Even then, Oliver had got the feeling that the poor retard hadn't been capable of making choices in his worst moments anyway: nobody with a gram of common sense threw chairs around and got their classroom evacuated because they *wanted* to be seen as a problem child or have their freedoms removed.

To that boy and to all of Oliver's primary-school classmates, choices had always been presented as a chance to decide between right and wrong. But that had never matched up with how Oliver had seen it. To him, choices had simply meant being in a position of power. If you had the ability to make a choice, you held a bit of power that others around you did not.

The only thing that could ever make you unreachable, Oliver, said McCormick's dead voice, *is your own choice to never be reached.*

Roth shook his head a second time, wondering how that man's thoughts were so good at entering his brain at inconvenient moments. Unexpectedly, he also found himself wondering what life must have been like for Ewan West, having those guiding thoughts planted in his head over the course of a year. Perhaps, for all his neurological faults, Ewan had become a better person because of McCormick's influence. Perhaps Roth could have become a better person too, if he had started the war on the opposite team. Perhaps in a simpler Britain, where there was no war, no Takeover and no clones, Ewan West and Oliver Roth could each have been McCormick's adopted grandchildren, learning the man's life lessons in parallel and growing together as young people. They might even have become proper friends.

Roth banished the thought, and remembered how his ten-year-old self realised he hadn't gone to the effort of shooting a squirrel once just to let it live.

The child version of Oliver Roth had chosen to reload the rifle and shoot the squirrel through the underside of its jaw. The squirrel's wobbling figure had rocked back with the impact of the pellet, and then frozen still.

It had been the first time Oliver had watched anything die. Anything bigger than an insect, anyway. He hadn't exactly enjoyed it, but it had been interesting to watch. The sudden *stop* of all movement had been the part that struck him most.

By Oliver's eleventh birthday, he had his own rifle. At the age of twelve, he had joined Marshall-Pearce's junior training programme. At thirteen he had been promoted to chief assassin and spared the horrors of Takeover Day, and at fourteen he had climbed the ladder to become Nicholas Grant's (provisional) Head of Military. He had kept himself out of captivity while his parents, schoolmates and teachers had been dragged into the Citadels, and he had kept himself alive as Iain Marshall, Keith Tylor, Anthony Lambourne, Adnan Shah, Sandra Zeigler and a load of other colleagues had died around him. It had to be said, Oliver Roth was one hell of a climber.

The phone in his pocket vibrated, and he answered.

'Yeah.'

'Oliver!' came Grant's enthusiastic voice. 'Give me news.'

'Heading towards Wheathampstead. Nothing interesting so far. A few of Nat's scout creatures are up ahead, and we're watching for signs of human activity. I'll call you when we find something. How's things back home?'

'Quite satisfactory,' came Grant's reply, in a relaxed manner that suggested he was probably lying back in his chair with his feet on his desk. 'Nat and Gwen touched down next to New Oxford last night, and will be spending the day training four hundred subjects. Tonight they'll be heading back.'

Roth shuddered. Six versus six in that Floor G slaughter chamber had been disturbing enough. Even after everything he had done in thirteen months of warfare, the image of Daniel Berry's snapping neck was slow to leave his mind. Four hundred conditioned people among the New London population would be more terrifying to watch than a real-life zombie movie.

'So,' Grant continued, 'I imagine it's a little early to ask when I can expect *you* back here.'

'Whenever you want me.'

'Remember your orders, Oliver. If you want to be the *permanent* Head of Military Division, you come back here once Spitfire's Rise is destroyed and not one moment before.'

'In that case, Nick, I have no idea how long I'll be gone.'

'Not a problem. Your provisions should last at least a week. If you need more, I can have some sent out. Cheers.'

Grant hung up without another word, and Roth huffed with enough anger to get a curious look from Pereira at his side.

But orders were orders. He was still accountable to Grant, and it kept him obedient.

His new job may have given him a lot of power, but he still missed the days of Iain Marshall. Before the man had vanished into McCormick's flames, the accountability had gone both ways. Marshall had been Roth's boss, but he had been equally accountable to Roth and nobody had even known.

Nicholas Grant would never find out about the assassination plot that Marshall had handled so badly. If Roth had known Marshall was going to die, maybe spilling the secrets beforehand would have been a lovely strategic backstab. It would have gained even more of Grant's trust, and countless rewards for exposing a traitor. But there was nothing to be gained from telling him now, and it was better to keep their relationship simple.

But keeping our relationship simple would involve wiping out the Underdogs.

Wait… did I just think of that as a bad thing?

It was the Mount Doom effect on Frodo again, Roth's

judgement getting more affected by the Underdogs the closer he got to them. Their sense of justice and love was so strong they were even at risk of getting through to a boy like Oliver Roth.

Oliver Gabriel Roth, now aged fourteen. The young man who could have avoided the whole war by walking past that squirrel.

Now there were a bunch of new 'squirrels', somewhere in the countryside north of them. And once again, Roth would have to make a decision on whether to take the shot.

'You OK, Oliver?' asked Pereira.

'Just wanting this to end.'

'Losing patience already? If you need a break, give the command and they'll stop.'

It was a lazy suggestion, but perhaps a kind one. Roth declined without words, and kept marching.

He came to realise that he felt accountable to Colonel João Pereira too. Not in a way that implied authority, but in a way that kept his social responsibilities alive. With another human around, there came the need to act like a human himself.

The previous night, he had been wondering whether Pearce had been truthful in claiming that his soldiers could heal a broken arm in a day and a half. And had Pereira not been present in his army, he would absolutely have put it to the test.

Instead he had waited until Pereira was at the other end of the camp, beckoned a clone over, and given him a shallow slash wound across the side of his waist that would lie hidden under his uniform. He was impressed when he called the same clone over to him the next morning and found that the injury had completely vanished, besides a few powdery marks on the inside of his clothes. But despite outranking Pereira, and despite the soldier making a full overnight recovery, Roth still

153

felt the need to keep the colonel from finding out what he had done.

Oliver Roth had always had an inquisitive mind, and he was becoming aware that other humans were helping him keep it in check. Without Pereira and his bumbling kindness, Roth would probably be removing clone kidneys by now to see whether they'd grow back.

Roth didn't know what it said about him, that he could commit horrendous acts against clones and enemy humans yet mind his behaviour around allies he barely knew. Maybe it meant he still had some level of respect for authority, even if not for people. Or maybe it meant he had more compassion than he thought. But either way it was far too complicated a subject to get into, especially so early in the morning. Roth brought up his thermal tracker to see how far ahead the scouting team were.

He gasped at the sight of the screen.

The scouting team were gone.

Not motionless and cooling down, as if they were twenty dead bodies. Just *gone*. Everyone else in the miniature army showed up on the screen perfectly, so there was nothing wrong with his equipment. Other than teleportation, or being chopped into so many pieces that they were too small to show onscreen, Roth had no ideas.

'All units,' he spoke into his radio, 'ready your weapons. Possible threat, half a mile northwest.'

Pereira ran over to look at the tracker, and wore the same look of confusion as Roth. Behind them, 480 clones raised their rifles and biorifles, and pointed them haphazardly at the lush green surroundings. Some of the clones hid behind trees that stuck out at the side of the road. Others took cover in the ditches and behind hedges.

Buzzes sounded in his radio; the simplified Morse-code-style buzzing that clone soldiers used as a replacement for vocal cords. Roth looked around to find which one of them was typing, but found every clone's hands on their weapons. Even the biorifle soldiers steadied their gun arms against their hand arms for balance and accuracy.

When the buzzing stopped, Roth realised what he had just been asked.

Do you want us to run back to you? We don't see any threats up here.

'Wait,' Roth said into the radio. 'Identify yourself.'

Buzzes sounded again, identifying the messengers as the missing team of scouts.

Oliver Roth paused and looked again at his thermal tracker, which still showed the scouts as having vanished into nothingness.

'Yes,' he said. 'Come straight back.'

There was a thirty-second pause, nothing around them but the whistling breeze, until twenty dots popped one by one back onto the thermal tracker screen. The scouting group seemed to be alive again.

'OK, stop,' said Roth, the bones of an idea forming in his mind. 'Turn around and walk back to where you were.'

The dots stopped moving, and then edged northwest again. Before long, they had vanished a second time.

'Cancel that,' he said, happy that he had subordinates who couldn't get away with being annoyed with him. 'Come back here.'

Moments later the scouting crew were back onscreen. Roth grinned.

'What are you thinking, Oliver?' asked Pereira.

'I'm thinking we're on the border of Underdog territory,'

he sneered, almost tempted to lick his lips. 'Colonel, is there such a thing as a device that can *block* thermal signals?'

'I imagine there could be. Why?'

'Because the Underdogs are led by a guy whose father was a major. On Takeover Day he raided the barracks and got out with a bunch of stuff. I think we just discovered how they kept themselves hidden so long.'

Pereira held a face that made it clear he couldn't understand Roth's grin.

'This is grave news then, isn't it? If they've got some kind of thermal blocker, we can't hope to find them.'

'Oh, we can. Our scouting team just gave me an idea that's going to win us the war.'

Chapter 13

The farmhouse was so much quicker to find in daylight. Ewan could ride his bike at full speed along the roads, held back only by the need to keep Kate and Jack close behind him.

On the outskirts of Thame, he saw it. No signs of life, as expected, which probably meant Rubinstein was there nonetheless.

Not much further down the road, he saw the tiny rope-shaped line Mark had told him about. He braked, parked his bike among the bushes, and waited for Kate and Jack to do the same. He then pulled the bushes to one side, and revealed the tiny stash of explosives to the surprise of his friends behind him.

'Bloody hell, that's NPN8,' he said. Evidently, Shannon hadn't recognised the type of explosive and Mark hadn't bothered to specify. NPN8 had a permanent place in Ewan's heart: not because of its sheer destructive power – less than a fistful of it being enough to remove a room's existence from the face of the Earth – but because of his painful memories of how McCormick had used the last of their supply. To Ewan, NPN8 was difficult to look at.

The little pile was only the size of a large bird's nest, but it would be enough to take down an airship if planted in the right places. Ewan was certain of it.

'Grab it all,' he said. 'We'll need it to take out the engines. And put the detonators in my backpack too.'

It felt horrible having that brand of explosives so close to him again, but he tried to remember the greater good, just like McCormick had. They made their way into the field, and Ewan gave a distant wave to the house. Rubinstein had probably seen them already.

Ewan, Kate and Jack, strolling into another mission together. It was the perfect team, so why was Ewan so nervous?

It was the three of us who broke out of the Inner City.

If we all die tonight, there'll be nobody left in the Underdogs who knows how the prisoners live.

Ewan looked around him, and realised he was not the only one enduring nerves.

'You OK, Kate?'

Kate nodded, a little too quickly.

'Yeah.'

'Really though?'

'It's my first mission in a month. I'm a little out of practice.'

Ewan looked over towards her face, and gave a smile which he meant to be sympathetic. 'You can be honest. It's your first mission si—'

'Since McCormick, yeah. And my second since Raj. And my third since Charlie… Me and him weren't very close but… we shared the Inner City together.'

A flood of memories about Charlie, good and bad, tried to wash over Ewan's mind. He blocked most of them out through sheer defiance, even in the knowledge that his Temper Twin deserved better than that.

'You know what all those missions had in common, Kate?' he asked.

'A crap ton of—'

'You survived. All of them. The Inner City, Oakenfold, the higher floors of New London... you always make it. You'll make it this time too.'

'You don't know that.'

'OK, fine. I don't. But the stronger you believe it, the more likely it'll happen.'

'It's never luck, right?' came Jack's voice from his other side. 'Even self-belief influences your actions for the better.'

'Right,' answered Ewan.

'I never was good at that,' Kate muttered.

'And yet you're still here,' said Jack before Ewan could think of a reply. 'Clearly you're getting something right.'

'Yeah. I'm brave.'

Ewan almost stopped in his tracks. He didn't think he had misheard Kate, but it seemed a little out of character for her to compliment herself.

'I've known for most of my life,' she continued. Her eyes were pointed to the soil, but they were determined eyes. 'Bravery doesn't mean never being afraid. It means being afraid and doing it anyway. I spend most of my life being afraid, but it doesn't mean much if I do things anyway. Besides, the fear of never seeing James again is bigger than the fear of... hey, why are we talking about why I'm not dead yet? It's pretty rude.'

'Oh come on, Kate,' said Jack with a laugh. 'That sounded like the start of an inspirational speech!'

'OK then, what about you? How on Earth are *you* still alive?'

Jack looked to the sky with his typical deep-in-thought expression. He seemed to find it a surprisingly difficult question.

'Being in the right places at the right times...' he said, 'single-minded relentless autistic focus… and keeping myself alive for the benefit of other people. And I don't mean that in a virtuous kind of way – honestly, it's a pain in the arse. And a pretty unhealthy attitude too, like I don't have any worth myself but my existence serves other people. But whatever, I'm rambling. Your turn, Ewan. Why haven't *you* died yet?'

They had reached the farmhouse. Ewan raised a fist to the door.

'Defiance,' he answered as he knocked. 'Pure, simple, bloody defiance. The kind of stuff they used to kick me out of schools for.'

'And now your biggest strength,' said Jack.

Ewan paused.

'Yeah…' he said. 'Now you mention it.'

Rubinstein opened the door, nodded towards Ewan and stretched out her hand to the others.

'Captain Emilia Rubinstein,' she said, shaking their hands. 'And you are?'

'Jack Hopper.'

'Kate Arrowsmith.'

Not wanting to stay in the open any longer than necessary, the team entered the farmhouse and sat around the dining room table.

Hopefully I won't screw up this conversation too.

'It's good to put faces to your names at last,' Rubinstein said to Kate and Jack. 'Just so you know, you and the rest of your group are *deeply* appreciated among Special Forces. And the United Nations too, although your existence is kept a closely guarded secret.'

'Sounds like we're back in special ed,' Jack said with a grin. 'Most of society pretended we didn't exist back then either.'

Ewan didn't think he would smile at that joke, but he surprised himself.

'I think you'll find your existence is now *much* more relevant and useful to mainstream society,' said Rubinstein with a clear tone of irony in her voice. 'When you free the British people, they might become interested enough to start listening to you.'

Does she… get it? She sounds like she gets it.

It was rare enough to find people who understood us back in the old days. Finding one now should have been impossible.

'Oh,' Ewan said, 'before I forget, we stole your NPN8.'

'Take it,' said Rubinstein. 'More useful to you up there than me down here. I assume you grabbed the detonators too? I hope you've got a good plan for sneaking them past the airship's security.'

'We're going straight through security?' asked Kate, her voice bordering on disbelieving laughter.

'Yes. Now listen carefully, because we don't have long. It's afternoon already and the airship launches at six.'

Ewan checked his watch. Half past two on June twenty-first.

Bloody hell, it's barely been twenty-four hours since we lost Gracie. Feels like a week.

'Once you leave here, you won't need to break into New Oxford. The airship's parked two miles north of it, which will give you a two-mile window to sneak into the procession of those who are getting on board.'

'Simple as that?' asked Ewan, also wondering what a literal two-mile window would look like. 'Really?'

'No, it's not. You need access badges and a senior staff member to vouch for you. So you'll be assuming the identity of three mechanical engineers. Apprentices of New Oxford's lead engineer, who's been in charge of them since Takeover Day. With his Citadel closing down, he's riding the airship to join the New London team and he's *insisted* his three apprentices come along. Thankfully, he's with us. Part of the Network, and the resistance against Grant. Oli's been instrumental in—'

'*Oli?*' Ewan snapped.

'Yes—'

'What's his last name?'

'Sharp,' said Rubinstein, a little taken aback.

Oli Sharp. I can cope with a name like that. I'll have to call him 'Oli Sharp' though, not just 'Oli'. Too close.

'Don't worry,' said Rubinstein. 'He's not ginger. He's a tall guy with dark hair and glasses. I'll refer to him by his last name if you want, though.'

Ewan focused his eyes on the wood of the table, and tried to process his thoughts. There must have been a million Olivers across Britain, and Roth had tainted his trust in all of them. Even from beyond his burning grave in the Experiment Chamber, the dead body of Oliver Roth still held a psychological grip over him.

'Besides having a name like that...' Ewan breathed, 'are you *sure* we can trust him?'

'Yes. Because if he's willing to stick his neck out and risk being caught sneaking you on board, he *must* be—'

'Leading us into a trap?'

'No. If he were planning to lead you into a trap, you can be pretty damned certain the trap wouldn't be on board an airship they can't afford to lose. Besides... Sharp's proven his loyalty already.'

Was that guilt in her voice just now? Or regret? Sorrow?

'How's he done that?' asked Kate.

'I said you'll be assuming the identity of his three apprentices. Which means the real apprentices have to be kept silent at all costs.'

Ewan looked at Kate in surprise, wondering whether she had worked it out. She looked like she had.

'He's killed them,' said Jack, in a voice that was grim but matter-of-fact.

'He tells me it was either that or leave them at risk of giving him away,' said Rubinstein, her shoulders hunched and her fingers fidgeting. 'Sharp killed three people he's known for several years, in order for you to take their places without being caught. He's been desperately hoping you'll show up tonight.'

'Did he *have* to kill them?' asked Kate.

'If he didn't, he'd be caught, captured and interrogated. Sharp knows how much he knows, and he knows how quickly he'll give it away when subjected to pain. Anyway, their uniforms are in the living room, along with their access badges. The badges have got names but not photos, so no worries on that front. The apprentices were all men but thankfully Sam had a gender-neutral name, so you shouldn't raise any eyebrows, Kate.'

Ewan looked at the door to the living room, his surprise controlling his actions.

'How on Earth did he get their stuff here?' he asked.

'Thankfully,' said Rubinstein, 'the ranger for New Oxford's eastern wall is also with us. The moment Sharp was done he gave the uniforms to the ranger, who's just about the only Network member who can walk in and out of the Citadel unrestricted. She's my main contact in New Oxford, and the one person I can meet face to face if I absolutely need to.'

Rubinstein rested her hands on the dining-room table and drummed her fingers, evidently keen to move things forward.

'Any questions?' she asked. 'If so, make them quick.'

'Yeah,' Ewan answered. 'Have you got a drinks bottle we can take with us? Preferably metal.'

Puzzled, Rubinstein rose from her chair, strolled over to the kitchen and removed one from the drawer under the dusty microwave. When she handed it to Ewan he opened his ruck-sack, fetched out the NPN8 and started packing it into the drinks bottle a fistful at a time.

'You mentioned sneaking this past the security scanners,' he said. 'This might work.'

'There's no way the scanners will miss that,' Jack muttered. 'It must be airport-level security there.'

'Sure, it'll get picked up by anyone looking closely,' Ewan answered. 'But the sight of a full drinks bottle won't surprise them. They'll be too busy checking our toolboxes, if we have any. And who expects mechanics to be armed anyway? We'll be forgettable extras in their eyes.'

'Pretty big gamble, Ewan,' Rubinstein said.

'Anyone got a better idea?' Ewan replied, casting his gaze around his small group of allies. 'Anyone?'

He was caught between hoping for a long silence that would prove him right, and hoping someone really *would* come up with that much-needed better idea. In the end, he got silence.

'As gambles go, this is the safest gamble we've got,' he continued, screwing the lid back on top and tucking the bottle into his rucksack. 'Their technology will be faultless, but the guards won't be.'

Rubinstein nodded, but her face didn't seem full of confidence.

'Right,' she said, heading over to the living room, 'let's get your uniforms.'

'What if they don't fit?'

'Then *make* them fit. Otherwise, go in your combat gear and helmets and see if they let you on board.'

Ewan bit his lip. There was little choice. He stood up, as did the others, and they followed Rubinstein into the living room.

'Just do it defiantly, Ewan,' Jack said with a humorous voice, nudging him with one elbow. 'I'm sure you'll live.'

'I wouldn't suggest that,' said Rubinstein, as she knelt down to open a cardboard box on the living-room floor.

'No,' replied Jack, 'it was a joke about what we were talking about earlier. The reasons we're still alive. Ewan's alive because he's defiant, I'm alive because I need to serve other people, and Kate's far too brave to die. And besides, she needs to find out...'

Jack fell quiet and looked towards Kate at his side, with an awkwardly apologetic look on his face.

'It's OK, Jack,' Kate replied, 'she probably knows already.'

'Knows what?' asked Rubinstein, bringing out the first of the grey uniforms from the box beneath her.

'My reason for being alive. I can't die until I find out what happened to James... my brother, I mean. And until I rescue him, if I still can.'

Something weird happened on Rubinstein's face, and Ewan noticed it clear as day. Her lips closed, she dipped her head further than necessary while picking up the next uniform, and there was just a flash of intense eye contact with Ewan before she did.

Ewan had never been good at reading people, but he knew how deceptive people acted. And what people looked like when they were being evasive.

What the hell do you know about James Arrowsmith?

Ewan kept his face as blank as possible. His brain screamed at him to raise the issue, and ask Rubinstein directly what she was hiding. But it didn't take him long to work out the four possible responses. First, Ewan could be wrong altogether, and it would stress Kate out for no reason. Second, Ewan could be right but Rubinstein would refuse to answer. The worst part of Kate's anxiety had always been not knowing, and it could disable her thought capacity for most of the night. Third, Rubinstein could tell them bad news about James, which would destroy his younger sister. And fourth, Rubinstein could tell them *good* news – whatever that good news could possibly be – and Kate would lose the motivation that had kept her alive for so long.

Ewan stayed silent. Whatever Rubinstein knew, she had seen fit not to mention it voluntarily. She must have decided that silence was the best option for Kate's wellbeing too, so Ewan bit his lip and decided to play along.

Once we're back from the airship… you and I need a word, Captain Rubinstein.

As Ewan walked through the forest, he came to realise how curious it was that he could distinguish late afternoon birdsong from regular birdsong. There was something elevated about it, as if the wildlife was trying to reach its daily word count before darkness fell. There was still plenty of daylight, even on the ground layer of the forest, but the heat of the day was gone. Once the mission began, they would be fighting in darkness.

Of course, the prospect of darkness didn't terrify him as much as being suspended thousands of feet in the air with no easy escape route, heavily outnumbered and barely armed. Thankfully, Jack ran up to him before the fear could start to circle around in his brain.

'Ewan,' he said, 'I can't keep it in anymore. Hope you don't mind, but I need to get this off my chest.'

'Sure?' Ewan answered, confused.

'Our last mission together was Oakenfold. I gave you advice about your mum, and you didn't like it. Well, I'm assuming you didn't. You seemed to hate me for the rest of the night. And since we left home this morning, the whole incident's been going around my head on repeat... I get circling thoughts like that all the time. You know what I mean?'

Like the fear of tonight's mission you just distracted me from? Yeah, I know what you mean.

'I've never hated you, Jack.'

Ewan didn't want to say any more, but Jack seemed to have run out of words. Or he wasn't sure how to deal with the answer. With Kate a fair distance behind and unlikely to break the silence, Ewan decided to tell him the truth.

'Talking about a dead mum is difficult,' he continued. 'You know that as well as I do. And the timing wasn't great either. We were just about to go back to school for the first time since Takeover Day. For the first time since Mum died.'

Since she got shot to death alongside my dad, aunt, uncle and little cousin, I mean.

'For what it's worth,' Jack answered, 'you're not alone. And it's not just my mum and her cancer either. Have you ever noticed how many of us have dead parents?'

'Or crap ones.'

'Ha, yeah...'

Ewan looked to the grass and mud beneath his feet, and began to brainstorm the dead bodies.

My parents... Jack's mum... Beth Foster, mother of Thomas... Alex's dad... and Lorraine's parents are probably gone too. There weren't many elderly people in New London.

And Shannon. Do the others even know her mum died when she was a child?

Ewan looked to the path ahead again, a slit of light between the trees marking the long-awaited forest exit.

If we're counting crap parents too, that would include Mark's. And Charlie's.

'You know what makes me jealous of you all, though?' he

said to Jack, already second-guessing his decision to go into detail. 'And what made me pissed off with you outside Oakenfold? The rest of you got to mourn your mums properly. I didn't.'

'Really?'

'Life changed too quickly for it. I was an orphan for a few seconds, a runaway for a few hours, and then I became a soldier for thirteen months. Nothing in between. I never got to slow down and miss her.'

The accelerating footsteps behind him told him that Kate was catching up. Somehow, he didn't mind her listening in. He even hid his envy of the fact that she still had a family. *Both* parents. And a brother, unless Rubinstein knew otherwise…

'Mourning is overrated,' Jack continued. 'I mean, yeah. McCormick was right. The pain of missing her really *is* worth the joy of having known her. But it still hurts, and I don't think you're missing out just because you didn't slow down.'

'I was talking to Lorraine about it yesterday,' Kate said from behind them. 'Her advice was pretty awful. She said the best way of coping with death is *not* to miss the person. But I think they deserve better. McCormick…'

Her words trailed off. The three friends walked in near-silence, accompanied only by the fading birdsong and the gentle percussion of the tree leaves above brushing themselves together.

'Well,' said Jack, 'before Mum died, she told me not to waste my days missing her. She wanted me to keep living my life. But I think you can do both.'

Ewan nodded. He'd never had the opportunity to keep living *his* life after his family were slaughtered, but he could imagine it being true for those who had the luxury of not becoming instant soldiers.

'What's it like, mourning a parent?' asked Kate. 'If you don't mind me asking, I mean.'

Even after losing Raj and McCormick within a few days of each other, she's still no expert on the wide world of mourning. Wow, is there no end to the sheer variety of pain that death can deliver?

Ewan looked at the gap between the trees close ahead, desperate to reach the edge of the forest on time but also reluctant for such a valuable conversation to end. Jack let out a long sigh, then gave his answer.

'Mourning is… it's made up of tiny little things,' he said. 'The things you never even noticed while they were alive, which suddenly just stop happening.'

'Like the dishes piling up?'

'Well, yeah, but the tiny personal things too. Like the way our dinner table was set. I used a spoon with my left hand, but Mum and Dad used their right hands. But every time she laid the table, Mum remembered to put my spoon the correct way round. Dad always got it wrong, all the way up to Takeover Day. It sounds weird, but having that spoon the correct way round each day was a little sign of how much Mum loved me, and it was one of the million tiny things I missed when she was no longer there.'

Ewan tried to think of the million tiny things that had vanished from his own life: the colours of his father's uniform, the taste of tarragon in his mother's shepherd's pie, the contrast in their tones of voice and their general personalities, and that somehow the contrast never led to tension or conflict. But it all felt too long ago for him to remember with any accuracy.

'Can I thank you, Jack?' asked Kate.

'For what?'

'I've been trying to process something since Raj and McCormick died. On the one hand I wanted to miss them properly, but on the other I'm tired of being emotionally crippled by it. Until you pointed it out just now, it never occurred to me that you can miss someone *and* live your life. That I can mourn them and fight anyway.'

Jack nodded. 'I'm not saying you recover, because you never really do. But you do kind of get your life back.'

Ewan looked over to her, and could see the beginnings of a smile on her face, as if the real Kate Arrowsmith was starting to make a return. Not just the Kate who could fight, shoot and survive, but the Kate who knew how to be happy. The Kate who seemed *alive*. Just in time too, as they were reaching the edge of the forest. He slowed down as he approached the gap in the trees, conscious of being seen by New Oxford soldiers on the other side. As Jack and Kate fell silent, Ewan took a moment to wonder whether he truly understood Shannon's pain as much as he had assumed. Ewan had lived through more than his fair share of mourning, but he hadn't spent the last decade missing the tiny things that Shannon must have missed, right down to how the bloody table was laid.

And all that time, while I told her I understood her pain, she must have known I didn't. And she never corrected me. Is that deceit, or is it love?

He forced his mind back to the mission, and peered around the side of his tree. It was time to begin.

Sneaking into the procession was easier than Ewan had predicted. The two-mile march of humans and clones between New Oxford and the airship's landing site was sparse enough for them to wait a minute or two, walk out from the trees and join in while nobody was looking. Apparently security was only a major concern *inside* New Oxford, especially as the Underdogs were thought to be several counties away.

All the same, Ewan got the feeling the relaxed atmosphere wouldn't last all the way onto the airship. He slowed down, encouraged Kate and Jack to follow suit, and allowed others to overtake them. Oli Sharp would catch up with them eventually. They had joined the procession pretty early, so they were unlikely to have missed him.

Ewan glanced across at his friends' uniforms and badges. The three apprentices had been young men called Tom, Damon and Sam. Thankfully, as Rubinstein had promised, Kate had been able to assume the identity of the latter without arousing suspicion.

They walked northeast, as slowly as they could get away with, Ewan wishing he could force Sharp's appearance through sheer will. It wouldn't be comfortable getting onto the airship without him.

Then it came into view. Over the brow of a hill, the airship appeared in the neighbouring valley. It was black from tip to tail, full of porthole windows like those passenger ferries of old, and absolutely enormous. Ewan wondered to himself how anything of that size was able to fly, and tried to picture the sheer size of the engines they were about to destroy.

The valley was buzzing with activity. Armoured vehicles scurried antlike around the front entrance, transporting humans from some kind of holding pen – clearly Crossland's chosen 400. At the other end of the ship, New Oxford equipment was being unloaded from a fleet of lorries and prepared for storage in the cargo hold. A swarm of helicopters rested around the airship's rear end, some inside the aircraft hangar and some in place to escort the airship from the front.

Then Ewan saw the airship's name, emblazoned on the side in white, large enough to be seen from a mile away.

'*Sheila*?' came Kate's voice.

'Seriously?' Jack laughed. 'The great Nicholas Grant builds the biggest airship the world has ever known, to use in a fiendish plan from the sadistic depths of Nathaniel Pearce's imagination, big and dark and imposing and absolutely bloody massive… and he calls it *Sheila?*'

'Sheila Grant was his wife,' Ewan answered, checking around for listening ears and finding none. 'She died a decade ago, when Shannon was about seven.'

Nobody made any further comment. Jack, given the fresh memories of their last conversation, looked particularly guilty.

Well, if they didn't know about Shannon losing her mum before, they do now. I guess she'd trust them with the info anyway.

The cognitive dissonance in Ewan's mind was too much to deal with: the fact that Nicholas Grant – who had committed horrific crimes against the whole of Britain, who had sent clones to murder his family, who currently planned to wipe out most of the planet's population – still loved his late wife enough to name an airship after her.

Love or not, he's dishonouring her memory.

They set off down the hill, and soon found that their slow walking had been unnecessary. A man who looked to be in his early forties, stood toying with his mobile phone, noticed their approach and smiled.

'Ah, good to see you finally made it!' he said, as if he had known them for years. When they came within handshake distance, Jack lifted his forearm but found it subtly pushed down by the fingers on Sharp's hand. 'I did tell you not to spend too long packing. Unless Damon was off for another one of his afternoon naps?'

He slapped Ewan on the shoulder with a joking smile. Even with no witnesses within hearing range, Oli Sharp was committed to character.

You killed three people earlier today. People you knew pretty well. How are you holding it together? Are you a psychopath, or an incredible actor?

It was probably the lure of the greater good. Ewan knew

enough about people to know that anybody was capable of just about anything, as long as they could justify it to themselves first.

'Right,' said Sharp, 'let's get the boarding out the way so Damon can sleep again.'

He set off down the hill, and Ewan felt a temptation to look at his friends' faces for reactions. But Sharp's act had consumed them too, and they walked along with him as if they truly were his apprentices.

Boarding the *Sheila* turned out not to be so difficult. Sharp's own confidence had influenced Ewan's, so he didn't show the nerves he otherwise would have felt when scanning a dead man's access badge in front of armed clones. 'Sam' and 'Tom' followed in turn, and the scanner found no hidden weapons in the rucksack. The NPN8 inside the drinks bottle was ignored, just like Ewan had predicted, and he did his best not to grin.

As Sharp guided them through the labyrinth of the airship's corridors, Ewan tried not to look too surprised at the airship's interior, in case Damon was supposed to know what it looked like. Whereas New London's Outer City was a maze of painted brick and metal panels, the airship corridors seemed to have been built with the lightest possible material: thin, holey metal walkways, walls that clanged with a hollow echo when hands were placed on them, and ceiling pipes that nobody had bothered to conceal with ceiling panels.

Sharp led them into a small room with a crude metal table, stools and a cupboard full of mugs. It wasn't a labelled room, but was clearly meant to be a staff room for maintenance workers, the biggest clue being the line of airship blueprints spread across the walls.

'Right, kids,' said Sharp, 'this is what you've got to look after. Six engines in all, pretty easy to find if you look at the maps close enough. I don't suspect we'll run into any problems, but it might be worth checking on them about half an hour into the flight.'

Even I can take a hint like that.

Ewan wondered what the need was for any delay at all. Most likely, the half-hour pause was to let the airship fly far enough from New Oxford to wipe out the chance of a safe emergency return, and to prevent air reinforcements from reaching them in time.

'Now if you'll excuse me,' Sharp finished, heading for the door, 'I've got to take my seat in the senior staff lounge. Don't worry, it's not half as comfortable as I'm making it sound. Have fun tonight.'

And with that, he was gone. Finally, Ewan, Kate and Jack could look at each other and check everyone's reactions.

'That guy scares me,' said Jack.

'I know,' said Ewan. 'But he got us here. Whatever it took, and however well he's taking it.'

After that they sat wordless, not even getting themselves a mug of tea. Jack studied the maps. Kate kept her eyes on the exit. Ewan's mind was too clouded to tell what he was trying to focus on.

They kept themselves in that state for the best part of an hour, until a rumble sounded from all around them. Particularly from below, but all around them just the same.

Ewan ran to the window, and stared through the falling darkness at the shifting grass.

'This is it,' he said. 'United by our differences.'

'United,' replied Jack and Kate, barely above a whisper.

Nicholas Grant's airship was taking off.

Chapter 14

Shannon checked her watch for the third time that minute. With Lorraine for company, time passed slowly. She was even quieter than usual.

A dark Boys' Brigade hall offered little in the way of recreation. Shannon's only way to occupy herself was to reach up her hoodie sleeve and fiddle with the edge of the bandage around her arm, wrapped there by Lorraine herself after Alex's savage bite. She hoped her fidgeting wasn't enough to draw Lorraine's attention: the sooner the bite was forgotten, the better off she would be.

It had been unfortunate, being Alex's victim after she had been so compassionate towards him during his confession. But Alex hadn't been in control of his actions and she knew it. Nonetheless, it would be good to iron out the awkwardness and make peace with him once they were back. Unless something more urgent happened on the airship to distract everyone, but she didn't like to think about that.

The phone rang, and Shannon answered. It was the unknown number again: one of Rubinstein's scrambled phones that she had donated to the team.

The thought of Emilia Rubinstein made Shannon shudder.

She trusted her professionally – the woman seemed to know her stuff and clearly wanted Grant dead so she could get back to her wife and daughters – but Shannon couldn't bring herself to trust her personally. Not with everything she knew, no matter how sympathetic she was.

This afternoon she was with Ewan again, this time without me. If she told him what I did on Takeover Day...

The thoughts entered and left her brain within a split second, before Shannon brought herself back to her senses.

'Hello?'

'Hey, mate,' said Ewan.

Mate?

'Yeah, just thought I'd let you know we've left. Launch happened as expected. Should be done by the end of the evening.'

Ewan spoke as if he were an entirely different person. It was acting, as well as a person like Ewan could manage.

'Yeah, OK,' Shannon replied.

'That's it really. Speak later.'

'Alright... bye.'

Ewan hung up. Short, and not entirely sweet. Then again, it was Ewan. Besides, Shannon wouldn't have wanted sweetness if there were the slightest chance of putting him, Kate and Jack at risk.

'I take it they're airborne?' asked Lorraine, her first words in at least an hour.

'Yeah.'

'OK, then I guess I can't put this off any longer. How's your arm doing?'

Oh no... she hasn't forgotten.

Shannon chose to be honest with herself, and realised that Lorraine would never have forgotten. All she did was take care of wounded soldiers. There was nothing else in her life to concentrate on.

'It's fine thanks,' she answered.

'Fine? That's curious. It was a huge bite he gave you, and it was filled with all the rage he could muster in the moment. Your skin was hanging off when it first happened.'

'You did a good job with the bandage. I don't feel a thing.'

'Hm.'

Shannon fiddled with the bandage again, and turned her face forward. But Lorraine wasn't done.

'The most useful part of being a nurse,' she continued, 'is how it teaches you to notice all the tiny details. Bruise placements, behavioural patterns, skin tones, dietary changes, everything. They're often the difference between saving a life and losing a patient. And in twenty years of nursing, I only ever missed a tiny detail once... on the night you first arrived.'

Shannon turned her head back to Lorraine, trying and failing to hide her nerves.

'You'd run halfway across Hertfordshire in bare feet,' Lorraine continued, 'and when you arrived there was no blood. A bunch of blisters were there when I bandaged you up, but the next morning you were walking around like nothing had happened. At the time, I figured it was just your physical strength. And some impressive determination, crossed with intense survival instincts.'

'Sums me up pretty well,' Shannon said, suppressing a nervous laugh.

'It does. Which is why your reaction surprised me this morning, right after Alex bit you.'

She's not worked it out... has she?

I guess it was always going to be Lorraine, if anyone.

Shannon continued the conversation, pretending nothing was wrong.

'I was pretty terrified, yeah.'

'So I saw. Your left hand went straight to the wound. But you weren't compressing it. You were *hiding* it. You seemed more concerned about our reaction than your injury.'

Shannon said nothing.

'It's been twelve hours since the bite, Shannon. Show me the wound.'

'No.'

Lorraine laughed; a strange kind of mocking laugh that Shannon had never heard from her before.

'No?' she asked. 'Why ever not? Seems like a reasonable request to me.'

'I don't want to.'

Lorraine leaned close to her, her eyes cold and serious.

'Either I'm right and we both know it, so you might as well show me. Or I'm wrong, and you can *prove* it by showing me. Either way, I'm asking to see the wound.'

Shannon took two short breaths, and then burst into tears.

She hadn't cried since her earliest days in Spitfire's Rise, despite the life she had fled to live there. For the last few months, someone had usually been there for her in her worst moments. But this time, the lady in the seat next to her showed no sympathy whatsoever.

'Show me, Shannon. I already know what to expect.'

There's no getting out of it now. Besides, if she knows the truth then there's nothing I can lose anyway.

Except Ewan. I can still lose Ewan. Especially if he finds out…

Shannon wiped her face with her left hand, before using it to tug her hoodie sleeve up to the elbow. She then tucked a finger underneath the bandage, and pulled it down.

The wound was gone. A faint scar remained, as if drawn by a white crayon.

The powdered remains of her half-day-old blood had turned to dust.

Shannon's biggest secret was no more.

'You're a clone,' Lorraine said.

It wasn't a question, but Shannon nodded anyway.

In the past, she had been told that confession felt therapeutic, and that a problem shared was a problem halved. But not the truth of her existence. She had never felt so naked, the entirety of her whole being on display in all its inadequacy and weakness.

'Who else knows?' Lorraine asked.

'If you were a clone would *you* tell anyone in this team?' Shannon gasped, choking through her sentence as she went.

'If I truly cared about their safety, I'd be honest with them.'

Shannon huffed, and pulled her hoodie sleeve back in place.

'Rubinstein knows,' she said with a sniff. 'It was the first thing she said to me. She knew who I was straight away. Knew my whole backstory from the intel on her phone. Right back to Takeover Day when...'

This is it. No going back.

'...when I killed myself.'

Shannon's tears returned at the memory of it. Memories of her first life were tricky: she remembered every fact and every feeling, but the sensory memories had not transferred. Smells did not remind her of her grandparents' house, and she had no memory of what a Sunday roast tasted like. She could not remember what her death had felt like physically, but the feelings of fear and horror were still etched into her brain.

'When the real Shannon Grant killed herself, you mean,' Lorraine corrected her.

'I *am* the real Shannon Grant,' she snapped, thrusting her angered face towards Lorraine's. 'I'm not the original, but I'm the real her. The closest the world has left to her. I have the same memories, personality, *everything*. They made sure of it. My father wanted his daughter back so badly...'

Coming back to life had been like waking up from a terrifying dream. Shannon must have been the only creature on Earth whose memory string went straight from her own literal death to standing upright in a cloning pod, naked but physically right as rain again. A transition from mortal weakness and total vulnerability, to perfect health and *still* total vulnerability. It had been horrible.

'I knew your father could make clones with memories,' Lorraine mused. 'It's what they planned to do with Alex. Doesn't surprise me that he can create female clones too, or clones with vocal cords.'

'Pearce could. My father commanded him to lift all restrictions when coming up with my model. My father may be a monster, but he wanted his daughter back... I think he wanted to make up for lost time.'

'And you abandoned him.'

'You're damned right I abandoned him. It was a better choice than the first four—'

She stopped herself. Not everything was Lorraine's business.

'Being a clone... it's not who I am. It's what I am, but not *who* I am. You know what I mean, right?'

Lorraine nodded. It was the first sign of sympathy she had shown throughout the conversation. Then again, it was hardly a situation she should have been comfortable with. One of Nicholas Grant's abominations had shared their house for nearly two months in total secrecy.

Someday I'll need to have this conversation with Ewan, she thought, reminding herself of what she had known ever since the night they had met. *I hope he handles it better than I think he will.*

She gulped. Now her secret was out to both Rubinstein *and* Lorraine, the day Ewan found out was likely to come sooner than she had planned.

'So you're not going to kill me?' Shannon muttered.

'No. Partly because you've proven yourself useful, and partly because it would take a lot of explaining. But mostly because I know you're still loyal to us. If you weren't, you'd have tried to kill me just now.'

'Why the hell would I do that?' Shannon snorted. 'You may be locking yourself in the clinic every day and refusing to engage with the people you claim to love, but the Underdogs still need you. And despite your judgemental nature and how you've forgotten what compassion is, I actually like you! You were good to me in the past, and I won't repay that with betrayal. But you knew that, didn't you? That's why you sat there and kept your handgun tucked in your pocket, having faith that I wouldn't shoot you first.'

Lorraine grinned, and leaned over to her.

'Your gun's been empty all night,' she said. 'I emptied it this afternoon before we left, just to see whether you'd try to use it once I raised the subject. I worked out your identity this morning after the injury, and I've had all day to plan tonight's conversation.'

'You must be bloody proud of yourself,' Shannon replied, lifting her gun out of her pocket and suddenly realising how much lighter it felt without bullets. She hadn't noticed when they had left Spitfire's Rise.

'I don't tend to feel pride,' Lorraine answered. 'I'm just happy when a job's done well.'

'Ha, as if you're ever happy.'

The silence stung. Shannon felt the weight of guilt on her conscience, and looked away from Lorraine.

'I'm sorry,' she said. 'I went too far with that.'

'So clones *do* feel sympathy and kindness.'

'I'm sure "real" humans do too. It'd be nice to feel it from you again someday.'

Crap, I went too far again.

Lorraine didn't respond with words, but with eyes. As she gave Shannon her coldest glare, she reached into her pocket and held out the clip of bullets for Shannon's pistol, handing them over to her with an icy silence.

'Thanks...' Shannon said, loading them back into her pistol and holstering it again. 'And if it's any comfort, this doesn't affect how much I want us to destroy my father.'

'I can believe that.'

Not nearly enough.

Shannon turned in her chair, and demanded Lorraine's eye contact. Fierce, unrelenting eye contact.

'I wasn't just the child he neglected so he could focus on conquest,' she snarled. 'I was the child he ignored to death. When Takeover Day came and he revealed his grand gesture of fatherly love, making up for years of nothingness by showing me what he was doing to millions of people, he broke me.'

Shannon was conscious that these actions had all happened to a girl who had occupied a different body, but she didn't care. She shared the same consciousness as that girl, and that was the same as *being* her. No matter what anyone said, not even Lorraine.

'What do you mean "a grand gesture of fatherly love"?' asked Lorraine, with the voice of a prosecuting barrister.

'He... he said he did it all for me. That everything he did was for the next generation who would live on in a new and better world. I never believed him – it must have been his way of justifying it all to himself – but when he showed me the screens on Takeover Day and revealed everything he had secretly been working on, soldiers in the streets and—'

'You didn't know about it in advance?'

Shannon tried to keep her temper and not yell. They were

supposed to be quiet in the comms unit with its thin roof and silent surroundings. But it hurt that Lorraine had assumed her to be a part of it all.

'I found out the same day you did,' Shannon said, her voice trembling but under control. 'He told me it was all for me... and it destroyed me. And that was *without* him telling me it would lead to him culling the world's population. I didn't give him time to explain his long-term goals – I ended it that day.'

When Shannon wiped her face with a finger, she found that her tears had stopped somehow. Was it anger? Her vulnerability making way for vengeful determination?

'But he brought me back,' she continued. '*Every* time I left him, he brought me back. As if it was his decision and not mine. As if his desperation to have his daughter back outweighed—'

'Every time?'

Shannon gulped, and decided to tell her. It may not have been Lorraine's business, but it was the first chance Shannon had had to talk about it since Lambourne was murdered. Talking about it was painful but cathartic.

'You don't really think I'm the first Shannon clone, do you? Takeover Day was thirteen months ago. I'm the *fifth* clone... the sixth Shannon Rose Grant who ever lived. And guess what the other four clones all did?'

'They killed themselves?'

'*They killed themselves.* Every single one. I don't remember it – they kept using the same memory bank they took from the original Shannon, so my lives as the other four never transferred. But maybe that's why none of them could cope... because the experience was new and fresh for each one of them. The sudden shock of having to cope with death *and* life as a clone... the inability to escape... all of them were programmed with the mind of a suicidal neglected teenager, so they all *acted* like a suicidal neglected teenager!'

Lorraine's hardened expression was faltering. Perhaps, just maybe, she was beginning to see the clone she had mistrusted all day as a real person. Lorraine shook her head in dismay, and gasped out a sentence.

'What kind of man can make the same person kill themselves five times?' she asked.

'Nicholas bloody Grant. That's who.'

'Good point,' Lorraine answered. 'So how come you survived?'

'Anthony Lambourne,' Shannon replied, trying to remember him but only seeing his final expression as Keith Tylor slashed his throat in that health centre. 'He had seen what happened to the others, and he tried to help me... He thought I was worth fleeing New London with, even though I was just a clone. Don't worry, I tried telling him I wasn't worth it.'

'What led to you fleeing New London?' Lorraine asked, no longer with the cold precision of a prosecuting lawyer, but not quite with the compassion of a former nurse either.

'Writing *Better Days*. The plan was to use the virus ourselves, destroy the clone factory, then flee New London and find you before anyone discovered who'd done it. But we were using Richard Unsworth's account when we wrote the software... I know you don't care who he is, but... one day we made the mistake of using his account while he was off work with food poisoning, and some security guy worked out he'd been compromised. My father's protocol was to close off and guard all essential areas, including the clone factory. We missed our chance...'

It was yet another excuse for Shannon to let herself feel inadequate. If it hadn't been for some New London chef undercooking a chicken breast without her knowing, the factory would have been destroyed quickly and with no obvious perpetrator. Anthony Lambourne would still be alive, safe in Spitfire's Rise. So would Charlie Coleman. And every innocent person at that health centre would not have been murdered.

'Anthony knew it was only a matter of time before they checked the CCTV and worked out we were in Unsworth's account. He knew that even if we ran away, he probably wouldn't live to bring down my father. But I wish he'd been connected to Emilia Rubinstein. Maybe he'd have found her instead of the health centre…'

Lorraine rested a hand on her shoulder. Which was unexpected, to say the least.

'If you hadn't found us that night, the war would already be over. The Underdogs are better off because you're a part of them.'

Shannon wanted to smile, but couldn't. She turned back to the desk in front of her, and bent her head down.

'Nicholas Grant was all the original Shannon had,' she said. 'Right from the age of seven, when Mum died. And he spent the next ten years pretending his daughter didn't exist. All of it leading to one big fatherly revelation, which killed her. Neither she nor the four clones that followed could keep themselves alive with a man like him controlling them. So to me, this war isn't just about saving the world.'

She lifted her head, and deepened her eyebrows.

'It's about me too, Lorraine. I'm going to be the clone who *won*.'

Chapter 15

Of the fifteen minutes they had spent in the sky, Kate had occupied at least ten of them looking out of the window. The English countryside beneath was about to vanish into the darkness of the evening, and it was better to appreciate the beauty from above while it was there. The rest of her world was ugly enough.

'Mind if I have a turn, love?' asked Jack from behind her. His words and his voice were bizarre and out of character; a forced kind of confident and self-assured. It must have been his Tom impression, mimicking his image of what regular, non-autistic people were supposed to be like.

'Sure.'

She stepped to one side and let him in, then sat back at the wobbly table next to her. Jack fixed his gaze on the countryside with the same fascination as Kate felt, except his was much more visible. His whole face had lit up like a Christmas tree, which Kate imagined was the right phrase.

Jack had never hidden his true self, for better or for worse. In their days at Oakenfold Kate had never really spoken to him, but still knew a lot about his personality. Perhaps the bullies at his old school had as well, and his inability to hide his feelings, his enthusiasm and his fears had contributed to him becoming the target he had been.

Kate could empathise, being transparent herself. Unlike Jack, though, she had hidden her true self with every molecule of energy she had… for all the good it had done. But however hard she tried to hide her personality, the bullies had seen through her and come for her anyway.

She glanced back to the table, where Ewan looked to be deep in thought. Ewan was probably the most transparent out of all of them. He hadn't exactly hidden his feelings well in his mainstream days.

But just because someone was transparent, it didn't mean they were easy to understand. All of Ewan's mainstream teachers had witnessed his vulnerable side on full display through his 'challenging behaviour', but none of them had meaningfully understood him. If they had, they might have taken steps to accommodate his anxiety, rather than report the incidents as 'violent outbursts' and act like their job was done. And Jack's personality may have been on full display, but his experiences weren't. Had it not been for Nicholas Grant's announcement in the Inner City, his two suicide attempts would have remained a secret to the other Underdogs.

And then there was Kate herself. As much as she tried to move on from her days of suffering in mainstream education, other people's lack of understanding was still damaging her – even years after she had left.

So there they were: three transparent but misunderstood Underdogs, trying to bring down an airship without people working out who they truly were. Kate wasn't sure whether their autism made them more likely to succeed or less.

'K-Sam,' said Ewan, remembering to use her cover name just in time. 'Want to take a look at the cargo manifest? We may need to look after some of this stuff.'

Kate had wondered why Ewan had spent so much of the last fifteen minutes reading something on a cheap tablet with a cracked screen, rather than mentally preparing himself for the night ahead. He passed her the tablet, which displayed a list of every object of value in the cargo hold, their details stored in bland-looking tables and graphs. Highlighted cells denoted each piece of cargo with mechanical elements, which must have been the reason the engineering team had been offered access to the manifest. Kate browsed the plethora of goods that would reach New London unless the Underdogs did something about it.

Equipment for handling a sudden increase in population, right down to the artificial fertiliser they'd use to expand and strengthen New London's farms.

One hundred canisters of poison gas, to keep the afore-mentioned population under control.

Ready-assembled cloning pods, along with enough piping and chemical storage tanks to build a whole new clone factory in New London.

We focused so much on the prisoners that we forgot about the hardware problem. New London and New Oxford are still being combined, and there'll still be consequences if we let it happen.

I know what Ewan's thinking, and I agree. Even if we take out Crossland and Pearce and kill the Acceleration project, Grant can still achieve most of what he wants to do tonight.

One way or another, we have to destroy this airship altogether.

Something churned in her stomach.

It was the worst possible moment to remember her child-hood travel sickness. It had lasted into her teenage years, but only seemed to impact her when something made her anxious. Taxi rides to Oakenfold had been—

Oh crap, too late.

'Bathroom,' she gasped, barely audibly as she staggered for the door. 'Don't follow me, I'm fine.'

She didn't see how Jack reacted, but Ewan's face looked gravely concerned as she ran past the table. Nonetheless, he respected her wishes and stayed seated.

She barged into the thin corridor, her footsteps clanging and echoing up and down the passageway as she ran. Her last meal was most of the way back up her throat by the time she reached the bathroom at the end. She burst in and threw up into the toilet bowl without having a moment to close the sliding door behind her.

Wow, stealthy move, came a voice inside her head. It sounded like one of her mainstream bullies, but she couldn't tell which one. There were too many to choose from.

But the voice was right. On a mission where standing out was the worst course of action, she had charged down a corridor to vomit graphically and audibly in a staff bathroom, one no bigger or more discreet than the toilet on a small plane.

She lifted her head up, turned towards the sink and found the mirror. Her face had lost most of its colour, but there were no vomit stains on her chin at least. She washed her face, spat out the remains, and headed back outside to see a smiling Oli Sharp waiting for her.

'Ha, you always were a bit queasy,' Sharp said with a sympathetic laugh. Like everything else though, Kate suspected the sympathy was also part of his acting.

'I'm fine,' she said.

'Well, better out than in. Once it's out it can hardly come up again. Right, Sam, could you pass on a message to Tom and Damon? I was heading to them myself, but you might as well do the job for me. I need to check Pearce's emergency escape pod. And the sooner I'm there, the better.'

There was some kind of hint in that, but Kate couldn't

translate it and Sharp couldn't afford to be any clearer.

'Sure,' she said.

'Tell them to start work as soon as possible. The engine rooms may need their attention sooner than they think, and they probably have less time than we thought.'

Kate nodded, coughing up a little bit more spit.

'Good,' said Sharp. 'Go straight to them. Don't bother fixing your appearance first. The hardware won't look after itself. Go, now.'

And with that, Oli Sharp was gone. Apparently towards the emergency escape pod, which Kate hadn't realised existed.

She walked back to the staff room, as briskly as she could without appearing panicked. When she returned, Ewan and Jack's first reaction was to ask if she was OK.

'Never mind how I am,' she answered. 'Sharp says we need to get to work. *Now*. He didn't say why.'

It had taken most of the day, but it was worth it. Oliver Roth looked down at his thermal tracker screen and grinned. It was beautiful.

Frodo probably thought the One Ring was beautiful too.

He shook his head. This was everything he wanted, even if he occasionally needed to purge McCormick's goody-goodness and remind himself. After all, eight of McCormick's army had died at Roth's hands.

Joe Horn, the Oakenfold retard he had killed with a fire axe.

Miles Ashford, the part-time PE teacher he had dispatched with a shotgun blast to the face.

Tim Carson, the former businessman who hadn't been fast enough to pick up the grenade and throw it back.

Beth Foster, whose nine-year-old son had been orphaned by one well-placed bullet.

David and Val Riley, who he had trapped at the end of a corridor after they had run out of bullets. Val had accepted his offer of a quick death in exchange for knifing her husband, and they had spent their last minutes on Earth relentlessly apologising to each other before she did it. Wow, it had got annoying. They had sucked the enjoyment right out of it by the end.

Ben Christie, who he had got with a sniper rifle without anyone knowing it was him.

And his eighth had been Charlie Coleman, who had been calling out for Ewan before he died.

When Oliver Roth looked back on his impact on the Underdogs, it was a record to be proud of. He had killed a quarter of their entire army personally.

For months I've been wanting to reach double figures. I always believed I could do it before my fifteenth birthday. But if I truly wanted to, I could achieve it by the end of tonight.

How much do I still want it though? I mean seriously, what I did to Val and David was bloody horrible.

Yeah. I do still want it. I came this far. And besides, my chest is still a scarred burning wreck thanks to the thermite fire. I landed on my front after Ewan shot me, so it's a borderline miracle I still have a face. Screw Ewan West and his merry men.

But at the same time…

Roth tried to push the thought out of his head, but it wouldn't budge.

…they've almost given me a reason to exist. What would I do without the Underdogs? Stay on Floor A eating junk food and getting fat? Go back to shooting squirrels?

It occurred to him that Grant would find things for him to do, and that ineffective staff members would always need disciplining. But that wasn't hunting. When the last of the Underdogs died, so would the only part of Roth's life that truly had meaning. Once his promotion was set in stone, his new role as Head of Military would quickly become unful-filling.

It was hardly a convincing reason to join forces with the Underdogs, but at the very least it gave him less reason to kill them. Mercy wasn't quite in Roth's nature, but...

A hand landed on his shoulder, making him jump.

'Is it time to go yet, do you think?' asked Pereira.

'We've walked in a fifty-kilometre circle today,' Roth mumbled. 'We can sit down for a few more minutes.'

It was no exaggeration. In the hours since the scouting team had first vanished off his thermal tracker, Oliver Roth and João Pereira really *had* walked just over fifty kilometres.

But it had been worth it.

The view on the thermal tracker screen made it *all* worth it.

After the incident with the scouting team, Roth had stopped his army for breakfast and made a few phone calls. First to Grant, to offer the latest news and ask if anyone on his staff team had basic knowledge of thermal blackout technology. The second phone call had been to a former army scientist who had known nothing of the sort, but had a knowledgeable contact somewhere in New Cardiff. The third and final phone call had been to a young Welshman who had given Roth far too much information and detail about the science behind thermal blocking, but had also given him the one detail he would find useful: its operational radius. The type of thermal blocker Major George West could have stolen would block out any decent-sized creature within five miles of its location. Roth had grinned, and awoken some secondary-school maths he used to know.

A five-mile radius. That meant a ten-mile diameter. Fetching up his smartphone's calculator, he had multiplied ten by pi to get the circumference of the thermal blocker's range: just over thirty-one miles. He had then converted it to kilometres using a method from his old school days, dividing by five then multiplying by eight. (The further away he stayed from the archaic and useless imperial system, the better off he would be.)

The calculator had read 50.265 km, and Roth had precisely 500 soldiers. Oh how he had laughed at the neatness of it all. All he had needed to do was march his army in a fifty-kilometre circle, along the exact border of the thermal blocker's range, dropping off a soldier once every hundred metres. Eight hours of walking and 500 drop-offs later, Roth and Pereira were the last ones left, back at the exact spot where that scouting team had vanished that morning.

Roth looked at the image he had created on the thermal tracker: his day's work was a beautiful, almost mathematically perfect ring of white dots, comprised of 500 clone soldiers in 500 locations around the border. Spitfire's Rise was technically surrounded: with hundred-metre gaps between each clone, of course, but *technically* surrounded.

Roth decided, just once more, to double-check his answers. He reached for his radio.

'All units,' he said, 'take ten steps forward. Now.'

The white ring of dots onscreen began to shuffle. And then they all vanished.

It was nearly but not quite simultaneous, with no more than a two-second gap between the first dot and the last dot vanishing – creating a flashing fadeout that almost looked pretty.

'All units,' he spoke again, 'take ten steps backward.'

A moment of nothingness passed, then 500 white dots popped into existence again and the ring of clones was back. Every soldier in Roth's clone army was precisely five miles plus a few steps away from Spitfire's Rise.

Roth looked at Pereira, who shared his grin.

'I have to admit, Oliver,' he said, 'you're far smarter than I gave you credit for.'

'Yeah, I'm pretty amazing,' Roth replied. 'Using a person's weaknesses against them is a pretty standard tactic, but it takes extra brains to use their *strengths* against them. Now, give me a few minutes.'

Roth smiled. After a full day's work, he had earned a moment of showing off. But as he retrieved his smartphone, he wondered whether he would have come up with the encircling idea had it not been for João Pereira. The man hadn't contributed anything in terms of good ideas, but he had kept Roth's feet on the ground and his brain in a sensible place. The influence of another human's company had been healthy, even if it was just Pereira.

Roth opened up his routefinder app. In his hours of resting from his eight-hour circular expedition, he had had plenty of time to find an app in the extensive Marshall-Pearce database that allowed multiple routes to show on the same screen at once – and which would allow straight-lined routes, displayed as the crow flies.

He copied the GPS coordinates of the clone at the very north of the circle, and the clone at the very south, and made a straight-lined route between the two points.

He then copied the coordinates of the clone furthest east, and the clone furthest west, and made another straight route between their locations.

He did the same with northeast and southwest, then northwest and southeast, and then several more times between other pairs of clones at opposite points of the circle. The more routes he drew, the clearer the centre point became. After fifteen or so straight lines he found that every one of them intersected at nearly the same point, all passing within ten metres of the same building.

Oliver Roth zoomed in, and laid eyes on the slate roof of Spitfire's Rise.

'We've found it…'

He copied down the coordinates, his thumbs shaking as he typed.

Oh, Nathaniel, he thought, *your hundred precious scouts and their oh-so-brilliant tech advances didn't help us a bit. Your biorifles added nothing either. My intelligence and deductive reasoning alone found the Underdogs, and I'd have managed it even without your assistance.*

He smiled at the thought of how Pearce's academic intelligence had been no match for teenage wits and battle experience. His smile dropped when he realised the Underdogs probably believed the same thing about their own victories.

'You realise,' said Pereira, 'that you've only found where the thermal blocker is. Not necessarily their—'

'That piece of equipment is so important they'd only keep it in their house, right next to them. Trust me, these are the exact coordinates for Spitfire's Rise.'

He reached for his radio.

'All units, please bring out your GPS navigators and type in this location. It's where we're all heading.'

He gave them a few moments, then read out the digits on his smartphone.

'Fifty-one degrees…'

He read out the full coordinates, latitude and longitude, in degrees, minutes and seconds. It looked alarmingly close to imperial measurement again, but it was the the only system their GPS devices would recognise.

'…and thirty-four point one seconds west. That is the location of Spitfire's Rise, and our target for the night.'

That was it. Even if Roth died of a heart attack at that exact moment, Spitfire's Rise was still doomed. Its coordinates were now in the open, known to 500 witnesses and a colonel.

Somewhere in the back of Roth's mind, an image materialised of Dr Joseph McCormick holding his teary face in his ageing hands.

Oliver Roth swept the image aside and returned to the biggest question of his life. He had spent most of his journey wondering what would happen if he actually reached Spitfire's Rise. He knew he would be faced with a metaphorical squirrel and air rifle once again, but didn't know whether he would make the same decision on a larger scale. The closer he got, the less he knew for sure, but one thing was certain: his actions there, positive or negative, would determine the person he would be for the rest of his life.

I don't want to do this.

But the truth of who I am is in that building. And I have to see it for myself.

It was time to close the net.

'March,' Oliver Roth said into his radio. He looked down to his thermal tracker, where the white ring of bodies shuffled inwards and disappeared from its screen.

Chapter 16

During his regular New London missions, the possibility of escaping the Citadel had always been in Ewan's mind. If worst came to worst, they had only needed to break out into the countryside and run home. That wasn't a luxury the strike team had tonight. It was more complicated on an airship.

But at the same time, the lack of an easy escape route also simplified it all. There was no complicated middle ground: they would either win the night, or they would die.

Ewan looked down at the empty mug in his hands. He wouldn't bring himself to eat or drink anything that had been touched by his enemies, but the mug served as a good fidget toy either way, and he needed to fidget his fingers after seeing that cargo manifest. It had been an unwelcome reminder that Acceleration wasn't their only concern that night: they could wipe it out completely and *still* end up with New Oxford and New London combining, just as Grant had planned all along.

Jack was stood at the wall, finalising a route plan from the maps in front of him. Ewan could read maps pretty well, but it was quicker to put his trust in Jack. It played havoc with his PDA-related need for control, but he knew how much speed mattered.

Kate was pale-faced, having mentally but not physically recovered from her travel sickness. At the very least, there was nothing else for her to throw up.

'Did Sharp give *any* reason why we needed to start so urgently?' Ewan asked, wary of how little distance had been put between the airship and New Oxford.

'Just "we may have less time than we thought",' Kate whispered back. 'And that he needed to check Pearce's emergency escape pod.'

'So he's bailing? He's taking the escape pod for himself?'

Kate shrugged. 'Either that or he's sabotaging it.'

Ewan nodded. Kate's suggestion made more sense. Someone as dedicated to his act as Oli Sharp wouldn't give himself away forever by stealing an escape pod and dropping down to Earth.

'Or maybe he's doing nothing with it,' said Jack, turning back towards them, 'and that was his way of telling us the escape pod exists.'

'You think so?'

'Why not? Normal people drop weird hints like that all the time. They don't even have to make sense. OK, take a look at this.'

Ewan and Kate joined Jack at the map, and he explained the route so quickly and clearly that Ewan remembered why it was such a good idea to bring him along in the first place.

'By the looks of the *Sheila*'s design,' he finished, 'it looks like it's heaviest at the rear.'

'Maybe it was the same with Grant's actual wife,' Ewan said, to laughter from the others.

Crap, he thought, *the woman I'm talking about was Shannon's mum. My hatred for her dad is so strong that I forgot about her for a moment.*

'The engines are split like the "six" dots on a dice,' Jack

continued, 'two at the bow, two in the middle, two at the stern. If you want to have the biggest impact as early as possible, I suggest we go for the stern ones first since they're carrying the most weight.'

'Which are the stern ones?'

'The back. Bow means the front. Port and starb—'

'Just say front, back, left and right,' Ewan replied. 'So we go for the back ones first because it's common sense, but we don't detonate straight away. We wait until we've planted all six and we blow them all at once. If we do one engine at a time we give ourselves away.'

Jack stared at him – an unusual, confused stare – and then spoke in a voice as if about to break bad news.

'It's not like you to have a concentration lapse, so I'm sorry if this is news to you. We may have a backpack full of NPN8, but we only have two detonators. Rubinstein had one for each side of the road.'

Ewan swore, quietly but with the foulest words he knew.

'So we're going to need other things to destroy the front and middle ones,' Jack continued. 'There's an armoury on the way to the stern – the back, I mean – and we'll see what we can pick up from there.'

The idea suited Ewan. Despite wearing a dead man's uniform, he felt naked without firearms in enemy territory. Other than their explosives in the drinks bottle, they hadn't been able to sneak so much as a knife on board. Even their traditional dental mirrors, so useful for peeking around corners, couldn't have been packed without raising suspicion.

'That's an aircraft hangar at the back, right?' asked Kate, pointing to the map.

'Yeah?'

'If we really need to, we could take helicopters and destroy the engines from the outside...'

It was a suggestion most other people would have laughed at. Kate had probably only suggested it in the belief that neither Ewan nor Jack would laugh at her, and she was right. It was a ridiculous and dangerous idea, no question about it, but any ideas were welcome at that point.

'The helicopters *will* have really simple controls, to be fair,' added Jack. 'Simple enough for a two-week-old clone to understand.'

'If it comes to it, maybe,' Ewan replied. 'Right now let's stay on the inside. If we go flying around out there we'll just get shot down by two-week-old clones, and I can't think of a more embarrassing way to die.'

Silence fell, and Ewan ran through the plan in his head one more time. It really was as simple and undetailed as he thought: go to the armoury and steal stuff, plant Rubinstein's NPN8 against the two rear engines, and sneak around destroying the other four with whatever weapons they had found by that point. There was nothing else to analyse, which made it harder for Ewan rather than easier.

'Right, let's get to work,' he said, rising from his seat. The others followed him out of the relative safety of the staff room and into the thin corridors. There was barely enough room for more than single file, as if they were walking through the centre of a submarine, but it felt safer with Jack leading the way. Within five minutes he had found the armoury, hidden behind one of the rare doors which looked shiny and sturdy enough to be secured.

'OK,' Ewan said, as the door slid open with a tap of his access badge against the pad. 'Let's do this quick. There's no good reason why maintenance staff would be here, so let's not get caught.'

'To be fair,' said Jack, 'you might have given us away just by using your badge to open it.'

'No other way of getting a keycard without combat. And let's avoid that if we can.'

On the inside, the armoury looked like a smaller, more impressive version of the cellar in Spitfire's Rise. The firearms were shinier – unworn by thirteen months of not being used in combat – and the other weaponry was more advanced, including one crate that gave Ewan the chills.

Acid grenades: for use on civilians.

'I bet they'll tear through the engines like flesh-eating bacteria,' said Jack. 'Take as many as you can carry.'

Ewan unzipped the backpack and filled it with eight acid grenades. Two per engine should be enough. He handled them with all the care expected of someone who literally had exploding pockets of acid strapped to his back.

'Anything else worth taking?' asked Kate. 'Besides the rifles, I mean.'

'Just take handguns,' Ewan answered. 'Easier to conceal.'

Armed and dangerous once again, the trio left the armoury, closed the door, and headed along the route to the first engine. Jack called it the port-stern engine, but encouraged Ewan to think of it as 'back-left'.

Halfway through their journey along the thin passageways, up and down miniature stairwells, and around tight unfriendly corners, Ewan realised that his pulse was somehow higher when he acted as a spy. Sure, he was an expert at masking his anxieties (up until the point they overwhelmed him, at least), but being exposed and fired upon – as deadly as it would be – would feel much closer to his comfort zone. He wondered what that said about him, and about the young man he was becoming.

Ewan found the door to the first engine chamber – a tatty stencil-painted door with bog-standard keycard access – and opened it.

Bloody hell, this room's loud.

Kate was already mid-grimace, her sensory issues repelling her from the room and all its chaotic droning bedlam.

'You can keep guard if you like,' Ewan said to her, or rather shouted over the noise of the engine. She nodded, and Ewan followed Jack inside.

The room was a wide-open chamber, the size of an average house. Most of it was empty, besides a line of tall metal cupboards and lockers across the wall, which perhaps contained engineering or maintenance equipment. Like the lowest corridors of New London, the room was no prettier than it needed to be, leaving its main focus to be the swimming-pool-sized hole in the middle of the floor that led into the open sky below.

The engine itself hung underneath the hole, just beneath the main body of the airship. The gaps between the connecting metal pillars and the engine beneath them revealed the darkened Oxfordshire countryside, far below.

'One of us is going down there,' Ewan said.

'Is that your way of asking me?'

'Didn't mean it that way. Why, you up for it?'

'I'll do one of them,' said Jack. 'Neither of us should have to go through this twice.'

'Agreed. I'll go first.'

Despite everyone overestimating his leadership qualities, there was one principle Ewan was proud to hold onto: he refused to command his friends to do anything he wouldn't do himself. He was going down there.

He looked around and saw a maintenance ladder at the edge of the rectangular hole, which led straight down to the curved surface of the engine. He gave the backpack to Jack, after removing half the NPN8 from the drinks bottle, and took a long breath.

He was halfway down the ladder when he felt the chill of the outside air. Three quarters of the way down, he felt the wind. He had to pause and give himself a moment to accept the very real risk of sliding over the curved edge and falling several miles to his death.

Ewan looked as closely as he could at the engine's complex design. Perhaps Jack would have been the better person to do the first engine after all.

Sticking the explosives on the windy exterior would be too risky. But there was a panel, barely visible, halfway along the engine. Ewan wouldn't have much in the way of handholds, but then again it had probably been designed for mechanics to fix it on the ground. When he looked carefully, there were bits of metal that stuck out along the centre of the engine's casing which led all the way to the panel, with finger-sized holes in the middle of each of them. Ewan thought the design was strange, but decided to take what he could get. He lowered himself down to the engine, so slowly that he wondered if they'd even destroy the first two engines by the time they reached New London. Once he had lain flat on the engine, he used the protruding metal points to drag himself along the curved metal, and after what felt like five noisy minutes he had reached the panel. The task would be simple: open the panel, stick the NPN8 inside, plant the trigger in the plastic, and climb back up.

He did so with ease, thanks to his singular focus distracting him from the peril he was in. But once it was planted, he closed the panel and his distraction was gone.

Ewan panicked. His body started to shake, and he clung onto the metal points for dear life until he had calmed himself down. Once the trembling had settled, he continued his journey forward to the opposite ladder, and climbed back up into the relative safety of the engine room.

He collapsed onto his back on the chamber floor, ignoring the voice in his head that told him he wasn't safe at all. It may have been less windy inside the room, but he was still on an airship full of people who would want him dead the moment his cover was blown.

'Ewan,' came Jack's voice.

Well, I guess there's no point in using our fake names while we're planting actual NPN8 on the ship's engines.

Ewan looked up, and found his friend removing one of the detonators from the backpack. 'How does this work?'

At first, Ewan did not answer. The sight of the detonator, cigar-shaped with a protected clear-coloured button at the top, brought back some dreadful memories.

I'm going to hate using those again.

For a moment, he was back in that tiny stairwell. He and Alex were sat next to Kate, trying to help her feel less alone.

'Ewan?' asked Jack.

'Yeah, sorry. You type in the six-digit passcode, and push the button. That's it. I'll set the code to 123456. Pass it here.'

Ewan rose to his feet, and Jack passed him the detonator with confusion on his face.

'Did you ever get your emails hacked in the old days?' he asked. 'Because that's a dangerously easy code to break. Gracie once got her Instagram hacked because she just set it to the word "password", thinking that nobody would—'

'It's not like they're ever going to use this against us,' Ewan interrupted, pressing the bottom-right button and securing the passcode. 'Besides, if they come for us suddenly, we won't have time to remember anything complicated.'

Ewan double-checked the strength of the protective cap, and was satisfied that the button wouldn't be pressed inadvertently in his backpack. In theory it wouldn't detonate without the code being entered anyway, although his paranoia tried to convince him otherwise.

'OK, engine number two.'

They made their way back into the thin corridors to find Kate waiting for them. She followed without a word, most likely grateful for the brief quiet she'd get during the journey between engine rooms.

The second engine room wasn't difficult to find, nor did Jack seem to have any reservations about taking on the task Ewan had been so afraid of. With Kate on guard again and Ewan keeping as close to the walls as he could manage, Jack headed over to the lockers at the end of the room and fetched out a harness and long rope.

'What's that?' asked Ewan.

'You weren't meant to climb down there unassisted, you know,' answered Jack, putting the harness over his body and fastening it in place. 'I tried calling down to you, but you didn't hear me.'

Ewan watched in embarrassment as Jack hooked the rope into his harness and tied one end to a pole next to the ladder, tying the knot to perfection. He took the NPN8 and trigger piece, climbed onto the curved engine and moved along the metal, slowly but safely. He clipped the rope into the sticking-out metal pieces as he went, which turned out to be miniature carabiners rather than handholds, and made his way to the panel far more quickly and calmly than Ewan had.

Ewan tried to come up with other excuses for why Jack was performing better than him. The one he rested on was that Jack had no traumatic memories attached to NPN8, and could keep a straight head when handling it. It wasn't like he'd played a part in blowing up his surrogate grandfather with the stuff.

Come to think of it, it must have worked in McCormick's favour that Jack was in the countryside that night finding us a house. If he'd been part of the strike team and McCormick tried giving him the detonator, he'd have worked everything out on the spot.

Ewan took the second detonator and set its code to 123456. He had cleared the envy from his face by the time Jack reached the top again.

'Well done, mate,' he said. 'Any ideas on how we acid-grenade the other four?'

'No idea,' replied Jack as he removed his harness. 'Maybe it's a case of getting the timing right. We're definitely not climbing down, pulling the pin and dropping them in the panel. I mean, we could do it once each but we'd run out of heroes with one engine left.'

They joined Kate back in the corridor, and Jack paused for a moment to visualise the route to the middle engines in his mind. He headed off, wordless.

Ten minutes passed, with no signs of the journey being close to an end.

Jack's not lost, is he?

'Are we nearly there yet?' Ewan asked.

'It's not the easiest route,' Jack answered, before a familiar voice interrupted him.

It came from the speakers overhead. Oli Sharp was addressing the whole airship.

'Calling mechanical engineers Sam, Tom and Damon,' he began. 'You are needed urgently in the staff room.'

The voice may have been Sharp's, but his manner had changed. He hadn't sounded that formal face to face.

'Please attend at once,' Sharp finished, 'as there is a very sensitive matter to be discussed.'

The speakers fell silent. The Underdogs looked at each other, puzzled.

'They let Oli Sharp use the whole airship's speaker system?' asked Ewan. 'They don't let regular staff do that, do they?'

'Did anyone else hear the nerves in his voice?' asked Kate. 'I'm not great with voices, but I know anxiety when I hear it.'

Without warning, Jack lunged for Ewan's backpack and pulled out the detonators. Before Ewan or Kate could react, he had typed in both codes, flipped both plastic caps, and crushed both red buttons under his thumbs.

Jack, what the hell are you doing?!

An enormous *boom* rumbled through the airship. The walls shuddered around them, painful groans echoing through the metal corridors. A moment later, the airship began to list to one side.

Chapter 17

'What the bloody hell was that for?!' Ewan yelled at Jack, grasping against the wall in an effort to stay on his feet. The airship continued to rock and moan around them as Jack shouted his response.

'They obviously got to Sharp! And if they got to him, they've either found the NPN8 or they were going to. I figured they wouldn't put him on the radio until they'd disarmed it, but either way there was nothing to lose.'

The rocking of the floor beneath them became less violent, although it was still difficult to balance on the tilted metal.

'Looks like we only got one of them,' Jack continued. 'They must have disarmed the other.'

'How can you tell?' asked Ewan, as Jack cast the redundant detonator to one side and returned the other to the rucksack on Ewan's back.

'For starters, only one of the detonators switched off after use,' Jack answered. 'That, and we've tipped back and to the left – not just backwards. The right-hand engine is still going.'

Ewan looked down, and saw the discarded detonator

rattling away from his feet as the floor continued to tremble. There was no arguing against Jack's analysis.

'Whatever,' he replied, 'we need to find Sharp.'

'But it's obviously a trap!' said Kate.

'Trap or not, we need to find him. If he's been snatched, it's only a matter of time until he talks. And when he does, Emilia Rubinstein dies... along with everyone Sharp knows in the Network. Come on, let's find him.'

Ewan prepared to run, but his footing was unsteady on the slanted floor beneath him. As he started to walk rather than jog, with Kate close behind, he tried to calculate how a man as in-character as Oli Sharp could possibly have been caught – if, in fact, he had been. Maybe he had snooped around in areas above his pay grade. Maybe people had got suspicious when his apprentices used their access badges to enter the armoury. Maybe someone had found the bodies in New Oxford. Maybe—

'Do you need all three of us?' asked Jack.

'Why?'

'Because one of the NPN8 batches didn't explode. Which means there's a bunch of clones walking around this ship with a pile of plastic explosives. If we want to stand a chance of blowing up—'

'Yeah, OK, I get it. You get the NPN8 back, we'll get Sharp. Meet you in the corridor outside the middle-right engine.'

Ewan didn't wait for a reply before running. Kate said some words to Jack, which Ewan couldn't hear, before she started to follow.

'Pretty sure we can find the staff room from here,' Ewan called over his shoulder.

'It won't be a safe journey,' replied Kate.

'Of course not. Either Sharp's captured and guarded in the

staff room... or this is all part of his weird communication, and we'll *still* have to fight our way to the staff room to find him.'

Ewan poked his head around the end of the corridor, and found four clones heading in his direction. Their feet clanged aggressively on the metal panelled floor, and the furious expressions on their faces indicated that the biological switch in their brains had been activated and they were now in 'war' mode.

Their assault rifles opened fire towards Ewan's face, and he ducked back behind the corner just in time. He leaned around again once their gunfire fell quiet and returned fire with his handgun. He was more rushed than usual, afraid of giving the clones too many chances to fire back. Not because of the risk to his life, but because he and Kate would need their automatic weapons. Better to kill them before they ran low on ammunition. He got two of them before needing to reload.

Kate leapt out underneath him with her head inches above the floor, and finished off the other two before they could lower their rifles towards her. Ewan looked down, surprised at her quick thinking, and ran to the hopefully well-loaded assault rifles in the dead clones' hands.

'Thanks,' he said, making sure not to thank her too loudly.

Wait, why wouldn't I thank her the way she deserves?

The same reason I'd lie to Rubinstein about competitive shooting, I guess. Pride, and not wanting to look vulnerable in front of people I'm accountable to.

But that's my problem, not Kate's.

'Thanks,' he repeated as he knelt down by the bodies, this time loud enough for Kate to hear. He passed her one of the assault rifles, and picked the other for himself along with a clone's radio.

He lifted it to his mouth, but Kate's hand slapped itself over the microphone.

'You're not going to talk, are you? You'll give us away!'

'We just killed four clones, Sharp's probably been captured, and a bloody engine just blew up. They know we're here.'

'And you want to prove them right?'

'Let's see how long we can string them along for.'

He raised the radio to his mouth.

'Mr Sharp?' he said. 'It's Tom. Would it be quicker to do this over the radio? I'd rather deal with that big explosion—'

'Tom?' came a sneering, vaguely familiar voice. 'Ewan, weren't you supposed to be Damon?'

Ewan froze. The condescending question confirmed exactly who it was.

Nathaniel Pearce…

'Oh yeah,' Ewan replied. 'My mistake. Let me start again.'

He decided that humour and overconfidence was the best way to mask his panic.

'Very funny,' replied Pearce. 'But sure, if you feel you have the time to chat, go ahead.'

'Oh I'd love a chat,' Ewan said. 'I don't get to talk to my enemies often, but it always turns out well when I do. I met Keith Tylor face to face and he died minutes later. I spoke to Iain Marshall over the phone and he died that night. And now I'm talking to you.'

'You think I believe in that kind of destiny?' scoffed Pearce. 'Keith and Iain died through their own bad judgement. Besides, your face-to-face meetings with Oliver Roth haven't exactly gone in your favour.'

Wait… the last one did. I killed him in the Experiment Chamber on Floor F. The whole room was on fire, and…

A panicked thought flashed through Ewan's brain, fighting for his attention. But Pearce continued to talk, and Ewan stayed focused.

'I don't need to be afraid of teenage failures with guns,

when I have a workable plan, sharp wits, and *even more* guns. Gwen and I have already won: we just need to go through the motions.'

'Underestimating your enemies. Smart move.'

'Ewan, you're an autistic boy with demand avoidance issues and huge gaps in even the most basic learning. Your brain's a blunt instrument.'

'Sledgehammers are blunt instruments too. But have you noticed how they get the job done?'

He looked towards Kate with a grin, seeking approval for his witty comment. But she was pointing towards the end of the corridor with an urgent expression in her eyes, mouthing something.

Pearce said something through the radio, but Ewan decided not to care. He looked to the end of the corridor and saw the shuffling shadows. He ran straight for them.

The thought in his head about Oliver Roth still fought for his attention. Pearce had spoken about him as if he were still alive.

When Ewan looked around the corner, Oli Sharp was being bundled out of the staff room by a horde of clone soldiers: thirty of them at least, most of them staggering along the slanted floor, some holding the walls for balance. They must have received word that Sharp's allies weren't taking the bait, and had been told to transport him back to somewhere secure.

Ewan opened fire with his assault rifle before any of the clones saw him. About half a dozen fell down before he took shelter. Kate arrived at his side and joined the fight, but her rifle bullets ran out after three short bursts.

'Watch my back,' Ewan whispered, as Kate retrieved her handgun and faced the other direction. Ewan peeked around the corner just in time to see half the clones remaining, and Sharp fighting with all his strength to escape their grasp.

It was a different Oli Sharp to the one they had seen throughout the mission. This man was afraid for his life and it showed across his sweaty face: in fact, it was the first sign of real honesty Ewan had seen from him all evening. He looked like a man who might have truly regretted – perhaps even *hated* – the task of killing his apprentices. Like a man who wanted to pray for forgiveness. But the biggest sign of his newfound sincerity was his sheer *terror*. Terror was a difficult emotion to conceal, no matter how good a person's acting was.

Sharp knows how much he knows, Rubinstein's words echoed in Ewan's brain. *And he knows how quickly he'll give it away when subjected to pain.*

With that in mind, his desperation to escape did not surprise Ewan at all. It wasn't just an effort to save himself. Ewan sprayed ammunition into the clones at each side of Sharp, offering him precious seconds to escape with. But the man was only athletic enough to perform a five-metre run, weaving around the dead clone bodies on the path beneath him, before another two clones grabbed him from behind. An arm wrapped itself around his neck, owned by a clone that wanted to use him as a human shield.

Ewan aimed at the less-sheltered clone and pulled the trigger. His assault rifle clicked.

Crap, just handguns again...

If he had counted right, he only had four bullets. For somewhere between eight and ten clones, the true number impossible to observe in such a thin corridor. Either way, the mass of bodies moved backwards, Sharp at the rear of a procession that moved away from Ewan. He and Kate would not be able to follow once they were around a corner and out of range.

Ewan's mind had to work like a calculator, in terms of both logic and speed. Oli Sharp was reaching out, struggling against the grip of the clone behind him, his eyes meeting Ewan's and nonverbally pleading for help.

Ewan knew exactly how to stop the interrogation that Sharp feared so much.

'*Ewan, hel—*'

He raised his handgun a little higher, and fired before Sharp could work out what he was doing. The bullet cracked through Sharp's forehead and killed him stone-dead.

Ewan turned to run before the image of Oli Sharp's corpse could solidify in his mind. The clones behind him had paused in disbelief, and Ewan took advantage of their hesitation.

'Run, Kate. Now.'

'What about Sharp—'

'He's dead. *Run.*'

Kate didn't need telling again. Her lack of questions suggested that she had worked out the truth. In a way, Ewan was glad.

They reached the end of the corridor before the remaining clones pushed their way past Sharp's body, turned the corner and opened fire.

Daniel Amopoulos couldn't resist interrogation, Ewan thought as he sheltered himself. *For all his physical strength, he still gave away our names.*

Alex didn't resist it either.

By putting a bullet through Sharp's brain, I probably saved everyone in the Network.

Maybe it was true, maybe not. But either way, it was a comfortable sentence for Ewan to keep telling himself.

'We said we'd meet Jack at the middle-right engine room, yeah?' shouted Kate.

'Yeah. Assuming we can—'

The radio at Ewan's waist began to sneer.

Oh bugger off, Pearce…

'You were planning to kill him all along, weren't you?' the voice said, in a tone that gave away the annoyance its owner felt. 'Nice gratitude for helping you aboard.'

'Nah,' said Ewan. 'If I could've saved him I would've done. I just *predicted* I'd end up killing him.'

Ewan took a moment to wonder why he was even engaging Pearce in conversation. Perhaps it was just to take the opportunity to say out loud that he wasn't quite a cold-blooded murderer.

'You found it pretty easy, didn't you? I'd bet money he wasn't your first human kill either.'

No, he was my fourth. Polly Jones, The Lord, Steven Elcott, and now Oli Sharp.

He shook his head. That figure became six if he counted inadvertently blowing up Joseph McCormick, and taking Iain Marshall with him.

'If I were you,' Ewan ended up answering, 'I'd worry about how easy I'll find it when it's *your* turn to die.'

'As if you'll ever get the chance. But just so you know, Ewan West... your actions just now say a lot about your personality. Your behaviour in recent months has been interesting to watch.'

'You're beginning to sound like Gwen Crossland. And trust me, that's not a compliment.'

'I'm far from having Gwen's psychological expertise, but allow me to plant a thought in your head. Feel free to think about this before bedtime, if you survive the night.'

Kate turned left down the next corridor. Ewan followed, unthinking.

'I'm guessing you've been the leader of your little clan since McCormick got obliterated,' Pearce continued, the anger in his voice suggesting how badly he'd wanted Sharp alive. 'And it's clear how quickly you've lost control. Not of your soldiers, but of yourself. Not everyone does well at leadership, so don't blame yourself too much for struggling. But do blame yourself for putting a bullet in Sharp's forehead. Whoever you used to be before Takeover Day, you're not that person anymore.'

'Good. That person sucked.'

'Either way,' finished Pearce with a smug laugh, 'enjoy the conversation in your head tonight.'

Ewan dismissed Pearce's words as best he could, and looked towards Kate. During the conversation she had done most of the navigating, and seemed to have done a good job of it. The tilting of the airship's back-left corner gave away which direction they were facing, no matter how many corners they turned. Kate reached a downward ladder, knelt down to inspect the floor below, and started to descend.

'Pearce, I'm a little busy right now. Would you mind shutting the hell up?'

Ewan didn't wait for an answer, and tucked the radio back into his belt before following Kate down the ladder.

Half a corridor later, they saw Jack running towards them. He had the NPN8 in one hand, with three assault rifles slung over his shoulder. His other hand held as many ammunition magazines as he could carry.

'The platoon had barely left the engine room when I found them,' he gasped. 'I got our NPN8 back, and even had time to raid the armoury on the way here. Did you save Sharp?'

The look on Kate's face must have given it away, but Ewan answered regardless.

'No,' answered Ewan, 'but I saved every good person he knew.'

'Ah, I get it. By killing him before he could talk.'

Ewan gave Jack the nastiest glare he could, but he was interrupted by a flash of navy-blue uniforms in the corner of his eye.

He leapt forward, wrenched one of the assault rifles out of Jack's grip, turned it around and fired over his friend's shoulder. The first of the oncoming clones fell to the ground, and Ewan's heart froze as the surviving squadmates followed. He looked forwards and backwards along the corridor with terrified eyes, and realised that the corners behind them were too far away to reach in time. They were totally exposed in a narrow corridor with zero shelter points – an easier target than an autistic child in a crowd of bullies.

But Kate had leapt to one side, and rammed the full weight of her body against the door next to her. Ewan hadn't even noticed the bathroom door, but followed her and Jack inside. Jack handed a rifle to Kate and hurriedly shared out the ammunition magazines, then ran for the back walls.

'It's a dead end,' said Kate, 'but we'll live longer.'

'Stuff that,' said Jack, bursting into one of the cubicles and ramming the butt of his rifle against the corners of the nearest metal panel. 'Follow the plumbing. It'll lead somewhere.'

Ewan kept his weapon pointed to the door. The clone platoon was probably halfway to them already.

Jack kept hitting the panels. *Thud. Thud. Thud.* After the fifth or sixth strike, the tone of the smacking noises began to change. He was denting the metal, at least.

'Kate,' Ewan said, 'I know this is a really bad time to ask you a question, but I *need* to ask it before it takes over my head completely.'

Kate took her eyes away from the bathroom door, just for a moment.

'What could possibly be distracting you at a time like this?'
Thud. Thud. Thud.

'Something Pearce said. How would you interpret this sentence? "Your face-to-face meetings with Oliver Roth haven't exactly gone in your favour."'

Thud. Groan. Clatter.

Ewan looked behind him and saw a gap where the metal panel had been. He looked forward again, and the bathroom door was halfway open. He and Kate spewed ammunition into the corridor, and another batch of ill-prepared clones fell to the ground.

'Come on!' yelled Jack. By the time Ewan had turned around, Jack had clambered through the gap, grabbed onto a pipe of some sort, and started to slide down it like a fat and uncomfortable fireman's pole.

'Isn't it obvious?' said Kate, running into the cubicle and reaching out for the pipe herself. 'He doesn't know you think Roth's dead.'

She swung her legs around the pole and held herself in place with the strength and skill that only a gymnast could have, and stared at Ewan sympathetically.

'It means you didn't kill him, Ewan. Whatever happened to him in that Experiment Chamber, he came out alive.'

Ewan wanted to be angry. He *wanted* to feel anger, so much. But there was no time. The next group of clones were already advancing over their fallen comrades. Once Kate slid down far enough, Ewan leapt through the gap and caught onto the pipe, reaching back and finishing off any clones stupid enough to get within six feet of the cubicle door.

The gap was narrow, only twice the breadth of Ewan's shoulders, and the warm pipe occupied its fair share of it. He secured his arms around it and stared downwards to the floor – far, far below.

Beneath him, Jack was gone. He hadn't fallen, as far as Ewan could tell. He had just vanished. Ewan slid down as fast as Kate's body beneath allowed him to, and soon saw what had happened. A quarter of the way down the long pipe there was a small channel leading to an air vent, short but wide enough for three people. Kate reached over to the channel and was grabbed by Jack's outstretched hand, and Ewan followed them both as energetic footsteps sounded in the bathroom cubicle above. The trio reunited in the cramped space, and began the long process of catching their breath. They were alone, far from any engines, and in utterly unnavigable territory. But they were out of reach. It was the safest place they could be, albeit the least productive.

'Did I hear that right?' asked Jack. 'Is Oliver Roth still alive?'

'Probably, yeah,' snarled Ewan. 'Turns out cockroaches really don't die. Not even ginger ones exposed to fire.'

There was a moment of silence. Not because there was nothing to say, but because none of them had the motivation to talk about such a depressing subject.

'Well,' Jack said to break the silence, 'alive or dead, he's not here. It's not worth worrying about until we get home, so let's focus on the here and now.'

'Yeah?' answered Ewan. 'Then what's on the other side of that metal grille?'

Jack took a glance between the metal slats, and his voice took on an even more serious tone.

'People,' he answered. 'Ununiformed... I'd say suspiciously close to four hundred of them.'

Ewan crawled up to the grille and looked for himself.

Jack was right. The 400 New Oxford hostages lay on the other side, not far below them.

And at that moment, a clone above them dropped the first grenade towards their shelter.

Chapter 18

Ewan's hands slapped themselves over his ears as the grenade clattered between the central pipe and the thin walls around it, then exploded not very far below. The pipe began to creak and groan, cutting off all hope in Ewan's mind of using it to descend further.

'Their grenades can't land in this side tunnel,' shouted Jack, 'the chances of throwing a grenade down the chamber and getting it into the hole next to us is—'

'They don't *need* one to land in this tunnel, you numpty!' yelled Ewan, scrambling back towards the metal grille. 'They just need to pull the pin, and drop it at the right time to explode *next* to the tunnel. We need to ge—'

Another grenade went off, this one louder, hotter and more frightening. The clones' estimates were getting more accurate.

It never failed to surprise Ewan how much more competent clones became with their brains switched to war mode. With most humans, anger made them less effective at just about everything except brute strength.

That's the case with me, anyway. When my brain goes into anger mode—

220

'There's only one way out...' said Kate, confirming what Ewan already knew.

For all his reservations, Ewan decided it was better not to waste time. He pushed aside his bitter memories of the last time he had stood among a crowd of prisoners, and flung his body towards the grille.

It came off in one blow, and Ewan glanced over the crowd of 400 humans below him.

Every single one of them was staring, bewildered, in his direction.

They must have heard the grenades.

The crowd ducked at the rumble of grenade number three. Ewan felt the hot wind on the back of his neck and through his hair, and both his friends screamed behind him. He welcomed the screams: they were proof his friends were still alive.

The third grenade turned out to be a blessing in disguise. The prisoners close to the front must have seen the panic on Ewan's face and worked out he was no threat, despite his uniform. A number of them approached the wall and raised their hands, almost like an evangelical congregation welcoming a saint. Ewan took the leap of faith and landed in a crowd of hands. After he was lowered to the ground, he looked up to see Kate and Jack also rescued in turn.

Clearly the New Oxford crowd are nicer than the New London crowd, he thought.

Give it time, said the other side of his brain. *Nobody's taken away their food yet.*

Ewan, Kate and Jack stood next to one another, silent and confused. Of all the scenarios they had prepared for aboard the *Sheila*, a face-to-face meeting with the prisoners had not been one of them.

'So,' said a young man close to the front, wearing a faded

black-and-red shirt that he must have worn every day for the last year, 'would you like to tell us what's going on?'

The compassion in the faces around Ewan had turned to fear. Perhaps they had not expected three people in staff uniform, all of whom held automatic weapons.

'I'll, er, try to keep it simple,' Ewan replied.

He looked across at his vast audience. Even during his most embarrassing public meltdowns or most destructive moments in school, Ewan had never had this many people watching him.

He took a deep breath, and tried to address the crowd. Part of it would involve cutting out details. Part of it would involve outright lying.

'We're activists against Nicholas Grant,' he said. 'We're going to commandeer this airship and take it back to New Oxford. We were chased here, and... well, I'm guessing you've not found a way out yet?'

'Are we in danger?' came the voice of the man in the red-and-black shirt. 'There was an explosion a few minutes ago, and the floor was tilted for a while.'

Ewan lifted his heels up and down to check the floor beneath him, and realised for the first time that the airship had balanced itself out again. Perhaps at some point during the chaos, the other back and left engines had increased their power to compensate for the one they had destroyed.

'Yeah, there was a big fight out there. But you're safe now. Looks like we're steady again—'

Not bothered about interrupting him, Jack leaned over and whispered into his ear.

'Ewan, we need to sit down.'

'Huh?'

'Look up. The moment Crossland sees us, we're dead.'

Ewan looked upwards and saw an array of windows along

the top of the prison chamber. They were the only noticeable feature in an otherwise bland cube, without even so much as a visible door.

At that moment, there were no faces at the windows. Regardless, Ewan followed Jack's advice and sat down with him and Kate on the metal floor. There was bemusement in the crowd around him, but he had stopped being afraid of normal people's disapproval a long time ago.

'Right,' said Jack to the crowd, in an authoritative voice which caught Ewan off-guard. 'Before we say or do anything else, I need you all to answer me this. What's your trigger song?'

As difficult as people were to read, the entire crowd's collective reaction made Ewan's job easier. Every visible face showed immediate confusion, and looked at Jack as if asking for further information.

'The song they used to brainwash you,' Jack elaborated. 'What was it?'

No answers. Not one voice. A few of the crowd shrugged shoulders, but most stood in abject cluelessness.

'*Brainwash?*' asked a woman in the background, her voice tinged with panic.

Ewan had to think fast.

'Yeah,' he answered. 'Are you the half who got brainwashed, or the half they left alone?'

The crowd were looking at each other, their confusion a huge relief. Ewan's lie about an extra group of prisoners would be worth it to avoid mass hysteria.

They had no idea what Jack was talking about. They've not been brainwashed yet. They probably don't even know what they're doing here.

Thank bloody hell for that. They can't do to us what Alex did to Gracie.

It didn't mean they had gained Ewan's trust. But he felt less threatened around them. Just a little less.

'OK, never mind,' said Jack with a timid voice. Ewan could not tell whether the embarrassment was real or acted. 'Have any of you seen *any* kind of way out?'

'No,' a man at the front answered. 'We've found nothing. Not because we haven't been looking, but because we *know* there isn't one.'

The man spoke with the academic confidence of someone who might once have been clever. Perhaps a scientist or mathematician or something. Either way, he sounded smarter than someone who hadn't showered in a year had any right to.

'We got lowered into here by a lift on the floor above,' the man continued, running his fingers across a forehead that shone with sweat, which he wiped off against his torn jeans. 'The ceiling's the only way out, but good luck getting up there. I'm Scott, by the way. Scott... Murdoch.'

He seemed reluctant to offer his last name at first. Perhaps he had said it to take the rare opportunity of introducing himself to someone trustworthy. Scott reached a hand outward, which Ewan couldn't think of a reason not to shake – other than the remaining forehead sweat, which he ignored as it touched his hand.

'Damon,' he answered. 'They're Sam and Tom.'

It was better to keep it simple. He had already told them they were 'insiders', which was much easier than claiming to be special needs kids from several counties away who were allied with a Special Forces woman working with the United Nations who had a couple of insider contacts (one of whom he had shot in the head just minutes earlier). The truth was complicated, and time was short. Besides, Ewan wasn't planning to be around long enough for them to find out much.

No... that's not why you're keeping your identity a secret.

The faces of the Rowland family crossed Ewan's mind without his permission. Patrick, Aidan and Benjamin, whose bodies would have been disposed of by a mobile incinerator unit two months ago. And Ruth Rowland, who lived with their absence – assuming she was still alive. Ewan had all-too-clear memories of the last time he had formed an emotional bond with Grant's prisoners.

He looked across at Jack and Kate, neither of whom were glaring at him for lying about their names. As his only two living friends who had witnessed the horrors of Inner New London, they probably felt the same about this crowd as he did, and were thinking about the same dead friends.

The three of us, alone again in a crowd of prisoners. This doesn't feel right without Charlie.

Ewan shook his head, and reminded himself of the comment Scott had just made. There was no way out of the chamber. He rested his head against the wall, and dared to close his eyes for a couple of moments. Even if nothing else, his confinement would mean a few moments of well-earned rest. As long as it didn't turn into too many moments, the break would be welcome.

'So... what are your names?' asked Kate. 'I know you're Scott, but...'

'Tona,' answered the woman behind Scott: the one who had panicked at the mention of brainwashing. She had piercings above her eyes, and one of her ears held a thin metal bar that ran between two separate piercings – an 'industrial bar', as another Oakenfold student had once told Ewan they were called. Ewan even saw a tongue stud as she spoke.

'Zane Rafique,' said another young man – the one in the red-and-black shirt – with a cheerful tone to his voice that suggested he could have been an entertainer in his previous life. Whatever his profession, something in his manner told Ewan he'd have been enjoyable company in a better world.

'What were you in the old days?' Kate asked.

Kate... why are you making boring small talk at a time like this?

Regardless, Ewan listened to the crowd's answers. He had been right about Zane, who had been a DJ at school discos and weddings before Takeover Day. Tona – Tona Loving, as her name turned out to be – had been a climbing instructor, a job which hadn't helped her to escape her current situation in the least. Other people calling out had included a criminology student, a heart surgeon and a charity shop manager.

Ewan was sceptical of the last few, and wondered how many were lying in an effort to push themselves up the ladder of people worth saving. He was surprised that none of them claimed to have been canonised by the Pope. He smiled when Scott admitted to being an architectural historian, not any kind of saint but someone who probably studied cathedrals.

Ewan looked at Kate, who seemed comfortable with pushing the conversation further, asking about their families and giving warm responses in return. At that moment, he realised why.

Since dropping into the chamber, Ewan's mind had been focused on the practical side of the mission. The prisoners had been no more than an obstacle, especially when they revealed their uselessness by saying there was no way out, and Ewan would quite happily have dismissed their existence if he were able to. But Kate...

Kate was interested in their humanity.

Ewan watched, with the foundations of a smile on his face, as the tatty crowd in front of him slowly became real people. They responded to Kate's warmth and compassion, and shared details about who they were beyond their simple roles as Nicholas Grant's prisoners. Scott had wanted to be an architect before heading into architectural history instead, choosing a part-time course to spend more time providing for his mum. Zane had been a dog lover, having owned six in his old house, and joked about how his personal pack was probably still out there ruling the backstreets of Oxford. Tona was a young woman who had kicked cancer's arse – twice.

There were smiles all around Ewan as the short summaries of their life stories unfolded – perhaps the conversation was helpful to them as well as the Underdogs.

It ended when Jack shook him by the shoulder, with urgency in the grip of his fingers.

'Hm?'

'Ewan,' he whispered, 'look up.'

Whatever Jack had noticed, it had taken so much of his concentration that he had forgotten to call him Damon.

Ewan rose to his knees, looked up, and saw her.

Gwen Crossland. Gwen bloody Crossland, stood at the upper window. It must have been her, going by the descriptions Ewan had been given. There she stood, only tall enough for her shoulders, head and solitary waving hand to be visible. She smiled, sweetly, in Ewan's direction.

'Crap,' Ewan whispered back. 'Houston, we have a Womble…'

Scott, Tona and Zane turned around, as did everyone in the crowd who saw the horror in the Underdogs' faces.

'I just realised…' Kate said. 'You know how nobody here remembers being brainwashed? Or knows their trigger song?'

Ewan's eyes widened. He realised too.

'Neither did Alex,' Kate finished. 'Right up until…'

Gwen Crossland's waving hand vanished beneath the window, perhaps to some control panel. Then speakers hidden within the walls started to buzz.

Two seconds later, they were playing 'Seven Nation Army'.

Ewan looked back at the crowd as they turned to face him. Like monsters who had just been made aware of helpless prey in their midst, Scott, Tona and Zane and the other prisoners lifted their clenched fists and bent their knees. The chamber was filled, wall to wall, with faces of pure unadulterated rage. Murder was in their eyes.

Ewan breathed, but no words came out.

Without warning, 400 people lurched towards him.

Chapter 19

Ewan shot Scott in the thigh. The plan had been to knock him unconscious with the butt of his assault rifle, but by the time Scott was close enough everyone else would be too.

Ewan looked up, and found that the gunshot hadn't discouraged any of his enraged opponents. Scott Murdoch fell to the ground, and before he could get up again he was trampled by a crowd of other prisoners surging over his body.

An attacker in Ewan's peripheral vision sprang out to his left. This time he had no choice but to uppercut him to the chin at close range, and threw his unconscious body towards the crowd ahead of him. The body fell to the ground and became no more than a small obstacle like Scott, which the crowd ignored as it approached.

Dun, du-dun dun dun dun, dun, continued the music.

To his right, Kate was fighting Tona Loving. They were evenly matched in strength and physique, the gymnast against the climbing instructor. Kate's rifle was at her side, the combat purely hand to hand: like Ewan, she refused to kill an opponent even if they were hell-bent on killing her. Perhaps, also like Ewan, she was wondering how long the goodwill would last.

Kate head-butted Tona in the face, and threw the punch of her life as she staggered backwards. Tona fell out of view into the crowd, which ignored her and ran for Kate regardless.

While Ewan looked, someone grabbed him from behind. In response, he bent over forward with such speed and strength that the prisoner flew over the top of his shoulders, into the faces of two frontal attackers.

I'm still wearing the backpack, he realised. There was an idea somewhere in there.

With 390-something enemies remaining, Ewan gulped and pointed his rifle forwards. He could already hear gunfire at his side, from either Kate or Jack.

Ewan opened fire, carefully, one bullet at a time, into the feet of those approaching. Prisoners fell around him, snarling rather than screaming, and even once they were on the floor they continued to crawl their way towards him. Ewan turned and ran to a different section of the wall, as the backpack idea solidified in his head.

The backpack was still slung over one shoulder when Zane Rafique struck his side, grabbed his neck and hurled him to the floor. As his rifle flew from his grip Ewan yelled most of the breath out of his lungs… which he would have tried to avoid if he'd known Zane would strangle him.

Jack White continued to sing and play guitar, as Meg White thumped the drums in the background.

Ewan's eyes, already blurring, landed their gaze towards the top row of windows. Gwen Crossland was still there, and Ewan was sure he could see one of her hands lifting a cup of tea to her lips.

Ewan pushed back against Zane, to no avail. At that particular moment, fighting the enraged DJ was like fighting an angrier, stronger version of Mark. To his left, three more

230

prisoners had arrived and were kneeling down. He was sure one of them was Scott…

Somewhere behind Zane, Jack appeared in Ewan's line of sight. However he had survived the onslaught against him, he had found some time to help Ewan. He bent down to Zane, and did the last thing Ewan expected.

He started to tickle Zane. Ewan recovered from his surprise just in time to watch Zane flinch and loosen his grip, then struck a closed fist into the man's chin. He leapt to his feet, grabbed his assault rifle from against the wall, and started to shout.

'Keep them busy!' he yelled towards Jack. 'And away from the corner!'

'How the hell am I supposed to keep them away f—'

'You're a clever guy,' Ewan yelled, opening his backpack, 'just do what you can!'

He ran for the corner, firing bullets into the feet of the prisoner attacking Kate, and dropped the backpack on the ground beneath him. He reached inside, and without time to double-check for other useful tools they were about to lose, started to pull pins out of acid grenades. He looked behind him and saw the NPN8 sticking out of Jack's pocket, and breathed a sigh of relief. The explosions from eight acid grenades would obliterate the backpack and plenty of the room around it.

'*Fire in the hole!*' he yelled, running back to Kate and Jack. Before they could work out what he had done, there was an almighty *boom* and a fierce crackle, like a firework had gone off next to his ear. Ewan turned just in time to see the last of the backpack stripped away into nothingness, and a fountain of clear liquid splatter against the floor and walls. Globs of it spat out sideways, smacking across the bodies of enraged prisoners. This time they did scream, and the sound of them was frightening.

Ewan knocked out another prisoner, who seemed not to care about his nearby wounded counterparts who writhed and twitched and called out with wordless voices. Ewan tried to ignore them too: as horrifying as it was, it was no time for remorse to take over his brain. He and his friends remained in mortal danger.

'OK, follow me!' he yelled at them, running back to the corner as the bubbling and fizzing noises faded. The metal floor had all but vanished, leaving nothing but the loose ceiling of the storey below. Ewan took a running jump, and fell through the empty space where the floor used to be. There was a blank moment of vertigo, a painful whack against his back, and when he opened his eyes again he was underneath the chamber. Jack and Kate leapt down too, and helped him to his feet.

Ewan looked upward, his sense of balance returning. He thrust his rifle upwards in an approximate direction, expecting the enraged prisoners to follow them.

Instead, the snarls and yells continued above, with nobody paying attention to the hole in the prison floor.

'They're not...' said Kate.

'They are,' said Ewan.

With no fearful opponents on their floor and their anger still burning, Crossland's 400 prisoners had started to attack each other.

The noise resembled what Ewan imagined a prison riot to sound like, only with more groaning and savagery. Every few seconds a yell of real pain would pierce the air – whatever the prisoners were doing, they were putting each other through more pain than the Underdogs had.

Eventually Crossland appeared to have had enough, and the music stopped.

Seconds later, the cries of horror began. Then came the

tears of guilt, and yells of pain from 400 people who had done unspeakable things to one another.

'We need to run,' Ewan found himself saying. 'Find the next engine while they're sorting out this chaos.'

Ewan knew it wasn't just a strategic decision. Being in that spot placed enormous moral demand on his shoulders; and even without the pressure of demands, his sensible side knew there was nothing they could do to help anyway.

Kate and Jack ran down the corridor and Ewan followed, jogging backwards. He kept his eyes on the ceiling hole just as Zane Rafique fell through, landing awkwardly onto the floor with a yelp.

'Guys—' he shouted, before the gunfire began and bullets thudded into his back.

Ewan chased his friends to the end of the corridor, certain that their lives were only saved by the half-dozen prisoners who also tried to escape, meeting the same fate as Zane.

Just two months earlier, Ewan had run through New London's Inner City at a speed he couldn't remember reaching before, and only to escape the visual impact of the scene around him before it took root in his head. He did the same again, putting as much distance between him and the prisoners' screams as possible.

Five minutes and a long series of thin and twisted metal corridors later, he began to feel comfortable focusing on the mission again. Jack had done most of the navigating, and they were closing in on the next—

The clone patrol opened fire too early, and the teenagers had time to shelter back behind the corner. Less than a hundred metres from the next engine room, their path was blocked. And going by the number of bullet holes in the thin wall next to them, there were far too many clones to handle.

'Even if we get in,' Jack said, 'have fun climbing down onto the engine and trying to get out alive.'

Ewan booted the wall as hard as he could, immediately thankful that he hadn't broken any toes in his rage. If this engine room was guarded, the others would be too.

'We're screwed,' he said.

'We're not screwed,' said Kate, her voice not matching up with her words. 'We just need to change our strat—'

She stopped talking as a noise came from Ewan's belt, out of the speaker of the radio he'd forgotten he was carrying.

'Let's hear it for Ewan West,' came a sneer from Nathaniel Pearce, 'leader of the free British army, protector of the innocent, and demand-avoidant little arse. Things aren't going your way, are they?'

Ewan looked at his friends. Both of them were shaking their heads. Ewan agreed: there would be no advantage in talking to Pearce. He pointed down the corridor they had come from, and they retreated back towards the centre of the ship.

'Early reports say that twelve people died in the chaos,' Pearce continued. 'Twelve living humans from New Oxford, who would still be alive if it weren't for you.'

They'd have died brutally in New London if they hadn't died here...

'*Thirteen* humans including Oli Sharp, of course. Sixteen including his apprentices. Still, even though we had to reveal the prisoners' hypnosis to them, it won't make much difference. They can't do anything to stop what will happen to them, and three hundred and eighty-eight people will do almost as much damage. That's four hundred minus twelve, in case you couldn't work it out.'

Ewan switched off the radio. Pearce wasn't going to give him anything useful, and the man's words were beginning to hurt.

His PDA-inspired defiance was rising to the surface. He could feel it, he knew Pearce had caused it, and he didn't care. He wasn't going to fight the rest of the evening on Pearce's terms.

'Rubinstein was wrong,' Ewan snarled to his friends. 'We haven't lost those prisoners yet. We don't have to play by the rules and let them die.'

'You won't want to hear this, mate,' said Jack, 'but those prisoners aren't the priority.'

'No, but killing the engines is no longer an option. We won't stop this airship from reaching New London, so we might as well make sure nothing bad happens to the prisoners once they get there. And the only way to do that is by getting to Gwen Crossland.'

'Even if we kill her,' said Jack, 'there's still the crap ton of hardware they've got on board. You read the cargo manifest. Do you want all *that* to reach New London?'

Ewan didn't have an answer.

'Ewan…' said Kate, seemingly afraid of her own words. 'I do have one last idea for the engines.'

The tone of her voice gave Ewan the feeling he wouldn't like the idea.

'Yeah?'

'Remember earlier when I mentioned the helicopters?'

'*No*,' he replied with a firm voice. 'I mean, I do remember, but the answer's no.'

'We could still do it,' Kate replied. 'The odds aren't great, but we stand a better chance out there than we do in here.'

'Three good shots and we're all dead.'

'Actually,' Jack began, to an instinctive huff from Ewan. He hated most sentences that began with that word. 'We don't need *all* of us to go out in helicopters. The map said there are minigun turrets along the side of the ship.'

Ewan nodded, unsurprised, remembering a little fact that his father once told him. Major George West may not have been a naval officer back when the United Kingdom had armed forces, but he had gone into fine detail about how even aircraft carriers always had built-in armaments. It came as no surprise to Ewan that Grant's biggest transport ship was also armed.

'If one of us flies the helicopter and shoots up the engines,' Jack continued, 'the other two can take a minigun on each side, and use them to wipe out the rest of the guarding fleet. The only question is…'

Ewan had no time to open his mouth.

'I'll do it,' said Kate.

He should have seen it coming: that Kate Arrowsmith, whose life's purpose seemed to be to throw herself out of her comfort zone in the name of anxiety conquest, had volunteered for a mission that she probably wouldn't survive. Ewan looked at Jack, who seemed equally concerned.

'Kate—'

'Jack, I'm the better soldier and you're the better planner. It has to be this way round. And Ewan's too angry to get it right. I'll head for the hangar at the back of the ship, take a helicopter and join the guarding fleet. Once you're at the miniguns, let me know and I'll open fire.'

There was silence. Nobody liked the idea, but equally they knew their options were limited.

'Once we're at the miniguns?' asked Jack. 'We're closer to them than you are to the hangar. We'll get there first.'

'You won't,' answered Kate. 'We both know Ewan's already made up his mind.'

She looked at him, only narrowly avoiding eye contact. Ewan wasn't sure whether it was for her comfort or his.

'Good luck killing Gwen Crossland,' she whispered. 'I

know you'll say it's not luck, but tonight we'll take anything we can get. Save the prisoners if you can. I'll be waiting.'

She gave him a hug, and did the same to Jack. When the embraces ended, the tears on her face revealed that she wasn't acting as a soldier embarking on a mission, but as a friend saying a likely farewell.

Kate turned and fled down the corridor. Once she had vanished, Ewan turned to Jack and found his expression mirroring his own.

'If Grant loses Pearce and Crossland,' Ewan said, 'his scientific future is dead. They're both on this airship. What we do tonight could change the rest of the war.'

He headed for the nearest metal spiral staircase, and started to climb. His sense of direction was probably good enough to find the room overlooking the prisoners' chamber. First things first, he knew it was upward.

Jack followed, and spoke with a quaking voice.

'I'm not going to lie to you, Ewan. I don't think we'll save the prisoners *or* take out the engines. I just hope the deaths of Pearce and Crossland will be enough of a victory for you.'

Chapter 20

As if being an accidental traitor wasn't enough, Alex hated the embarrassment that came with being tied to a chair. More than that, the embarrassment of the moments when he was released from it.

Mark retied the ropes so much tighter than Shannon had. It was painful to the point that Alex almost regretted asking to use the loo in the first place. He had only been released with both Mark and Simon on guard with loaded weapons, his hands remaining tied except for when he had literally needed to use them. It had been humiliating, but even then he had understood. He had stopped deserving equal treatment when Gracie had died by those same hands.

Simon was still pointing the gun in his direction as Mark retied him to the chair. The lad didn't look particularly comfortable, leaving Alex to wonder if he really would shoot him if it came to it.

Mark finished his work and climbed back down the trapdoor without paying a moment's attention to Alex. He did, however, say a few words to Simon.

'I'll get some dinner sorted. Stay here until you're certain he's secure. I'll feed him when I'm done with ours.'

They know I'm risk-free in this room because there's no music around. But even then, I'm still tied to the chair. To be fair though, I did ask to be.

As soon as Mark was gone, Thomas leapt up the stepladder and into the farm, taking careful footsteps across the planks at the side of the soil.

'You OK, Alex?' he asked.

'About as good as I look.'

'Oh... sorry.'

Alex wanted to make some kind of joke in response, like, 'Wow, I'm that ugly, am I?', but he didn't have the energy. His capacity for jokes had long died out.

At the back of the room, Simon sat himself down cross-legged and held his pistol lightly in one hand, pointing it towards the wall with his finger far from the trigger. Thomas, however, sat so close that an untied Alex could have kicked him from his seat.

'So...' the boy said, 'what do you want to talk about?'

Even now, he was socialising. And knowing Thomas, it was meant for Alex's benefit rather than his own.

You're still a person, Thomas had said earlier, *even if people don't treat you like one.* It had been such an obvious fact, but Alex appreciated that someone had bothered to say it.

With that in mind, it didn't take long for Alex to think of a talking point.

'I never told you what happened to me on Takeover Day, did I?'

'No...?'

At the back of the room, Simon looked up in fearful interest.

'I was fetching a wholesale order from Luton,' Alex began. 'Luton's a hell of a long way from Brighton, but there were delivery problems and my boss sent me up north to fetch it all. By mid-morning I had a van full of hardware and a long drive home, so partway back I stopped at a supermarket to get lunch. A little place in a commuter village. And I queued up with my sandwich, crisps and drink for three quid fifty...'

Alex raised his eyebrows, and came to realise how the £3.50 meal deal was one of the tiny things he missed so much about a world that had died.

'...but it was like half the bloody village was there. And the one guy on the till was this kid who looked about seventeen and barely knew how the contraption worked, and *wow* he was slow. So twelve whole minutes later I'm stood there, having my three items scanned by this lad who's acting like he's afraid the food will bite him if he moves too fast, and when he hands it back to me, my sandwich is warm. Seriously – he took so long to scan it, all the cold of the fridge wore off.'

Thomas seemed to be smiling, just a little.

'So I did what I thought was fair,' Alex continued, 'and asked him if I could replace that sandwich with a cold one from the fridge. Because obviously, you know, I *paid* for a cold one. It was his fault the sandwich turned warm. Besides, I thought it'd make him realise he needed to hurry up and not keep his customers waiting. You know what I mean?'

Thomas nodded.

'But then,' Alex continued, 'the lad paused, looked at me like he'd never seen a black guy in his village before, and hung his mouth open as if I'd just threatened to sue him. Or lamp him one. And he stuttered out some words about how he'd need to call the manager and get permission. He got on the speaker and called his boss over, the queue behind me was getting annoyed at *me* rather than him... and I didn't want to give in and walk out with my substandard room-temperature sandwich, but I was looking at another ten minutes of waiting for a cold one. And just when I was in the middle of wondering whether my principles were truly that strong... the gunfire started.'

Alex looked across the room, to find forlorn expressions on Thomas and Simon's faces.

'Anyway,' he said. 'You know the rest. I ended up here. But ever since then, I've yearned for the days when the worst thing about my day was a warm sandwich, and some kid being slow at the till. I still wonder what happened to that slow lad sometimes. I wonder if he's alright.'

'I remember Takeover Day,' Thomas piped up. 'Me and Mum—'

'Thomas,' Alex interrupted, 'I'm sorry to cut you off but... I *need* to finish this. You can talk to me about Beth as much as you want afterwards, alright?'

Thomas dipped his face, and nodded.

'Because something else happened in that supermarket,' Alex continued. 'Something I'll never forget for as long as I live. When the gunfire started, everyone froze. But guess what they did once they saw armed soldiers? They fled the supermarket and ran as far as they could... but looting the store first, and taking as much stolen food as they could carry. People were legging it with three or four loaves of bread. Maybe some were thinking about survival in the long run... but I'm sure the stupider people fleeing with bottles of wine just wanted free stuff.'

Alex had predicted the shock on Thomas' face long before it came. But there was more than just shock: the boy seemed heartbroken. As if he were learning for the first time that grown-ups could be just as bad as the worst kids at his school. Alex almost felt guilty for putting the thought in a mind as pure as Thomas', a boy who still saw humanity as how it needed to be, instead of how it really was.

'Everyone stole everything?' the boy asked. 'Even when people around them needed help?'

'I mean, a *few* of them were honest and left empty-handed. And hell, I'd already paid for my food. But for some people, it doesn't take much to remove the good from them. Most people know how to be all nice and polite and say the right things, and smile along and pretend they're interested... but they don't mean it. The whole "nice and polite" thing is called diplomacy, and it's something most people just have in their day-to-day lives. Except the Oakenfold guys... no offence, Simon. But when authority vanishes, people reveal their true selves. The Oakenfold crew are just less pretentious about who they really are. Gotta admit, I admire that about them.'

He looked up at Simon and Thomas, and hoped that his secret was safe. Under better circumstances, he would never have admitted to feeling admiration for his younger house-mates.

'But the reason I'm saying all this, Thomas... you need to understand how *good* you are. How uncorrupted, how... I mean, you wouldn't have done that. It never would've occurred to you. You too, Simon. You're good people, and I mean that. Genuinely.'

Alex closed his eyes. Truth be told, he didn't want to watch their reactions. A man like him, raised under the uncompassionate watch of Dean Ginelli, had never felt comfortable around other people's emotions.

In the darkness, Alex found himself wishing he had grown up with Thomas' moral values: the kind that would even lead the boy to socialise with a dangerous killer, just to make sure the killer didn't feel lonely. But experience in warfare told Alex such goodness would have put him at risk.

If I were as good as Thomas, I'd have died long ago.

Alex opened his eyes again, trying to rid his brain of its natural next thought: that if the war lasted long enough for Thomas to become a teenage soldier himself, he doubted the boy would have the stomach to put up a good fight. Even in self-defence.

Simon stood up at the back of the room and headed for the exit. He lowered himself down the stepladder, so that only his face remained visible to Alex, and opened his mouth. It stayed open for what felt like a long time, like the lad was building up to something.

Eventually, it came.

'You are good man too, Alex,' Simon said, half whispering, before dipping his head below the floorboards and escaping before Alex could respond.

Alex looked at Thomas. Thomas looked at him. Both were in astonishment.

'You've not heard him talk either?' asked Alex.

'No... He must like you.'

Simon was no liar, but Alex doubted the accuracy in his words anyway. Alex had *never* seen himself as a good man. But all the same, he hadn't been among those who had looted the supermarket that day. He had spent his next year fighting for the freedom of those same looters. And despite all of his rudeness, sarcasm, and need to be seen as stronger than he was, it had taken a woman like Gwen Crossland to make him do something properly terrible.

He would never be as good as Thomas Foster, but he didn't need to be. And at that moment, it was enough to watch Thomas just being Thomas.

'OK,' Alex finished, smiling at him from the chair. 'I did promise. Talk to me about your mother.'

The attic of the Boys' Brigade hall had been an insufferable place to spend the evening. Shannon had endured enough with Lorraine's first interrogation, but it hadn't ended there. It would have been tolerable if their conversation had ended with the words 'I'm going to be the clone who won', but Lorraine being Lorraine, she had wanted more. *However* much information she had, she always wanted more.

Shannon's evening probably hadn't been much more pleasant than Ewan's, however he and the others were doing. She had been the victim of a continuous stop-start conversation: Lorraine would ask a sensitive question about a topic she hated, a ten-minute conversation would follow, silence would fall out of nowhere, and she would spend the next ten minutes afraid of the next question. Shannon didn't blame Lorraine for asking so much: she was protecting her friends, of whom Shannon had once been one.

Perhaps they were still friends. It was difficult to tell when Lorraine was in protection mode.

Shannon had hated her existence, even back in her original body, following a lifetime of apathy from her father and the untimely death of her mother. Being a cloned version of that self-hating girl, raised back to life again and again, seeing herself as a lab experiment rather than a person...

Well, technically I was right.

Nathaniel Pearce had certainly taken every opportunity to remind her. But when she thought about it, nobody else had treated her as lesser. Not because she was a clone, anyway. Then again, nobody else had had the chance, since only four people in New London had known the truth about her: her father, who had driven her to suicide; Hannah Marshall, who had witnessed her death; Nathaniel Pearce, who had brought her back five times; and Anthony Lambourne, who had run away with her.

Could I have told anyone else? In those clone lives I have no memory of?

No, there was nobody else I would have trusted. Which means there's only one way Emilia Rubinstein could possibly have found out the truth about me.

She swept the thought aside, and got back to her worries. Everything she had said to Lorraine had been true. She was the closest thing the universe still had to the original Shannon Rose Grant, who had suffered an undeserved but predictable death on Takeover Day...

She clutched her hands against her hair, and reminded herself not to think of that first body as if it had been someone else. She and the 'original' Shannon *were* the same person: the trauma was still alive, transferred across half a dozen brains.

She remembered her earliest years spent with her mother, and the vacuum that had been left when that beautiful woman died. Shannon occupied a body that her mother had never hugged, but lived with a brain that suffered the same bereavement. In her mind, that trauma gave her the right to claim her original body's identity.

If Shannon were to live with the pain, she would take the humanity that came with it.

'So, Shannon,' Lorraine said, bringing her back to reality.

Shannon let out a huff, and didn't care whether Lorraine heard. The interrogation was about to restart.

'Yes, Lorraine?' she answered with fake enthusiasm.

Lorraine stared at her with unfriendly eyes. Her face had not been friendly for a while, but until then it hadn't quite been antagonistic either.

'How old are you?' she asked.

Shannon responded with her hardest glare.

'I'm seventeen years old,' she snarled.

'Your body, I mean.'

'I know what you meant. And I'm *still* seventeen, whether my body agrees or not. I live every day with the impact of those years, so I can at least claim they happened to me.'

'OK,' said Lorraine with a sigh. 'How long have you existed in your current form?'

Shannon sighed, and decided it wasn't worth the fight.

'This body existed for four weeks before Anthony Lambourne and I escaped.'

'So you're now...'

'Two and a half months down the line.'

'Which means you've got, well...'

'Lorraine, why don't you just ask "when's your expiry date?" and be done with it?'

Shannon had shouted, for the first time that evening. Of all the topics they could have discussed, from her previous suicides to her relationship with her father, her impending mortality was the one she was most afraid of.

'Shannon,' Lorraine said, 'if you have less than two months to live, Ewan deserves to know.'

'Yeah. I'll tell him.'

'Sooner rather than later. Give him enough time to deal with the news.'

'*I'll tell him.* On my terms and not yours.'

'Never mind my terms. Do what's right for *him.*'

Shannon tried to avoid looking at Lorraine, but in the corner of her eye she saw her leaning forward.

'I've known Ewan for more than a year,' Lorraine said. 'And this last month, he's started to lose parts of himself.'

Shannon kept silent, and tried to pretend she hadn't noticed the same.

'The boy's had an even tougher life than I've had,' Lorraine continued. 'To start with there's his upbringing, his special needs, a lifetime of being seen as worthless by most of society and unreachable by *six* different schools. Kids like Ewan aren't *meant* to be given a fair chance. They're born at the bottom of the social food chain, and constantly reminded of it. And even if you ignore that, this war has just about destroyed him. His whole family were murdered. Then he was put in charge of strike team after strike team and watched his soldiers die, while McCormick – as much as we loved him – got to stay at home and chisel their names into a wall without seeing their bodies. Then he watched his best friend get murdered. Less than a month later he lost his surrogate grandfather. Now he's at the helm of a broken crowd of diminished Underdogs, and everyone he loves is dead.'

She leaned closer for her final sentences.

'Except you, Shannon. So please, treat him gently.'

Lorraine stopped talking, her monologue concluded. Perhaps she would have stayed silent for another ten minutes, had Shannon not responded.

But against Shannon's better judgement, she did.

'I love Ewan,' she answered, 'but he's not the only one who's suffered. I've got a story too.'

'Ewan has—'

'Ewan does *not* take priority over me,' Shannon snapped, the first of many tears forming in her eyes. 'We're perfectly equal, and we have more in common than you could possibly know. I spent my life being overlooked too. I grew up feeling useless. And from the day I woke up and got told I was a re-cycled human, Dad and I *both* saw me as even less than I was before.'

Shannon decided not to stop the tears. They were coming either way. Lorraine looked on, her face motionless as if reserving judgement.

'Please just remember,' Shannon continued, 'I'm afraid too. Believe what you want about what I am, but I feel human emotions just like you do. Pearce built me that way. And *this affects me*. I may have been grown in a lab somewhere but I'm still a teenage girl who misses her dead mum…'

Shannon wanted to look at Lorraine's face, and check whether she had remembered how to be sympathetic. Instead, she kept her face lowered to the desk in front of her. When she spoke again, she whispered as if speaking to the desk itself.

'If Ewan survives the night, I'll tell him the truth when he gets home. But I need your support, not your judgement.'

She closed her eyes, and took advantage of Lorraine's silence. Shannon had spent most of her life having her emotions ignored, but she knew that the clone versions of her would have fared even worse if their origins had been public knowledge on Floor A. Perhaps people would have assumed she didn't even *have* emotions. Other people's perceptions of clones had been another reason, beyond the more obvious ones, why she had hoped her friends in the Underdogs would never find out the truth.

Kate had told her the stories of how people's attitudes towards her changed once they found out she was autistic. Ewan had said similar things about people who found out he went to Oakenfold. Even that prisoner family in the Inner City had reacted with embarrassment on the Underdogs' behalf. All of the negative assumptions ran to the front of people's minds: that they must be stupid, that their opinions are automatically misguided or not worth listening to, that they should be seen only by their afflictions, real or imaginary.

Shannon found herself with similar fears. As soon as the others found out the truth about her, they would see her with all their preconceived ideas about the clones they had spent more than a year shooting. The isolation she had felt in New London was following her to Spitfire's Rise.

Maybe I should ask Lorraine for advice on coping with isolation. She must be a bloody expert by now.

A thought struck her. An important one.

If I really do want Lorraine's support rather than her judge-ment... I should offer her mine first.

When Shannon thought about it, Lorraine's background had been tough too: a long, sad story that had started with the suicide of twelve-year-old Joey Shetland and ended with the death of McCormick, and her life had never got much happier between the two events. It was easy to see her as the bitter recluse rather than acknowledge the strength she must have held onto for twenty years before finally breaking in the midst of war. In a failing army of vulnerable teenagers, Lorraine Shepherd deserved compassion and accommodation too.

Shannon took a deep breath.

'I *can* forgive you,' she said.

Lorraine looked over to her, curious.

'For what you did with McCormick. You asked me for forgiveness that night. You can have it.'

Shannon turned to Lorraine, almost afraid of what her reaction would be. Not everybody took forgiveness well. When their eyes met, the nurse's face displayed shock rather than anything else.

'The reason I struggled to forgive you before was that I loved him too. The same way the rest of you did. But I don't hold it against you, and... I *can* forgive you. And I do. I hope that gives you the peace you deserve.'

Shannon saw Lorraine smile, for the first time since before it happened. Lorraine actually had a pleasant smile when she gave one, and Shannon felt compelled to smile back.

'Thank you, Shannon,' she said.

No more words were said. No more were needed. The attic fell into total silence, the air around them filled only with the noise of the gentle breeze outside, and the rustling of...

Wait, what's going on out there?

Through the thin, uninsulated tiles of the attic, the footfall of several people could be heard behind the wind. Shannon looked at Lorraine and cupped her ear. Lorraine took the hint and listened too.

There were only four Underdogs left at Spitfire's Rise, one of whom was tied to a chair. However many pairs of boots marched along the road outside, there were more than three.

Shannon took her pistol and headed for the ladder. If enemies were coming for them, hiding in the attic would be a terrible strategy. Once on the ground floor, she jogged light-footed to the window that overlooked the street, and gasped in terror.

There were ten clone soldiers in total. They were walking past the Boys' Brigade hall as if Shannon and Lorraine didn't exist, but walking with visible *purpose*. The soldier at the front held up a GPS device – similar to the one she and Ewan had taken from Luton Retail Centre a month earlier – clearly leading the group towards a specific point.

They were marching in the exact direction of Spitfire's Rise.

Impossible…

Lorraine appeared behind her. When she saw the passing clones, her face fell.

'They're heading for…'

'Yeah.'

Before the platoon of ten vanished from view, a second group of ten clones appeared, also led by a soldier following a GPS device.

'We need to follow them,' Shannon said.

Lorraine didn't object. As vital as the comms unit was for the strike team, Ewan and the others could defend themselves. There was no way of communicating with Mark and the others inside Spitfire's Rise, thanks to the McCormick-era rule of keeping all telecommunications equipment powered down inside the building. Ironically, that rule had existed to protect their location.

Their two handguns wouldn't be enough to take out at least twenty clone soldiers. But it was marginally better than nothing. Shannon and Lorraine headed for the front door.

In the rush to prepare themselves for a stalking mission before the platoon vanished into the countryside, there was no time for a phone call to Ewan. There wasn't time for a voice-mail either. Shannon had enough seconds to find the number of one of Rubinstein's borrowed phones, and the text message she sent was three words long.

Don't come home.

Chapter 21

Something moved around in Ewan's pocket, perhaps a vibrating phone. Or maybe it was nothing. It was difficult to tell in the middle of a gunfight.

The last clone fell, thanks to Jack attacking from a second angle. If Ewan had counted the floors correctly, the stairs guarded by the platoon would be the last before they reached the altitude of Crossland's observation point. Ewan followed Jack up to the next storey, confident that the mother of Acceleration was only a few corners away.

'Ewan?' came a voice from the radio. 'Jack?'

It was a relief to hear Kate's voice, and to have the assurance that she wasn't yet dead.

'Talk to me, Kate,' he said.

'I'm getting close to the hangar,' she said. 'I don't know if I should steal a helicopter now and join the others outside, or wait until you're ready...'

'Wait a few minutes,' Ewan replied. 'We're about to cause a distraction.'

Footsteps sounded from another group of clones. The groups were coming thicker and faster, assuring Ewan that they were closing in on Crossland. And she had to be running out of bodyguards.

Their victories over the oncoming platoons of clones came as no surprise to Ewan. They had just fought their way free from a sealed room with 400 murderous opponents, whom Ewan saw as a far deadlier threat – and he could feel the thrill of his gleeful defiance telling him that it wasn't a question of whether he and Jack could blast their way through the clone platoons but merely how long it would take. Besides, the corridors were getting wider now: areas with important human staff appeared to be roomier and more comfortable, and it gave him and Jack a less cramped space to wage war in.

Once the next group were dealt with, the final clone fell to his side to reveal a room with a fridge at the end of the path.

'Staff room,' said Jack. 'Maybe there's another map there.'

They ran for the room, noticeably higher class and with more effort put into it than the mechanics' staff room, and sure enough there was a map on the wall. Not one with schematics or blueprints, but one for less skilled humans – the type who worked in management. Each room was labelled, including one simply called the 'Control Room'. It must have been Crossland's observation point: it lay directly next to a blank rectangle, which signified the empty space above the prison floor several storeys below.

Ewan huffed. He and his friends had almost died in that nondescript blank rectangle.

'Do you think Pearce is there too?' he asked, pointing to the control room on the map.

'No,' answered Jack. 'Acceleration is Crossland's thing. Pearce will be on the bridge.'

'Whatever. His time will come.'

Ewan set off. The route was simple enough for him to

memorise, and they had fought most of the way already with speed and efficiency that had impressed even him.

Two corridors and three more dead clones later, the final approach was quiet. Ewan remembered his first conversation with Rubinstein, during which she had mocked the idea of wiping out every single clone on board. It may still have been a ridiculous idea to clear the whole airship, but as he approached the door to the control room he couldn't help but smile at how quiet the area around him was. The remaining human staff were probably hidden away in their offices, considering themselves too important for combat. There was an eerie silence on a floor that should have been infested with clone soldiers, the only audible sounds being the faint rumble of engines below and the breathing of himself and Jack. They might as well have been in space.

The last clone's keycard worked against the door. When they ran inside, Gwen Crossland was stood at the control panel, looking indignant.

Ewan had been expelled by half a dozen headteachers who had worn similar faces, and given him identical stares of authoritarian disappointment. Crossland was not scared of Ewan and Jack breaking into her control room and cornering her with automatic weapons. She wasn't even worried. More than anything else, she just seemed annoyed at the inconvenience.

'You two brats have caused me a considerable amount of trouble,' she snarled, as much as a composed woman like her knew how to snarl.

Ewan was unwilling to enter a hero-to-villain conversation when all he needed was her dead body. He fired his first bullet. Crossland saw the shot coming and leapt behind the nearest swivel chair, the bullet only catching her side.

'If you kill me,' she shouted, 'all of the prisoners die too!'

Ewan had the perfect kill shot: the plastic swivel chair would have no impact on his bullet. But her comment made him hesitate.

'Yeah, how's that?' yelled Jack.

'Walk to the window.'

'No. Just tell us.'

'No. *You* walk to the window.'

Wow, Ewan thought, *she's an ageing unarmed woman in a room with people who want her dead, and she's still refusing to compromise.*

Jack took cautious steps towards the row of windows.

Even without her hypnosis skills she knows how to manipulate people.

Jack reached the window, and his jaw dropped.

'Ewan… they're getting angry.'

Ewan opened fire against the window frame, shattering the glass panel to Jack's shocked yelps and Crossland's vague interest. Once the soundproof frame was gone, the opening notes of 'Seven Nation Army' thumped into the control room.

'I switched it on a moment before you broke in,' Crossland said. 'Let me out, and you'll be able to turn it off.'

Ewan knew he couldn't shoot her dead. Equally, he couldn't let her go. That option would be even worse, because *more* than 400 innocent people would die if she lived.

'You don't have long, Ewan. Take off your rifle and slide it across to the wall.'

The very fact that she had told him to do it made him reluctant to do so. But his conflicted PDA instincts were already too busy defying Emilia Rubinstein, who had told him he couldn't save the prisoners.

Ewan took off his rifle and slid it along the floor, out of both his and Crossland's reach. It clattered against Jack's, which had been cast there the moment she had asked.

Jack's speedy obedience told Ewan how fearful he was of the sight he was witnessing.

Crossland bolted from her hiding place behind the swivel chair and limped for the door, with one hand clutching her side as it bled.

'How do we stop it?!' Ewan yelled after her. There was no reply.

Ewan ran for the window, and saw it unfolding. A crowd of worn prisoners, already bloodied from their previous horrors, had risen to their feet and were leaping at one another again with dreadful groans.

Ewan's eyes went straight to the control panel. There was no guidance, no instruction manual, no labels on the buttons.

He pushed buttons randomly. It was a stupid strategy, but inaction was worse than whatever mistakes he could make.

After the tenth button was pushed, Ewan noticed something. Not only was the music still playing: nothing else had changed either.

'Go after her,' he snapped at Jack.

Jack ran for his rifle, and then for the door. The chances of him finding her were minimal and Ewan knew it. The chance of finding *any* success in *any* of this was minimal.

Ewan took a glance out of the window. Tona Loving was losing a sadistic wrestling match against a younger woman, and the industrial bar was missing from her ripped ear. Scott Murdoch stood on his wounded leg, seemingly blind to the pain of Ewan's bullet to his thigh. He was punching the face of a prisoner who must have been twenty years older than him.

Some of the bodies were already motionless. Ewan was running out of time.

Ewan reached for the far-left side of the control panel, and pressed every button, pulled every lever and twisted every dial in order from left to right. As expected, nothing changed and Meg White's drums continued to thump.

At the edge of the control panel's metal surface, Ewan saw something that didn't look right. Some of it was damaged, perhaps attacked with something small. Only then did Ewan see the discarded screwdriver at the near wall.

Ewan lifted the metal surface and saw the ripped remains of the wiring underneath. Nothing of the sea of wires remained connected to their respective buttons.

He had been lied to. He could have shot Gwen Crossland behind her bloody swivel chair and the prisoners would have been just as condemned.

You complete and utter bloody...

She had manipulated him, and he had been gullible or desperate enough to fall for it. Ewan ripped the metal surface clean off the control panel, and lobbed it across the room with the loudest and most aggressive yell he could make, full of obscene language that would have made his mother cry. It could have progressed to a total meltdown were it not for Jack's sudden voice from the doorway.

'Anything?'

Ewan turned around, about to scream at him for giving up his search so quickly, before he saw Gwen Crossland gripped in one of his arms.

Once again, she wasn't afraid. Only annoyed.

'How the hell did you find her so fast?'

'I followed the breadcrumbs,' Jack answered, pointing his rifle tip at the blood droplets on the floor.

'Bring her to me.'

Jack marched her over, to the tune of the White Stripes and the screams and groans of dying prisoners. Ewan couldn't ignore it, as much as he tried. He pointed at the open control panel and the mess of disconnected wiring.

'You tore apart the controls…'

'Yes,' she replied, her lips pursed.

Ewan's brain was awash with grief, which he wouldn't allow himself to show.

'Why?'

'To buy myself time before you worked it out. If I die, Acceleration dies with me. But there are plenty more people living in New Oxford. The loss of four hundred is negligible.'

'Tell us how to stop it,' Jack snarled from behind her.

'You don't seriously think there's a way to stop it?'

'No,' said Ewan, 'I believe you. But I can buy them some time.'

Ewan wrenched Crossland away from Jack's grip, and fixed his hands under her armpits. His rage, which must have been comparable to the rage felt by the prisoners below, gave him the strength to lift and separate her from the ground. He ran – physically *ran* to the smashed window, launched his arms through the empty frame and released her.

Gwen Crossland fell through the chamber with a petrified scream. Just for once, she was scared. Ewan looked down as she fell with a satisfying *whack* onto the top of some already-dead prisoners. She survived the fall, just as Ewan had hoped. Not because of any sadism, but because he needed her to live for a little longer.

He had noticed during his own time in the chamber that while the prisoners were enraged, he, Kate and Jack were their only enemies. The Acceleration victims hadn't turned on each other until there'd been no other targets.

Crossland had no time to get to her feet. Alone in a sea of her own prisoners – up close and no longer just observable test subjects – she watched, aghast, as most of them stopped attacking one another and stared at the spot where she had landed. They didn't seem to hold any grudge against their fellow inmates next to them, whom they had been locked in mortal combat with just seconds earlier. Tona and her attacker released each other and looked to their right, Scott and his opponent to their left. Then the crowd advanced, and Crossland screamed.

Jack stared, dumbfounded. Ewan had no time to deal with his friend's emotional reaction.

'I'm open to ideas, Jack,' he said.

'Go for the speakers,' Jack replied.

Ewan leaned into the chamber through the broken window, and listened for where the music was booming from. There were no speakers visible, nothing obvious protruding from the walls. 'Seven Nation Army' was being blasted out from somewhere inside the walls themselves.

As Tona reached Gwen Crossland first and snatched her by the throat, Ewan fired his rifle bullets towards air vents, gaps between wall panels, anything that stood out. On his left, Jack had got to work with the wiring. If anybody in the Underdogs could get the wiring right it would be Jack, but with all the technical skills in the world he would still be hopeless if it came to guesswork.

Crossland had fallen silent. The prisoners had too. Ewan had not seen the details, other than blood across one of Tona's twitching hands, but she must have been dead.

Moments later, the crowd attacked each other again. Ewan's distraction had bought them an extra thirty seconds at most, not that they had helped. As Ewan kept firing into random places across the chamber, and as Jack played with the controls in the face of futility, they knew how the situation would end. Ewan's tears fell in advance.

The man who had briefly paused his attack on Scott struck him again. He fell straight to the floor, thanks to the gunshot wound Ewan had given to his thigh, and never rose again.

Tona finished off her previous opponent, but was surprised by another prisoner from behind. Paralysed by the shock of another piercing being ripped from her skin, she didn't last more than twenty seconds.

Three minutes passed, the chamber beneath growing quieter with every death Ewan couldn't prevent, until the last cries died out and he and Jack were left alone above a chamber of corpses. A couple of silent winners crawled or twitched among the bodies, none of them looking like long-term survivors.

Rubinstein was right, Ewan thought to himself, trying and failing to ignore the truth: that the woman who acted like she knew better than him really *had* known better than him.

Of course, his logical side knew about the small victory. The only woman capable of brainwashing her victims into killing one another had been killed herself, and her only surviving victim was safely tied up in a secret location in Hertfordshire. The Acceleration project was as dead as Gwen Crossland.

But the anger remained. It was a hollow victory, and only the death of another scientist would fill the void.

'Pearce next,' he snarled, heading for the door.

'Ewan…' said Jack through his own tears. 'We can't go for him yet.'

Ewan remembered why. He had forgotten about it in his fury, but even with the prisoners dead, the airship and its enormous cargo hold full of hardware would still need bringing down – otherwise Grant would look at the night's destruction, shrug his shoulders, and combine New Oxford with New London anyway.

But hopefully they'd be able to kill Pearce at the same time as bringing down the airship. It was a shot worth taking.

'Kate needs us,' said Jack.

Chapter 22

Kate took tentative footsteps towards the hangar entrance, like a child sneaking downstairs past her bedtime. She was undetected, for now. It would only take one clone to walk through that side corridor and her cover would be blown, but there were no better places to shelter within half a mile.

'Kate,' came Jack's voice from her radio.

'Yeah?' she whispered.

'Crossland's dead. Ewan and I split up and we're heading for the miniguns. I'm about a minute away, and Ewan—'

'Already here,' Ewan interrupted. 'Go get them, Kate. We've got you covered.'

Ewan's encouraging words didn't match the dulled tone of his voice. Not even close. Kate's father had once taught her that was one of the warning signs of someone hiding something.

Kate decided not to ask about the prisoners.

'I'm going in,' she whispered. 'Unless they recognise me and shoot me, I'll let you know when I've flown outside. If you don't hear from me in the next five minutes...'

'Sure. Go for it.'

Kate took the deepest breath her lungs knew how to take,

and put on her most convincing expression of fake confidence.

She walked through the hangar entrance as if nothing was wrong, even lowering her assault rifle to her side and holding it with loose fingers. One way or another she would be seen by the clones and humans inside, but being seen was different to being noticed. Her enemies would register the presence of a nervous human, but not a regular mechanical engineer doing the rounds.

Kate walked past ten or so clones running in the other direction towards the hangar's main exit. Perhaps Pearce had reassigned them after the news of Crossland's death, supposing he had seen it on CCTV or something. They paid her no attention on their way past, and Kate was reminded of a lesson her uncle had told her – one that she had never been able to put into practice before that moment – that you could get away with almost anything as long as you did it confidently.

She looked at the open exit at the back of the hangar, as wide and tall as a house and connected to nothing but empty night sky. She walked past the line of parked helicopters along the side wall, and chose the one closest to the edge.

The cold and the wind struck Kate harder the closer she got to the exit, but by far the most disturbing part was the sound. Loud noises had never been handled well by Kate's brain, and the merciless roaring air currents were a timely reminder that whatever happened in the coming minutes, it would *not* be quiet.

Kate opened the door to the cockpit, still unnoticed by the remaining clones and mechanical staff, and clambered inside.

Well whatever I was expecting, I wasn't expecting this...

In the library back at Oakenfold, Kate could remember the accessible computer: the one for students with physical disabilities, sight issues and so on. The screens had been bigger, parts of the keyboards had been colour-coded with large letters, and the whole setup had been designed for ease of use no matter who the user happened to be. Inside this helicopter designed for clone pilots, Kate believed she had found the equivalent.

The controls were so simplified that even a teenage novice like Kate could find her way around them. Everything from the ignition switch to the weapons system was as easy to understand as noughts and crosses, and within three minutes of inspecting the dashboard, Kate was ready to give it a go.

She rested her assault rifle beneath her seat, and looked out of the curved windscreen at the gap to the sky. It was time.

James… unless a miracle happens, this might be the last thing I ever do for you. I hope I do a good job of it… and I hope you're safe, wherever you are.

And McCormick… Raj…

Kate knew that time wasn't on her side, but she took a moment anyway to recognise something important. Not important to the mission, but to her.

Back in comms, Lorraine had tried convincing her not to miss the dead people she had loved. In return she had argued that every dead loved one was another reason to fight, but putting it into practice hadn't been simple. Ever since the AME shield, Kate's personal journey had been about finding ways to mourn the dead and fight well at the same time. And, preferably, claim her personality back too.

Now at the controls of a helicopter, moments away from launching a battle in the skies, Kate came to realise that she had succeeded. All night she had missed the people she loved, whilst becoming once again the warrior she needed to be. Bereaved but brave, Kate Arrowsmith was back.

With another deep breath, she pushed the ignition button.

The helicopter roared to life. Kate leapt and screamed.

Unlike the accessible computer, the helicopter had not been designed for those with sensory issues. She took a moment to settle herself and for her hands to steady again. Then, as the first of the curious faces turned in her direction, she started to fly.

The initial hover must have looked clumsy enough, but the flight towards the exit could have looked disastrous for all Kate knew. Nonetheless she continued, tricking herself into feeling as confident as she could, and flew outside. The floor vanished beneath the helicopter, exposing the vast dark blankness of Oxfordshire countryside beneath her.

If I push the wrong button, I'm dead. And I'll have time to panic for whole miles before I hit the ground.

She hoped her flight path didn't look as wobbly from the outside as it felt on the inside. Whether it was her nerves or the sensory overload, some type of shudder was flowing through Kate's hands and the joystick was translating it into awkward movements. She rotated the helicopter by 180 degrees and lined it up with the back of the airship, now separated from her by at least a hundred metres of nothing but air.

I must be the only person who could sit inside an ultra-simplified helicopter, accessible enough for a barely experienced clone, and still look stupid flying it.

Kate decelerated, and her helicopter fell into line with four others. Presumably, four more would be guarding the airship's bow, or stern or whatever Jack had called the front.

She looked back at the hangar, and caught a figure in human uniform talking into a radio. She didn't have long.

Kate had spent so long concentrating on the immediate task of stealing a helicopter that she had briefly forgotten why she had done it. The plan that involved shooting five engines came back to the forefront of her mind. She reached for her radio.

'Guys? I'm ready if you are.'

'Go for it,' said Ewan. 'No time to lose.'

'Wait, just one moment... are you *sure* you want me to do this? If I get everything right, the airship crashes with you on it.'

'Pearce has an escape pod, remember? ...Sharp mentioned it.'

Kate nodded to herself. The boys at least had a vague plan to look after themselves. It was time to bring down the *Sheila*.

She aimed the helicopter's guns towards the remaining back jet, with the help of aiming visuals built into the windscreen glass. On the other side of the ship its parallel jet was no more than an empty space, destroyed by Jack's quick thinking before anyone could remove the NPN8. Kate turned her eyes back to the engine they had failed to destroy, and opened fire.

Bloody hell, those guns are loud!

The sensation of the noise felt physical: not just a sound in her ears, but like metal ball bearings rattling around her cranium. Kate kept her hands steady despite the pain, and the bullets did their job. The second rear engine exploded with a beautiful but overwhelming *boom* and a sizeable fireball to match. The helicopters around her started to sway, reacting with the clumsiness of four jump-scare victims.

The airship leaned a little further backwards. It looked a subtle change from a distance, but Kate knew it would be chaos to everyone inside.

I am so useless, she thought to herself as the yellow-orange light beneath the engine faded and the falling components vanished into the dark. *I should have gone for the side engines. If all of them fail on the same side, the ship's doomed.*

As the saying went, hindsight was always twenty-twenty, whatever the hell that was supposed to mean.

Kate tightened her grip on the joystick and turned her helicopter ninety degrees to the right. The helicopter beside her had only half-turned, and the bullets she fired smashed straight into the cockpit. The strobe light of the muzzle flash illuminated the pilot as he jerked back and forth, his body dotted dark red.

Kate flew upwards as her dead enemy tipped towards the ground, the other helicopters aiming for her with singular focus as if their colleague had never existed. A minute later there would be a violent explosion on the grass below, but nobody would be paying enough attention to witness it.

Kate flew along the side of the airship, taking the slim chance of reaching the next engine before combat began. But the remaining three helicopters were not far behind. The painful *tpat-tpat-tpat* of minigun fire echoed in her brain, and streaks of light shot past her left side like aggressive shooting stars. Kate, short on brainpower and on seconds, decided to manoeuvre. It would be shaky and unpredictable, but perhaps that would be to her advantage. The enemy pilots had probably been trained for combat against people who knew how to fly.

She rotated halfway around whilst dropping her altitude dramatically. Once she had fallen out of the helicopters' line of sight, she tilted herself backwards to point her weaponry upwards. She could see the trio of helicopters now, one out in front and the others supporting it from behind.

Her helicopter shook as she tilted, and a stall warning appeared on the dashboard. She would not be able to tilt far enough back to return fire against her attacker above. Instead, she rattled bullets into one of the support helicopters further behind, which gave a limp explosion and wobbled downwards until it was out of view. Two enemies left.

Wait… there were half a dozen more in that hangar…

The front helicopter shook at the distant sound of more ammunition. The muzzle flashes on Kate's right came from the side of the ship. One of the boys had opened fire with the side minigun.

The whole helicopter plummeted in front of Kate, then dropped out of view like a disconnected elevator. In the split-second Kate had to react, she noticed there were no blades connected to its main body. She looked up in time to see the airship's guns spit bullets into the topside of the last helicopter, hacking away at the top axle until the force of its own spinning ripped it apart. The blades flung themselves chaotically through the air, and the helicopter beneath fell like a boulder towards the fields below.

'Small weak spot,' came Ewan's voice over the radio, 'but it kills them dead if you hit it.'

'What's going on?' asked Jack.

'Just wiped out the rear guards. What are you doing now, Kate? Going for the middle-right engine, or back to the hangar? I'd head for the hangar, so you can wipe out the other copters before they come out.'

'But the engines are the prio—'

'If you're dead, you can't shoot the engines. Make your choice but do it quickly.'

Ewan was right, and Kate knew it. Leaving the hangar alone would be a death sentence for her. She slowed down her helicopter until the airship had overtaken her, and spun around in front of the hangar exit. One helicopter was already moving towards the open air, and another two had their blades rotating. Clones were scurrying around next to the idle ones too. Kate opened fire at them all.

She had never seen a body split in half by minigun fire before. In the space of five seconds she saw it three times, and ignored the voice in her head telling her about the likelihood that one or more of them might have been human. Five seconds of ammunition was all she needed to disable all the aircraft inside before she flew away again, hoping and praying that her friends wouldn't end up relying on that hangar for their escape.

The air was mercifully empty as she flew back towards the middle-right engine, but bloody hell, it was slow going. Her helicopter wasn't much faster than the airship itself, and the relative velocity looked no faster than a brisk walk.

Yet another reason why I'm useless… why I pretty much deserve to fail at this.

I should have joined the helicopters at the front before I gave myself away, then slowed down and shot the engines as they flew past.

If nothing else, the idea made her realise her brain was stabilising again. The bellow of the spinning blades above still sent a continuous string of shudders down her body, but it was a constant, unvaried drone. Kate's world may have been loud and terrifying, but at least it was *steadily* loud and terrifying.

After at least a minute – a long time by battleground standards – the next engine came into view. It was close enough to see but not close enough to fire at with any accuracy, and Kate got the feeling she would need to conserve her ammunition.

Just a little closer. A hundred metres or so, then four engines would become three.

Then she saw the podcopters.

Her mouth dropped open as a dozen egg-shaped death machines were spat out of the side of the airship, through gaps in the hull too thin for her to see. Lighter, more agile and deadlier than any helicopter could ever hope to be, at least twelve of them were heading in Kate's direction.

'*Ewan?!*'

'I see them. Hold tight.'

Ewan's opening wave downed three of the podcopters. The rest fired upon Kate, bullets roaring towards her before they were even in range to aim accurately. Kate understood. Only one bullet needed to hit the right place. Who would care about the thousand that missed?

Something else was coming from the hull. Five or six of them, dark and flat. Kate could only see them because they were an even darker shade of black than the night sky.

Jetpods… the Mark Two podcopter models. They actually exist.

The day she had escaped the Inner City prison, Ewan and Charlie had raided an officers' sector for valuable information. Among the findings, Kate had seen an early set of plans for a new one-man aircraft – urgently put into production after a traditional podcopter had been taken down by a teenager leaping on its back and messing with its minigun.

The jetpods were no longer theoretical designs: they were right there in front of her, bursting into the night sky. Horizontal, half human-sized, probably flown by half-sized clones like the one she had seen in the sniper rooms a month earlier. Armed with lighter weaponry, faster and more agile, powered underneath by small jets rather than propellers on—

Two jetpod bullets shattered the left side of Kate's windscreen. They punctured the passenger seat and came to rest somewhere in the back of the helicopter. Kate fought against the cold wind that grabbed her face, and fired back. She caught three podcopters and two jetpods before Ewan released a second wave that downed several more.

Not enough, though.

'Crap. I'm out, Kate. Get away from there.'

'I can't reach the engine…'

'Reach the *other* middle engine. Jack's got enough ammo to

protect you. Come back for this one after the other clones go down.'

Kate had started to move before Ewan had finished talking. She dipped her helicopter and fled underneath the belly of the airship, pursued by all of her surviving enemies. Before she got too far, two more regular helicopters appeared at the left-hand side – exactly where she was heading. They opened fire too.

Podcopter bullets from behind. Helicopter bullets from the front. Black jetpods buzzing around her like flies over a corpse, lining up against the windows for a shot directly at her head. Outnumbered, undefended, low on ammunition. Every sensible part of Kate told her that she was dead.

The clones knew it too, and were closing in. For all of Kate's historical bravery, for all her achievements and all the demons she had conquered, scores of bullets struck her engine anyway.

Smoke billowed into the cockpit. Red lights went off across the panel of simple controls, and loud noises attacked Kate's brain. Her helicopter was doomed, moments from destruction, and held no respect for what type of soldier she had been. Despite her efforts during thirteen months of war and all the personal achievements she had accomplished, Kate was under no illusions. Good soldiers died in explosions just as quickly.

Kate looked out of the shattered windscreen and saw one of the other two helicopters flying in for the kill. A jetpod had lined itself perfectly on her left, the barrel of one of its guns inches from forehead height.

Kate had been brave for a long time. But she had never had much in the way of defiance. Her next move contained a level of defiance that would have made Ewan proud, had he been in a position to witness it.

Not even bothering to check the gap between her blades and the airship above, Kate used the last of her helicopter's power to rocket herself upwards and out of the jetpod's range. The nearest enemy helicopter flew ever closer, not even pausing in surprise.

Kate undid her seatbelt, let out a whimpering cough against the smoke, and reminded herself that once upon a time she had been a gymnast. Then she clambered out of the window, struggling through the slash marks from the glass against her hands, and made the mistake of looking down. The drop would either be three metres, or several thousand.

She jumped. Her feet hit the flat surface of the jetpod, but she knew better than to rely on them for balance. Her knees were bent, her hands lay flat against the metal, and her teeth gritted without her permission. The pilot beneath her had no idea how to react, and no time to make a decision. Kate leapt again, forcing herself to ignore the freefall that was sure to happen if she missed the second helicopter.

Even at her most terrified, her skills on the horizontal bars remained through the power of muscle memory. In another world she could have made it to the British Championships, if she hadn't been suffering through mainstream education at the time. Instead, her years of gymnastics expertise culminated in her leaping from a floating jetpod onto the landing skid of a helicopter in mid-flight. She gripped the skid so convincingly she could almost feel the chalk on her hands, then lifted her legs and wrapped them around the skid too, clutching it tightly with all four of her limbs. She tilted her head, and saw the upside-down image of her jetpod victim tumbling through the sky.

That could have been me.

Except I would have just fallen. That aircraft will be back as soon as the pilot regains control.

271

Above, her original helicopter gave up the ghost and exploded on its way down. Its light revealed the swarm of podcopters, jetpods and the remaining hostile helicopter, all lining up like a firing squad.

Kate knew they would shoot. They would wipe out one of their own helicopters in exchange for one Underdog. The clone inside would be collateral damage by anyone's standards.

She thought of James.

Perhaps he had been dead all along. Since Takeover Day, when Mark had shouted 'get bloody running, they're not worth it'… when she had followed the others across the field just minutes later. When her brother and the Block One students had been confronted by armed soldiers and forced to follow instructions they might not have even understood…

Maybe James had been killed that day, and her whole war had been for nothing.

Without warning, the helicopter she was clinging to spun round, its miniguns blazing with noise that almost made her faint. She looked to her side and saw podcopters cracking open like dropped eggs. Evidently the clone inside the helicopter, deep in war mode, did *not* see Kate's life as worth losing his own for.

The pilot put up a resistance worthy of any Underdog – not that Ewan would ever accept a clone into Spitfire's Rise. With no enemies remaining and the helicopter having sustained minimal damage, Kate almost felt guilty for climbing to the door, hauling it open, wrapping her hands around the clone's head and breaking his neck.

The clone had deserved better. But then again, so had James.

Kate replaced the clone's joystick hand with her own and kept the helicopter steady, then sat on the dead clone's lap and shut the door. The rattling of the helicopter's frame and the roar of the blades attacked her senses again, but this time she knew what to acclimatise to. Besides, it wasn't half as loud as the outside had been.

She suppressed a swear word, upon realising her assault rifle had gone down with the previous helicopter. Even if she landed safely, she would be unarmed once she stumbled back into the hangar. But that would be a problem for later, after she had shot the other engines. She had almost died half a dozen times, yet four out of the six engines still remained.

'Jack,' she gasped with tears in her voice, 'I'm coming for the middle-left engine. There's just one helicopter coming from underneath the ship, and it's me.'

'Get here quick,' Jack answered, with a tone that seemed indifferent to the hell that Kate had just gone through. There was no way he could possibly have known the details. 'There's another few helicopters at the front of the airship, and they'll get to you pretty fast.'

I don't even need to get all six engines, Kate thought. *Just a couple more would bring it down, surely. This, and one more.*

She focused her aim at the middle-left engine, and fired.

Her bullets never made it. They caught the second wave of podcopters leaving the hull. As Kate came to realise that *both* sides of the airship had spaces for them and the jetpods, the podcopters fell from the sky to reveal their allies behind them, positioning themselves in a defensive formation in front of the engine.

The minigun on the side of the airship opened fire, bringing down the frontal helicopters as they came. Jack even took out a few podcopters that strayed from the crowd, but was powerless to stop the rest: the miniguns were designed never to turn far enough to hit the airship's own engines. Kate opened fire with the last of her ammunition, most of which had been used by the dead pilot in the seat beneath her, and destroyed one or two. The other five or so returned fire, and hit Kate's helicopter.

'What's going on?' asked Ewan.

'They're attacking her again!' Jack screamed. 'And she's out of ammo!'

Kate watched the group of jetpods heading under the ship and flying towards the hangar. Perhaps to stop her from ever landing back on the airship, or perhaps to attack her from behind.

Either way, she was never coming back aboard.

'I can't land...' she gasped.

'Kate,' said Jack, 'you know we love you, right?'

Kate's heart fell. Jack's warm words were an admission of defeat. At the upper end of the *Sheila*, Kate could see the last three guard helicopters abandoning the front of the airship and flying straight for her.

'You can't land,' Jack continued, 'you can't kill any more engines, and you can't stay where you are. You'll have to evacuate. Just fly away.'

Ewan started yelling something, but Kate couldn't make out his words. He was angry at Jack for the mere suggestion of giving up.

'I'll catch as many of them as I can while they're chasing you,' Jack finished, his voice wavy with pre-emptive mourning. 'Just fly. Find somewhere safe away from all this. Go as far as the helicopter will take you.'

Kate's feeble resistance was taken away when a podcopter bullet smashed her side window.

'I love you guys too...'

She turned the helicopter around, unarmed and ashamed, and flew as fast as she knew how to. The *Sheila* continued its voyage to New London with four engines out of six remaining, and two of her last surviving friends stood alone against however many clone soldiers Pearce had left.

She had failed. Failed the mission. Failed her friends. Failed her brother who may or may not have been dead all along. But she flew anyway, looking back at the airship as it grew smaller behind her, listening to Ewan's screams across the radio as they began to fade. Once she was out of range, she was unlikely ever to hear his voice again.

The three approaching helicopters gave chase, matching her speed perfectly. They were not close enough to open fire, and unwilling to waste ammunition now the threat to the airship was gone. They just tailed her at a constant distance, awaiting their moment. Maybe Kate's fuel would run out first, and they would kill her. Maybe they would shorten the gap metre by metre, then open fire and kill her. Maybe they would run out of fuel first, open fire out of desperation, get a lucky shot and kill her. Maybe they would run out of fuel, miss all their shots, and reinforcements would fly in from the nearest Citadel and kill her.

Or maybe she would live a little longer. At some point during the night or early morning she would escape, touch down at a place she had never seen, unarmed and without a map, wandering around until she starved to death.

She looked at the three helicopters behind her, and wondered whether a faster death would be better than a slow one. She raised her radio next to her ear, and listened as closely as she could to Ewan's and Jack's crackled voices until they stuttered into nothingness. Once they were no more than static, Kate found herself trapped in an empty universe, nothing left in her life except overwhelming noise and pitch-black emptiness below.

Her friends were gone. But the pain of missing them would always be worth it for the joy of having known them.

Kate Arrowsmith flew onward, her thoughts drifting to McCormick and to Raj, who perhaps weren't far away. And as she and her hunters left the *Sheila* far behind, her thoughts drifted to the memories of watching *Doctor Who* with Mum, Dad and James.

Her world had been beautiful once. Even in her worst times, it had been beautiful.

Chapter 23

No matter how loud Ewan shrieked into the radio, no response came back. Jack was silent, having given up several minutes earlier.

'*Kate!*' Ewan yelled with a hand on the minigun controls to steady himself. '*Bloody answer!*'

The distant creaks in the outside corridor might have been general flight noises or clone footsteps. But Ewan didn't care. One of the last people he trusted was probably dead, and the threats to himself were the last thing on his mind.

'*Kate!*'

He grabbed the sides of his head and started to pull his own hair. Alive or dead, Kate was gone.

And let's face it, the odds of her still being alive are...

'Ewan,' came Jack's voice in the radio, 'we need to find each other.'

'We need to find *Kate*.'

'Ewan, for as long as we've fought this war it's usually been *me* telling you the stuff you don't want to hear. And I'm doing it again. Whatever's happened to Kate, it won't make any difference here. She could be alive in the distance or dead in the distance, but *here* it's just us and Pearce. You're in the mood for vengeance, right?'

Ewan deepened his eyebrows. Jack had one thing right, at least.

'I'll meet you back at the point where we split up,' Ewan snarled. 'We'll come up with a plan from there.'

Ewan tried to pretend he had the slightest idea what he was doing. The engine mission was over. Attacking them from the inside had been so impossible that sending Kate out in that bloody helicopter had literally been their best idea. And even then, she had only destroyed one of the engines before vanishing off the face of the Earth.

Ewan hated the thought of changing his plans. Not out of defiance, or a stereotypical autistic fear of change, or even the pain of admitting he had failed: if they gave up on the engine plan, they'd have lost Kate for nothing.

He left the empty minigun behind him and stormed back into the airship corridors, slowly rebuilding his habit of checking for clones and caring about whether they came for him. The tilt in the floor had returned following the death of the second back engine, and Ewan found himself brushing his hand along the walls as he stumbled along. The instability beneath his feet would remain for the rest of the mission.

Within three minutes, he arrived at the base of the stairwell where he and Jack had split up earlier, to find his last ally already waiting for him.

Ewan marched straight up to Jack and punched him in the head.

'*Argh*!' yelled Jack, one hand nursing his temple and the other held up to shield himself. 'What the hell was that for?'

'You told Kate to fly away. She's missing because of *you*!'

'If it weren't for me she'd have died five minutes ago. And you know it.'

278

Ewan wanted to hit him again, but his friend was right.

His anger subsided, and the guilt hit him. Jack had not deserved to be punched. A better Ewan would have known that.

Ewan's lungs and trachea constricted, and his eyes felt heavy. He was almost in tears, outnumbered on an airship miles from anyone he trusted except Jack. His brain wasn't working the way he wanted it to, and in all the confusion his enemies were *still* trying to kill him.

Ewan found his hands grabbing behind Jack's shoulders, and he pulled himself close. Unexpectedly, Jack accepted the hug, and even seemed to tolerate the tears. It was like the punch to his head had never happened.

It was Jack in a nutshell. Tolerant and understanding, even at his own expense.

'I'm losing it, Jack,' Ewan said, sobbing. 'It's like I can feel my own brain falling apart...'

'Sounds familiar,' replied Jack. 'And it's OK to feel weak at moments like this.'

'No it's *not*,' Ewan snarled, clenching his fingers. 'Can you think of a *single* moment when it'd be *more* important to keep a level head? We're trapped in the air with a mad scientist, his boss literally wants to murder most of the world, and pretty much *everyone* who can put up a fight is dead!'

When Ewan let go and stepped back, he saw Jack's face pointed to his boots. Evidently, even Jack Hopper's greatest logical powers couldn't find a suitable response.

'McCormick thought I'd make a decent leader,' Ewan continued, 'so did Shannon... but *I* ended up being right. I just can't do it. Even back in my best days I couldn't have done it... How the hell was I supposed to lead us after McCormick died? I lost a part of myself once he was gone.'

'We all did. We all noticed you were suffering too. And

none of us judged you for it. Except Mark, maybe, but he's always been a numpty.'

Ewan let out a short burst of despondent laughter. He barely understood why.

'Before this war,' Ewan continued, reverting back to his comfort zone of misery, 'I was a problem child with special needs and behaviour problems, or some kind of monster or whatever. For a while during this war, I was the best person I'd ever been. But now... there's not much of me left. Whatever good parts I had, whatever McCormick made me to be...'

He leaned against the wall, and fixed his eyes to the metal floor. If any clones came, Jack could handle them. And if he didn't, Ewan was fine with them taking him to meet his family, in whatever afterlife there might be.

'Even the Oakenfold Code doesn't apply to me anymore,' Ewan finished. 'My problems *are* the person now. They're all that's left. This war will be the end of me, Jack... Even if we win one day, whoever comes out the other side won't be *me*. I'm collapsing, and it can't be stopped.'

Jack laid a hand on his shoulder. An uncomfortable one, as if the lad didn't know how to show affection naturally, but Ewan tried not to tear his shoulder away. His friend was trying to be kind.

'Then look at it logically,' Jack answered. 'If you're going to collapse either way, make sure you collapse in a way that rescues millions of others.'

'Is that how *you're* coping?' Ewan asked him. 'Cold logic?'

'If it works, it works.'

'*Is* it working though, Jack?'

Ewan noticed himself speaking softly. He knew he wasn't asking to be confrontational, but to be supportive – in his own, stressed-out, ineffective kind of way.

'I know you're struggling too,' Ewan finished. 'You think I haven't noticed your fingers? You haven't stimmed them since you found out Gracie was dead. Not once.'

Jack looked down at his own hands, as if inspecting them for himself. He let out a sigh, most likely recognising how Ewan was right.

I can't just leave it there, Ewan thought. *I can't just make him depressed, as if dragging him down to my level improves anything.*

He reached around for a relevant thought, and found one that had circled around his head through the journey to New Oxford. One that might make up for his crap advice back home.

'Look, about Gracie...' he began.

'What?' said Jack.

'You said you feel guilty for not being the person she wanted you to be. But... did she let you be who *you* wanted to be? When you told her the truth, did she accept it and keep you as a close friend, or did your rejection become the main headline of your whole friendship?'

Jack joined him in staring at the floor, and rested a spare hand against his brow.

'You weren't in the wrong for not being attracted to her,' Ewan finished. '*She* was in the wrong for not accepting who you are. You're a good guy, Jack, and I wouldn't change a hair on your head.'

'Except when you're punching it?'

'Look, I said I was sorry.'

'Technically you didn't. But I'll take your words as an apology now.'

'Fine. Just... please know that you don't have to feel guilty for who you're not. Be proud of who you actually *are*, because that's what matters.'

Ewan rested a hand against the wall, and tried to work out

whether his words had come from his dad or whether they were McCormick's. He was astonished when he realised the advice was actually his own original content. Collapsing or not, a part of Ewan could still think for himself.

He took three long breaths, each one deeper than the last, and stood himself up straight. Whatever had happened to Kate, and whatever would happen to him, he and Jack had work to do.

'We won't be able to take out the other four engines,' Ewan said, beginning to walk. 'That's not me being negative, it's just the truth. But you've still got one lot of NPN8, right?'

'Yeah. What are you thinking?'

'We can't take this ship down. But someone else can.'

Exhausted, demoralised, and with his brain barely able to function, Ewan had made it to the front of the ship. Other than a light bullet graze to the forearm, he was even uninjured. Jack had been even more fortunate, with no wounds whatsoever. Their ammunition had been replenished every time a fallen clone dropped his rifle, and there had been plenty of rifles to choose from.

There must have been scattered bands of remaining clones – and human staff – in other places around the airship. But so far, the ones they had fought had been uncoordinated and disorganised, isolated and easy to pick off. Ewan reached the entrance to the bridge, exhausted after the uphill journey (and wishing they had destroyed the engines at the front instead of the back), and he hoped that they wouldn't need to hang around for long in a room with only one exit and dozens of potential pursuers.

When he tried the last clone's keycard against the door, he was met with a predictable red light and an unfriendly buzz.

'Looks like we're going in the exciting way. Jack?'

Jack was already kneeling down next to him, spreading the NPN8 in a vertical line along the crack in the entrance door. It wouldn't stand a chance.

Once the metal trigger was in place, the duo ran around the nearest corner and covered their ears. Jack pressed the magic button on the detonator, and Ewan's ears were assaulted by the echoes of the loudest explosion he had ever heard.

A split-second of that noise must have been the last thing McCormick ever heard... unless the explosion was faster than sound, and he was dead before it reached his ears.

Jack was the first back into the corridor. He ran to the empty remains of the entrance, firing his bullets into a small crowd of unprepared, disoriented bridge soldiers. Ewan followed, taking out what he hoped were the last of them.

Ewan had pictured the bridge invasion to be a moment of glory: a grand entrance that wouldn't feel out of place with a trumpet fanfare and a leap onto a podium. Instead he was focused too intensely to enjoy himself, apprehensive about Nathaniel Pearce's possible last lines of defence.

The NPN8 explosion had not damaged the control panel, which must have been at least forty metres from the disintegrated entrance. However, the soldiers that had stood in front of it had been put down by Jack.

'So what do we do?' Jack asked. 'Point the *Sheila* towards the ground and hope not to die when we crash face first?'

'Before anything else, we look for extra clones. This room's *big*, and if Pearce is anywhere in our reach, he'll be here.'

Jack began his search, and Ewan headed towards the control panel to double-check the bodies of the fallen.

On the way, he noticed the size of the windows before him: pure wall-to-wall glass the length of a sports hall, the entirety of the darkened countryside before him. The breadth of the glass – across the whole scope of Ewan's vision – made him feel like *he* was flying, very slowly, unimpeded by gravity or the elements.

Somewhere on the horizon there lay a grey line: even the gargantuan Citadel of New London looked small from a distance. Ewan looked to his left – which he assumed was north since they were flying east (or 'right' on the atlas at home, which Ewan believed was east) – and wondered whether Spitfire's Rise was somewhere in view too.

Despite his pain, he recognised the complete lack of helicopters blocking his view, and smiled. Kate had done a good job before she…

The window was tall as well as wide, the ceiling high enough for the bridge to have room for an upper floor too. Ewan turned around and saw it, its balcony hanging over the back half of his own lower floor. His lower level was wide enough for a miniature army by itself, but clearly a ship as enormous as the *Sheila* needed a control bridge the size of a small hotel.

Jack was halfway up the stairs when Nathaniel Pearce leapt out from behind a support pillar, knife in hand. The man shrieked as he dived at Jack.

Jack had no time to defend himself, except to raise his rifle in an attempt to block the knife. The force of Pearce's body toppled him backwards and they fell down the stairs together, rolling, clattering and yelling in pain, until they reached the bottom.

'*Jack!*' Ewan yelled, as if yelling would help.

Pearce recovered first, and Ewan had no clear shot as Grant's Chief Scientist hauled Jack to his feet. The man was too smart to stab Jack to death so far away from the exit, so instead he pressed his knife against Jack's throat, his other hand grasping the teenager's dishevelled hair with strength that made him wince.

'Ewan West,' he sneered, his shrieking voice having reverted back to his typical smarmy tone. 'I believe this is the first ti—'

'*Take the shot*, Ewan,' Jack interrupted.

'Shut up, Jack.'

Pearce grinned. 'I believe this is the first time we've met face to face,' he continued. 'And I have to say, I'm disap—'

'*I mean it*,' Jack interrupted again. 'Better to have Pearce dead than keep me alive!'

'You're worth more than you think, Jack. You always have been.'

'You could cripple Grant's entire scientific framework with one bullet! Two at most, if you need to get me out of the way—'

'Not happening, Jack.'

'There's a good boy,' Pearce said, in a patronising voice that made Ewan feel afraid rather than defiant. 'Now, I saw what you did to Gwen on the security feed. That wasn't nice. But if—'

'*Just bloody kill him, Ewan, you bloody, bloody numpty!*'

'Watch your language, Jack.'

Pearce let out a disgusted rasp. When Ewan focused on him again, he noticed he had moved five or so steps closer to the obliterated doorframe.

'You know, it's rude to keep interrupting a man mid-speech,' Pearce said.

'We don't *care* about your bad guy speech,' said Ewan.

'Fair enough, I'll make you care. Lower your weapon or I'll slit your friend's throat. If you do as I say, I'll release him unharmed once I'm at the exit.'

'Yeah, sure you will.'

All the same, Ewan checked the distance between Pearce and the exit. If he truly believed there was a chance of Jack living, he would let Pearce go in an instant. In a world with so few trustworthy people, Jack Hopper of all people needed to live.

'Why *wouldn't* I let him go?' Pearce continued. 'You're both dead either way. You killed the only people on board who know how to fly this thing.'

'Then why shouldn't I just take his suggestion and kill you both now?'

'If you were willing to let him die you'd have killed him already. *Put your gun down*, Ewan.'

Jack coughed. The tug on the back of his head and the metal of the blade on his throat must have given him a tickling cough...

Ewan had an idea. Like most of their ideas that night it would probably fail, but it was better than giving in to Pearce.

'Jack,' he said, 'remember what you did to save me from Zane?'

Jack didn't move, didn't nod, didn't speak. But his eyes widened.

He moved immediately. His arm shot up to the arm which held the knife against his neck, reached under the armpit and tickled as hard as he could.

Pearce flinched, and the knife moved away. Jack pushed his arm forward and made an attempt to pull out of the grip, but the hand that grabbed his hair remained too tight to escape. Ewan bolted across the bridge towards them as they staggered around, clumsy and uncoordinated, before Pearce made an attempt to stab Jack in the chest.

Jack was fast enough to deflect his arm, but not strong enough to deflect it to one side.

The knife landed somewhere in his face, and Jack screamed horrendously.

'*No! Argh, Ewan!*' Jack called out, in a voice like Ewan had never heard from another living soul. Pearce let go and ran for the exit, knife in hand, taking full advantage of the distraction. Ewan fired a couple of shots, his hands trembling too much for a decent aim, and Pearce vanished unharmed.

As Ewan had promised himself, he put Jack first and allowed Nathaniel Pearce to run to his escape pod unimpeded. In front of him, Jack had collapsed to the floor.

'*I can't see*,' he wailed. 'He *blinded* me. I can't see anything from it. Ewan, *help*…'

Ewan finished his run by skidding on his knees to Jack's side, then took a look at his face and wished he hadn't. Tears streamed from one of Jack's eyeballs and something black trickled from the other. Half of his face was a bloody mess: a border of dark red blood surrounding his damaged eyeball, surrounding the trail of whatever the black stuff was. His healthy eye rolled around in utter panic, a mood not reflected by his other side. It was like the wounded side of his face had already died, offering no more than an occasional eyebrow twitch.

'Pearce has escaped, hasn't he…'

'I tried killing him, Jack.'

The guilt attacked Ewan without warning. Guilt that Nathaniel Pearce was still alive. That Grant still had the brains to create horrifying plots from the ugliest depths of science. Guilt that Ewan had suggested a way for Jack to get out, and his idea had cost him an eye.

He tried to remind himself that it was Pearce's actions rather than his own that had cost Jack that eye, but the idea refused to stick.

'This eye's blinded, Ewan… I'll never see out of it again for as long as I live…'

Ewan didn't have the words to respond, nor the bandages to dress the wound. All he could do was remove Damon's uniform shirt, reducing himself to a vest, and offer it to Jack to compress against the wound.

'I'm going to die, Ewan...'

'You're not,' Ewan answered. 'It's a crap situation, but you'll live.'

'Even if I survive I'll die another day... someday in combat, when my vision lets me down...'

'If that happens, it's still a win. Because it means you survived tonight. Come on, have some determination. It's your brain that's always made you awesome, not your eyes.'

Jack sobbed, and offered no words. Ewan was grateful when he pressed the shirt against the dead side of his face, concealing the wound and all its ugliness.

'Besides,' Ewan continued, 'if you were going to die tonight you'd have died already. If he'd managed to get a full-on stab, that knife would've gone right into your brain and killed you instantly.'

Beneath him, Jack continued to sob. Ewan wondered whether he'd gone too far, but it was no more than the truth.

Unexpectedly, the phone rang from the control panel. Ewan hesitated, but saw more opportunities in answering it than ignoring it.

'Do you mind if I...' Ewan asked.

'Go,' said Jack. 'Do what you need to do...'

Ewan let go of his friend, slower and more gently than he had expected, and once his hands had left Jack's body he ran at full pelt towards the control panel. With his eyes cast across the vast English countryside again, he answered the phone.

'Calling Ewan West and Jack Hopper,' came the voice, 'are you both still alive?'

I've heard that voice before. Twice.

The last time I heard it, we'd just blown up McCormick.

The first time was when he read out my name to the whole of New London, and told everyone to kill me.

'Nicholas bloody Grant,' Ewan snarled.

'My middle name's Francis, actually,' Grant replied. 'It was my father's name. He was an egotistic gentleman, but he made me who I am. Anyway, how's your evening going?'

Ewan looked back towards Jack, who rolled himself over and cried on the floor as his eye continued to leak. Then he looked at the empty space next to him, where Kate should have been.

'Well, we commandeered the airship you used to desecrate the memory of your dead wife,' he answered, mentally apologising to Shannon for referencing her late mother. 'Pearce has been chased away, Crossland's been killed by her own creations, and thousands of New London prisoners are safe from being murdered. I'd say it's been a good night.'

'Even though, let's see… your little girlfriend is missing in a damaged helicopter, Nat just called to tell me he's blinded your best mate, you shot that traitor Oli Sharp in the head, and the New London prisoners are only safe because Gwen's subjects killed each other. If that's a *good* night for you, I'd hate to see a bad one. Or even a mildly annoying one.'

Ewan swore under his breath, removing the phone from his mouth as he did so.

'Ewan? Don't go quiet on me. I've looked forward to this chat for a while.'

'Alright,' Ewan answered, reaching into his brain to switch on manipulation mode. 'Nat didn't blind my best mate. My best mate was murdered by Oliver Roth two months ago. And I'm looking forward to getting my revenge.'

'Oliver's looking forward to bringing his kill count into double figures,' Grant replied. 'So rest assured, he can't wait for the reunion either.'

Confirming that Oliver Roth really is still alive. Thank you, Nick.

'Oh, and while I'm at it,' Ewan continued, 'Kate was never my girlfriend. Your lovely daughter is my girlfriend, and she absolutely hates you.'

Grant wasn't offended.

In fact, he laughed.

'Oh, I've known for a while. Ever since you made that "great kisser" comment to Iain. And it's no big surprise she sees something in you… she always was a little faulty. Maybe she inherited that personality defect. Not from myself or Sheila, of course.'

'What the hell's that supposed to mean?'

'Ask her yourself if you survive the night. It's better coming from her than me. Besides, you wouldn't believe me if I told you.'

Several nasty, spider-like thoughts tried to crawl around in Ewan's brain. Before the anxiety could take root, he was distracted by a yell from Jack. He was still crying, perhaps having compressed the shirt too tight against his burst eye.

'So what's your plan now?' asked Grant. 'What are you planning to do with a near-empty airship, now you can no longer rescue anyone you value?'

'Well what do you know, you wouldn't believe me if I told you either.'

'Try me.'

'What would *you* do in my position?' Ewan said, with determination and laughter blended in his voice. 'Screw you, Mr Grant. With all my heart, and for every dead member of my family, *screw you*. You deserve what you get tonight. Farewell.'

Ewan hung up the phone, as quick as he could before Grant had a chance to reference his mum, dad, aunt, uncle or cousin Alfie. He had probably memorised their names, in order to use them against him.

He looked behind him again. Jack was stood on his feet: knees bent and arms waving around for something to cling onto, but stood on his feet. Wow, he was brave. Ewan ran towards him and offered him a shoulder to wrap his arm around.

'I'm sorry, Jack,' he said. 'Really, truly sorry. If I hadn't suggested—'

'Blaming yourself for other people's actions,' Jack whimpered. 'You're worse than me. What did Grant say?'

'He just called to taunt us. Didn't work.'

'He wouldn't have called up just to chat… he would have wanted something. Did you give him any clues about your plan?'

Ewan grinned, as much as he could grin under the circumstances. 'I confirmed what he already suspected. That was enough. Jack… if you were to keep parachutes on board this airship, where would you keep them?'

'I'm not in a thinking mood right now…'

'So… you haven't worked out what's going to happen?'

'Ewan, *please* just make it easy for me.'

Ewan walked to the front of the bridge with Jack hanging onto his shoulder, and showed him the beauty of the darkened countryside. Even through one eye, it must have looked incredible.

'Jack, what's the most obvious thing two "terrorists" can do with an enormous airship under their control? Especially when they're desperate and can't do anything useful on board?'

Jack thought for a moment, and sunk his head.

'You let him believe it.'

'He'd already decided what to believe. I just let him confirm it to himself.'

They had discussed the idea with Rubinstein, just briefly, back when the whole horrifying mission had been nothing more than a set of theoretical plans. Rubinstein had dismissed the idea altogether, but now the prisoners were dead and there was nothing left to lose. It was worth a try.

Ewan would *never* have used the airship as an enormous missile to destroy New London's western wall, regardless of what Grant believed. Not out of fear of losing his own life, but because it just wouldn't work. Grant would blast his wife's airship out of the sky before seeing his lead Citadel damaged.

'I think I know where to find the parachutes...' Jack moaned.

At that moment, a wailing noise sounded from one of the control panels. Ewan ran over to it, and found himself to be proven right. All along, they had never needed to bring down the airship themselves.

The bright and loud '*INCOMING MISSILES*' warning showed that Nicholas Grant was capable of doing the job alone.

Chapter 24

Ewan ran down the corridors with one arm pointing his rifle forwards, and the other stretched out to his side just in case Jack needed to grab on to him. His half-blind friend was slow and uncoordinated, but coping brilliantly under the circumstances.

'Keep going, Jack, you're doing well.'

'Of course I'll keep going. What else am I going to do?'

Ewan didn't like people who provided fake encouragement, or reassurance based on nothing. He preferred people to be honest rather than offer false positivity. He reminded himself of those people as he spoke to Jack... but in all fairness, Jack really *was* doing well.

There were no clones along the journey to Pearce's escape pod. Ewan was almost disappointed: he wanted at least one opportunity to check how accurately Jack could aim. Then again, his friend had been through enough – and was about to go through even more.

Ewan found the entrance to the escape pod's tiny chamber, and found the outer door still open. Inside was a tiny airlock, now sealed shut, and an assortment of emergency resources around its sides.

Including six parachutes.

Ewan plucked out two of the parachutes, and looked through the airlock window. He found the outline of a downward tunnel, which must have led to the bottom of the airship. The escape pod itself was missing.

'He's gone,' Ewan growled.

'We can still find him before Grant does,' gasped Jack. 'His parachutes will be open and we'll just watch where they go…'

Jack fell silent as Ewan threw one of the parachutes in his direction. He caught it approximately, his depth perception gone forever.

Ewan and Jack shared mutual expressions of fear. With the parachutes in their hands, their immediate future began to feel real.

'I don't think I can do this…' said Jack.

'Me neither. But guess what, we're doing it. Let's get to the hangar.'

He didn't stick around for a debate. Jack's objections would only be out of fear, and the missiles were coming. Ewan started to run, and Jack followed behind him.

'Why didn't Pearce take the parachutes with him?' Jack shouted.

'Because the escape pod has its own, duh.'

'No, I mean, why didn't he take them so *we* couldn't use them?'

'Because he thought we were planning to stay on board. He thought we were too stupid to predict Grant's missile attack.'

Or that we'd be too scared to jump anyway.

He might even be right about that.

The hangar was the best place to run. Not only would it have an opening into the sky too big to miss, but Ewan held on to the faint hope that a functioning helicopter might still be there.

They arrived to the sight of a total ruin: a metallic graveyard of advanced technology, with clone bodies strewn around the helipads and bits of helicopter debris rolling along the tilted floor towards the hangar exit. Ewan sighed. Kate had done far too good a job of defending herself in the sky.

Hopefully she's still out there, keeping herself safe... despite her guns being empty.

Ewan scanned the wreckage. None of the helicopters remained intact. He and Jack would have to jump.

Ewan found himself slowing down the closer he got to the edge of the airship. The view across the countryside was so much more frightening with the wind around his face. He had long acclimatised to the tilt towards the back of the ship, but it became uncomfortable once again when he saw how the decline led directly into thin air.

'Still can't do it,' said Jack from too far behind him.

'Come here, Jack. I'm not leaving you alone, and I'm not dying here either.'

As Jack approached, Ewan looked over the edge. He thought it would be better to get the shock out of the way early, but instead he was struck with a devastating sense of vertigo at the sheer *nothing* that appeared beneath the platform he stood on.

'I can't jump...' Jack said.

'You're at least putting it on.'

Ewan demonstrated how to put on his parachute, and prayed to whoever was up there that he was doing it right. He was high enough in the sky for his prayers to be heard louder, and close enough to Raj for the lad to put in a good word for him. Once the straps were tightened and the backpack was fastened the best way he knew how, he checked Jack's too. He was taking longer, nowhere close to overcoming his struggles with hand-eye coordination. With Ewan's help his parachute was fixed in place, but Grant's missiles must have soared miles closer in the time it had taken them.

When Ewan turned back to the exit, his toe nudged a small cylindrical piece of metal – most likely a chunk of dead helicopter. It rolled towards the edge for half a metre before it fell into the sky and instantaneously vanished from view. No dramatic tumbling through the air, and no sound whatsoever: it just disappeared, never to be seen again. A shiver ran through Ewan's spine at the merciless nature of physics, which he and Jack were soon to entrust themselves to.

'Right, Jack,' he said, 'listen carefully. I'm going to tell you what to do.'

'What… you've skydived before?'

'No. You've got to be eighteen before they let you do that. But my dad told me a bunch of stuff, and I watched a ton of YouTube afterwards.'

'Oh bloody hell…'

There was no condescension in Jack's voice. Just fear.

'Once you're out there,' Ewan began, 'give yourself time to get used to freefall. It'll feel different to anything you've felt before, but you've got loads of time. A minute, easily.'

'Where's the cord?'

'Here. But don't pull it right away. You need to freefall most of the distance. On the way down, spread your arms and legs wide. It'll increase the wind resistance and slow you down a bit. You'll have more time to think.'

'When do we pull it?'

Ewan bit his lip. He knew the numerical answer was two to four thousand feet, but he had no perception of how high that actually was. It would be guesswork.

'Just after I do,' he answered. 'We'll keep each other in sight and once I've pulled it, you do the same.'

'I'm scared, Ewan.'

Ewan could no longer hear Jack's faded voice over the wind. But by the shape of his lips, that was probably what he was gasping.

'Once your chute's open,' Ewan said, louder to make sure he was heard himself, 'keep yourself vertical. Stand up straight. Some handles will deploy with the parachute and you can pull them left and right to navigate yourself. Go for a nice flat field, and *whatever you do*, pull your feet up when you land. If you hit the ground with your legs, you break them.'

Jack had his mouth half-open, as if trying to ask a question he couldn't find the words for, but Ewan knew they didn't have time. Jack had one of those brains that needed to know every single detail before taking any plunge, so that the plunge felt more like a gentle easing into a pool. But by the time he'd be done asking questions, the whole airship would have exploded around them.

'And in answer to your *final* question,' Ewan said, 'they work almost one hundred percent of the time. As long as you follow what I said. There's an emergency cord too. Ready?'

An evil thought occurred in Ewan's mind: one that he refused to recognise as his own.

Pearce didn't need to steal these parachutes. He just needed to sabotage them and wait for us to use them.

'I'm not ready,' said Jack, 'but I'm doing it.'

Ewan was no longer so sure himself, but as he and Jack lined up their toes against the yellow and black warning zig-zags on the hangar floor, he decided to go for it. Given a choice between dying on a burning airship or dying through a sabotaged parachute, he would choose the death with the better view. He imagined Jack would too, but decided not to put the thought in his friend's head.

'Three... two...'

'I can't do it!'

'Tough crap. Three... two... one...'

Ewan wrapped his arm through Jack's, held him tight, and ran off the side of the hangar's exit into the night sky.

Holy blood-pissing hellfire!

Outside the airship, the world changed. Ewan's perception of everything around him was thrown into disarray, and the roar of the *Sheila* fell silent, replaced by aggressive winds and absolutely nothing else.

Ewan's body tumbled around, upside down and round in circles, and the grip of Jack's arm revealed his friend was going through the same. Right up until their grip broke, and Jack vanished somewhere into the night air.

However long Ewan West would live – minutes, weeks or even years – he would never be able to describe the feeling of freefall. In people's day-to-day lives, they were only aware of the 360 degrees surrounding them, and saw the world in terms of front, back, left and right. People didn't spend much time looking up or down. Out in the empty sky, a whole *sphere* of directions hit Ewan's consciousness at once, the intensity of the surrounding sky enveloping him.

It was frightening beyond words. It would have been enthralling or exciting, except death was rising towards him at over a hundred miles per hour. Ewan already had visions of his parachute failing, his body pancaking against the ground, and his dead remains being eaten away by crows or foxes while the rest of the world didn't even notice.

Ewan levelled himself out, faced downwards and lay flat on his belly, stretching his arms and legs out as far as he could. He coughed and gasped for oxygen: up to then he hadn't even realised he was holding his breath. Perhaps it was instinct. Humans weren't *supposed* to be able to breathe in conditions as inhospitable as this.

Once his freefall had stabilised, Ewan took a look at the vast expanse of Oxfordshire beneath him. Eighteen months ago, the streetlights and lit houses would have made the view beautifully patterned and elegant. Instead his eyes were met with pitiless, apathetic darkness.

Except for a few circular flashes of white. Far below and somewhere to his right, Nathaniel Pearce's pod had activated its parachutes. Ewan tried his best to analyse its trajectory and predict which village it would land in, but wasn't able to do so accurately.

Meanwhile… where the hell was Jack?

Ewan's question was answered straight away, as the only other shape in the sky flickered beneath him. Jack had fallen a little faster, but had straightened himself out too. By the looks of it, he was trying to steer himself towards Pearce.

Jack's body fluttered between darkness and light, and Ewan had a nasty feeling about what that meant. He rolled over onto his back just in time before the shockwave and noise hit him, and saw the *Sheila* ablaze in the sky above. Grant's missiles pummelled into its bridge, its sides and its underbelly, with merciless exploding force. Several of them hit the remaining engines, finally concluding the Underdogs' work. The airship seemed to halt in the sky before it tipped forwards. Ewan turned around, with a satisfied smile on his face for the first time that evening.

The burning airship lit up the countryside as if Oxfordshire had its own miniature sun. The ground was hardly bright, but little details could be made out. The flailing of Jack's arms and legs were perfectly clear.

He won't see me when I pull the cord…

Ewan gulped, stretched himself pencil-thin, and tipped downwards.

The wind was even more intense at maximum speed. Ewan had once heard the phrase 'terminal velocity' used in his physics class – something to do with how fast a falling object could possibly go – and this must have been what it felt like. He just hoped it wouldn't be *literally* terminal for him.

He caught up with Jack in what felt like twenty seconds, and dipped far enough below for his friend to see his demonstration. Then, without thinking, he pulled his cord.

His worries about Pearce's sabotage had been unfounded. His body rocked around, and when he came to his senses he was upright in his harness, swaying to and fro with a fully opened parachute above his head. The noise of the wind had stopped, and the world was quiet. He felt the cold against his bare arms and vest: the natural chill of night rather than the intense wind. Even the crackles of the airship above didn't seem—

Jack fell past him at a speed he had never seen a human travel. He continued to fall, the ground close enough for pathways in people's gardens to be visible.

Pull it, Jack… come on, bloody pull it…

Has Pearce sabotaged…?

It took too long for comfort, but Jack succeeded. Ewan's last ally, partially blinded and scared out of his wits, had operated the parachute to perfection. It opened beneath Ewan with no visible problems, and moments later it changed direction. Jack was already navigating towards the escape pod.

Ewan looked in the direction Pearce's escape pod had been, to find empty sky. It seemed to have already landed: something white and oddly shaped had appeared on a village green somewhere.

A huge piece of debris roared less than half a mile from

Ewan's parachute. Parts of the *Sheila* were falling around him and Jack.

If I get hit right now, it'd be the worst luck ever.

I'm not beginning to believe in luck, am I? I don't want to, but I can't see what else can help me...

The pieces of debris started to strike the ground, several hundred metres apart from each other. Ewan noticed one heading towards the same village green: it careered straight into a neighbouring house which exploded under it.

As tragic as it would be for the homeowners if they lived long enough to be freed – if they *were* ever freed – the destruction made things easier for Ewan. Wherever he landed, he would head in the vague direction of the village and then follow the light of the fires. Pearce wouldn't be far away.

The ground was close. Horribly close. Ewan had been afraid of the fall but *terrified* of the landing. And Jack would hit the ground first.

To his credit, Jack had found a decent-sized field. Ewan didn't have the remaining altitude to change course and follow him, so he aimed for another field across the road. The overgrown rows of its crops were becoming progressively more detailed in the vague moonlight.

Ewan saw Jack land. He didn't see the details, didn't hear any shouts of pain, but equally didn't see any movement afterwards. Jack was on the ground, his welfare a total mystery. Ewan squeezed his fingers tight against his harness. As Kate had always said, the worst part of any type of anxiety was *not knowing* something.

It was a cruel irony, Ewan realised, that he didn't know whether Kate was alive either. The worst part of her absence was not knowing too.

The wild crops in the field reached up to grab Ewan. He lifted his legs and gritted his teeth.

When he landed it was a soft impact: his relatively slow speed and the cushioning of the sagging wild crops helped him. Ewan rolled over, checked his body for anywhere that hurt, and laughed aloud when he realised the truth: that he had leapt out of an airship thousands of feet in the sky, used a parachute with nothing more than YouTube training and his dad's words of advice, and got out unscathed. His only wound was the bullet-graze to his forearm, which he had long forgotten about.

He unclipped every clip and unfastened every strap he could find, and crawled towards the freedom beyond his parachute. Ewan West stood in an actual field with his hands clutching his head in disbelief, the soil beneath him feeling odd against his boots. He looked to the sky at the airship he and his friends had spent the evening on, now no more than an enormous fireball that broke into pieces and disintegrated into the countryside.

Ewan tried not to think of the contents of the airship that would also be spread around the countryside. Namely the bodies of Scott, Zane, Tona, nearly 400 other innocent prisoners, Oli Sharp, countless clone soldiers, and Dr Gwen Crossland. Plus any remaining human staff members who were sure to die somewhere between the sky and the ground.

Ewan looked into the neighbouring field and found the other white parachute motionless among the long grass.

'*Jack!*'

Ewan knew he didn't have to focus on his own safety. No clones would be around, and Pearce was at least a village away. Ewan ran across the road, leapt into Jack's field, ran at full pelt towards his parachute and scrambled underneath.

'Jack…'

Jack was moving, at least. He winced and whimpered, and

when Ewan rose to his knees to lift the parachute upward, he saw Jack's hands clutched against his side.

'Are... a-are you OK?' Jack gasped and spluttered.

'I'm fine,' said Ewan. 'You?'

'My side... Don't worry, I'm not dying. Just winded. But bloody hell it hurts... I lifted up my legs like you said, so my arse hit the ground first. I rolled badly and bits of me hit all over the place.'

At that moment, Ewan had a horrible thought. When his father had taught him about lifting his legs, he was talking about the dive that Ewan had planned to do after his eighteenth birthday. It would have been a tandem jump, with an instructor strapped to his back, since Ewan would have been unqualified to jump alone. In a tandem dive it was always the instructor who did the landing rather than the passenger. All the passenger did was lift their legs and wait for the instructor to do the difficult bit.

Long story short, Ewan's bad guidance would be responsible for whatever injuries Jack had sustained. But Jack said he was going to live, and Ewan had faith in him.

'Go get Pearce,' Jack said with a cough. 'Leave me here. I'll be safe.'

Ewan looked at Jack's belt, and saw his pistol still strapped to his waist. Incredibly, it had survived the fall without separating from him. If someone came for Jack, he could defend himself for a while. Ewan checked his own belt and found the same: the rifles may have been too awkward to carry on the journey down, but he still had a gun with eight bullets.

'Well done, Jack,' Ewan said. 'You did yourself proud. I mean it. Truly.'

'You too, Ewan.'

Ewan initially thought it was a generic polite response, but

Jack was staring into his face – his remaining left eye holding the seriousness of two regular eyes combined.

And, perhaps through the joy of surviving a fall from an airship, he was stimming his fingers once again.

'You may not feel proud of yourself,' Jack continued, 'but believe me, this was one hell of a mission to lead a strike team through. No matter what happens next, no matter what's already happened, you did a bloody good job leading us. Now go get Pearce.'

'I'll take out his eye first if you want,' Ewan said with a wry smile.

'Don't focus on revenge. Focus on making him dead. I don't care how.'

Ewan reached out an arm, and he and Jack shook hands. It wasn't a hand-clasp like they often did, but a true adult handshake. Perhaps they really were growing up. Ewan smiled at his friend in genuine admiration, before turning and crawling back out from under the parachute.

As he got to his feet again, Ewan thought that maybe Jack was right. He often was. Ewan had spent the last month wondering what McCormick would have thought to his lacklustre leadership, and had always made the assumption that his mentor would have been disappointed with his lead soldier's shortcomings. But maybe, just maybe, the soul of McCormick would have looked upon him just as the physical man had always done: deeply proud of every single accomplishment Ewan had achieved, against odds that had always been set against him.

And maybe, just maybe, Ewan wasn't as bad a person as he kept telling himself.

But it wasn't the right moment for pride. Not just yet. Ewan remembered the urgency of his situation, sprinted back for the road and followed it towards the neighbouring village.

Gwen Crossland was dead. Acceleration had died with her. The airship was a gargantuan burning wreck plummeting towards the ground. Only one piece of Grant's plan remained alive: the inventor of the clone soldier, and the architect of every horrifying creation the Underdogs had ever fought against. If Grant's Chief Scientist got back to New London, the chance to stop their master plan may be lost forever.

Ewan ran for the village in search of Nathaniel Pearce, and he did so alone.

Chapter 25

Oliver Roth could see Spitfire's Rise a few hundred metres away. According to his GPS coordinates, it was the house with the white paint on Church Lane. The one surrounded by hundreds of clones.

It was a posh-looking house with old-fashioned architecture, far from the squalid slum he had expected the Underdogs to be occupying. More than anything else, it looked like a house that had been loved, both before and after Takeover Day. Despite the struggles of isolated living and the cramped conditions, perhaps the rebels had managed to live a comfortable life inside its cosy walls. Until tonight, at least.

Roth looked down at his hands, and remembered the eight Underdog lives they had taken away. They had used everything from a sniper rifle to a fire axe to reach that number. Within minutes, Roth hoped to finally crack double figures; there had to be plenty of them inside, and killing two in a surprise attack would be easy enough.

And they would be even easier to find with him and Colonel Pereira standing on the trapdoor to their escape tunnel. Roth looked down at the grassy square that had stood out just a little too much during his perimeter search: he had predicted that a group led by a mathematics lecturer would have been too smart to use the front door, and a trapdoor had been the most obvious alternative. It must have taken them months to dig that tunnel into the neighbouring field, only for Roth and Pereira to use it as their entry point.

'What are you thinking, Oliver?' came Colonel Pereira's voice from behind him.

He probably meant the question in a strategic sense, asking what Roth's plan of action was. But in the literal sense, it was a complex question.

Oliver Roth was thinking about a squirrel he had killed at the age of ten. More specifically, he was thinking of the thought process that had gone through his mind: the opportunity he had been presented with, the total lack of consequences there'd be to his actions, the curiosity about what it would look like if he did… and the little voice in his head that told him he could still *just walk away*.

Age and experience hadn't made that little voice of reason any louder. Within four years, Oliver Roth had gone from killing a squirrel to slaughtering human combatants.

And yet, McCormick had reached out to him that night.

A few months ago he had tortured a man called Adnan Shah – the Chief Architect of the northern wall – and Roth's performance had gone beyond what Nathaniel Pearce had commanded. He had been far too creative, and the poor man had died a week later.

And yet, McCormick had insisted that Oliver Roth was salvageable.

He had brought the decapitated head of Raj Singh into a meeting, and used it as a prop to prove a point to his superiors.

And yet, McCormick would have happily taken him in as an Underdog if they had escaped New London together that night.

But McCormick was dead. Adnan Shah and Raj Singh were dead. McCormick's detonation had killed Iain Marshall and brought Roth right to the top of Grant's military pyramid. Nearly *everyone* Roth had come into meaningful contact with had been killed, and he sat on a throne built upon other people's dead bodies.

Oliver Roth came to realise the truth: that the world had become a worse place because he had been in it.

'Oliver?' asked Pereira. 'What are we going to do?'

He's right behind me. I could draw my knife, spin round and slash his throat. I could tell 500 clones to head further north, say that I made a navigation error and tell them Pereira's staying here just in case. I could blame his death on Ewan or whoever, and people would believe me.

I have that kind of power now. I have that kind of influence. I can get away with anything, good or bad.

It was the squirrel situation all over again. He was back in that forest not far from his house, a rifle in his grip and the assurance of no consequences. Now, just like then, the events of the night would be decided by what kind of person he truly was.

'You *are* listening to me, right?'

Roth realised he wouldn't kill João Pereira. The fat colonel was a decent man, and had served him well as his human companion. Having Pereira around had kept him away from his worst impulses. After all, what would Roth have done in the countryside with an army of clones without any humans watching him?

'Yeah,' Roth answered. 'Just give me a moment to think.'

'What's there to think about? Just order them all to open fire against the house, wait until it's pretty much crumbled, then invade and finish off any survivors.'

Roth looked ahead. Five hundred clones surrounded

Spitfire's Rise. Half of them – including all the biorifle soldiers – lay at a distance of a hundred or so metres, to protect themselves from returning fire and crumbling debris. The other half – including the hundred hawk-eyed scout clones – formed a second perimeter in case another exit tunnel existed, although Roth suspected he had found the only one.

Everything in his life over the last thirteen months had led him to this moment. And McCormick was still dead. But Grant was alive, and waiting for him to come home.

I have a choice between keeping my lifestyle the way it is, or honouring a dead man and his friends who wouldn't accept me anyway.

Besides, these guys have already lost the war. They were doomed from Takeover Day and anyone without special needs would have known it.

You know what? Screw it. Killing that squirrel was the best thing I ever did. If I hadn't gone down that oh-so-horrible path, I'd be trapped in New London with Mum and Dad and the rest of them. That squirrel died for me to rise above everyone else, and I've made its sacrifice worth it.

Roth didn't claim to have much wisdom, but he knew people were defined by their actions, not their thoughts. He had no control over McCormick's appearances inside his mind any more than he had a choice in breathing. But he *could* choose how he reacted, in the full knowledge of who it made him.

Oliver Gabriel Roth had decided who he was.

He reached for his radio.

'All units on the inner perimeter,' he said, 'open fire.'

There was a short silence between the end of his order, the switching of 500 clones to war mode, and the subsequent sputter of bullets. In those seconds, Roth had just enough time to pocket his radio, cup his hands around his mouth, and call

out with his loudest voice towards the white building on
Church Lane.

'*Surprise, retards!*'

The house before him was pummelled with hundreds, perhaps thousands of bullets per second. In the dead of night, the
white house began to fade towards darkness as its paint was
chipped away. Somewhere in Heaven, if Roth could possibly
have believed in such a place, McCormick's soul must have
been crying. Roth ignored the thought: his conscientious side
was dying by the moment anyway.

Five seconds of watching was enough. He opened the
grassy trapdoor and dropped himself into the makeshift
tunnel.

'We're going in?' asked Pereira from above. 'I thought we
were waiting here for them to escape?'

'This building's not collapsing until I've seen its insides.
Come on, we'll kill them faster this way.'

Roth switched on the torch at the front of his rifle as
Pereira dropped onto the wooden floorboards behind him.
The tunnel didn't seem to have an opposite entrance: just
muddy wall to muddy wall, stopping at a dead end. Roth continued his walk anyway. The tunnel must have served *some*
purpose: the Underdogs had always been smarter than Grant
had given them credit for.

He edged towards the end of the tunnel, shining his rifle
torch around, suspecting a trap. He approached the mud wall
at the end, wondering if there was more to it than met the
eye.

'Oliver?' whispered Pereira behind him.

When Roth shone the torch on the far-left side of the door,
he saw a gap in the mud. One that could only have been made
by human fingertips.

Is that... a door handle of some sort?

Oliver Roth may have been quick to work out that the rebels had decorated the muddy entrance to conceal it, but he was too slow to move when the door rammed outwards into his face.

The young man behind the door must have been trying to evacuate through the tunnel, perhaps just as surprised as Roth when they collided. But the lad with the funny-shaped face recovered before Roth could come to his senses, and snatched the assassin's rifle from his loosening hands.

As the boy took aim and laid his finger on the trigger, Roth had no time to do anything except leap backwards. He fell onto his back along the muddy floorboards as the figure at the door shot half a dozen rifle bullets, straight through the air where Roth had stood one and a half seconds earlier. Most of them struck Pereira in his Kevlar, but one burrowed through his voice box.

There had been no time for Roth to breathe, let alone call out and warn Pereira. The colonel had been doomed before he could even bend his legs to move, and his body collapsed to the floorboards, landing on top of Roth. There was a moment of eye contact between the assassin and the boy with Down's Syndrome who had disarmed him, before Roth hauled Pereira's own rifle from under his body. Seeing the threat, the boy slammed the door shut again.

Bloody hell, Colonel João Pereira just got killed by the Down's kid.

A set of weak, erratic coughs revealed that Pereira wasn't yet dead. One of his hands reached for the side of Roth's head, perhaps looking for comfort or guidance, but Roth pushed it away. There was no time for niceties when his life was on the line too.

Roth crawled out from under his colleague with his assault rifle in hand, scrambled to his feet and charged back for the mud-covered door. When he reached it he lined his back against the wall – positioning himself behind where the door would open – and waited.

Perhaps the Down's kid was waiting for Roth to open the door himself. Or perhaps he knew Roth wouldn't be that stupid. Either way, the bullet-storm in his house above ensured that there was no other escape.

The door burst open again, the muddy side stopping an inch from Roth's face and concealing him from view against the wall. The boy, not giving his enemy a millisecond to fire first, released a stream of bullets along the tunnel. Roth responded with three bullets of his own which burst through the mud and wood of the door. A yelp sounded, and his enemy fell to the tunnel floor. One more bullet in his back finished the boy off.

Roth looked down at his ninth Underdog victim, and saw how young he had been.

That was… what was his name again? Sam or Simon?

Roth glanced back down the tunnel. Colonel Pereira was no longer moving. He must have died during the wait for the door to open. Roth knelt down to the dead teenager on the floor to snatch his own rifle back, holding a level of grudging respect for him. The boy with Down's Syndrome had lasted thirteen months as a guerrilla soldier, and his final achievement in life had been disarming an assassin and defeating a colonel in single combat.

But a surge of adrenalin was seeping into Roth's brain. Without Pereira to watch over him, the final restriction on his animalistic personality was gone. Alone in Spitfire's Rise, with nobody he was accountable to, he could be whoever he wanted.

Roth realised he couldn't carry both rifles at once, so he ripped out the ammunition magazine from one of them and tucked it into his pocket before casting the empty weapon aside. He stepped over the boy's body, leapt around the door and entered the cellar just in time to see a bulky pair of legs vanishing up the stairs to the ground floor. It was one of the men. Roth was pretty sure it was Mark. He smiled: Mark Gunnarsson was one of the Underdogs he had been looking forward to duelling.

The cellar was loaded with weapons: shotguns, knives, grenades, assault rifles, and enough of them to make Roth's bedroom armoury look timid in comparison. But the Down's kid had needed to disarm him rather than use his own weapon, and Mark had run up the stairs rather than face him: two seemingly clear signs that the firearms were emptied of bullets. Maybe the Underdogs had decided that impulsive special needs kids were safer with their guns and ammunition stored far away from each other. But Roth's combat instincts told him to look for other reasons Mark could have been running, and he found one.

Roth looked to the floor, and spotted the grenade two metres from his feet. He ran and booted it to the corner of the cellar, where it exploded with a sound that sent his ears ringing, but did him no physical damage. Roth checked the number of grenades on his own belt, and grinned.

Before he went upstairs, he checked around the room one more time. It was lit with a single bulb: somehow, the rebels had electricity. There were two other exits made from make-shift wooden doors, but Roth didn't see them as time-sensitive targets. Not while Mark was running around, almost certainly without a firearm, in the main part of the house. Besides, if any rebels were hiding in those two rooms they were welcome to escape, skip over two dead bodies and get shot by the perimeter clones outside.

'All units,' Roth said into his radio, 'cease fire. I'm inside the house. Repeat, cease fire.'

He crept up the stairs with his rifle pointed forward, wondering whether Mark would be waiting outside the top door to knife him in the chest once he entered. When Roth burst through the door he found Mark nowhere to be seen. Perhaps he had hidden behind a sofa, sheltering from the bullets of several hundred clones.

Roth decided not to play hide and seek. He fetched out his own grenade and tossed it into the living room.

The explosion sent a fireball through the room where the Underdogs must have socialised together, cried together, and celebrated their victories together. The dying part of Roth that cared about such things made a little wail, but was blocked out by a manly scream from the far end of the living room. Roth charged for the doorway and fired rifle bullets towards the figure vanishing into the kitchen, who leapt off his feet like a desperate goalkeeper and landed behind the wall. Roth's bullets missed.

'*Try again, ginger twat!*' Mark yelled.

'Oh – it's like that, is it?!' Roth yelled back, spraying ammunition across the walls. Even if he wasn't lucky enough for them to hit the figure on the other side, it would scare him. It'd be good to see a man like Mark getting scared.

Roth ran into the kitchen and a hunting knife flew past his face, embedding itself into the peeling wallpaper with a solid *thunk*. Roth grinned as he turned, knowing that Mark may have wasted his only weapon. There was no way he had a firearm if he was desperate enough to throw a knife. Mark himself was nowhere to be seen, but surely in the kitchen and in the direction the knife had come from... and unarmed again.

Gunfire sounded outside. A lot of it.

Bloody hell, why are clones so, so stupid?! When I said cease fire, I meant it!

It was coming from outside the nearest window. Thankfully, the bullets didn't seem to be hitting the building. Roth reached for his radio regardless.

'All units, I've already bloody told you, *stop*—'

Mark emerged, running at full pelt from the utility room, and barged straight into Roth. There was no time for Roth to do anything other than squeeze his rifle as tight as he could, ensuring Mark would not pull it from his grip. Roth found himself slammed against the kitchen doorframe with the force that only a hardened youth offender could deliver, and as he fell to his knees Mark made a running jump for the window.

It shattered upon impact, and must have carved up Mark spectacularly. But despite his special needs background, Mark wasn't stupid. He'd have known he stood a better chance of survival by leaping through glass shards towards gunfire than he would have done against Roth unarmed. Especially when the gunfire seemed...

Roth stood up and ran for the smashed window. By the time he peeked through the empty frame Mark had already reached the road, staggering through his glass injuries past a row of dead clone bodies.

What the hell killed them?!

A pair of muzzle flashes answered him, lighting up further clone bodies as they fell to the street. They were single flashes rather than strobe flashes, hinting that the Underdogs' reinforcements had nothing more than basic pistols.

Roth picked out a second grenade and launched it as far as he could. It didn't reach Mark before it exploded, but it shone a light on his two friends. In the split second of grenade light Roth saw who they were. One was the older lady, and the other was...

Bloody hell... she really is still alive.

In the short-lived grenade flash, Shannon Grant made eye

contact with Oliver Roth, and used the moment to convey just how much she *hated* him. Roth grinned back. No matter how much she had achieved, even in saving a wounded Mark, Shannon had still chosen the losing side.

The trio had clearly run out of ammunition. They ran for the dead bodies of the clones to steal their assault rifles, but further gunfire chased them away. Shannon, Mark and the old lady were forced out into the countryside, without weapons and under pursuit.

Roth turned and made his way back to the cellar. With Mark gone from the building, there was no reason to keep his remaining clones from attacking.

'All units,' he said as he descended the cellar steps again, 'those who aren't busy with the three rebels can open fire again.'

Roth's soldiers did as he commanded, the rattling of bullets sounding above him once again. It was time to check those other two exits.

He opened the door to one, and found nothing but a petrol generator. That answered the question about their electricity. He walked to the other side of the cellar, opened the other door, and found a tunnel that led to a stepladder at its far end. Roth followed the path, confident that his soldiers weren't firing upon the neighbouring house.

He rose up the stepladder and found a man tied to a chair.

The man looked familiar: black, short hair, muscular. But the devastation in his face was new to him.

This is Alex Ginelli. We've met on the battlefield a few times. But he always seemed in better spirits than this. Then again, he wasn't tied to a chair.

I don't remember that massive scar on his cheek, either.

Alex looked up, aghast. The image of Oliver Roth in his

home must have horrified him beyond words. And with good reason, since he was utterly helpless to do anything about it.

He thought I was dead, too. Right up to this exact moment. I'm watching the expression of a man finding out that his deadliest enemy is still alive, and is going to kill him. Yeah, this was worth the wait.

'So, Alex…' Roth began, 'why exactly are you tied to that chair?'

Alex gasped. The tears were already in his eyes.

'Let me guess,' Roth continued, half-remembering some details in a report he'd been made to read. 'You were a victim of Acceleration, your mates found out and now they're afraid you'll kill them.'

The first of Alex's tears dripped onto the soil beneath him. Up to that moment, Roth hadn't realised that the room was a farm. The sprouting vegetables looked surprisingly good; no surprise, after thirteen months of practice.

Alex coughed out a sentence.

'Ewan's going to *kill* you for what you did tonight…'

'Oh no, you mean kill me for real this time? Maybe you should focus more on your last words. Or waste time thinking about how much of a failure you are. Makes no difference to me. In a few seconds it won't make a difference to you either.'

Alex's facial expression didn't change, which Roth found annoying. In fact, even the flow of his tears seemed to stop.

'I played my role in this war and I played it well,' Alex said strongly, like he meant it, but unable to hide his despondence. 'A year of successful missions… I killed far more clones than you've killed humans… I even made it to Floor C one time…'

'Wow, impressive,' said Roth with a sarcastic laugh.

'It doesn't matter what Gwen Crossland did,' Alex said, daring to look into Roth's eyes. 'I still achieved more in my life than your squeaky-voiced pre-pubescent arse ever will.'

'And yet, here I am, about to put you out of your misery.'

'There is no misery. I worked out a while ago that my journey as an Underdog is over, and I've had plenty of time to make peace with it. So do what you're going to do, piss off back to your fancypants fortress, and tell Gwen Crossland she's a bitch.'

Roth offered a sympathetic expression, and spoke softly.

'Don't worry. I'm sure she knows.'

There was a moment of solemn silence, and then Alex let out a grieving laugh. Roth laughed too. The laughter ended when he saw Alex making one final brave struggle against the ropes surrounding him, and decided enough was enough. He shot Alex with two bullets: one in the chest and another in the head.

The dead body of Alex looked sad rather than terrified. Roth took a moment to try to remember the reports he had read about the Ginelli Project, and the psychological profiles they had contained. If he remembered rightly, Alex had died the way he had lived: alone.

And that was it. Ten dead Underdogs by Oliver Roth's hands. It had taken him more than a year, but he had finally reached double figures. His dying voice of decency tried to make him feel less proud, but Roth leapt back into the tunnel again with a renewed sense of achievement. Besides, he could go home again the moment he was finished with the building's infrastructure.

'All units,' he began as he entered the armoury and replenished his supply of grenades, 'cease fire once and for all. I'm sweeping the rooms and burning them. Repeat, cease fire once and for all.'

Roth entered the main house again, now full of creaking noises, wooden splinters and plasterboard across the floor, and headed straight upstairs. He strode from room to room, systematically opening doors, checking for survivors, throwing in grenades and covering his ears. The first bedroom was set on fire with an incendiary grenade for maximum effect. He destroyed the disused bathroom with a regular grenade, since nothing flammable lay within. The other bedrooms were each set alight by an incendiary grenade on the bedsheets.

The last upstairs room – a clinic of some sort – was destroyed in a similar way.

Stood on the landing, Roth looked upwards and decided to cover all possibilities. He opened fire across the ceiling in case survivors remained in the attic, before concentrating his fire against the hatch. The single grenade he tossed upwards sent the ceiling into collapse, and he leapt back onto the stairs just in time.

The same little voice of decency, which had spent the last five minutes gasping for breath, told him to take a closer look at the boxes which fell from the annihilated attic. He was sure some of the photos displayed a younger version of Joseph McCormick. The man must have used the attic to store his personal effects, suggesting he had a heartfelt connection to the place before Takeover Day.

There must have been answers, but Roth didn't care about objects so close to burning. Almost nobody else on Earth cared about the fate of McCormick's things either.

Roth headed downstairs as the upper floor burned behind him, then he gave the ground floor the same treatment. As the house heated up, he could almost feel the word 'provisional' burning away from his contract. He smiled at the thought. The role of Head of Military was his for good.

The more rooms he destroyed, the more the fires began to overwhelm him. It was time to quit while he was ahead and use the escape tunnel, perhaps paying his final respects to Colonel Pereira as he stepped over his body.

Double-figure kills, the whole of Spitfire's Rise burning down, and probably the end of the whole war. Not bad for a night's work.

And so what if my ninth Underdog kill was a boy with Down's, and number ten was a man tied to a chair? They chose to play war games, and they were bad enough to lose. I can't be blamed for that.

Oliver Roth descended the cellar steps for the final time, coughing as he went. When he took a moment to inhale a shallow amount of cellar air, the choking sounds continued.

But it wasn't an echo of his own coughs. They were too high-pitched.

Roth was not the only one coughing.

He lifted his rifle, and ran down the stairs as fast as he could. If the last Underdog in Spitfire's Rise had a gun, the cellar steps were a dreadful place to be caught.

Roth landed on the cellar floor, and found a terrified child frozen next to the exit.

The boy was wide-eyed, with a short shock of jet-black hair and a bottom lip that trembled in fright.

Crap, the list mentioned a child too.

I think his name was…

'Thomas?' Roth asked.

The boy nodded. At least, Roth thought it was a nod rather than his head shuddering through fear. Roth kept his rifle raised, and the boy stepped backwards until the back of his head touched the wall behind him.

Roth had walked through the cellar twice, but not noticed the significance of that wall until Thomas had backed up against it.

UNDERDOGS MEMORIAL WALL
In loving memory of those who fought and
gave their lives in the Great British Rebellion.

Some of the names were far too familiar.

Ben Christie, read one of them.

Charlie Coleman, read another.

David Riley and *Val Riley* were also present.

'Please…' Thomas mouthed in front of him.

That was when Roth noticed *Beth Foster* among the names, and came to the realisation that the boy in front of him was already one of his victims. He was looking into the face of a child he had orphaned, next to the memorial for his deceased mother, underneath his house which burned to the ground above him. The boy had lost his ability to speak, but his face communicated everything it needed to.

Damn it, Thomas, why didn't you move a few seconds faster? I can't pretend I didn't see you now!

The boy must have been in the farm when Roth had invaded. Probably keeping Alex company right to the end. That compassion had got him into deep, deep trouble, and Roth was unwilling to let compassion do the same to him. As haunted as he felt with Thomas Foster stood before him – a boy who had already suffered so much at his hands – he had made his decisions about compassion and he had made them permanently.

Oliver Roth looked at his last chance of redemption, and shot him in the chest.

Chapter 26

Ewan slowed down as he approached the village, his ribs tightening around his lungs. Pearce must have had at least ten minutes to lock himself down and call for reinforcements, while Ewan had been exhausting the last of his energy reserves.

Walters Ash welcomes careful drivers, read the sign at the side of the road.

Ewan focused on the fires ahead, and tried to ignore the fact that he had no idea where in England he was. That even if he won the night, he would struggle to complete the journey back to Spitfire's Rise.

He had walked through abandoned villages in the dead of night before, but never without a torch. Most assault rifles had them fixed on, but he was armed with only a basic handgun.

It didn't matter. There were billowing clouds of smoke from multiple fires, and one of them had to be next to the village green.

Ewan didn't take long to find it. Lit up with the orange-yellow glow of the fires from the destroyed house, the village green sat with its overgrown grass and underused bandstand. Somewhere in the middle lay a fluttering collection of white parachute nylon, pushed away from the entrance of the escape pod.

Ewan hid against the wall of the nearest house, sheltering himself from any surprise gunfire, and tried to think.

If I were Pearce, where would I run to?

Don't bother trying, said the negative side of his brain. *Nathaniel bloody Pearce has always been smarter than you.*

Whatever, said the side he hoped was the real him, *he's never had my combat instincts. If he can think of a good hiding place, I can think of it too.*

Ewan looked around again, and wished he wasn't alone. With Jack in a field far away and Kate's position and welfare completely unknown, he had never been so alone in the battlefield.

Whatever county we're in, he thought, realising for the first time that they must have flown out of Oxfordshire before the end, *I don't have long. He just needs to make a quiet phone call and the cavalry will come for him. And I won't be able to defeat a whole army with a single pistol...*

He had to think fast, but it didn't take him long to establish some facts. The escape pod would have been able to broadcast its GPS coordinates, and Pearce would feel much safer waiting nearby than making a run for another village. Even if he believed Ewan and Jack to be dead, a man like him would take few risks: Pearce's quickest hope of rescue would be waiting for a miniature army to head for the escape pod's coordinates, then emerging from his hiding place once he knew he was safe.

'You're not far away...' Ewan breathed.

Ewan looked at the range of buildings that surrounded the village green. Among the ones in his line of sight, there was a lot of variety. Posh residential homes, quaint shops, a pub and a church hall to name a few. He tried to work out which would offer the best shelter, but had no obvious ideas. Besides, half the buildings weren't visible from his spot against the wall either. To see them all, he'd have to head to the centre of the green and expose himself to gunfire.

There probably wasn't much time. If Pearce's rescuers came in helicopters, they could be there within twenty minutes and Ewan wouldn't stand a chance. He had to act, and fast.

He had one ridiculous idea. Ridiculous to the point of being dangerous. But it would force Pearce to expose his position, and as soon as he got over his fears it would feel like the best thing to do.

Run to inspect the escape pod, and pretend I don't think he's nearby. Have a nosy around until he shoots at me, and then he's given away his position. Easy... unless his bullet hits me.

Pearce was a scientist, not a marksman. If he had a clear shot at Ewan, there'd probably be only a fifty-fifty chance of the bullet striking him.

But still, that meant once Ewan was at that escape pod he had a fifty percent chance of being shot. And even a minor wound could stop him from escaping before reinforcements arrived and finished him off.

Ewan took deep breaths, and remembered what kind of man he was facing. What Nathaniel Pearce had done to him, and to the world.

He had punctured Jack's eye with a knife.

He had conspired with Gwen Crossland to murder tens of thousands of civilians, an atrocity only prevented by the death of 400.

He had invented AME, only defeated after the deaths of McCormick and Raj.

He had created the clone soldier. The biorifle soldier. The Alex clones. All of them. Every type of creature that had tried to kill Ewan over the previous year had been because of

Nathaniel Pearce. Even his dead family had been killed by creatures grown in Pearce's factories.

The man needed to die. Not just out of revenge, but to stop his next set of atrocities which were certain to happen if he ever made it home.

With that in mind, a surge of irrational courage took root in Ewan's brain, and he charged for the centre of the village green.

'Pretend to be stupid, pretend to be stupid...'

Ewan knew that in Pearce's opinion, he and his friends would still be no more than armed retards. Putting himself in the firing line would be exactly what Pearce would believe a special needs teenager would do.

Ewan stood next to the parachute – presumably silhouetted against its white background – and tried to look like he was peering inside. When the first bullet came, he would need to have one eye towards the windows and watch for the flash.

Nothing happened.

Ewan looked deeper into the escape pod, to find a little screen reading '*DISTRESS SIGNAL SENT*'. And even then, no bullets came.

The fear of being shot by a mad scientist began to fade. Pearce was unlikely to take the shot if he hadn't done so already. Perhaps he couldn't.

'Crap... I am such a numpty...'

Perhaps Pearce had been right about Ewan being no more than a glorified special needs child. In order for a bullet to be fired in his direction, *Pearce would need to have a gun.* If he'd been armed with a pistol to begin with, he would never have leapt at Jack with a knife.

But if he was around and close to a window, the figure of Ewan next to his escape pod would be unmistakable.

Ewan hit himself around the head, three or four times for

good measure. Pearce might not even have seen the parachutes in the sky. Ewan might have given himself away for no reason.

No, not for no good reason. I've got a good view of half the village here.

Every building around the village green lay in plain sight, lit up to varying extents by the burning house. Ewan's instincts told him to look for the odd one out, and he found it within seconds.

It was the pub. The one with the closed door.

Every other building within sight had an open door, left at least ajar from the raids of Takeover Day. The attack on this village must have been particularly brutal: back in Hertfordshire, where Ewan wished he could just teleport home to, most villages contained at least some houses whose doors had been closed by the invaders as they left.

It wasn't certain, but it was likely. Pearce, in his own panic, could have burst into the pub and instinctively closed the door behind him.

Ewan raised his pistol, and marched for the door. The search would last between ten seconds and ten minutes depending on how good Pearce was at hide and seek. But it would be well-lit inside the pub, thanks to where it stood in relation to the fire.

Maybe I should just torch this place too. Let him burn.

It was a nice thought, but not workable. Ewan needed a confirmed kill, not just a hopeful burning.

Ewan ran up to the door and booted it open. In a village this quiet, he would be heard no matter how silently he crept. And he wanted Nathaniel Pearce to be *scared* in his final moments.

But Pearce didn't even seem nervous as he spun around from the wall right next to the entrance door, and swung his knife towards Ewan's face. Ewan's hand, without his brain's permission, dropped the pistol to focus both empty hands on the knife. He swore at his own biological reflexes for making him cast away his main weapon, and gasped at the sight of the knife creeping forward towards his right eye. He could still see a little of Jack's blood and eyeball fluid on the blade.

'Not this time, you test-tube-born creepy bloody arsewipe!' Ewan yelled, pulling his hands close to his chest. Pearce's body followed his arm, unbalanced, and Ewan sent his knee thundering into his groin. With Pearce weakened and bent over it was easy to wrestle the knife from him, but Ewan's stomach dropped when he saw Pearce's hand grabbing at the fallen pistol.

Ewan thrust the knife through his upper arm, ripping through his clothes, skin, muscle, blood vessels and whatever else was in there, until a red spike protruded from the arm's other side. Pearce yelled in agony and fell backwards onto the floor. He scrambled to his feet as Ewan reached for the pistol himself, and was at the neighbouring table by the time Ewan aimed.

Pearce grabbed a year-old pint glass, its contents long evaporated, and took a desperate swing at Ewan with a high-pitched squawk that only a wounded nerdy scientist could make. Ewan didn't shoot him: he just caught the glass on its way down with his free hand, pulled it from Pearce's grip, and shoved it with full force into his face. It shattered upon impact, and left searing deep wounds across a face that had spent too much of its existence grinning.

Ewan let the remains of the glass fall to the floor as Pearce staggered back against the barstools, cradling his face with both hands – one still twitching from the knife that remained inside his arm. He was defeated, and bleeding a well-deserved amount of his own blood.

'Ha, that was my first bar fight,' Ewan gasped. 'I'm guessing it was yours too. I've done farts that fought harder against me than you did.'

'Doesn't matter...' Pearce moaned, the words from his savaged mouth dulled and approximate. 'No matter what happens tonight, this war was never yours to win...'

Ewan raised his pistol.

'Yeah,' he said, 'well I hope that brings you some comfort. Now let's talk. You don't have long.'

Ewan motioned his eyes towards the knife in Pearce's arm. The blood flow out of the wound had increased. Ewan must have severed an artery.

'I bet that hurts like hell,' he said. 'And as satisfying as it would be to watch you suffer... if you want a quick end, I'll give you one.'

Pearce trembled, then squeaked from the pain of trembling. The look on his mangled face seemed forlorn: he must have known Ewan would only end his life quickly in exchange for something.

'We both know you were never part of Grant's plan for the benefit of humanity,' Ewan continued. 'Grant's messed-up idea to take over the world and bring down its population... you never believed in that. You just believed in a nice existence on Floor A and life's little luxuries.'

'What's your point?'

'My point is, why would a man like you *care* what happens after he dies? The world could win or lose, Grant could succeed or fail or whatever, and it'd make no difference to your dead body. The only thing you'll care about for the rest of your life is how comfortable you are before you go. Tell me the next stage of Grant's plan, and I'll give you what you want.'

Pearce grinned, his bloodstained teeth visible in the light of the fire outside. Even now, with his life ending the way it was, he *still* found a moment to grin.

'You're wrong, Ewan,' he said. 'There is something I'd be happy to stretch out my last moments for. And it's watching your grieving, war-torn face as you realise what kind of person you've become.'

Ewan kept silent. Was he really about to get morality lessons from a monster like Nathaniel Pearce?

'Did you notice how easy you found it to defenestrate Gwen Crossland?' Pearce asked.

'De-what?'

'You threw her out of a window, you may remember. I was watching from the bridge's CCTV... Did you notice how easy you found it?'

'Had to be done.'

'And shooting Oli Sharp through the forehead. Did you notice how easy it was to kill the man who sneaked you on board? A totally harmless man who was passionately loyal to your cause?'

'Had to be done.'

'And all the other human staff that must have died along the way?'

'*Had to be done.*'

'And glassing me in the face, knifing me through the arm... making my last moments horrible for me?'

Ewan smiled.

'I didn't have to do that. But bloody hell was it satisfying.'

Pearce smiled back, as if he were playing chess and his opponent had just blundered.

'And that's the problem, isn't it?' he said. 'Remember the person you were before McCormick got destroyed?'

Ewan didn't answer.

'There may have been a time, Ewan West, when you

would have found tonight difficult. Not just in a teenager-with-learning-difficulties-on-an-airship kind of way, but in a moral way. The younger version of you would have refused to do some of the things your modern self has done tonight.'

'Maybe that's why I'm so good at winning now.'

Pearce looked straight into his eyes. Ewan knew better than to look away, as painful as it was.

'I just want you to know,' Pearce said, 'that whether your body dies tonight or next week or even in sixty years' time… the best version of Ewan West is already dead. Little bits of him died with his friends one by one, until McCormick blew himself up and took the last of you with him. Whoever ends up killing you physically, you died mentally long ago.'

Ewan barely bothered to hide the misery on his face. He didn't even try to deny it in his own mind; he had confessed the same, nearly word for word, back on the airship with Jack.

There was very little of him left as a person. But perhaps that would make his next task easier. His finger landed on the trigger of his pistol.

'But just before you kill me,' Pearce gasped, 'one quick question. Just out of curiosity. Is Shannon still alive?'

The mention of her name, even from a dying enemy, caused Ewan to shudder.

'Alive and better than ever. Why?'

'Wow… and I saw that moment of panic just then. She's still someone you care about, isn't she? Is she still a great kisser like you told Iain?'

'If that's meant to be a threat—'

'Oh come on, Ewan. What kind of threat could I possibly offer in this position? It's just entertaining that she's still alive… for now.'

Ewan pointed his pistol towards Pearce's forehead.

'If you want the bullet you only need to ask,' Ewan snarled.

'Then give me the bullet. And when you next see her, ask her what she did on Takeover Day.'

The expression on Ewan's face must have matched Pearce's expectations, as he began to laugh. It was laughter with sobbing tones, but still laughter.

'And how the hell do I know you're not just making stuff up on the spot?' Ewan asked.

'Believe what you want right now. Just watch the expression on her face when you ask her the question. You can read faces, right?'

Ewan could read Pearce's face at that moment. Apparently there was satisfaction to be found even during a slow death. Pearce was doing what Ewan had done through all his years of growing up losing board games: rather than face the horrifying concept of something not going his way, he just made up his own truth and pretended he had won.

Pearce had lost, but in his own way he was still winning. The look in Ewan's eyes must have confirmed it.

'It'll be hilarious when you find out,' Pearce finished. 'If you'd known from the start, you'd never have allowed her within twenty miles of you.'

'Lying won't save your life.'

'Then shoot me.'

Ewan shot him.

One bullet, straight through the forehead. And since Pearce's last sentence had been said with such daring bravado, he had died with a grin on his face.

But it didn't matter. Nathaniel Pearce was dead. Ewan had hoped the victory would be more satisfying, but Pearce had stolen that feeling from him. All he had in his mind was worries about Shannon, and defeatist thoughts about his mental wellbeing.

Second to staying alive, it was exactly what Pearce had wanted.

Ewan shook his head, and took the radio from his pocket.

'Can you hear me, Jack?'

They were possibly out of range, but it was worth a try. When Jack didn't answer, Ewan walked to the front door, hoping he would get a better signal outside. He took a final look at Nathaniel Pearce's body before he left – sunken against barstools, a knife through his arm (which Ewan took a moment to steal for himself), a carved-up face and a bullet in his forehead – and wondered whether the man had been right about Ewan being the real monster.

'Jack?' he said as he walked back into the street.

After a moment of silence, he heard a voice that almost made him collapse with relief.

'Still here, Ewan,' said Jack. 'And doing OK. What's up?'

'I found Pearce and killed the crap out of him. His backup's coming though. You fit to start running home?'

'Argh, I dunno. Ask me again when you reach me. Do comms know about Pearce yet?'

'Calling them now.'

'Great. And you might want to call Rubinstein afterwards. She deserves to know.'

'Good idea. Oh, and one more thing for bonus points,' Ewan said, looking at Pearce's knife as it lay in his grip – the one so grievously used against Jack, now stolen for himself. 'Guess what I'm holding in my hand right now?'

'Your radio?'

'Other hand, you numpty.'

Jack didn't need long to think, and Ewan was almost disappointed when he guessed correctly.

'The knife Pearce used to puncture my eyeball. I appreciate

the effort, Ewan, but get out of there fast. You don't want to be around when reinforcements find his body.'

Ewan nodded. Jack wasn't one for sentiment during important moments, and as usual, he was right.

'Got it. See you soon, Jack.'

Ewan put his radio back into his pocket and started a brisk walk to the edge of Walters Ash. He reached into his other pocket and found Rubinstein's scrambled phone – unused for most of the night – and felt guilty about leaving Shannon and Lorraine in the dark. The last they had been told, Ewan, Jack and Kate had only just arrived on the airship. Comms had probably been worried sick about them.

Ewan brought the phone in front of his face and wondered how to phrase the night's events: that Pearce and Crossland were dead, that the airship had been shot down on Grant's own orders, that Acceleration was dead and cremated... and that Jack was injured and Kate missing. It would take them a long time to process the magnitude of everything that had happened.

When Ewan pressed the home button on the phone, an undetected text message showed up on his screen. That surprised him: the Underdogs almost never exchanged text messages. Once a plan was texted, there was written proof of its existence. But the message stared at his face regardless: one that had been sent by Shannon several hours earlier.

Don't come home.

Chapter 27

Dawn had arrived, but Shannon hadn't slept. Even if she *had* been tired enough, Ewan's catastrophic meltdown in reaction to her phone call would have haunted her dreams. She had been the one to tell him that his home had been burned to the ground, by the same assassin who had killed his Temper Twin, and that three more of his friends had been murdered while it happened. There had been disbelief, then yelling, then swearing, then a meltdown that had been terrifying to listen to. She had felt powerless, witnessing his desolate sadness from so many miles away, unable to even put a hand on his shoulder.

She looked at the clogged road around her. She didn't want to get out of the car, but knew she'd have to leave at some point. Lorraine had climbed out of the passenger seat earlier in the night, the moment she had seen the burned-out tank in front of them. The dead husk of the Challenger 2 blocked a whole carriageway of the M1, unmoved and unchanged from the day Mark had destroyed it during the escape from Oakenfold.

'How did you blow it up?' Shannon asked.

'Why do you care?' Mark muttered. 'Both the people I saved that morning are dead now.'

Shannon had not yet accepted Ewan's vague, angry news about Kate. Then again, she had barely accepted the death of Simon or the others either. She had not seen their bodies, so her head still held the undisturbed image of Simon's smiling face and the delightful sound of his huffing laughter. Alex's cocky attempts at charm, clashing with his recent, unashamed vulnerability. Thomas' entire beautiful being, and his unbroken voice that would never be heard from again.

Mark left the car, gasping as he hauled himself from the driver's seat. His glass wounds were no longer bleeding, but they were evidently still painful. Shannon had no choice but to follow in order to continue the conversation.

'Why are we here?' she asked.

'Because it's the only place I knew for certain we could drive to. If we'd kept running, Lorraine would have collapsed and been shot.'

There hadn't been much time to think, running from a crowd of clones with nothing but two empty pistols. Once they had put enough distance between them and their attackers, Mark had found the nearest car and hotwired it like a man with experience. They had driven to Harpenden and met the M1, hoping Mark knew what he was doing. Evidently, he had.

'So what's the plan now?' asked Shannon, her voice barely above the level of a grunt.

'We call Ewan and Jack, and we agree on a meeting place.'

Shannon shuddered. The thought of talking to Ewan again...

She needed to change the subject, and there was something on her mind which had to be addressed. Mark had told them he was the sole survivor of the storming of Spitfire's Rise. But Shannon remembered the stories about Takeover Day: how Kate's brother and all the others had been abandoned on

Mark's orders, with the words '*get bloody running, they're not worth it*'. Shannon didn't trust him as the only witness.

'Mark,' she began, 'you're *sure* the others are dead, right?'

'Bloody hell, Shannon, how sure do you want me to be?'

Shannon looked over to Lorraine – who had seemed transfixed by the burned-out tank from the moment they arrived several hours earlier – sitting motionless on the road as if trying to ignore the rest of the world. Perhaps she had finally witnessed an event that had destroyed her willingness to confront the ugly truth: after twenty years of nursing, and the suicide of a former student that had led her there, Lorraine Shepherd had finally endured something that detached her from reality. Thinking about the path ahead would involve thinking about leaving Thomas behind, whom she had spent every single non-comms-duty hour sharing a home with for thirteen months.

With Lorraine distracted, Shannon whispered to Mark.

'You can be honest. We both know it's too late to go back and save anyone now. Did you *know* they were all dead?'

'I saw Simon's body with my own eyes,' Mark said, resting his back against a neighbouring car. 'We were playing chess when we heard the gunfire around us, so we ran for the armoury together. He found Roth coming down the tunnel and tried to hold him off. The lad must have died while I was in the generator room, grabbing the thermal blocker to take with us.'

Shannon's eyes widened, and she stared up into Mark's face as aggressively as she could.

'*Oliver Roth* was shooting at Simon, and you ran for the thermal blocker?!'

'Simon didn't need to kill Roth. He just needed to fend him off. And there was me thinking ahead, making sure we couldn't be scanned after we escaped. Anyway, Alex was tied to a chair in the farm. There was no saving him. Roth was clearly going to go exploring and find what we'd done with the neighbours' house. And Thomas had been keeping Alex company all evening. Bloody righteous child probably wasted his chance to escape and spent ages trying to untie him, not realising the knots would be too tough. A good kid, but I figured his kindness would be the death of him one day.'

Shannon wanted to punch him. Really, *really* wanted to punch him. But the Underdogs had suffered enough for one week. Four dead friends (including Gracie, whose death now seemed like a year ago), Kate missing, Jack grievously wounded, and their home burned to the ground.

Mark was gazing into the sunrise, hands in pockets, with a look of genuine sadness on his face. Even that annoyed Shannon. Every dead body in Spitfire's Rise had once been a better person than Mark, and *he* had been the one to see another sunrise.

'If it makes you hate me less,' he finished, 'I hung around the cellar long enough to let Roth see me running up the steps. I made him chase me. I couldn't save Alex and Thomas, but I could grant them extra seconds of life. Even if they weren't particularly good ones.'

Shannon didn't have the energy to respond. She walked over to Lorraine and joined her in gazing at the dead tank.

'I don't suppose you've got any ideas on where to go?' Shannon asked. 'Anywhere we can hide?'

'I've not been further than comms since your daddy imprisoned everyone I love,' Lorraine answered, not shifting from her sitting position on the tarmac. 'Your original body's daddy, I mean. How the hell would I know what to do now?'

There was no way of progressing the conversation. The Lorraine who could think with sober judgement was now absent, resorting to cheap cracks about Shannon's existence rather than offering ideas.

Back in comms, I saw her smile at me. After a month of isolated hell, she was on her way back to us. There was promise in her face, right up until we heard those passing clones.

But now she's gone again. Robbed of the recovery she was just about to start.

She walked over to Mark again, hoping he would offer something productive.

'What about the house in Lemsford?' she called over to him as she walked. 'Where Ewan and the others sheltered—'

'The one invaded by the Alex clones? No thanks. Besides, Grant flattened the place.'

Shannon sighed. Somewhere in her memory she had a faded vision of Alex telling her and Lorraine about the end of that report, with the execution of Dean Ginelli and the obliteration of Lemsford. He must have told Mark too, at some point between getting his memories back and his untimely death.

'OK... what about the house Jack found for us a month ago? On the night of the AME mission?'

'Other than Jack, the only people who ever saw it were Simon, Gracie and Thomas. Guess what they all have in common?'

'What if Jack met us—'

'Even with Jack's memory, he'd only find it by retracing the route from Spitfire's Rise. He won't like the idea of heading there first. Oh, and apparently the house was crap.'

'What about just picking any random house? Anywhere, in any village close by?'

'Close by Spitfire's Rise you mean? Even if some random house were suited to our needs, which Ewan will say it won't be, let's at least play it safe and camp a few counties away.'

Shannon had hoped for *something*. Anything that would have prevented her from vocalising the thought in her head. But no other ideas came from her two allies.

'I know a place,' she whispered.

The sun had set by the time they arrived. Shannon had slowed down towards the end of the journey, trying to delay the return home.

Once upon a time, I walked to school down this road. Back when I had a mother. Back when I thought I was the most special thing in Dad's life.

When she turned the final corner onto a row of terraced houses, she saw it. She was home, for the first time since she had been forcibly moved into New London... five bodies ago.

'You grew up here?' Mark muttered in disgust, and with pain in his voice from having walked all day on glass-shredded legs. 'When you suggested your dad's place, I thought we'd be sleeping in a mansion.'

'My father kept us in the cheapest house he could get away with,' Shannon answered, looking down at the wonky road where she and her streetmates had once played football. 'He didn't have the time or desire to move us anywhere bigger. To him, home was where his office was, nothing more.'

'Huh... that sounds more autistic than most of Oaken-fold.'

Shannon gritted her teeth, feeling the insult on Ewan's behalf.

'Dad wasn't autistic. He was too unfeeling and uncaring for that.'

She jogged forward before Mark could answer, and reached the unlocked porch of her old house. When she opened it she found that Ewan and Jack had already arrived, and were sat on the tiled floor in wait for her. Both were wearing New Oxford staff uniforms, although Ewan was down to his vest.

Jack's face...

There was no time to show Jack any condolences. Partly because Lorraine had pushed in front of her and started talking to him about combating infection risks. But mainly because Ewan had already leapt to his feet and thrown his arms around her.

Shannon had no idea how to react to the hug. A day earlier, back in that wonderful time when Spitfire's Rise had existed and Alex, Simon and Thomas had all been alive, she had promised Lorraine she would tell Ewan about her true identity. She was yet to decide whether to keep that promise.

Nonetheless, she hugged back. Ewan seemed almost dead on his feet, and he needed all the support she could offer.

'You're bloody brave, you know,' he gasped. 'Coming back here.'

It was a glimpse of Ewan's better side. No comments about her house, or her working-class upbringing despite her grandfather being an oil tycoon and her father being a dictator-in-waiting. No judgement of her for the lives she had failed to save at Spitfire's Rise. Prioritising her feelings over his own.

Ewan had his faults, and his whole psyche was falling apart. But when he was good, he was good.

'You waited in the porch?' she asked him.

'It was locked. And I wasn't going to break into your childhood home.'

Shannon ended the hug, grateful to Ewan, but surprised that he thought this place was some kind of cherished holy site for her. It was Heaven and Hell in equal measure. She walked outside, knelt down and moved a loose brick on the outside of the porch, where she found her faded silver key to the front door. Her father's home had been the one house on the street without its door knocked in by clones, and thankfully they had left its surroundings alone too.

'You have a key?' asked Jack as she walked back into the porch.

'Hid it here the day we moved into New London. A part of me always hoped I'd be able to run away and come back here. I just didn't think it would take so long.'

Shannon Rose Grant opened the front door, and saw her childhood again. It looked just as bleak as it had felt at the time. The hallway looked identical: her father hadn't even bothered to take the photos off the walls when they had moved to the Citadel. She found the living room with its usual blank neatness, and when she walked into the kitchen she found it in good shape, all its food having been removed long before Takeover Day.

Shannon started to cry, and she didn't understand why. Her brain – her complex, artificial but brilliant brain – was filled with a dozen conflicting emotions that she couldn't identify.

'Are you struggling?' came Lorraine's voice from behind her. The woman's nursing instincts seemed to resurface at the sight of someone who needed her help.

'Yeah,' Shannon gasped.

Lorraine rested a tense hand on her shoulder, and joined her at the window to the back garden. The grass was predictably overgrown, but Lorraine couldn't have known how similar it was to the old days. The garden was a place Nicholas Grant had never deemed worthy of his attention.

'Honestly, cry as many tears as you need to,' said Lorraine. 'I spent thirteen months wishing I could go home. But now we've lost Spitfire's Rise, I'm not sure I ever want to see my old house again. I want the memory of it to stay untainted...'

the one good thing from my life that this war won't ever take from me…'

Lorraine's voice trailed off. Shannon didn't answer; she was still wondering whether coming home had been a good idea at all. But like McCormick had once told her in that hand-written letter, at some point she would need to face her past. And an unoccupied house seemed like a good start.

'The truth is,' Lorraine continued, her voice catching in her throat, 'it still doesn't feel like we've actually left. It feels like at the end of tonight, we're going to go back to Spitfire's Rise where the others will be waiting…'

Shannon turned away from the window, and tried to look at Lorraine's face. It was dipped too deep to see her expression.

'Whatever future you want after this war,' Shannon replied with the hint of a hiss, 'it's not far away. My father won't win because we won't *let* him. He doesn't get to win without our permission.'

Shannon recognised the naivety in her words, but ignored it. To her credit, so did Lorraine. Shannon turned for the living room, where the others had gathered. Lorraine followed and the group united in the fading evening light.

Me. Ewan. Jack, Mark and Lorraine. The last of the Underdogs.

Unless Kate's out there somewhere, far away and looking after herself.

'I don't know about you,' said Ewan, 'but I've not slept well this week.'

Jack, Lorraine and Mark each nodded. Shannon didn't move. She saw the little look Ewan had given her, whether he had meant it or not.

Within ten minutes, each Underdog had their own bed or sofa. Mark had been the least opposed to sleeping in Nicholas Grant's old bed. He had not even seen it as a satisfying tres-pass; all he had seen was a double bed with enough room to stretch out. His sleeping bag in Spitfire's Rise had never had that.

Shannon's own bed had just enough mattress space for two people, and neither she nor Ewan could cope with being alone that night. They lay under the covers, Ewan's hand in hers. He had never done that before.

After half an hour's unsleeping silence, Shannon dared to speak.

'I'm sorry, Ewan. They were people I loved... but I know you loved them longer than I did.'

For a good twenty seconds, Ewan didn't answer. But his fingers tightened, suggesting he wasn't ignoring her. In the silence, Shannon's mind conjured up the image of Simon. He was wearing that smile that showed how dutiful and loyal he had always been, and his bulky hand was patting her shoulder in reassurance. According to Mark, he had been dutiful and loyal to the end. She pictured Thomas, felt the warmth of his hugs, and tried to reconnect with how his company had always been a distraction from the harshness of the world. Finally her memory fell on Alex... the version of him who had bitten her arm in uncontrollable rage. The man who had spent his remaining hours on Earth trying to help his friends using his memories while tied to a chair. The hero Alex had died as, not the hero he had lived as.

'The worst part is,' Ewan murmured, 'they died without ever knowing we won. If they'd lived just a bit longer, they'd have seen the victory for themselves.'

It was typically defiant talk from Ewan. But perhaps he believed his own words.

'Have you had any ideas yet?' Shannon asked. 'About how to make it happen? Because seriously, I want to know how to destroy him once and for all. Just being in this house has reminded me how much he needs to die.'

'I'll come up with something during the night,' he answered. 'When I'm not having nightmares.'

Shannon laid her head on her pillow, freshly brushed of its own dust. Ewan, almost in reaction, sat himself up straight.

'One last thing,' he said, his face turned away from her and pointing towards the far end of the room. 'You need to know what Pearce said before he died.'

Shannon gasped, and it must have been audible.

She remembered Nathaniel Pearce far too well: that creepy smiling scientist who would laugh under his breath whenever they passed each other on Floor A. Who would casually refer to himself as her 'creator', and would occasionally remind her that her future lay in his hands, her existence his own to control. She had been a rare case of an experiment he could run *everywhere*, not just in his laboratories.

Now he was dead, but Shannon felt no weight off her mind.

'He told me to ask you what you did on Takeover Day,' Ewan said. 'And to watch the expression on your face when I asked. That's why I'm looking away from you. I don't want to know.'

Shannon wiped her tears, and waited for Ewan to continue. He couldn't possibly have finished.

'I know what kind of past I've had,' he said, 'and I've lived most of my life wanting people to not judge me for it. And… this week I lost most of myself. Almost everyone I care about is dead or missing, our home is destroyed, and everyone's turning to *me* for leadership, as if I was ever good at it. One more bit of bad news might just destroy me forever.'

Ewan fell back and collapsed next to Shannon, his dulled eyes looking to the ceiling.

'Whatever you did on Takeover Day, whoever you killed or whatever shocking thing it's meant to be, I don't want

Pearce to win by letting it get in our way. If it stands a chance of coming between us, I don't want to hear it. I just…'

His hand squeezed tighter.

'…I just want to live on believing you're perfect. The one perfect thing in a world built without people like me in mind.'

She squeezed his hand back.

'It wasn't built with me in mind either,' she answered. 'Maybe that's why we fit so well.'

'Yeah,' finished Ewan. 'Maybe.'

No more words were said. Within two minutes, Ewan's breathing changed to a hypnotic, trance-like pattern that suggested he had fallen asleep.

Ewan was right. He and Shannon had the perfect relationship. But given her own experience of creation, Shannon didn't believe any two people were 'made for each other' in the traditional sense. She had abandoned a life of luxury to *escape* the man she had been made for. She and Ewan had become closer than she ever thought she could come to another person… and it was set to last for a maximum of two more months.

In killing Nathaniel Pearce, Ewan had doomed Shannon to her mortality. Once her current incarnation died, there would never be another Shannon Grant.

But that was OK. There would never need to be. No matter what happened, no matter how she spent the time she had left on Earth, she was going to fulfil her promise to herself. Shannon was going to be the clone who won.

Chapter 28

Oliver Roth was becoming accustomed to his desk's new position. Marshall had always positioned his own desk on the other side of the room, but this wasn't Iain Marshall's office anymore. It was Oliver Roth's. And as Grant's official, *permanent* Head of Military, he had bloody well earned it.

Roth rested his feet on the table: no shoes, no socks. He had earned that too, and his feet needed to breathe after a long day's walk through Hertfordshire.

Shortly after midnight, Nicholas Grant walked into Roth's office with a bottle of champagne and two glasses. But the expression on his face didn't offer a sense of celebration.

'Evening, Nick,' said Roth. 'Take a seat.'

Grant did so, and held the refrigerated champagne bottle against Roth's bare foot. Roth flinched from the cold, took the hint and sat properly.

'I didn't think you'd want champagne on a night like this,' Roth said.

'What do you mean? My prodigal son has finally returned.'

I'm not prodigal. I'm no Bible scholar but I know the prodigal son volunteered to leave home. He wasn't sent away and forbidden to return until he had killed a child, a Down's kid and a man tied to a chair.

Roth stared into space. When he thought about it that way, his evening at Spitfire's Rise had been a much easier fight than he remembered. Barely in his top ten, and certainly the fight that had yielded him the greatest reward.

'So yes, it's definitely a champagne night,' Grant continued. 'But it's one of those bittersweet champagnes, to reflect the bittersweet truth about where we find ourselves tonight.'

'Yeah, makes sense.'

Roth gave himself the appearance of a boy who mourned Nathaniel Pearce, Gwen Crossland, João Pereira, the loss of an airship and the death of Acceleration. But in reality, he was annoyed about having to drink bloody champagne. Adults kept saying it was an 'acquired taste', whatever the hell that meant, but to him it tasted like sparkling urine at the best of times. And a bitter champagne stolen from an abandoned house in a nearby village would be especially unpleasant.

Roth jumped at the sudden *pop* of the cork. Grant had opened the bottle faster than Roth thought he would, thanks to his usual inimitable enthusiasm.

'So the rebels have been taught an important lesson, even if they've yet to be extinguished fully,' Grant said. 'Tell me, how did you manage to find them in the end?'

'They were using a thermal blocker,' Roth replied as he watched his champagne glass being filled. 'I just worked out where its borders were, made a circle around it, and attacked the building in the middle.'

'Smart lad,' Grant replied. 'Did you find the blocker they were using?'

'No. The house was burning down around me.'

Roth and Grant clinked their glasses, and Roth swallowed a small sip which he pretended not to hate.

'So they could have escaped with it,' said Grant as he drank half the glass in one gulp. 'Or just left it to burn. Either way, I'll get my thermal scanners going and see if we can detect the survivors. If we don't find them straight away, we'll just repeat your trick again.'

Roth nodded, unsure whether his trick could be repeated at all. If the Underdogs had any sense they'd keep themselves on the move, and the blocker would be with them, its radius borders ever changing.

How many Underdogs are left, anyway? he wondered to himself. *A few days ago Nick said there were ten, but I killed three last night… Shannon, Mark and the old lady are still alive, and at least one of the airship team was alive to shoot Nat in the face… so there could be as few as four, or as many as seven.*

Roth huffed at the uncertainty. Despite his promotion, he still considered himself an assassin. And assassins performed better with specifics – especially knowing how many scalps still needed collecting.

But there was a world away from the Underdogs too, and Roth wanted to know what his home was going to look like.

'So what happens next?' he asked. 'I mean, who's Chief Scientist now?'

'Richard Unsworth,' said Grant, gulping the other half of his glass.

'Who?'

'Someone who worked with Nathaniel on the AME project. He did data entry, mostly. Not half the scientist his predecessor was.'

Those details were enough to awaken the memory in Roth's mind. Unsworth had been the man who had his account hacked by Ewan, the night they had lost all their research. New London was obviously desperate for remaining scientific minds, if their prime choice for Chief Scientist was a man who'd almost been thrown into the Inner City for a devastating data breach. The Underdogs weren't the only side who had been irreparably damaged over the last few days.

Then again, Roth thought, *we're the side with reinforcements. Ewan, if he's still alive, will only have a handful of soldiers for the rest of his war.*

The thought didn't bring much comfort. Roth knew that any Underdogs left alive were probably the stronger ones, since he'd only managed to clear up the young and the weak at Spitfire's Rise.

Grant refilled his glass with champagne, and replaced the sip at the top of Roth's. Roth rolled his eyes, blatant enough for Grant to have noticed if he'd not been gazing at the bottle's label instead.

'Hmm,' Grant muttered. 'Hannah clearly isn't a champagne woman. Still, supermarket brand is better than nothing.'

Roth perked an eyebrow, and wondered where he had heard that woman's name before.

'Hannah?' he asked. The name sounded familiar, but he couldn't quite place it.

'Yes,' answered Grant. 'This was a gift from her. She must have asked someone to raid—'

'Hannah who?'

'Hannah Marshall. Iain's wife. Or used to be. She's trying her charms on me, now that Nathaniel's gone.'

There were too many names in too many sentences. Roth looked as confused as he could, hoping that Grant would elaborate. Grant finished his second glass and stared in Roth's direction, a little more light-headed than before.

'You know the rules, Oliver,' he said, pausing to burp before he explained further. 'If an employee gets killed, their families are thrown into the Inner City. Hannah and her daughters were VIPs so we kept them here after Iain's death, but she must have feared we'd get bored of them one day. She started dating Nathaniel publicly just *days* after Iain's death! Privately, of course, they'd been dating while he was still alive. Always good to have a backup plan, and Hannah was smart enough to know it.'

'And you don't think it's suspicious that she's suddenly attracted to *you*, now that Nat's dead?' asked Roth, taking a second sip out of duty alone.

'Oh, she isn't attracted to me. But she *is* trying to get with me. And why would I say no? With Sheila and Shannon both dead, I'm free to start looking around for new wives and daughters.'

Roth looked at Grant, to double-check whether he was significantly drunk. Either he was, or he had just experienced a surprising memory lapse.

'Nick,' he said, 'I told you on the phone yesterday. I saw Shannon at Spitfire's Rise, rescuing Mark Gunnarsson. *She's still alive.*'

Grant paused, then gave a misshapen quirky grin.

'Ah yes,' he said. 'So she is. My mistake.'

He didn't give Roth enough time to think his words over, instead leaping back to his feet and readying himself to leave the room.

'I hope you're ready for the next stage of the plan,' he said. 'Without Nathaniel or Gwen, it's going to be a bumpy ride to save humanity.'

Saving humanity… wow. So that's why we're killing so many people.

'What do you mean?' asked Roth.

'I wanted to conquer the world with technology and science,' said Grant, finishing a third glass which Roth had not even noticed him pour. 'But with my best scientists gone, it's going to have to be conquered through more traditional means. Sheer numbers. Reproducible numbers. Not long from now I'll send a clone army across the Channel D-Day style, and slaughter everyone in France outside of Paris. I *would* start with Ireland, but that would give mainland Europe a chance to guard their coastlines. We'll keep the army alive with the supplies they find in France, guard the eastern French border like a twenty-first century Maginot Line, then invade Spain and kill everyone outside of Madrid. Then Portugal except those in Lisbon, then the low countries except those in their respective capitals, then Switzerland... which may be tricky to conquer, with all those mountains of course... I won't bore you with everything now though. I'll give you the night off.'

And with that, he was gone. Already semi-drunk, Nicholas Grant marched out of Roth's office and along the Floor B corridor, presumably to his own living quarters to drink some more. Roth looked at the world map mounted on his opposite wall – which had appeared there without his permission while he had been away – and came to realise what it was doing there.

Roth placed his glass of champagne at the other end of the desk, rested his bare feet on the wood again, and wondered whether he was OK with Grant's master plan to 'save humanity'.

All in all, he was probably OK with it. If he were the kind of person to disagree with such a plan, Thomas Foster would still be alive. Roth had known all along that his odyssey to Spitfire's Rise would reveal the truth about his personality, and he was glad to have come to a deeper understanding of himself.

I told you who I was, he said to the imaginary ghost of McCormick.

I told you I was unsalvageable. You should have believed me.

*

Ewan didn't need the Memorial Wall anymore. He knew it off by heart.

Sarah Best, who used to help Kate in French.

Callum Turner, who came up with the Oakenfold Code.

Joe Horn, who... did he play chess? Something about showing off...

He had told McCormick about this habit once. Of not just remembering people's names, but also a detail about each person. Without those details to personify them, they would become nothing but etched names on a wall buried under a burned house.

Elaine Dean. She was... she walked dogs, I think.

Arian and Teymour...

Ewan opened his eyes. Outside Shannon's bedroom window, the sun had started to peek over the horizon.

She lay next to him, more peaceful than he had ever remembered seeing her before. Even for a warlike girl like her, it was easy to look peaceful while unconscious through sleep.

Arian and Teymour... ah, screw it.

Ewan stared at the ceiling, and a tear crept onto his cheek. Nicholas Grant may not have killed him, but he had removed the best parts of him. When Ewan thought of his fallen friends, all he remembered was how each of them had died.

Still, it was better than not remembering them at all. He started again.

Sarah Best, who died four days into the war. The clones pinned her down in a supermarket aisle while we raided it for food.

Callum Turner, who ran out of insulin a week after we arrived.

Joe Horn, who got a fire axe to the back of his head. The first time we met Oliver Roth.

Shannon started to shuffle around next to him. The sunlight looked to be waking her up too.

Elaine Dean, who had gone with Jack and the Shirazi brothers to steal a generator so we could have electricity. Died instantly from a bullet to the head without even knowing she was being attacked.

Arian and Teymour Shirazi, who fought like hell to keep themselves alive. Jack was the only one who made it home that day.

Shannon put her arm around him, and Ewan sighed. It was time for him to pretend to be human again.

'When are we heading out?' she asked.

'Ten minutes from now.'

'Good,' she replied, delivering her last word with surprising enthusiasm for someone so tired.

Rosanne Tate, fortunate enough to die of old age in Spitfire's Rise.

Miles Ashford, the second victim of Oliver Roth. Shotgun blast to the face.

Chloe Newham... bloody hell, it was Keith Tylor of all people who got to her.

Shannon swung her legs off the bed, and rose to her feet. Ewan did the same.

'I can wake the others if you want,' she said.

'No, it should be me.'

He paused.

'You can come with me if you like, though.'

She must have heard the vulnerability in his voice. Ewan was grateful that she stayed by his side as he walked through the house, waking Mark and Lorraine in turn. She stood positioned behind him at the bedroom doors, allowing him to look like he wasn't relying on her.

Tim Carson, who died in a grenade explosion during a normal boring gunfight against Roth. Around the time when gunfights became normal and boring to us.

Roy Wolff, who died of a mild stomach cancer that could have been cured in a half-decent hospital. Wow, his death screwed up Lorraine.

Mike Ambrose... who took his own life.

He reached the downstairs sofa and woke up Jack. He took a deep breath when his friend turned around and revealed his punctured eye.

'Morning, mate,' Jack said.

'Morning. How fast can you get ready?'

'I'm basically ready now. Hardly came here with much, did we?'

'Good. Shannon, you know what to do.'

Wordless, Shannon headed for the front door and walked outside onto the street. She seemed to have no problem with exposing her position, as if she didn't care whether she lived or died anymore.

Beth Foster... shot a few weeks after last Christmas, by the same psychopath who would go on to murder her orphaned son.

David and Val Riley, who...

He didn't need to think about it. They all remembered what Roth had done to them in their final moments.

Mark walked into the room as Jack scrambled to his feet. It was unusual to see Mark in that combat-ready pose – the stance he usually took when about to leave for a mission – without a single weapon in his hands. Ewan and Jack had finished their mission with a handgun each and a stolen knife, the rest of their arsenal burned up back home.

'So you've come up with a plan now?' Mark muttered.

'Yeah,' Ewan muttered back, although the word 'plan' was an exaggeration. 'There's only one friendly place in this whole country that we know about and Grant doesn't.'

'Rubinstein's place.'

'Yeah, that's it. We go to Emilia's countryside farmhouse and ask for shelter. From there, we'll see if the Network or the UN or whoever are willing to work with us.'

It was a weak plan and he knew it. They all knew it, but

neither logical Jack nor critical Mark was willing to point it out. In the silence, Ewan continued his mental list.

Sally Sharpe, the second and final victim of Keith Tylor.

Svetlana Karpov, shot while we tried breaking into New London on an ammo raid.

Ben Christie, who enjoyed an instantaneous death thanks to Roth's sniper rifle.

Lorraine walked into the room, her face confused and annoyed.

'Would you mind telling me what Shannon's doing out there with those cars?'

'She's stealing fuel. Use your imagination, you'll work it out.'

Lorraine didn't answer. She probably thought Shannon's little plan was a strategic misstep, and it was difficult to argue. But Shannon had earned whatever joy she could pick out of this whole mess.

'Am I going to like Captain Rubinstein when I meet her?' Lorraine asked, to change the subject.

'*You* might,' said Mark. 'Her first impression on me was pretty crap.'

Ewan wanted to smile, but just couldn't.

Rachael Watts, who died in a car crash as the two of us fled New London. She thought she'd save time by not stopping to put on her seatbelt.

Daniel Amopoulos, captured and tortured to death in exchange for our names.

Charlie Coleman, my Temper Twin and best friend, murdered in an officers' sector by Oliver bloody Roth.

There were clumsy footsteps in the porchway as Shannon stumbled back into the house with a washing-up bowl full of petrol. She smiled at Ewan as she walked past. Perhaps this really was helping her self-esteem.

Ewan walked into the kitchen and raided the drawers for bladed weapons. He found a wide range of kitchen knives, all of the highest quality metal and still shiny after a year. More than enough for two each.

'Ewan,' called Jack from the living room. 'If Shannon's doing what I think she's doing, we need to head outside.'

Raj Singh, who hadn't escaped Oakenfold in time... blowing himself up by running through the AME shield. The only shield Grant ever managed to raise.

Dr Joseph McCormick, who bought us an extra month in this war by destroying the last AME computer.

He left out the details of McCormick's death that troubled him most, and any memory of the remote control in their hands.

'Yep,' he replied to Jack, gathering the ten sharpest knives together and dumping them into an old supermarket carrier bag, double-bagging for good measure. 'Let's gather on the road.'

Behind him, Jack, Mark and Lorraine headed for the porch. Ewan opened the back door into the garden and walked to the shed: if there were unused paint pots anywhere in the house, that's where they would be.

He found a pot of plain white inside the shed, and nodded to himself. He grabbed the pot and the largest brush he could find.

By the time he had reached the road, there was already a strong petrol smell emanating from the front porch. He found a spot on the road, aligned with the house but a safe distance away, and knelt down.

Gracie Freeman, killed by Gwen Crossland hypnotising one of our friends.

Kate Arrowsmith... we don't even know for sure that she's dead. But let's bloody face it.

He had not made peace with it yet. But he was beginning to.

And finally, Alex Ginelli, Simon Young and Thomas Foster... murdered in their own home by Oliver Roth. While I was far, far away, leaving them all to their deaths.

He knew it was illogical to blame himself for what Oliver Roth had done, but his mind was far from caring about logic. He wiped his eyes, his recitation of the Memorial Wall concluded, then rested the bag of knives on the tarmac to free both hands. He dropped to his knees, flipped the lid off the pot and started to paint.

Five minutes later, Shannon had finished her work indoors. She walked out of her childhood home forever, with a kitchen tool in her hand. When Ewan looked closer he recognised it as a gas ring lighter.

'You sure you're OK with this?' Ewan asked as she stood next to him. It was a stupid question, but it needed asking.

'I *want* this,' she answered. 'And I want you to do it.'

She thrust the lighter into his fingers. Ewan jerked his hand away out of instinct, and looked at Shannon in surprise.

'Drowning my home in petrol was my half of the revenge,' she continued. 'You've earned your half. Go on – take away a part of my father's life, just like he took away part of yours. And next time we break into New London, we'll take everything else.'

The others lined up next to them. Ewan, Shannon, Jack, Mark and Lorraine stood in a neat row, knowing they were about to witness some sort of ceremony. A cremation, by the smell of it.

Before it happened, Ewan thought the occasion deserved a few words.

He took a deep breath.

'McCormick sheltered us in his home for over a year,' he

began. The opening sentence was enough for all four faces to
gape at him in surprise.

'Yeah,' he continued. 'Spitfire's Rise was McCormick's
home. He was sheltering us personally, and I knew all along.
When we arrived on Takeover Day, I scouted in front of the
Oakenfold group and found him and his partner cowering in
their house. Her name was Polly Jones. She was the home-
owner, and McCormick was her long-term guest. She was
taking care of him after the death of his wife… and in a meltdown, I shot her dead.'

Hardly an inspiring speech so far, came a voice in his head
which sounded a little like McCormick.

'I don't even remember it happening,' Ewan continued. 'I
remember running into Kimpton… our village was called
Kimpton, by the way… I remember bursting through their
door looking for shelter, and I remember the first time I heard
McCormick's calm, soothing voice. But Polly wasn't interested in keeping things calm. She started yelling, then there's
a blank spot in my memory, and the next thing I remember…
McCormick was holding onto her corpse on the living-room
floor.'

Shannon offered to grab his hand. He declined.

'Nobody else ever knew. I tried to wipe Polly from my
memory, and spent a year avoiding the slightest thought of
her. McCormick kept it quiet too, because he didn't want to
reveal whose house we lived in. So Polly was left forgotten,
and McCormick pretended he was new to the house too.'

'Why are you telling us this?' asked Mark, not one to shy
away from interrupting a speech.

'Because Polly deserved better than to get shot by a violent
teenager and have her existence forgotten. McCormick
deserved better than to have his best friend killed and pretend
it never happened… even taking her killer under his wing and

raising him as a surrogate grandson. I could have deserved better than losing my family... but ever since I shot Polly I've deserved nothing. I've never pretended otherwise. But the rest of you? You've all been to Hell and back, and so did every Underdog who never made it here.'

Ewan closed his eyes, and tried to remember the faces of those who had died under his and McCormick's leadership. But he had never been good with faces.

'If any of you need more motivation to nail Nicholas Grant to the wall and paint the countryside with his guts, this is what you should think about. The simple fact that *you deserve to win this*. Don't think about the billions of people who depend on us. None of us can deal with that much pressure. Think about your own need to succeed... and your right to get what you've earned.'

He ended his speech, not looking at his friends' faces for reactions. Then he stepped towards the end of the petrol trail Shannon had left for him, knelt down and set it alight.

Nicholas Grant's house – Shannon's childhood home – took less than three minutes to become a thunderous fire that burned so dramatically it had its own roar. The street around them lit up from flames rather than sunrise, and loud clatters sounded inside from the walls and ceilings that collapsed into the inferno.

To his side, Shannon was crying. But Ewan recognised her expression. Those were angry tears.

He reached out his arms, and the final Underdogs linked hands.

'To honour those who gave everything they had,' Ewan called out with angry tears of his own, 'we will give everything *we* have. To honour the dead we will free the living... united by our differences.'

'United,' shouted his last friends.

Shannon was the first to turn and leave. The others followed, and Ewan didn't bother to look back. He ignored the burning house they were leaving behind, and ignored the words he had painted onto the road.

He hoped that one day before the end, Grant would read them for himself and be afraid.

NICHOLAS GRANT
OLIVER ROTH

THE UNDERDOGS ARE COMING

THE
UNDERDOGS
WILL RETURN.

For the latest updates about the Underdogs series,
visit the author's website at chrisbonnello.com
or the series' Facebook page at
facebook.com/underdogsnovel.

Read on for an extract from the fourth and final book
in the series, *Underdogs: Uprising*…

Ewan took the knife from the desk, gripped it tight, and ran back into the corridor.

Oliver Roth was stood at the far end, with his own knife in his hand.

'You know,' Roth shouted, 'I'm almost impressed at how well you're holding yourself together. You *must* know you've lost the war now.'

You can't see the inside of my head. I'm not holding it together at all. You have no idea how broken I am.

'Still,' Roth continued, 'at least you can die knowing that you kept fighting to the end. You had a life that'd make *anyone* feel sad to watch, but you gave it your best shot.'

Roth started to walk towards him. Ewan walked forward too.

'It's funny,' Ewan replied as they drew closer to one another, 'people used to mourn my existence. They used to wonder who I could have been if I weren't autistic, if I didn't have PDA, if I hadn't gone to Oakenfold. I used to dream about the answers myself. Right up until these last few weeks.'

He passed the door to Roth's office, wondering whether something of McCormick remained in there to listen to his self-reflection, and kept walking. Shouting distance became talking distance.

'But now I'm grateful,' he continued. 'Because I've realised... if all those things hadn't happened, I could have turned into *you*.'

Roth grinned as he walked.

'You did,' he replied. 'We're the same person, remember? I'm just winning.'

'That's not what you said. You said we're both irredeemable, and I'm not arguing with that. But we *are* different. And I'm glad I avoided growing up and growing old with your crap excuse for a personality.'

'I'm sorry you missed out on the experience.'

'Don't be,' Ewan finished, slowing to a halt. 'I'm bloody serious. You don't have to feel sorry for anyone in the world who managed to avoid being you.'

Three metres away from him, Roth halted too. Together, they raised their knives.

Unbound is the world's first crowdfunding publisher, established in 2011.

We believe that wonderful things can happen when you clear a path for people who share a passion. That's why we've built a platform that brings together readers and authors to crowdfund books they believe in – and give fresh ideas that don't fit the traditional mould the chance they deserve.

This book is in your hands because readers made it possible. Everyone who pledged their support is listed below. Join them by visiting unbound.com and supporting a book today.

Shawn Brooks
Mark Broomhead
Darren Brunton
Richard Buck
Ali Burns
Fred Byrne
Ruth Byrne
Kristen Callow
Megan Campbell
Tiffany Campbell
Leo Capella
Dana Carswell
Tom Catton
Tom Chappelle
Lewis Chawko
Katharine Childs
Marlowe Chong
Billie Clarke
Eliza Clarke
Finn Clarke
Noah Clarke
Ryley Clarke
Lynn Clunie
Lou Coleman
Nick Collins
Tanja Collins
Lara Compton
Denise Cone
Lara Conner
Barb Cook
Dawn Cooper
Gina Cotterill
Anita Coulson

Andrew Cowan
Dawn Louise Cox
Emma Crabb
Stephanie Crook
Rachel Cropley
Heather Cueva
Haley Jo Cutrone
Vic Cutting
Julia Dando
Jim Darby
Rose Darroch
Alexander Davis
Tegan Davis
Carly Day
Robyn DeCourcy
Nancy Delapenha
Leon and Xander Delsaint
Charlotte Dent
Bhanu Dhir
Jane Di Lieto-Danes
Alex Diviney
Helen Doody
Sam Dooley
Linda Douglas
Ilja Drost
Hannah Dunbar
Patrick Dwyer
Annabelle Edge
Emma Ellard
Helen England
Sarah Erickson
Julie Erwin
Finley Evans

Elijah Farris
Josephine Marie Fernandez
Robin Finlayson
Kirsty Finn
H Fish
Matthew Fleming
Claire Flowers Smith
Mary Ford
Danielle Fowler
Georgina Fox
Oliver Fox
Joel Francis
Alex and Joshua Frost
Graham Fulcher
Erin Fulton-McAlister
Julie Gagnon
Therese Gallop
Jennifer Gholap
Jackie Giles
Claire & Sam Giroux
Benjamin Giroux #oddtoo
Sue Goldman
Jess Gomersall
Mia Grace
Jane Gray
Kären Gray
Liliana Greenfield
Clare Griffiths
Evelyn Griffiths
Lois Groat
Matthew Guzik
Amanda Hacking
Susie Halliwell

Paul Hallybone
Jared Hamblett
Imogen & India Hancock
Steve Hanlon
Carl Harding
Becks Harper
Georgia Harper
Nye Harris
Christiane Hart
D. Hartman
Abi Harvey
James Harvey
Kai Hawkins
Bonny Hazelwood
Matthew Heale
Geraldine Heaney
Amanda Heitmann
Emily Heitmann
Jane Hendricks
Tim Herman
Charlotte Hester-Chong
Jaime Hodgson
Odette Hofstedt
Jana Hopfinger
Michael Howard
Michelle Hughes
Kristiaana Humble
Christina Hummel
Tracy Humphreys
Katie Jean-Louis
Nikay Jennings
Danielle Jiang
Kendra Johnson

Christ Kacoyannakis
Marie Kaltoft
Dorina Kasapi
Keepa Family (Ren Angela
    Jacob Dylan Keisha)
Zachary Keita
Charlotte-Ann Kelly
Susan Kelso
Richard Kemp-Luck
Kathryn Kerr
Cleoniki Kesidis
Jonathan Key
Dan Kieran
Karen Kitching
Jennifer Knab
Annie Knowles
Sigve Kolbeinson
Jessica Lambert
Jane Langdon
Kris Larsen
Ester Larsson
Charlotte Le Brecht
Barbara Leaf
Ben League
Jemma Lee
Sarah Lewins
Gary Lloyd
LondonGaymers (A. Rider's
    Second Family)
Theo Lote
Eve Loving
Michelle Ludlow
Helen Lupton

Jodi Lynn
Helen Lynne
Hester Lyons
Tanya Maat
Katie Mabberley
Emma Maher
Making Momentum
Davis Mamantov
Kim Marie
Raleigh Marmorstein
Max Marnau
Leo Marson
Lucas Marson
Benj W. Martin
Emma Martin
S.I.S. Martin
Andrew Maynard
Jonah MCA Roberts
Zara McBurney
B A McGilvray
Jennifer McGowan
Paige McKay
Connall Mclellan
Paul Micallef
Lesley Michalska
Elias Miller
Andy Milligan
Carl Mills
Gesine Milne
Karen Mitchell
John Mitchinson
Kim Mockridge
Jorik Mol

Fiona Moncur
Andrew Morris
Kelly Morris
Owen Morris
Rachel Moseley
Anouska Mullan
Colin Murphy
Layla Murphy-Plant
Rhel ná DecVandé
Carlo Navato
Sam Neal
Basti Needs
Susie Niewand
Misty Nodine
Hegedüs Norina
Becs Norman
Alexandra Nudds
Linda Nudds
Joe O'Brien
Margaret O'Neill
Chris O'Prey
Alexander Ogden-
   McKaughan
Adam Oliver
Tiff Ost
Kristin Pack
Jade Page
Barbara Paier
Heather Palmer
Aaron Parker
Aelswith Parker
Mary Parker
Mark Parratt

James Paterson
Laura Paulikaite
Phillip Perry-Walden
Kendra Petkau
Melissa Phillips
Nye Phillips
Dylan Phipps
Tamara Piper
Justin Pollard
Anaïs Pollet
Anya Pollock
Chelise Popoca
Chris Purdum
Holly Rafique
Karen Ralston
Brendon Reece
Louise Reid
Nick Rich
E C Rickett
Monica Rickett
Alex Rider (An Aspie, Not A
   Teenage Spy)
Clare Riley
Elvire Roberts
Eitan Rosa
Rose and Kit
Luca Rossi
Riko Ryuki
Gabby Saj
Beth Saunders
Mary Anne Savage
Joshua Schlanger
D'Art Schmitz

Matthew Searle
Katherine Seers
Jeffrey Segal
Callie Shackleton
Jo Sharp
Karen Shephard
Sue Shilson
Roslyn Sim
Eilidh Skinner
Michael Slater
Bruce George Smith
Caryn Smith
Chad Smith
Sidsel Soendergaard
Helen Souter
Jane South
Beth Stevic
Stockdale Family Australia
Victoria Strudwick
R Stumpf
Ashleen Sweeney
Jenny Sweeney
H Swingler
Paula Swinscoe
Jessica Szucki
Liza Taylor
Rachael Moon Taylor
Daisy Tempest
Naomi Thornley
Merindah Thornton
Pete Tiley
Sarah Tillman
Caddie Tkenye

Donna Trett
NdiVisible Tui (invisible
    disability/neurodiversity
    blogger)
Emily Turner
Su Underwood
Irene Valdez
Zuleika Van Dieren
Kyle Waddell
Andrew Walden
Barry John Walden
Julie Walden
Mark Walden
Gavin Walker
Mari Wang
Cathy Wassell
Cassie Waters
Merryl Watkins
Juliana Watson
Laura and Rowland Webb
Weekes Boys
Rosalind Weinstock
Jeremy Wenham
Wernersville Public Library
Cameron West
Sandy Wild
Carol Anne Williams
Kat Williams
Vicki Wingrove
Wendy Wofford
Ben Wood
Hannah Wood
Lydia Woodroff